PRAISE FOR THE LANE WINSLOW MYSTERIES

"Iona Whishaw is a writer to watch." —*Globe and Mail*

"Relentlessly exciting from start to finish." —*Kirkus Reviews*

"There's no question you should read it—it's excellent."
—*Toronto Star*

"The setting is fresh and the cast endearing."
—CrimeReads

"An enthralling mystery." —Historical Novel Society

"This series . . . continues to get better and better."
—Reviewing the Evidence blog

"Complex, suspenseful, and deeply felt, this is a smart series for the ages." —Francine Mathews, author of the Nantucket Mysteries

"Rich with intrigue, humour, murder and romance."
—Kerry Clare, author of *Mitzi Bytes*

"Fantastic . . . readers will stand up and cheer."
—Anna Lee Huber, author of the Lady Darby Mysteries and the Verity Kent Mysteries

"Wonderfully complex." —Maureen Jennings, author of the Murdoch Mysteries

"Exquisitely written, psychologically deft."
—Linda Svendsen, author of *Sussex Drive* and *Marine Life*

"A simply riveting read by a master of the genre."
—Wisconsin Bookwatch

"The 'find of the year' . . . this mystery series has it all!"
—Murder by the Book

"A series that's guaranteed to please." —Mercer Island Books

"Full of history, mystery, and a glorious BC setting . . . a wonderful series." —Sleuth of Baker Street bookstore

"Seriously good storytelling that continues to earn its place among the finest mystery writing in Canada."
—Don Graves, Canadian Mystery Reviews

A MATCH MADE FOR MURDER

THE LANE WINSLOW MYSTERY SERIES

———————

IONA WHISHAW

A MATCH MADE FOR MURDER

A LANE WINSLOW MYSTERY

TOUCHWOOD

TouchWood Editions
touchwoodeditions.com

This book is a work of fiction. Names, characters, places, and incidents are either
products of the author's imagination or are used fictitiously. Any resemblance to
actual events or locales or persons, living or dead, is entirely coincidental.

Edited by Claire Philipson
Cover illustration by Margaret Hanson
Typeset by Lara Minja

LIBRARY AND ARCHIVES CANADA CATALOGUING IN PUBLICATION

Title: A match made for murder / Iona Whishaw.
Names: Whishaw, Iona, 1948- author.
Description: Series statement: A Lane Winslow mystery ; #7
Identifiers: Canadiana (print) 20190186461 | Canadiana (ebook) 2019018647X |
ISBN 9781771513265 (softcover) | ISBN 9781771513272 (PDF)
Classification: LCC PS8595.H414 M38 2020 | DDC C813/.54—dc23

TouchWood Editions gratefully acknowledges that the land on which we live
and work is within the traditional territories of the Lkwungen (Esquimalt
and Songhees), Malahat, Pacheedaht, Scia'new, T'Sou-ke and W̱SÁNEĆ
(Pauquachin, Tsartlip, Tsawout, Tseycum) peoples.

We acknowledge the financial support of the Government of Canada through
the Canada Book Fund and the Canada Council for the Arts, and of the Province
of British Columbia through the British Columbia Arts Council and the Book
Publishing Tax Credit.

This book was produced using FSC-certified acid-free paper,
processed chlorine-free, and printed with soya-based inks.

PRINTED IN CANADA AT FRIESENS

24 23 22 21 20 1 2 3 4 5

For my delightful grandsons, Teo and Tyson, in the hopes of encouraging them in the idea that it is never too early, nor too late, to do things you love.

CHAPTER ONE

November 1947

LANE'S FIRST IMPRESSION WAS OF the whiteness. The mid-afternoon sun, which she had always thought of as golden, bleached everything here to the purity of bones. The endless desert had given way to adobe and wood houses that seemed to lie low away from the sun, and then to the white of the station they were approaching.

Her honeymoon. It was ridiculous and wonderful. A year and a half before, she had arrived at King's Cove, a tiny hamlet an hour outside of the city of Nelson, in the middle of British Columbia, and moved into her beautiful house among her eccentric neighbours with no other object than to lose herself, and her memories, and put the war behind her. The danger of dropping out of airplanes into occupied France carrying weapons and encrypted messages began to seem more and more like a life that had happened to someone else. The misery of her first love affair had been swept away, almost against her own better judgement, by

Frederick Darling, inspector of the Nelson Police.

She looked at him now, his dark hair slightly tousled from leaning against the window, and her heart skipped. They'd had a bad start, she had to admit: he had arrested her over the death of a man on her property. He was extraordinarily reserved, not to say impenetrable, but he had come, very slowly and most reluctantly, to accept that she had some skills that were invaluable in some of his other cases. And she in turn had come to appreciate his profound sense of justice, and his philosophical turn of mind, perhaps a product of his surprisingly academic background. She had not expected a degree in literature from a policeman. She wondered if either of them had realized how completely they were falling in love. She smiled. She was pretty sure his sidekick, Sergeant Ames, had. She wouldn't have been surprised to learn it was he who had pointed it out to Darling.

"Not terribly punctual. It's gone two forty-five," she said, consulting her watch. The train screeched, as if protesting at having to slow down, and then stopped and hissed. People began to stand up, stretch, and reach for their bags. It had been a long day's ride from Los Angeles.

"You want precision on a honeymoon. How delightful!" Darling said. "It's hotter than blazes. I'm overdressed." He took his hat off the seat and fanned himself. "Well, shall we?"

A porter appeared as they stepped off the train. Lane paused and took a deep breath. She loved arriving in a place she'd never been. Warmth emanated from the tiles of the platform and off the white walls of the station, and a breeze made the movement of air almost sensual on her face.

"Can I get your bags, sir, ma'am?"

"That would be lovely, thank you," Lane said. "What is the temperature today?"

"A balmy seventy-eight, ma'am." The porter touched his cap briefly and led the way to the baggage car, pushing a trolley.

"You see, darling, a perfect summer day at home. My husband thinks it is too hot," she continued to the porter, following him, her handbag over her arm.

"Oh, no, ma'am. This is just how we like it. Summertime? Now that's a punishing time in Arizona. It can get up over a hundred. You just wanna crawl under a rock like a lizard. Vacation?"

"Honeymoon," Lane said, embarrassed to feel her cheeks flushing.

"Well now, that's something! Congratulations and welcome to Tucson. Will you be needing a taxi?"

"Yes," said Darling, "thank you." He reached into his jacket for some coins.

The station platform felt ghostly in the white afternoon despite chattering travellers getting on and off the train. Lane and Darling followed the porter into the station, where it took her a moment to adjust to the darkness. Inside, the shade contrasted sharply with the blinding light of the street visible through the windows. Sharp, she decided was the operative word. Sharp shadows, sharp light, sharp lines.

"Where shall I tell the driver y'all are headed?"

"The Santa Cruz Inn," Darling said. He produced the coins and the porter tipped his hat, turning a beaming smile on Lane.

"You have a wonderful honeymoon, you hear?"

"YOU MADE A conquest there," Darling remarked, settling in the back seat of the cab after asking to be conveyed to the Santa Cruz Inn. "I wonder how Ames is getting on?"

"Don't be silly. We've only been gone four days. This is a complete vacation from mayhem. We're going to get along like a house on fire because I won't be interfering in anything. I plan to lie by the pool with an improving book during the day and make up for it by swilling cocktails in the evening. I hope they have cocktails."

"They got cocktails, ma'am," the driver interjected from the front seat. "You got the best there. All the actors go there. Very swanky. Pretty new, too. My sister Consuela works there, cleaning."

"Oh, is it far?" she asked—the driver looked Mexican, and Lane had expected him to speak with an accent. She gave herself a stern mental correction.

The driver took a moment to honk at someone, slowed down to wait for a tram to go by, and then turned onto Sixth Avenue. "It's a few miles out of town, just east, but I could drive you just a couple of blocks near here to see the old part of town."

"Why not?" Darling asked, when Lane gave him a nod.

Lane looked at the town outside the car windows. They passed a massive pink building with a red-tiled roof and a huge mosaic green and yellow dome. A row of columns connected by arches provided a long, shaded walkway. She could just see the courtyard beyond the arches.

"What is that wonderful-looking place?" Lane asked.

"That's the county courthouse. This here is the old part of the city, called the Presidio. The Spanish came here first, and you've got some very fine houses in here. I'll just drive you along Fourth Avenue so you can see. It won't take a minute."

LANE THREW HERSELF onto the bed of their suite. "This is heavenly! We were right to pick this. All this lovely adobe. It could almost be Mexico. I feel like I have been transported to a completely foreign place. And this weather! It is hard to imagine that somewhere in the world it is this warm on the ninth of November. We'd be in our wool shirts at home."

Lane had seen the travel brochures for Tucson at the travel agency on Baker Street and had been attracted to the sunny desert landscape, perfect for a honeymoon as November ushered in the damp cold of a British Columbia winter. "We could go to a dude ranch," she'd said, spreading the brochures across the table one evening.

"Are we dudes, do you think? I have decidedly negative views on dressing up in chaps," Darling had said. "You know, I have an ex-colleague who moved there in '37. He might have an idea for a less energetic holiday. I'll write to him." And indeed, his ex-colleague, now the assistant chief of police in Tucson, Paul Galloway, had recommended the Santa Cruz Inn, adding that it was a favourite of Hollywood movie stars.

"You *have* been transported to a foreign place," Darling pointed out. While not of a demonstrative turn, he was quietly relishing the sunny warmth, not to mention a completely new sensation to him: the feeling of truly being on holiday, with no responsibilities and nothing to do but enjoy the company of his new and beautiful wife. He hung his jacket in the closet and rolled up his shirtsleeves. His tie was already discarded on the dresser. He looked at the suitcases.

Lane smiled. "Let's not unpack now. Let's just get out the things we need for tea. I'm astonished they have a good old English tea here, and," she glanced at her watch, "it's on in fifteen minutes. I don't want to miss it; we can see who our neighbours are."

Darling kicked off his brogues and lay down on the bed, scooping her into his arms. "I don't care who the neighbours are." He kissed her in a way that suggested they stay put awhile, which Lane found almost irresistible.

"We should see if we can find Consuela, the cabbie's sister," she said through his kiss.

"I've never met a woman with less sense of occasion. You are not easy to love."

"I'm sure you knew that when you married me. Come, up you get! We didn't come here to while away our time in bed."

"I should have thought that was exactly why we came," Darling protested, swinging his legs onto the floor.

They walked along the brick path past neat rows of flowers and green lawns, to where a fountain splashed in the centre of a large lawn surrounded by palms and other trees Lane couldn't identify.

She clutched Darling's arm. "Oh, listen!" she exclaimed, holding up a finger.

He duly tilted his head. "To what, in particular?"

"That cooing ... mourning doves! One of my favourite birds ... we had them in England." They stood together in

6

companionable silence and became aware of several types of birdsong, the soft cooing predominating. Lane sighed happily. "They always sound so peaceful. I feel as if nothing bad could happen in a place where they are."

The library—modelled, Lane decided, on some fantasy European manorial room with dark ceiling beams and a long wall of books—was abuzz with quiet chatter and the clinking of cups. The women were in bright summer dresses, some sporting wide-brimmed straw hats and others pert little numbers with wisps of veil set at becoming angles. A couple of younger men in pale linen trousers stood by the massive unlit hearth with their elbows on the mantel, smoking pipes. The place had the confident, quiet feel of money.

"Those two by the fireplace look just like the brochure," Lane whispered. "Do you think they stay there permanently on the off-chance they'll be photographed? Oh. What have you got? I missed those." She pointed at a pair of tiny scones on his plate.

"They're over there. You're not having mine."

Lane left the little round table they had managed to get and went to where the scones were laid out, wondering if it would be greedy to take two.

"This is gorgeous, sweetie," said someone nearby. "I don't think I've ever seen nothing ... anything like this. You're spoiling me, you know that?"

Lane turned with her scones and a woman, possibly in her mid-thirties, with frizzy, nearly white bleached-blond hair in a pre-war Bette Davis style. She was wearing a deep ruby shade of lipstick that Lane wasn't sure about for the time of day. The man she giggled at, the man she held up her china cup to toast, was considerably older. Lane would have said he was into his seventies. He was slight and perfectly dressed in white slacks and a blue blazer, and his full head of white hair was brushed and Brilliantined into a side part. She could see a heavy embossed gold ring on his right hand and a simple wedding band on his left.

"A bit spring–winter, that couple, wouldn't you say?" she whispered to Darling, pointing surreptitiously with her buttered scone a few moments later.

"I would. But would it be any of my business?"

"Perhaps not, but we were interested in finding out who our fellow denizens are. I think it's rather sweet, really."

"I believe it was you who was interested in our neighbours," he said. "I bet he's being taken for everything he's worth."

"Or he's taking her for everything she's worth," Lane said.

"She doesn't look like she's the one with the money," Darling countered.

"Are you telling me the only thing women value is money?"

"I wouldn't dream of it," Darling said, selecting a petit four. They chewed contentedly for a few moments, and then a young couple came up to them, smiling. The woman was lovely, Lane thought. Tall and slender with golden hair twisted into an elaborate knot. She was wearing a simple, graceful, cap-sleeved linen dress with pale-blue stripes.

"I think you folks are our neighbours. I saw you come in earlier. We were just leaving to go have a dip. Isn't this grand?"

Darling and Lane stood up. "I'm Lane, and this is my husband, Frederick Darling. How do you do?"

"I'm Ivy Renwick, and this is Jack. We're from Wisconsin. We don't get anything like this place back home! We just came yesterday."

Darling nodded and shook hands with them. "We don't much either. We're from a little town in British Columbia."

"Oh, my! Canadians. You're a long way from home. What brings you out this way?"

Jack Renwick had pale, straw-coloured hair and very genuine blue eyes. Darling liked him at once. "Honeymoon," he said with a slight touch of apology.

"Hey! Us too. We got hitched just before I shipped out in '44, and we never got a chance to have a honeymoon, so we're having it now," Jack Renwick said.

"We should meet for cocktails and then have dinner one night. I saw Clark Gable checking out just as we were arriving. He was staying in one of the villas!" Ivy Renwick said. "What about tomorrow?"

AMBLING THROUGH THE garden later, Darling said, "I can't think when I've met a more perfect couple. I suppose we will have to follow through and have dinner with them tomorrow?"

They stopped by a little planting of cactus. "You say 'perfect' as if they were boring."

"I'm not saying that, but they do seem almost too good to be true and are probably regretting the impulse to socialize already. I know I am," Darling said. "Apparently the Native people in this part of the world could peel and eat these things." He was pointing at a cactus helpfully labelled *nopal*. "Which reminds me: Should we go for a swim before we get ready to go to the Galloways' for dinner? I suspect the temperature starts to go down smartly when it gets dark."

"SWEETIE, I'M GOING to the lobby. They have some jewellery in a glass case for sale, and I saw this gorgeous silver bracelet." Meg Holden stood in the doorway of the villa with one hand on the doorframe, as if she were trying to still her own restlessness.

Rex Holden was stretched on the bed, his loafers and blazer off and his blue and white ascot loose around his neck. *The Greek Coffin Mystery*, an Ellery Queen that Holden had found in the library, was resting on his chest. He was gazing at his wife, his eyes narrowed in an attempt to bring her into focus. She was the prettiest thing he'd ever seen, he thought, as he always did, but this thought, comforting though it was, did not completely dispel his slight sense of disquiet. He had tried to trace this disturbance and had been wholly unsuccessful. His friends at the golf club in Phoenix were clear: she was too young, too dim, a gold digger who would run through his money, but Holden had not minded any of these things. In fact, it was what he had expected, and he had plenty of money for her to run through. Looking at her now, he felt himself almost grasp what unsettled him. It was something in the alertness in her body, as if ... but then it was gone.

"Don't go crazy. I'm not made of money." He said this with patient affection.

10

"Yes, you are, silly!" She left the door and went to sit on the bed beside him and stroked his cheek, an activity that necessitated putting Ellery Queen to one side so he could look at her. "Just kidding. Anyway, it was so sweet of you to let me take some money to my aunt. She could never get her operation without it. I'll be sure to be real careful about spending." She got up and returned to the door and gave him a large smile. "I saw a real cute bolo tie with a horse head made of turquoise. Maybe I'll get you that as a surprise!"

"I don't think I'm going to be very surprised," he said, but she was gone.

THE CAB PULLED up at a long low adobe house west of the university. It was built close to the property line, allowing only for a row of ocotillo along the fenceline. Four small, deeply inset windows punctuated the street-side wall, and a wrought-iron gate showed the way up some broad stairs of brick-red tiles. The wrought-iron lamp illuminating the entranceway cast a warm light. Before Darling could knock, the door swung open, and a tall man emanating lean power was upon them.

"Fred! As I live, it's good to see you! Good trip?" He shook Darling's hand vigorously and gave him a resounding pound on the shoulder.

Lane, standing just behind Darling, could not suppress a smile. She had never heard anyone call her husband Fred nor seen him in a social situation requiring shoulder pounding. She was surprised that Darling's friend was English—had he told her that?

"Excellent, thank you. Good to see you, Paul. You're looking well. May I present my wife, Lane. Lane, Paul Galloway. He did a brief stint in Nelson, where we worked together. He took me under his wing when I first got there. A London man. He is the assistant chief of police here."

"For my sins. Chief is off on health leave, poor fellow, so I'm more or less in charge of the whole operation now." Galloway had released Darling's hand and now opened his arms as if he were planning to embrace Lane, his face wreathed in smiles. Instead, to her enormous relief, he offered a hand to shake.

"Mrs. Darling, what a pleasure. Fred, you dog! Where did you find this lovely creature? She must be a saint, putting up with your gruff self." Still holding her hand and pulling her close, he said in a stage whisper, "Always took himself too seriously."

Thank heavens, Lane thought, if this man's unbridled enthusiasm was the alternative. She had just retrieved her hand when she became aware of a woman standing perfectly still behind their host. Lane nearly gasped at her beauty. She had jet-black hair, pale skin, and piercing blue eyes; she was wearing an emerald-green silk dress that was fitted to her slender waist and then hung in an exquisite flare of silk that seemed to catch the light. Blimey, she thought, I could be meeting Vivien Leigh.

"This is the wife, Priscilla," Galloway put his arm around his wife's shoulder and pulled her into the group. "My old chum, Fred Darling. He's a police inspector now, up in Canada."

Priscilla smiled and offered a hand. "You'll have a lot to talk about, then. Please do come in. It's still warm enough that we can have drinks on the patio." She spoke with a clipped English accent, her voice pitched low.

Lane wondered if she modulated her voice and adopted this posh accent, which couldn't quite hide her Cockney roots, deliberately, to add a little weight to her delicate frame. With a touch of regret, Lane reflected that Priscilla's pretense made her seem more vulnerable, not less.

The house had a spacious rambling quality that made it feel, Lane thought, extremely expensive. The foyer was tiled and dropped two steps to a sunken living room full of English chintz furniture; it was in sharp contrast to the Spanish Colonial feel of the house itself, but together the two styles somehow seemed to work.

"Come, Lane. Let's get the boys out onto the patio, and you and I will put the drinks together. Martinis? G and Ts? What's it to be?"

"A couple of G and Ts," Galloway said. "That do you, Fred? And don't let Fernanda near them. Hasn't got a clue," he confided to Darling, leading him through French doors out to a patio illuminated with gentle light from candles set on a large dark wood table near a tiled fountain that burbled in the centre of the courtyard.

In the kitchen a plump, middle-aged woman in a blue uniform and white apron and cap was assembling something on the counter.

"Fernanda, did you put the glasses out as I instructed?" Priscilla wasn't unkind, exactly, but she spoke in a peremptory manner that caused Fernanda to turn toward her mistress but not look at her.

"Yes, Mrs. Galloway. They're on the tray. I cut some limes for you." A plate of cut limes, releasing their citrus fragrance into the kitchen, sat by the tray upon which glasses, a bucket of ice, and a bottle of tonic sat next to a luminescent blue bottle of gin.

"You're very beautiful," Priscilla said, turning to Lane and then beginning her preparations with the gin. "When did you come over?"

Lane glanced anxiously at Fernanda. It would have been unthinkable in her household not to thank the servants. Absolute courtesy had been her grandmother's gold standard. She gave her a quick smile and was rewarded by Fernanda turning away to open the oven.

"I came over right after the war, in the spring of '46. Gosh, only last year! I feel like it's been ages since the war ended. I bought myself a little house in the middle of nowhere. You?"

"And collared a very handsome man. He looks kind, for a policeman. Is he?"

"Yes, very kind," Lane said. She saw Priscilla's neat sidestepping of the question about her own background and wondered suddenly if it was her husband who expected her to disavow her London roots. "What can I do?"

"Fernanda, are the canapés out?"

"Yes, ma'am. I put them on the table."

"Can you stick a sliver of lime on each of the glasses, Lane, then we'll be ready to hop." Priscilla put the drinks on a small silver tray and led Lane toward a door that opened onto the courtyard. "Are you planning to have children?" she asked.

"I haven't given it a thought. We've only just got married." Perhaps Priscilla herself was thinking about it, Lane speculated.

The courtyard smelled of orange blossoms from trees Lane could just see in the shadows beyond the light. Over them, the dark velvet night sky was beginning to populate with stars. Lane, looking skyward, was about to exclaim at the loveliness of the place when Galloway spoke.

"To old friends and new ones. Cheers." The ice in the glasses gave a soft rattle, and the four of them touched rims. Galloway winked at Lane and drank.

"Not bad, Pris. You'll get the hang of it. A touch more gin in the next one," Galloway said, and then he laughed. "My girl used to pull pints in a London bar. Met her during the war. Makes a fine gin and tonic, I think you'll agree."

"Very good, indeed," Darling said.

Lane smiled and lifted her glass, thinking the ratio of gin could not go any higher. She glanced at Paul Galloway and realized she was trying to place him in some social context. She had at first found his accent almost soothing—sounds of home, she realized—but there was something else. A sense of superiority, she thought, or was it simply confidence? She was surprised when she turned toward Priscilla to see her hostess looking flushed and angry, but in another moment, Lane attributed this to the uncertain light.

CHAPTER TWO

SERGEANT AMES WOULD NEVER HAVE known about the crime if he hadn't, after some considerable thought, found an excuse to drive out to the Van Eyck garage near Balfour. The temperature had dropped suddenly, and though it was sunny, he was sure he could smell the first snow in the air. The stand of pale-skinned aspens behind the wooden house and garage still had a few hardy yellow leaves clinging to them after a good wind the night before.

Ames was grateful it hadn't snowed yet. He pulled up onto the grassy parking area in front of the garage in the maroon car he drove for the Nelson police and tried to look nonchalantly like a man with a car in need of service. Instead of seeing Tina Van Eyck and her father hard at work on the car currently parked in the service bay, he found them standing in front of one of the two large, newly painted doors to the service area. Marring the new dark, barn-red wooden door was the word *Bitch* scrawled in messy black paint.

Tina turned as Ames got out of the car and put her hand up to shade her eyes from the bright November sun. Her blond curly hair was wrapped in its usual workday turban, and she had a wool shirt of thick brown plaid over her boiler suit.

"It's hardly a police matter," she said by way of greeting. "Dad, did you call him?"

"No, I didn't. Good morning, Sergeant. You see what's happened. We never had this sort of carry-on before the war," Marcus Van Eyck said. He looked more anxious than his daughter, who just looked cross.

"Good grief!" said Ames. "When did this happen? What does it mean?"

"You have to ask?" Tina said with no little sarcasm.

"No, I didn't mean that." Ames felt himself blushing and unsettled by his own fumbling response to Tina's obvious anger. "I meant why did someone do this?" Most of his previous meetings with this competent, self-assured lady mechanic had made him feel like a blithering idiot. It still surprised him that she'd agreed to come with him to Darling's wedding the month before.

"It happened sometime in the night," her father said. "Paint's dry." The mechanic walked along the edge of the building, moving the long yellow grass aside with a stick, searching for something that might help him understand why this had happened. He went around the side of the garage and exclaimed, "Aha!"

Tina watched him, frowning. "I wish he'd leave it. I don't want you involved. The police are unlikely to do a blind bit of good, in my experience."

But Ames hurried after her father. "Don't touch any-thing, sir." He found Mr. Van Eyck looking down at a small can of paint and an old paintbrush that was worn nearly to the end. It looked as if a fleeing vandal had tossed them there, splashing paint against the wall and over the ground where the tin had fallen.

"Here. I've got a box in my car. I'll collect this stuff and bring it back to the station. We can see if there are finger-prints." Ames took a large blue handkerchief from his pocket and scooped up both the brush and the metal handle of the paint can and carried them to the car. Hesitating for a moment about how he was going to unlock the trunk with one hand full, he turned and found Tina approaching the car.

"I wish you wouldn't concern yourself with this," she said.

"I'll just have a look-see. Maybe we can track it down. This is vandalism, and it is my job after all. You don't want it happening again. You wouldn't mind getting my keys, would you? In the ignition . . ." He felt sheepish in the face of her terseness. But she was angry, he reminded himself. He tried to imagine someone writing *Bastard* across his office door, but somehow it wasn't the same.

Tina came back with the keys and pushed and turned the latch to get the trunk open. There was a small wooden apple box in the trunk in which he kept a pair of clean and carefully folded overalls in case of a messy crime scene. He watched her remove them and fold them next to the box. Then he deposited the evidence, deciding to leave his handkerchief in place.

"Since Dad claims he didn't call you, it means you came out on your own. Was there something you wanted?" Tina asked as she handed Ames back his keys.

"Well, the car. I mean, I thought I could ask you, or your dad of course, to give the car a once-over, you know." It sounded ridiculous even to him.

"No doubt the police department has a contract with one of the local garages, which, I assume, you'd like us to break? Was there something needing the feminine touch? The transmission, the carburetor?"

Ames, wondering now how he had imagined anyone would buy his excuse for coming out, stood silently looking at his shoes, his finest two-toned brogues, and felt acutely embarrassed that he'd worn these on purpose to impress. A girl less inclined to be impressed by a pair of shoes, he realized, he was unlikely to meet.

"I did wonder," he tried. "You know, because of last month and the wedding ..."

"Look, Sergeant, if you manufactured this flimsy excuse to come out here and ask me out, let me put your mind at ease. I had a good time at your boss's wedding, but it was a once-only thing. I don't even know why I agreed to go with you, to the wedding of a policeman at that. For one, we've got nothing in common, and for two, I've got work to do. Or do you think I should meekly give up my job and flit around you like a butterfly?"

Stifling a desire to point out that they weren't that different, Ames said, "But I don't want to get you out of your job. Why would you think that?"

"You're a man, aren't you?" She smiled suddenly, as if

her anger over the sign was dissipating and had been replaced by the amusement of baiting Ames.

"Well, yes. But I still don't see how it follows that I want you out of your job." If he was honest with himself, he would admit that when he first met Tina Van Eyck in the summer, he'd held the firm view that a woman should not put a man out of a job, as Tina's return from England had put a young mechanic out of work in her father's garage. A conversation with Lane Winslow, a rescue by Miss Van Eyck over the matter of a flat tyre, and an almost accidental date had shifted his view somewhat.

"Look," Tina said, "I have a couple of school friends, with good office jobs in town, who've been handed their pink slips. You know what they were told? That they ought to be happy to get back to their kitchens. That if they really need to work, they should try to find jobs more suited to women. I don't mind the fellows coming back to their jobs, nothing wrong with that. But not every girl wants to hang around in a kitchen. I don't." She looked pointedly at him, sounding, perhaps, a warning note. "And as for *that* . . ." She pointed at the garish insult on the bay door. "That sort of thing can't put me off. I lived through the London Blitz. Poor Dad is more upset than I am. And, if you want the naked truth, I've got no use for the police."

Ames saw that Mr. Van Eyck was coming out of the garage with a can of red paint, and, at a loss for an adequate response to Tina's words, he moved to approach him. "Sir, could you hold off on that? I'd like to go back to town and get my camera and snap a photo of it. This guy may be aiming this just at your garage, but he may go on to deface

20

other properties. It would be good if we had a record."

"Oh," Mr. Van Eyck said uncertainly, looking at his daughter. It was clear he wanted to spare her feelings by removing the offensive word.

Tina walked Ames back to his car. "You don't have to take a picture," Tina said in an angry whisper, glancing back at where her father was putting the paint down. "I already know who did this. It's a guy from near Willow Point. Barney Watts. He came with a car a couple of days ago, ignition trouble. He seemed nice, but the minute my dad was out of sight he made a pass at me. I gave him what-for, and he said some rude things. I haven't told Dad." Tina stopped and looked down, kicking at a clump of grass with her foot. "I don't want my dad to think he needs to be looking out for me."

"It's not your fault," Ames protested gallantly.

"I know. It's just the usual stupid stuff. But Dad would be upset. I don't want to have to try to calm him down as well."

"If I can get the man's address, I could go see him, but I still don't want you to clean off that paint, sorry, till I record it, just in case this Barney fellow isn't the one. Did you hear a car or anything during the night?"

"Just forget about it. I don't want anything done. And no, I didn't hear a thing. There was a pretty good wind, so I don't think we would have heard if someone had driven up. Anyway, I told you. Leave it. Dad and I will paint the garage and get on with our lives." They stood silently and watched Mr. Van Eyck leave the garage and go into the house. They both spoke at once, "I heard ..." she said, at the same time as his "I don't think ..."

21

"You go first," Ames said.

"I was just going to say I heard your boss is away. Are you running the show? What were you going to say?"

"It doesn't matter. Yes, they went to Arizona, so I'm as in charge as anyone in that place lets me be. The boys give me the gears from time to time, but they're okay."

Tina stood with her hands in her pockets and smiled again. "Look, it's a free country, so you can take the picture, because I do understand it might not be him and you have to have some record," she said. "But don't go see him. It would just make it worse. Trust me, police involvement will only muck it up. I can handle this."

"I don't exactly hold with the idea that not confronting a bully will make him stop. That's what the police are for. In fact, it's why I'm a policeman. It's against the law to deface other people's property. Simple as that."

"Yeah, well, I confronted him when he thought he could paw me, and that's the result," she said crossly, indicating the garish message on the garage door.

Ames drove back to town, his brow furrowed. He'd never really thought of how much of that sort of nonsense women like Tina had to put up with from men. If he were honest, he always assumed it was part of the deal. Men, he readily admitted, were awkward around women and probably didn't have a clue how to get their attention. He certainly found it awkward every day of the week. But there was a continuum. He was at one end with his fancy shoe gambit, and the men who thought women were there to be pawed, and worse, were at the other end. Worse, when he thought of domestic disputes that sometimes reached the police.

He was embarrassed to be anywhere on that continuum. He wasn't sure he was getting the whole story from Tina. And why her sudden antagonism toward the police? But there was one thing he was sure of: he felt a strong desire to protect her, and that didn't seem to be wanted either.

He thought about Miss Winslow, or Mrs. Darling really, now, and Darling. They seemed to have plunged into their relationship at some deeper level right from the get-go. He would have said from watching them that they seemed to be friends. Of course, Darling was always wanting to protect Miss Winslow. It was hard to make the switch, but she didn't like being protected much either. Ames drove off the ferry ramp on the Nelson side, disconsolately singing "You made me love you ..."

———

"THIS IS ALL right," Lane said, reaching across the table for Darling's hand. They had stayed in bed late and, afterward, had opted to have breakfast outside under the shady overhang of the interlaced branch ramada, looking out at the lawn and garden and listening to a fountain splashing somewhere nearby. They sat before the scant remains of their scrambled eggs, bacon, and fresh-squeezed orange juice. "I've never had juice like that in my life. I never want to leave."

"How would poor Ames take that?" Darling asked, drinking. It wasn't orange juice but Lane's auburn hair spread across the pillow in the morning sunlight that made him have thoughts of never wanting to leave. He brought

23

himself back and put his empty glass on the table. "So, what are you going to do while I'm with Galloway?"

"Lie around, I expect. I'll finish the *Arizona Daily Star*, there's an interesting article about American football that might help me understand it, and then go explore that bookshelf, with a view to lounging by the pool."

"Think of it as rugby with armour. Look, I'm sorry about this. I didn't feel I could turn down his invitation to see his office and discuss the sorts of cases they deal with here."

"Don't be silly. You'll love it. You can tell me all about it when you get back," she said, "over a sunset cocktail." Lane, who'd been used to spending a great deal of time alone, found she was looking forward to an uninterrupted morning of reading.

With Darling gone, Lane considered her next move. The library first, she decided. She emerged from their room, relishing again the gentle warmth of the morning, and was about to make her way on the brick path through the garden to the main building of the hotel when the door of the nearest villa opened just to the right of the building their suite was in.

"You relax, sweetie. I won't be long, and I promise not to buy anything!"

It was the woman with the very red lipstick and white-blond hair from tea the day before. Her hair, which looked more startling in the morning sun, billowed around her face in fuzzy curls. But the expression on that curl-framed face was in direct contrast to her cheerful singsong words. Her eyebrows were drawn together in worry, and her eyes darted anxiously, but she caught sight of Lane and smiled brightly, waving her fingers.

Lane waved back and then moved slowly toward the hotel's main building behind the woman. She seemed to be late for an appointment; she hurried, catching at the pale-blue cardigan that had slipped off her shoulder.

The library was cool and shaded, with a clean-edged slant of light from the morning sun cutting across the Turkish carpet and climbing the inner walls, in a way, Lane thought, a Dutch master could do justice to. She was the only one there, and the walls and thick carpet seemed to muffle sound, so the near silence was luxurious. A faint clattering of people leaving the breakfast room in the distance somewhere intensified the sense of quiet and solitude. It had an almost old-world feel to it, like the English manor house the hotel seemed so anxious to emulate.

Heaving a happy sigh, she turned her attention to the books. She would go for something utterly light, like an Agatha Christie, or her favourite, Dorothy L. Sayers. Much to her delight, she was quite quickly rewarded with a nearly new copy of *The Nine Tailors* incongruously shelved just past a whole row of Zane Greys. She had read it, but before the war, and she recalled there was a lot of business with bell ringing that might give her mind a little exercise. With her reading sorted, she remembered the blond woman's remark about some jewellery on sale in the lobby. Seeing nothing anywhere that indicated she needed to sign her book out, Lane went up the stairs and was about to go into the lobby when she wondered at a long corridor on her right.

Perhaps there was a reading lounge, or even a massage room to be explored. Turning in the opposite direction from the lobby, toward the thickly carpeted hallway, she stopped at the sound of frantic whispers. She peered around the corner and saw the young woman with the blue cardigan pressing into a tall man who was leaning against the wall. He had dark hair that flopped in front of one eye and a thick black moustache. He was exceedingly handsome—a character from one of those Zane Grey novels, Lane thought in a flight of fancy. He towered over the young woman and had his arms around her, pulling her in to kiss him. The blonde responded with a soft gasp and made as if to pull away but then settled into his embrace. Lane stepped back hurriedly and decided that jewellery and further exploration could wait. This man was certainly not the older man from the previous evening—the man she'd been certain was the young woman's husband. She suspected *The Nine Tailors* might lie unread next to her deck chair for some time while she ruminated on this very human development.

"IT'S GOOD OF you to have me along to your office," Darling said. When he'd left Vancouver for Nelson, Galloway had been a sergeant, and Darling remembered him as being quite a good policeman. He had a natural authority Darling had attributed in part to his being English. His accent alone seemed to cause the other men to defer to his views; he had a concise way of speaking and appeared to be able cut through confusion and distraction. At the same time, he had an open, friendly nature that clearly endeared him to the others. Darling had envied this quality when he was younger, and only with time had come to value his own more thoughtful approach to understanding the crimes he had to deal with.

He recalled in particular a case Galloway had worked on in Nelson: a man called Landon had been imprisoned for arson. Galloway had been decisive, and Darling had admired how logically he approached the evidence. Landon had been a disgruntled employee who had been fired from a local mill; he had been drinking heavily on the night of the fire and was unable to account for his whereabouts. Darling was surprised to remember the incident just at this moment. Like Galloway, he had believed the man to be guilty. Landon was eventually tried, and spent six months in prison, but on a routine domestic abuse call, Darling had stumbled on the true culprit lighting a second fire. It had been a cautionary experience for Darling. Landon had lost his job, and he was unable to find his footing after leaving prison and had left Nelson for good. Darling had always hoped he'd found work and a new life.

By that time, Galloway had already left for Arizona, saying the British Columbia climate was too gloomy. He'd obtained American citizenship, and signed up with the 34th Infantry Division in 1942. Darling remembered admiring Galloway's sense of confidence. He always said it was important to apprehend the guilty as quickly as possible, because in a small community, it made people feel secure and trust they were in good hands with their local police. It encouraged people to come forward on other crimes. It was only later, after Galloway was gone, that Darling asked himself how it could have been done differently. It didn't surprise him to see Paul in charge now. He had not lost that air of confidence.

"Nonsense. I'm proud to show it off!" Galloway answered, bringing Darling back to the present. "I dare say there are one or two things in our organizational approach that would be of interest to you. With the chief out of commission, it's all down to me at the moment." He led Darling through the back door of what he described as the city hall building and then downstairs to the basement. Windows set high up along one wall let in some outdoor light, but the room was largely lit by what seemed to Darling to be an inadequate few rows of fluorescent lights.

"This is where they keep us. Not very glamorous, and we swelter in the summer. As you can see, we have our lock-up over there. Drunks and vagrants mostly. More dangerous people go to the county jail. Anyone convicted goes up to the state pen." They made their way toward his office between a couple of desks. "Those two fellows are on the phone-in desks, and that's the dispatch," he said, waving at a desk near another door. Just outside the office, under a window, he stopped. "Morning, Sergeant Martinez. I'd like you to meet my pal, Inspector Frederick Darling. We worked together up in Canada. He's just got married to the prettiest woman you've ever seen! Down here on a honeymoon."

Sergeant Martinez, who was sitting at a desk under one of the two ceiling fans, stood up to shake hands with Darling. He was young, Darling thought, but had a look of such weight and seriousness that it appeared the entire fortunes of the Tucson police depended on him. His black hair was cut in a military style, and he had a thin black moustache. Perhaps it was the moustache that gave him his air of gravity, Darling thought.

"Pleased to meet you, sir." He shook Darling's hand, and then turned to his boss. "Sir, I've been through these arrest reports three times. The Griffin arrest and the accounting evidence aren't in the files. It was right in order last week. I myself sent it for filing. The case is coming up for trial. It won't look good if I don't have it."

"Then you better find it, hadn't you, or Jimmy Griffin will go scot-free. It won't do the department's reputation any good."

"Yes, sir. It's just that I had the notes and evidence locked in my desk while I was working on them. I did take it over to be filed, but Grace says it isn't there, and there's no record of it being filed."

"Then presumably it wasn't filed, was it?"

Back in his office, Galloway stretched back in his wheeled chair and shook his head. "You've heard the saying, 'can't get good help'? Case in point. These Mexican fellows are pretty fearless, and they speak the lingo we need for a lot of the crime we deal with, but they're sloppy as hell. See, now we're going to lose a big case against one of the local restaurateurs who runs a gambling business at the back of his building because Diego Martinez can't keep his paperwork in order. I was the one who pushed for his promotion, but I sometimes wonder if it was a good idea. Luckily I've got a couple of white rozzers that know their stuff."

Darling raised his eyebrows. "You surprise me. Sergeant Martinez appears to be concerned and thorough."

Galloway shook his head, laughing. "You never change, Darling. Always wanting to give everyone the benefit of the doubt!"

———

December 1946

MARTINEZ PULLED THE car in front of his house and let the dust settle. He could hear his son and daughter playing outside on the swing he had built for them in the backyard of their small adobe house. He was struggling. He had wonderful, improbable news for his wife, Rosario, and yet that same news had sparked an anxiety deep within him that he could not articulate.

"*Mi vida*," he said when he kissed her. She'd been standing in the kitchen watching the children and had turned, smiling, when he'd come in. He held both her hands.

"What is it?" Her face took on a worried cast. "Has something happened?"

"Sit." He sat down and pulled her down to sit opposite him, still holding her hands, kneading them. "Something amazing. I can hardly believe it. I've been promoted. I never thought when I took the exam that it would make any difference; you know how they are about us. But the assistant chief called me in to tell me today. Sergeant. Effective immediately." He didn't tell her how Galloway had gone on and on about how he'd had to go against the chief and the board to push the promotion through.

"I knew you would do it!" Rosario leapt off her chair and sat on his lap, throwing her arms around him. In the next moment she was up, pacing the kitchen. "We will celebrate, go out. I don't feel like cooking anyway! *Dios mio!*" She crossed herself and held her hands momentarily in a position of prayer. "I must phone Marta!"

"Rosi, just let's enjoy it. Don't phone anybody just yet. We can go out, sure, but ... I don't know."

She came to sit opposite him. "You don't seem that happy. Do you understand what a big thing this is? It's everything. You always said there'd never be a Mexican sergeant. What are you afraid of? I hope you don't think you don't deserve it! I won't listen to that. You are their best officer, and you know it."

What was bothering him? "It will probably mean longer hours," he said.

"I know, but it's going to be okay. I'm here. I'll look after things. I'm so proud of you, *viejo.*" She leaned over and kissed him again. "Okay, I won't tell anyone, only when you're ready."

He lay awake long into the night. He knew he was being ridiculous. It was something he'd dreamed about since joining the force and had watched as Anglo police officers— some not as competent as he was—were promoted around him. The thing he couldn't shake was, why him? And he couldn't forget Galloway's voice: "I took a big risk for you, buddy. I hope you appreciate that. You better not let me down." Why did Galloway seem to doubt his loyalty? Of course. They don't trust us. Well, he'd show him. He'd be the best, hardest working, most loyal damn sergeant in the history of the Tucson Police Department.

"**YOU WERE GONE** a long time." Rex Holden, usually unperturbed by his wife's coming and goings, was worried. She'd been gone for four hours. He normally didn't mind her little shopping jaunts. He had observed that she needed to be up and doing more than he did, and she never really went overboard.

"Oh, sweetie, don't be upset with me. I was so surprised. I was just looking at a cute handbag on sale here and my cousin Bernie turned up all upset, looking for me. You remember him from the wedding. He said my sister Lola was in trouble. I told you I have a sister here, didn't I?" A tear splashed on Meg's gloved hand, and she wiped it away hurriedly. She took off her gloves and collapsed on the love seat.

"My dear, whatever is the matter?" Holden got off the bed where he'd been reading the paper and sat by her, taking her hand.

Meg turned to him, unable to contain her tears. "It's so awful. My sister's husband left her high and dry. He cleaned out the savings and left her and the two kiddies with nothing. Her landlord has told her she has to be out by the end of the week, and her sitter said she won't work until she gets paid. I hate to ask you this, honey, but could we give her something to tide her over? Two hundred dollars would help her just get through this. I know it's a lot to ask. She has a job and everything, so it's really all she needs to get a sitter and that."

Rex Holden felt his heart swell. It wasn't too much to

ask. Nothing was too much to ask, if he could just get her smiling again.

"Come on," he said, standing and pulling her up. "We'll give Rog something to do. He can drive us to the bank, and then we'll go buy you something nice to wear, and we'll have a cocktail before dinner and look at the sunset. We can drop the money off to her on the way back. What do you say?"

"Oh, sweetie! You're a doll! It's going to mean so much to her." She pulled him close and kissed him. "Where would I be without you?" she whispered. She would have to tell him that Lola was too embarrassed to have anyone see the way she lived.

CHAPTER THREE

—————

DARLING FOUND LANE STRETCHED ON a lounge chair by the
pool under a striped umbrella. He pulled up a chair and
removed his hat and jacket. "I don't care if it is only sev-
enty something, it's hot. It's that relentless beating down
of the sun. How was your morning?"

"Exceedingly interesting." Lane put her book open and
face down on the round table next to her and sat up, looking
around to make sure they were alone. "I've discovered
something disquieting about our neighbours in the villa,"
she paused, looking into his eyes. "You know, I'd forgotten
how handsome you are."

"Try to stick to the subject." Darling smiled and considered returning the compliment. How very lucky he felt
to have persuaded her to marry him. "Now then, the disquieting villa people."

"To be honest I don't think I should say, outside here,
as we are. It's well past lunchtime. Ought we to get dressed?"

"As much as I'd like to gaze at you in that red bathing

suit, yes. And then should we go horseback riding or something? I understood from Galloway it is the done thing. He's given me the name of an outfit that hires out horses."

"You're not forgetting we are dining with that nice couple from Wisconsin?" Lane collected her book and towel and prepared to leave the pool. They walked past a row of new palm trees, and along the winding path to their room.

"All right, we're out of earshot. What did you learn about the villa people? By that, I assume you mean that May–December couple," Darling said, closing the door and pulling off his tie.

"Another May, or even April, has been introduced. I heard the woman leaving the villa with a giggling but loving adieu, promising not to spend too much money, and then she hurried off and met a very young man with a moustache in one of the corridors in the main building and, well, they got into a bit of a scrum."

"You followed her? You're absolutely without scruples, you know that?" Darling said with evident admiration.

"I didn't mean to see them; I came around the corner looking for the gift shop and there they were. I beat a hasty retreat and came out to the pool to think about it."

"Concluding?"

"That she is not particularly happy and seems to be carrying on a desperate affair with a young man with a moustache. Probably younger than she is."

"Let that be a lesson to you. A double life never did anyone any good. You ready?"

"Yes. Can we give the horses a miss, do it another day? I've just got stuck into my book and I might need a nap to prepare for this dinner tonight. We were up rather late last night," Lane said, pinning up one side of her hair, directing a glance at him in the mirror.

Darling, a slave to the curve of her cheekbones and the fall of her auburn hair, took her hand. "Right. Lunch and a lie down. Perhaps I can tell you about my morning. I'm not sure I'd go as far as 'disquieting,' but something like it."

The first rush of lunch eaters had come and gone, and they were able to get a table overlooking the cadmium yellow and moss-green-tiled fountain they so admired. The water glinted in the sunlight, and trees with yellow puffballs in full bloom—which Lane had learned were called sweet acacia—bobbed decorously in a gentle afternoon breeze.

"I think I didn't quite recognize the Galloway I knew before," Darling said, pulling apart a roll. "He was very informal, not to say slapdash. He introduced me to an earnest young sergeant as his 'pal.' I can't imagine introducing anyone to Ames that way. What was interesting is that this Sergeant Martinez looked to be a man of much more formality. He leapt up and shook my hand. He was in some distress because he wasn't able to find an arrest report and some evidence he needed for court. Galloway was dismissive of him when we were alone together. 'Good at the lingo and brave, but not really up to the job of a real policeman' sort of thing. Said he had white policemen who are more reliable. I don't think I would have suspected him of that sort of prejudice. I feel like he's not who I thought he was, if you see what I mean."

"I'm sure you get that sort of attitude at home. I think Constable Terrell must have to put up with that sort of rubbish," Lane said, referring to Jerome Terrell, the Nelson Police Department's new hire and the first black officer on the force.

"Yes, but not from me, is my point."

HIDALGO SHIFTED HIS behind on the wooden chair he used as his surveillance base across the road from the hotel. There was a field with a few scrawny cattle and some mesquite trees near the road that threw a little shade in the heat of the day. He hadn't minded the job at first, especially when he got a glimpse of her, but he began to wonder why a man would put his wife to work on a racket like that.

He sat up straight when a cab pulled up—not at the foot of the stairs up to the main entrance of the hotel but farther down, at the gate where the help went in and out. A young man in a nice suit got out and leaned into the car, saying something to the driver. The young man looked like an operator, Hidalgo thought. Maybe he was seeing one of the maids. A full ten minutes went by, and he was beginning to lose interest when the gate opened. He was startled to see that it was the young man ushering Meg Holden hurriedly out the gate and into the cab.

Frowning, he watched the cab disappear in a cloud of dust and make the turn at the end of the road that would take them back to town. This was new. He pulled out his notebook and jotted down the time. Should he wait till they got back? He tried to imagine Mr. Griffin's response. He'd be angry if he hadn't followed through. On the other hand, maybe this was something to do with Mr. Griffin, someone he'd sent to fetch her, and therefore none of his business.

JAMES GRIFFIN SAT at his desk in a dark and cluttered office at the back of his restaurant. He'd come in through the front door, as he did every morning, just to revel in the size of the place when it was empty and quiet and be comforted by the redolence of stale cigarettes and liquor that spoke of the restaurant's popularity. He lit up a Fonseca cigar and leaned back in his desk chair and contemplated the ceiling.

He'd have to lie low for a bit and not move any money around—he'd have to lie low for a bit, period. He was pretty sure he'd closed the tap at the nursing home. His man on the inside had taken care of the other. The only fly in his ointment, really, was his wife. He always hated this part of the business—her being with someone else. Of course, she was loyal as loyal as could be and always glad to be back with him, and maybe he shouldn't be going out to see her as much as he did. He was doing it more than he had in the past. He should stop. It was just making him mad.

The knock on the door made him jump. "What?" he barked.

Hidalgo came in and shuffled in front of the desk.

"Spit it out," Griffin said. "You have something to report?"

Opening his notebook, Hidalgo began to read. "At two forty-five today, a cab pulled up to the back gate—that one you go to, sir. A young man in a white suit got out, entered, and approximately ten minutes later emerged with Mrs. Holden, your good wife, sir, and entered the cab. They drove east and then turned south at the corner."

"Come again?" Griffin said, leaning forward.

"At two forty-five, a cab pulled up—"

"I heard you, you moron!" Griffin shouted, standing up. He began to pace behind his desk, and then wheeled on his henchman. "It didn't occur to you to jump in that car I provided and see where the hell they were going, I don't suppose."

Hidalgo gulped. "I thought it might be something to do with you, you know, like you'd sent someone to pick her up."

"Is it likely I'd send an oily, overdressed gigolo to pick up my wife?"

Hidalgo could think of no safe answer.

"I'm surrounded by idiots! You go back out there, and you follow next time that happens. Got it?"

"Yes, sir."

Hidalgo drove back to the street around the corner from the hotel and parked, and then sat and lit a cigarette, relieved to be out of the storm front in his boss's office. And there was a lot to think about. If the man in the white suit wasn't one of Mr. Griffin's men, who was he? He tried to remember what he'd seen between them in the brief period between her coming through the gate and getting into the cab. Was she running something on her own? He smiled briefly at the thought of Mr. Griffin getting bested at his own game by his own dame. He was aware that his admiration for her had been growing, just on the basis of her looks, but this thought of her on the make behind her husband's back made him almost proud.

BEFORE DINNER, HOTEL management invited guests to watch the sunset from the roof of one of the buildings while staff served drinks. Darling and Lane, along with Ivy and Jack Renwick, stood looking west, holding martinis. The sky overhead seemed huge, and Lane could imagine the turning of the earth away from the sun. Bands of orange and gold stretched across the sky over the distant Tucson Mountains. As the sky darkened, the temperature dropped. Lane was glad of the cardigan she'd brought. She noticed some of the other women wearing shawls, elegantly slung across their shoulders. I must look into that, she thought.

Ivy Renwick, like Lane, was wearing a cardigan. "I never tire of the sunsets here," she said. "I mean, the sun goes down in Winnebago County, too, but it's just not the same. Of course, I don't usually have a martini in hand, either. I'm usually in an apron making Jack's dinner!"

"She makes a fine dinner, my Ivy," Jack said, putting his arm around his wife's shoulders. "I'm getting cold. What say?"

"Yes, do let's go down," Lane said. "I'm famished, though I've done nothing all day but lie around."

"I love your accent," Ivy said, as they came down the outside stairs to the poolside patio. "It's very sophisticated."

At their table, the waiter startled Lane by taking up her napkin and placing it on her lap for her. She glanced at Darling, and then looked away, afraid she would laugh at his discomfiture.

"Tell me, Fred, what do you do up in Canada?"

"I'm a police inspector in our tiny little town. You?"

Jack sat back and smiled. "I just got made president

and chairman of my electronics company. I mean, it wasn't meant to be mine, really, but when my dad died, he left me in charge. I just concluded a big contract with a local hotel that is adding a big convention centre." He looked down, turning his fork over and over, and then sighed; he seemed to be considering his next words. "I'm lucky, I guess, but it's sort of at my older brother's expense. He was supposed to be the one to take over the company, but he came out of the war a little funny, and I guess Dad didn't want to put him in charge. Honestly, I don't know how to square it, in some ways. All my life he's been the one. I was just going to go into engineering, maybe start a small firm of my own. The war changed everything."

"What about you?" Lane asked quietly, turning to Ivy, surprised by what looked like a momentary flash of ... flash of what, anxiety perhaps, on Ivy's face as she watched her husband talking. But it disappeared as she spoke.

"Well, I'm obviously a housewife now, since we married, though in the war I taught wire communications. That's how I met Jack originally; his dad's company hired me to coordinate the communications offices. He was a nobody then. His dad believed in starting his sons on the factory floor." She laughed suddenly, her face lighting up for a brief second.

She seems content, Lane thought. Happy to give up everything she did before to be his wife. She wondered how Ivy could go from really important work to keeping house. But, of course, that was what women everywhere were doing. Would it be as simple as that for her? She and Darling had discussed their domestic arrangements. She was certain he would never ask this utter domesticity of her, but did one just slide into it? The husband goes off to work, the wife stays home to tend the house, the garden, the meals. Perhaps it had its compensations. Time alone, so one didn't lose oneself completely, for example. The trouble was, she did miss it—not the war, exactly, or even the dubious thrill of jumping out of airplanes, but being useful. Offering her skills to help Darling and the police force solve some recent crimes had made her feel useful again. Would he leverage his position as her husband to stop this sort of activity?

Lane turned away from this disquieting line of thought, to find that Ivy had asked about what Lane did before she married.

"I'm a writer, of sorts. I worked in an office during the war, of course, nothing clever like what you did." Lane tried to sound dismissive to avoid any deeper questions.

"Oh, you shouldn't denigrate what you did. Every bit of war work helped, don't you think? I taught men things they thought I had no business knowing. I saw them looking at each other with 'who does this dame think she is?' written all over their faces, but after a while, they paid attention, when they found they had to work hard to learn what I already knew. I had a degree in engineering, which is the reason I got that job at the factory. I could do what a man could do, but for cheaper. It's why I got the war work as well. I had to break information into pieces that people without any college training could understand. The army let me stay on till the end, even though Jack and I were married."

"Do you miss it?" Lane asked.

"I miss being part of something bigger, the camaraderie. I was happy to discover lots of men who were very accepting of my role, and those of other women. But now we're thinking about a family." Ivy tilted her head a little and looked momentarily distrait.

"Oh! Are you ...?" Lane leaned toward Ivy and dropped her voice.

"Shhh. I haven't told him yet," Ivy said, giving her chin the slightest tilt toward her husband. "Not till I'm sure." She looked down and then glanced at her husband with a look that seemed far from that of a happy mother-to-be.

Dinner was brought out and the metal hoods ceremoniously lifted off their plates. After the appropriate exclamations of appreciation, Darling continued talking to Jack, and between her exchanges with Ivy, Lane could hear that they were discussing the older brother. She looked forward to hearing the full story from Darling later. She was surprised by how much the Renwicks talked about their personal lives. She could certainly not imagine any English person doing the same thing after having just met someone.

"This is so good. It's a treat to have someone cook for me!" Ivy said. "This is a real roast beef dinner!"

"I'm lucky. Both my husband and I are a little short of culinary skills, so we are learning together. He makes a wonderful steak!"

Ivy stopped her fork midway to her mouth and put it back on the plate, staring at Darling. "He cooks? But he's a police inspector."

"I think it relaxes him," Lane offered, now unsure about how uncommon her worldview might be.

"Jack is a saint, honestly he is, but other than grilling a hot dog outside, I wouldn't trust him near my kitchen!"

Jack smiled and took his wife's hand for a moment. "I'd be lousy, and that's the truth. Anyway, like she said, I'm not allowed near the place!"

———

"I DON'T SUPPOSE you could produce a respectable dead body for me to practice my skills on?" Ashford Gillingham said, standing in the doorway of Ames's office with a piece of paper.

"I told you, Gilly. No wrongful deaths till the boss gets back. Anyway, Nelson's a small town when all is said and done. People can't be murdered every day of the week. We'd be a ghost town in no time. Anything?"

"I picked up a couple of clear pads on the can," he said. "Middle finger, maybe, and thumb. I hand them over to you and go back to cleaning out my files and lining my tools up neatly. Done my job. Yours is to see if you have any matches."

Ames sighed. "I don't even have a matching crime on the records. I suspect this is a one-time thing. Miss Van Eyck thinks it was a man she had to put back in his place when he came to have his car worked on at their garage. I should go across and get his dabs and find out where he was between the hours of who the heck knows, but she doesn't want it followed up on."

"Van Eyck. Isn't that the name of the pretty blonde you turned up with at Darling's wedding? I admire your optimism, Sergeant, I'll say that! It's convenient that there's been an outbreak of crime on her garage door."

"Yes, thanks, Gilly. If there's nothing else, I've got work to do."

"Try not to make a mess of this one, too," Gilly said as a parting shot.

Ames knew he didn't mean the vandalism investigation, and he thought it an unfair characterization that he "made a mess" of his relationship with Violet Harding. He simply realized they weren't suited, not that he was going to satisfy Gilly with an explanation, which, after all, he wasn't entirely sure showed him off in a good light. Maybe he was being too choosy. How could anyone know right away what kind of person a girl was? What kind of person was Tina Van Eyck, for example? It wasn't enough that her smile made his heart flutter. Her initial fury about the garage door showed some depth of anger that maybe ought to worry him, not to mention her sudden antagonism toward the police. Where had that come from? She had originally struck him as attractively confident and sure, but he worried she might not be that different from Violet, who had seemed always furious at him for something.

———

"ARE YOU SURE you don't mind? It's almost the last time I'll abandon you. I promised Galloway I'd go for a drive around his district. I'll be back right after lunch, and we'll go for a ride at that ranch up in the hills that he recommended."

"I'll try to cope with just the pool and my book. I may even have a nap, since this place fairly cries out for afternoon napping. Or perhaps I'll send Angela and the Armstrongs a postcard. Shall I send one to Ames signed by you?"

"Don't be ridiculous. I'd never live it down, and neither would he."

"You're quite sweet when you're gruff. Have fun with Galloway, whom … well, never mind." Lane put her straw hat on, pinned it, and looked for *The Nine Tailors*.

"What?" asked Darling.

"It's nothing. It's unfair, really, I shouldn't judge on one meeting. I just don't think I quite like the man. I thought, don't you know, that he was being rude about his wife and she didn't care for it." She kissed him and swept out with her book and a towel.

Darling stood at the front of the inn waiting for Galloway in something of a turmoil. For one, Lane in her red bathing suit with her straw hat tilted over her left eye was hard to abandon, but he also became aware of something about being married to Lane. He was used to forming judgements, usually, he told himself, quite accurate ones, but he now had an astute and intelligent wife to provide a new perspective. He realized he'd had a feeling about their evening at Paul Galloway's home that he'd not been able to articulate, and Lane had just identified what he now saw to be true. As the police car pulled up and Galloway leaned over and called out to him to hop in, Darling wondered anew about his old colleague.

THE WATER IN the turquoise-tiled pool stirred and eddied in bands of luminescent blue and gold in the late morning sun. Lane, soothed by its beauty and the quiet talking and laughing around her, rested her book on her stomach and closed her eyes. The warmth of the sun on her eyelids, the gentle cooing of the doves, and the lapping, fading sounds that accompany the drifting call of a nap by a pool sent her into a doze.

Then two shots.

When they came, it felt like they had come from inside her, from some dream that had been wiped away by its own sounds. A scream and the scattering of birds, all rising at once in a panic, brought her fully to life, and she leapt up, suddenly aware that those few people who had been by the pool when she'd gone to sleep had all but disappeared. One older woman on the opposite side of the pool was on her feet, clutching her towel against her chest and looking frantically around.

"What was that?" the woman cried hoarsely.

"Stay here," Lane commanded. The scream seemed to have come from near the villa somewhere, and she ran around the hedge, toward the villa patio, wrapping her towel around her waist.

The Bette Davis blonde, her hands over her mouth, her face white, was staring down at the body of Jack Renwick, lying flat on his back, his chest rent by the bullets that had mowed him down. Lane rushed to the woman and took her arms and shook her gently to get her to stop staring at the dead man and focus.

"Run and get the office to call an ambulance and the police. Now!"

Lane's commanding tone seemed to bring the terrified woman around, and she stumbled toward the main building, sobbing. Lane knelt down and, stilling the turning of her stomach at the sight of the torn flesh and gory white shirt, felt Renwick's neck for a pulse. A pointless gesture, she knew. He was dead. One of the bullets had certainly penetrated his heart. A man from the front desk barrelled toward the scene, shouting, "Oh my God! Oh my God!" He leaned forward and appeared about to try to do something with the body.

"Don't touch him, please," Lane said firmly, reaching her hand out to block him. "The police will need him as he is."

The man, uncertain anyway, recoiled and looked helpless. The blond woman's husband came out of the villa, bemused, woken from a nap, and demanded to know what all the racket was, then stopped, aghast at the scene before him.

"You," Lane commanded, looking at the blond woman's husband, "can you get something from your room to cover him with?" She could have gone to her own room, right nearby, but she was reluctant to leave until the police arrived; she had learned during the war that it was better to keep people in shock busy.

"How could this happen?" the distraught front-desk agent cried, wringing his hands. The blond woman stood frozen in the doorway of the main building, a handkerchief up to her nose, reluctant to come any closer. The old woman by the pool hovered uncertainly near the hedge, craning her neck to see what was happening. Other guests who had been sitting down to lunch had come out and pressed up behind the blonde.

"How could this have happened?" the desk agent repeated.

That, thought Lane, is a good question. She turned and looked in the direction the bullets must have come from. She remembered they had been loud and very near. There was the low boxwood hedge between where they stood and the pool area, and a fence with a much higher planting of boxwood along the far side of the pool. That must be the road behind there, she thought. The growing scream of sirens became audible.

Where was Ivy Renwick?

CHAPTER FOUR

A MES WAS FINISHING UP SOME paperwork on a robbery at a local mining office and was feeling guilty that he'd not gotten out to photograph the garage door at the Van Eycks' as he'd promised. The call had taken up the whole morning because the burglar had unexpectedly not made an attempt at the safe but had gone through papers, pulling open drawers and scattering the contents across the office, and the secretary had been trying to figure out what, if anything, had been actually stolen. He was nonplussed at the knock on his office door.

"Constable Terrell. Do you have something on this break-in?"

"No, sir, but there's been an accident on the road just before the Harrop ferry. I've already contacted the ambulance service."

"Right," Ames said, jumping up to reach for his coat and hat. "Come with me. Casualties?" he asked, as they clattered down the stairs.

"The woman who called it in said there was one man in the car. She was a bit hysterical. She said she approached because the car was in a ditch, like the driver had lost control, and she said the man looked unconscious. She was coming off the ferry and saw it just before the main road. Car doors are locked. She apparently lives nearby and rushed home to make the call." By this time, he too had retrieved his coat and hat and was holding the car keys up.

Ames reached for them and then pulled his hand back. "Would you like to drive?"

"Yes, sir, if you like. I haven't driven this vehicle. Any peculiarities I should know about?"

"As a matter of fact, there's a kind of glitch when you throw it into reverse," Ames said, opening the door to the unfamiliar passenger seat. His anxiety about someone else driving what he thought of as his beloved car was somewhat ameliorated by what he considered a very proper question from Terrell.

As they drove the curve around the bottom of the hill the Nelson hospital was perched on, they heard the sound of a siren. "Should hit the ferry at the same time," Terrell said. A sleety rain began to fall, and he leaned forward slightly as the wipers worked inadequately to clear the windshield.

The ferry was heading away from town, bobbing on the dark green choppy water toward the north shore. They clearly had just missed it.

Terrell turned off the engine, and he and Ames sat watching it, the wake looking almost luminescent on the dark surface of the water.

"And that's that," Ames said. "Hurry up and wait."

"I have my thermos of coffee, sir," Terrell said, holding it up. "And two cups."

"That's pretty forward thinking of you, Constable. Any cookies?"

"No, sir. But I'll make a note for next time."

They sat, companionably drinking coffee, sweet and milky, just as Ames liked it. He looked about him at the bleak darkness of the lake and the gloomy bank of forest on the other side. It was a cold and deeply misty day. The kind of day that made it seem like the coming winter would last forever. He could see patches of snow already visible between the trees, and he sank into a kind of impatient melancholy. He wanted to ask Terrell about himself but wasn't sure how to go about it. They'd never had a coloured officer on the Nelson force. In fact, he wasn't sure he'd ever met a coloured person at all.

"Nice country, sir. It reminds me a little of Nova Scotia."

Pleased at this opening, Ames said, "Is that where you're from? How'd you find yourself all the way out here? I mean ..." But whatever Ames thought he was going to say next eluded him, and he quickly felt flustered.

Terrell smiled. "Not too many of my kind around here, is what you're thinking. I just wanted a change of scene. It's a big country. I heard there was an opening here, so I came."

"Right," said Ames quickly. "Right, well, have you, I mean, how are you finding it with the uh—"

"Oh, the guys are okay, sir. The inspector is great, everybody."

"Oh. Well, good." Ames thought about people's ability to be casually offensive about others in general, but polite when confronted with actual individuals.

"So you trained in Nova Scotia?"

"I was with the West Nova Scotia Regiment in the last two years of the war. Military police and reconnaissance. I was at university before that."

Ames nodded and opened his window to turn out the last drops of coffee in his mug. He shuddered and looked at his watch. He wished he had cigarettes, but his mother, perhaps because of the coughing and spitting death of his father, had made him promise never to take up the vile habit, as she suspected cigarettes were to blame. He smoked sometimes in the bar after work with the other fellows, but he could never really break his promise and take it up full-time. It would have provided a bit of spurious warmth now, though. Constable Terrell looked like a non-smoker.

———

THE HUBBUB OF the police taking over the scene and pushing gawkers away found Lane standing with the blond woman who was still distraught. Her husband, who had produced a blanket to cover the body, had been working his way around the melee to reach them but had been held back by a police officer.

"Thank you," Lane said. "You did the right thing."

"I've never been so frightened in my life! I was just saying hello to him and ... that ... that awful noise ... the way he fell like that ..." She began to sob with great ragged breaths.

"Sweetheart, what happened?" The woman's husband finally made it past the police officer. He put his arm around his wife, who buried her face in his chest. He looked at Lane, still uncomprehending. "I don't understand. What happened?"

"I don't really know, myself. I heard the gunfire and found Mr. Renwick like that. Can you look after your wife for a moment, maybe sit her down over there? I think the police may want to talk to her because they'll want to know what she saw. I'm Lane Winslow. What are your names? I can let them know."

This caused the woman to look up, panic evident in her eyes. "Oh, I can't, I can't talk to anybody. They can't make me, can they?" She looked imploringly at her husband and then glanced back at the scene.

Stroking his wife's head and offering a few more soothing words, the man turned to Lane. "I'm Rex Holden; this is my wife, Meg. I really don't think she can talk to anyone." The police had removed the bedspread that Holden had supplied to cover the body and were leaning over it taking pictures. Meg Holden looked away in horror and made a choking noise.

"Maybe if you just sit over there, I can get someone to bring her some water. If she was standing right there, the police are going to have to talk to her. I don't think there's any way around it."

Rex Holden nodded grimly and took his shivering wife to sit on the edge of the lawn on a seat that overlooked the fountain rather than the turmoil of activity around Renwick's body. The Holdens safely dispatched, Lane, conscious that her state of undress was hardly appropriate to the grim goings-on at a crime scene, approached a uniformed policeman who appeared to be in charge.

"Excuse me," she began.

"Just go inside, miss," he said impatiently, and then he shouted at an officer near the door. "I thought I told you to keep people away from here!"

"My name is Lane Winslow. I assume you are the officer in charge? I was the second person on the scene. Mrs. Holden, who is sitting over there, was talking to Mr. Renwick when he was shot. I've asked her to stay there in case you want to talk to her." Lane delivered this in an insistent manner to forestall any further attempt to dismiss her.

It seemed to work. The detective looked at her, then at the Holdens, and pushed his hat marginally back off his forehead.

"You know this man?"

"We just met. We're guests here, and we dined with them last night. His name was Jack Renwick and his wife is Ivy Renwick."

"Where's the wife?" The detective looked around briefly.

"I don't know." Just at that moment, Lane saw a movement at the door of the main building. Someone was saying, "Step aside." And then Assistant Police Chief Paul Galloway came through, and behind him was Darling.

The detective looked surprised to see Galloway but nodded. "Sir."

"What's going on, Sergeant? We heard it on the radio."

Darling nodded at the man who had been talking to Lane. "Sergeant Martinez," he said by way of greeting.

Martinez pointed to where the body was being photographed. "A man named Renwick has been shot, sir. That's all we know so far. This lady thinks she has something to add." He nodded toward Lane and then turned back to his boss. "She was second on the scene and knows the name of the deceased. I was just collecting some information from her. That lady over there was present when the man was shot."

Stepping past him, Darling thought Galloway had a peculiar expression on his face. Trying to take in the scene perhaps, he thought. Darling looked at Lane with a slight raise of his eyebrows that did not disguise the relief he felt at seeing her unharmed.

Galloway shook his head and looked his officer. "*This* lady, Martinez, is Inspector Darling's wife. Get someone to collect the information from the two witnesses, and you come with me," he said peremptorily and then turned to Darling. "You'll want to be here with your wife while someone questions her, of course. I'm going to have a look." Galloway went over to where the body was being photographed as if a murder scene was a casual daily affair. Sergeant Martinez talked to a man in uniform who was taking notes and nodded in the direction of Lane and Darling.

"You're unbelievable," Darling said. "I can't leave you alone for five minutes. Are you all right?" He reached out and took her hand.

"I'm fine, though my ears are still reverberating. The shots were very close. And before you ask, I didn't find him—poor Mrs. Holden over there did, or rather, was standing right by him when he was shot. What I'm really worried about is Ivy Renwick. It's going to be absolutely ghastly for her. She's—"

"Ma'am?" A young police officer with blue eyes tipped his hat slightly at Lane, interrupting her. "Sorry, ma'am. Officer Sandler. Do you mind?"

Lane was struck by how young and fresh-faced he looked. A bit like Ames. She couldn't help smiling, though she was aware of beginning to feel a little shaken up as her initial part in dealing with the emergency was over and the enormity of Renwick's death began to hit home. "Not at all. Where would you like me?" She looked briefly at Darling, who had been about to say something to her when Sandler spoke again.

"Maybe over here? You're welcome to come, sir." Sandler indicated the dining area under the ramada. Darling looked at Lane indecisively. He did, in fact, want to be there when Lane was questioned, not for the protective reasons Sandler no doubt had in mind, but more out of curiosity. He remembered the first time he'd met her and questioned her about a man found dead in the creek that served her house. He'd been quite dazzled, he'd realized later, by her clarity and sangfroid.

"Officer Sandler, can you ask one of the officers to get some water for Mrs. Holden? She's very upset," Lane said, looking toward where the Holdens were sitting with their backs to her. Holden had his arm around his wife, who was crying, judging by the convulsive bobbing of her body.

Sandler, who'd been about to sit down, went to the door and spoke quietly to one of the policemen keeping back the curious crowd.

He returned and opened his book. "Can you just tell me everything you can remember, Mrs. Darling?"

"I go by Lane Winslow," Lane said, pointing at where the officer had written her name as Mrs. Darling.

"I will have to use your legal name, ma'am."

Stifling a desire to suggest sweetly that perhaps her husband could give her version of the events for her, Lane said instead, "Of course. Lanette Evelyn Winslow Darling." This was no time to stand on principle.

She wanted to recapture the exact moment she had woken to the sound of the two gunshots, in particular, how close they had sounded. "I was dozing by the pool when I heard two shots, very close together, and then a scream. I ran in the direction of the scream and found Mrs. Holden looking terrified and Mr. Renwick as you found him. I sent Mrs. Holden to get the hotel to phone you, and I felt for a pulse, but obviously it was pointless." Lane stopped and waited for Sandler to catch up.

"You said you knew the victim?"

"Yes, my husband and I had dinner with Mr. Renwick and his wife yesterday evening. They are from Wisconsin."

"You said two shots."

"Yes. While I was waiting for the police to arrive, I tried to piece together where they originated. There's a thick hedge between the pool and the street over there. It struck me how nearby the sound was, as if someone was firing from the pool area where I was lying. But there was no one by the pool, except an older woman who jumped up when I did. I think it's possible they came from the street, through, or over, that hedge. I can show you what I mean."

Sandler looked in the direction she was pointing, and then toward where Martinez was talking to Galloway.

"If it was from the street, might there be any sign of the shooter?" Lane suggested.

"That's exactly what I was thinking, ma'am. Can you wait here?"

Mrs. Holden, still sitting on the edge of the garden with her husband, had turned and was watching Lane, and when the officer had hurried over to Galloway, she got up, extracted her hand from that of her husband, and approached Lane.

"How long is this going to take? I can't take this! I need to lie down. How long can they keep us here?"

Lane was sympathetic. It must have been horrific for Mrs. Holden to see a man killed right in front of her. "I don't know, Mrs. Holden. I'll ask the officer when he comes back if he can interview you and finish me up later. You must be in terrible shock."

"You got no idea! I near died of the shock. I don't know how you can stay so calm. Call me Meg, by the way. I'm still not used to *Mrs. Holden.*"

"I don't feel calm inside, Meg, I assure you!" This was true enough. She could still feel her own anxious heartbeats. "This is my husband, Inspector Darling. He's a police inspector in Canada, where we come from." Lane could see that as they talked, Meg Holden seemed less distraught. She wondered if after the initial shock, some of her distress was a show of sorts for her husband.

"Oh," she said. "Canada. I thought your accent was funny. Wait. Something's happening."

Meg and Lane looked over to the officers. Sandler was pointing toward the pool and Galloway, impatiently glancing toward Lane, nodded as if making a concession and dispatched two police officers to the pool area. Sandler started back toward them and then, seeing that Lane and Meg had been talking, moved quickly.

"You're going to have to go and wait there, miss," he said to Meg.

"Mrs. Holden was just asking me how long it would be. She's very shaken up because she was right by him when he was shot. Could you possibly interview her now? I'm happy to wait," Lane offered.

What Sandler might have offered in reply was forever lost because Ivy Renwick burst through the door and pushed past the police blockade, screaming.

"Jack! Jack! Oh my God ... I knew he was crazy!"

CHAPTER FIVE

"HOW DO YOU KNOW YOUR way around so well?" Ames asked, as they bumped off the ferry and sped north toward the Harrop turnoff. He'd have preferred snow to this icy, driving rain.

"When I first got here, I got out a map and drove the roads. One of the fellows showed me the extent of our outreach, so I thought I better get to know it. It's a habit from doing reconnaissance in the army, I guess."

Ames was silent for a moment. He had always been conscious of what he thought of as one significant difference between himself and his boss: Darling had been in combat, and he had not. He had tried to sign up in September of 1939 but was told he'd be required for policing at home. At nineteen he'd just landed a job at the Nelson Police, and though he had understood the need, he had felt keenly the envy of watching others, including his friends, going off on the big adventure. And he had seen how war had changed his friends when they returned. Some came home more serious, a little weary perhaps, but unwilling to fritter away their lives as they had seemed intent on doing as younger men. Some had returned as his father had from the Great War: damaged, angry, fearful in ways that seemed hard for them to get past.

"I wasn't able to sign up. They said I would be exempted for police duty here. I wish I could have."

"I wouldn't, sir."

There was something about the way Terrell said this that suggested he wished to say no more about the subject.

Terrell turned right down the road that led to the lake and the ferry landing and stopped the car in front of the listing green two-door Chevy. The ambulance was close behind. The listing car was at least a decade old. The icy rain was still slashing down. Ames got out, pulling his jacket around him, and strode to the car to look in the window.

"Doors are both locked. He doesn't look too well. We're going to have to break in," he said to the ambulance driver.

Ames gave the window a wipe with his lower arm to clear the water off. A man was slumped forward and against the door. His hat had been knocked off, perhaps as he fell forward, and was balanced on the steering wheel and dashboard. He certainly looked dead. The most the ambulance was going to do was take his body back to town. Still, there might be a chance he was unconscious.

"Go ahead," Ames said. "I should really put a crowbar in the car." Terrell had come up and offered Ames an open black umbrella, which was gratefully accepted.

The ambulance medic skirted the edge of the road and found a rock suitable to the job. He went around to the passenger side and smashed the window, then reached inside to open the door. Ames watched him gingerly brush the glass off the seat and lean in to feel for a pulse.

"Constable, could you get the camera?" Ames imagined the driver, taken suddenly by a heart attack, maybe clutching at his chest, losing control of the car. He's not going very fast because he's just come off the ferry, Ames thought, and he's going to turn at the top of the road. The car slides down the short embankment and comes to rest, askew, its nose in the dense underbrush at the edge of the forest. He slumps forward, or even keels over sideways toward the passenger seat because the car is listing steeply in that direction. Ames shook his head slightly. This man was leaning forward, with only his right arm fallen, his hand open, on the seat beside him. His left arm seemed to be jammed between himself and the driver-side door. His position went against gravity and logic.

The ambulance driver backed out of the car and shook his head.

"Dead." He wiped his hands on the back of his already rain-spattered trousers. "Most likely a heart attack. Strange that he's leaning against the door like that. It's like he was trying to get out in a hurry and couldn't."

Ames walked around the listing car, hunkering under the umbrella. "Nothing in the position of the car suggests he could have been injured by sliding into this ditch. We'd better get his wallet and confirm who he is. We'll take a few shots, and then can you load him up."

"Yes, sir!" said the driver with an exaggerated military salute, and then he made a beeline for the ambulance, pulling his hat down against the sleet.

"Oh, for God's sake, this downpour is all we need! Terrell, give me the camera."

The sudden clanging of the ferry gangplank made them both look up. Two cars were coming back to the north side. Both of them slowed down. The driver of the first one, a man in his fifties, stopped and rolled down the window, leaning his elbow on the ledge.

"Something wrong?" At an impatient honk from the car behind him, he waved his arm to have them go around, but Terrell, holding his black umbrella, moved to the second car and pulled out his identification with his free hand and asked the driver to wait.

Ames approached the driver of the first car, pulling out his own card. "I'm Sergeant Ames and that is Constable Terrell. Do you recognize this car? It's likely he was on the other side earlier today."

The man looked at Terrell, frowning, and said, "Oh." And then hesitated.

"Sir, I'm going to go have word with the ferry driver," Terrell said. "The guy in the other car is trying to get to an appointment in town."

"Thanks. I won't be a moment," Ames said. He turned back to the driver. He could feel the rain on the backs of his trouser legs. "Recognize the car?"

"I'm surprised to see one of them on the police force."

"I'm surprised you can't answer a simple question," Ames said. "Yes or no?"

The man turned his attention back to the car. "Well, no, now you ask. Is something wrong with the guy inside?"

"Do you live in Harrop or Procter?"

"I live out Ymir way, but I go visit my sister in Harrop. What's wrong with him?"

"Thank you, sir. I'll ask you to move on now, if you don't mind."

The man drove off, peeling onto the main road as if to show his ire at being kept out of the goings-on.

Ames waited while the second car pulled even with him. "Thanks for waiting, sir. We're just trying to find out if anyone recognizes the car here. Did you see it on the other side?"

The driver, an older man with his wife, turned his mouth down and shook his head. "Don't think so. Isn't one of ours. Is that someone in it?"

"So you don't recognize the car?" Ames pursued.

The man shook his head, but his wife, who had opened the passenger window and was staring through the rain at the car, said, "I recognize that licence plate."

Ames leaned down to look across her husband at her. "Ma'am?"

"It's unusual. I noticed it at the train station the other day."

Ames stood up and looked at the plate. It was white with green numbers. 65-018. He couldn't see how it was remotely unusual. "In what way?" he asked.

"Oh, well sixty-five minus eighteen is forty-seven. You see the small 'forty-seven' down the side, for this year."

Astounded that anyone would go to the trouble of doing sums to find a licence plate out of the ordinary, he leaned down again. "Are you certain, ma'am?"

Her husband shook his head. "The wife loves puzzles. And she used to teach mathematics, if you can believe it, back in the day, before I married her. So if she says it, you can count on it." He chuckled, and Ames guessed he'd made that joke more than once. The man looked at Ames impatiently. "Anyway, is that all? We're going to have to hurry."

"When did you see the car at the station?"

"I like to have coffee with friends a couple of times a week at that little café near there. I've seen it most days, I think, only I just noticed the numbers about a week ago," the woman answered.

Ames took their names and then touched the brim of his hat. "Thanks, sir, ma'am." He looked back to where the ferry sat idle in the drenching rain. Terrell was leaning into the tiny cabin holding his umbrella and talking to the ferryman. Ames turned back to the scene. The medics were inside the ambulance smoking. Ames slid the camera bag out of the police car—Terrell had replaced it to keep it dry—and took out a couple of flash bulbs to illuminate the inside of the damaged car. He stepped to the now-gaping passenger door and, propping the umbrella on his shoulder and the roof of the car, gingerly leaned in to snap some photos.

Terrell came back and walked around to where Ames was trying to get a close-up of the man's torso. "The ferryman is adamant that that car was not on his ferry today, either going or coming," he said.

Ames frowned and pulled himself upright, looking back toward the ferry. "That's odd."

"Yes, sir. I thought so as well. But I did find something else, if I can show you."

They walked toward the lake and then Terrell stopped and pointed. What Ames saw was a clear indication that a car had swerved violently in a way that left gravel splattered in an arc as it evidently had turned away from the water. Recent traffic had obliterated some of the tracks, but the swerve picked up again at the other side of the road and nearly disappeared off the side.

"Good catch, Constable. So it looks like someone must have sped down this road toward the ferry stop and then swerved violently so that he was heading back toward the main road. It could have been anyone, but my money is on our corpse up there." They walked toward the other edge of the road.

"He turns violently to stop himself from going into the lake, swings around facing back up the road and nearly goes off the edge *here*." Terrell pointed. "And then somehow he gains control of the car enough to get back on the road here but loses it again up there where we found him."

"So what we have is a dead man, in a locked car that is positioned as though it has come off the ferry. But it hasn't. Instead it's careened around and back up here. No car keys in evidence, by the way, though they may be on the floor under the seat or somewhere, and I think the way he's slumped, almost against the driver-side door, is a bit strange."

"I'm wondering if he felt some sort of attack coming on and turned down here to be off the main road? Then he realizes he's headed for the drink and turns the wheel desperately and ends up over here."

Ames looked up and tried to imagine this. It certainly looked plausible. "The way his left arm and leg are jammed between the door and the steering wheel may have kept him from falling onto the passenger side, either when he died or when the car tilted when he went into the ditch."

Pictures done, the medics took the dead man onto a stretcher and put him in the ambulance.

Ames searched the man's car and found nothing, except to note it had an unpleasant but vaguely familiar smell, as if he hadn't given the car a good cleaning in a while. They'd have to get into the trunk when they got the car towed to the station.

"You boys can help yourselves to his pockets," one of the medics said.

Ames climbed into the back of the ambulance and gingerly went through all of the dead man's jacket and trouser pockets, but they were empty. Frowning, he jumped back onto the road and repositioned his umbrella, looking at the space between the two vehicles.

Terrell called out from the car. "No sign of the keys, sir."

"And no sign of a wallet. Something is very strange here."

"Do you mind if we get going?" asked the driver. "We'll drop him at the hospital morgue and you fellows can figure out what to do with him after."

"Yes, of course."

As the ambulance drove off, Ames began looking around the car. "No wallet. No keys. Doors locked. Trunk locked. We'll have to get into that when we get the car back. Was this a robbery?"

"Man's dying of a heart attack or something, someone's with him, takes advantage of the situation by robbing him. But why not just roll the driver out and take the car as well?" Terrell asked. "A hitchhiker?" He too began a search, focusing on the shrubby edge of the forest.

"A hitchhiker would have taken the car too," Ames suggested.

"Unless he can't drive," Terrell said.

Ames walked toward the turnoff onto the main road. I've got a ride with someone who's suddenly keeled over with a heart attack; I've robbed him, he thought. I've locked him unnecessarily inside the car. I need to get away. Have I grabbed the wallet and stripped its contents and thrown it into the bush, or have I taken it with me?

He was surprised when he found it. It hadn't even been thrown, just dropped at the corner where the main road met the ferry turnoff. It was sitting in a pool of water that had gathered in a depression at the side of the road.

"Got the wallet!" he shouted down to Terrell. He pulled out his handkerchief and picked it up, shaking the water off it, and started back down to where the car still sat, forlornly tilted at the side of the road, as if it were already beginning its journey into decrepitude.

"I was looking for keys as well," Terrell said, "but nothing doing. It must have been someone he picked up. But why would someone take the keys? Do a lot of people hitchhike along this road?"

"That's a good question. I suppose some must. Not everyone owns a car."

Being careful not to put his fingerprints on it, Ames

opened the wallet. It was empty of cash. This increased the likelihood of a robbery but illuminated very little else. In a second pocket was a thick folded paper.

"God, this bloody awful rain. Hop in," Ames said, dropping the wallet onto the seat and collapsing his umbrella. Once back inside the police car, he pulled the wallet out with his handkerchief, laid it on the seat between them, and opened the thick card carefully. It was soaked through, but still perfectly identifiable as a British Columbia driver's licence.

It was a 1941 licence issued to one Barney D. Watts, complete with address of same.

———

"IT'S BEEN A horrible day," Lane said. She and Darling had dressed for dinner, but now sat listlessly on the end of the bed, in the grip of the same miasma of bewilderment that seemed to have overtaken the whole inn. "I'm not even sure I'm hungry. And I can't imagine how poor Mrs. Renwick and Mrs. Holden are feeling. Police have told both of them they can't leave. And I'm feeling a little guilty because I can't stop thinking about whether either of them has something to do with it."

"And here we go," said Darling, taking her hand. "Look, the place was awash with police officers today, right on the scene. It's nothing to do with us. And starving ourselves is not going to achieve anything but making me crotchety. Come. *Avanti*." Darling stood up and pulled Lane to her feet and folded her in an embrace.

"Of course, you're right, darling," Lane said from his

shoulder. She lifted her head and looked into his eyes, something she had an affinity for as much as he did for her cheekbones. "But, don't you—"

"Ah!" he said, raising an admonishing finger. "Dinner."

The dining room was subdued, as if the spectre of the death that had taken place right outside the window had instilled a fearful reluctance in the hotel guests to be noticed by the fates. When Lane and Darling were being ushered to a table, the room fell quiet for a moment, and then people leaned in to talk quietly and pretend not to look at her.

"We missed our drink with the sunset," Darling said. "A cocktail?"

"Won't it look unfeeling?" Lane asked.

"We can ask the waiter to hold the tiny umbrella and any other frivolity. In fact, we can ask him to put it in a mug, if you like. If anyone needs a drink, it's you. None of these people had to spend the afternoon being questioned by the police or attempting to keep poor Ivy Renwick from disintegrating. And Mrs. Holden too, for that matter."

The waiter dispatched for strong drink, and the steaks ordered, Lane sat with her chin resting on her hand. "I can't shake these two things: Meg was meeting a young man with a moustache on the sly, and Renwick apparently has an unstable, shell-shocked brother who could quite probably be angry about the family company going to his younger sibling."

"And you think," Darling raised his eyebrows in a show of incredulity, "that these things are related?"

"I'm not saying that, certainly, but they are ... I don't

know ... *circumstances*. How often have you said that secrets lie at the heart of every murder?"

"Never. And anyway, the possibly angry brother is no secret. Renwick told us quite openly about him. And may I remind you that Wisconsin is very far away. However, since you are so insistent on using dinnertime conversation that could better be spent on other topics, did you tell Officer Sandler either of these things?"

"I didn't. I was being asked to describe what I saw and heard. Anyway, I didn't think of it till afterward. And it's a dilemma, isn't it? Meg's liaison is most certainly a secret, and if it has nothing to do with Renwick being shot, then it's none of my business and revealing it would likely do untold damage to her marriage. And as to the other, you're right. Wisconsin is far away. But more importantly, Sandler asked Ivy if her husband had any enemies and she said he hadn't, that he was very well respected by all who knew him. Ivy told me the brother is on the way and should be here tomorrow. Apparently, she called him in a panic because she didn't want to have to cope on her own. The police will no doubt question him then. I'll go see both of them in the morning to make sure they're all right," Lane said, brightening slightly at the arrival of their drinks, about which none of their neighbours batted an eye.

THE MORNING, A symphony of golden sunlit colours and birdsong, found Lane sitting outside on the deck in a chair with her feet on a stool reading *The Nine Tailors*. As if on cue, a church bell nearby began to ring. She closed her eyes to listen. She was a child again, listening to the bells on

Sundays from the churches in the nearby village. Approaching footsteps interrupted her memories, and she looked up to see a hotel maid carrying a tray toward the villa.

"Good morning," Lane said, smiling. "Is that for the Holdens? They probably need it; I don't think they ate last night at all."

"Yes, ma'am. Mr. Holden ordered it."

"I'm sorry, I don't mean to delay you, what is your name?"

"Consuela Ruiz, ma'am."

"Oh, does your brother drive a taxi in town?"

The woman smiled and nodded. "Raúl, yes. You know him?"

"Yes, he drove us here from the train station."

The woman hesitated a moment longer. "But I better get this to the guests."

"Yes, of course. I was only going to ask if anything was ordered for Mrs. Renwick, next door here?"

"Oh. I don't think so."

Lane got up. "Okay. I'm going to see how she is getting on. Can you stop by when you've finished with the Holdens? I might ask you to bring something for Mrs. Renwick."

"Of course. You are a very kind lady to think about her."

Lane knocked lightly on the door of number 27 and called out, quietly. "Mrs. Renwick? Ivy? Can I come in?" She heard a shuffle from inside and let out the breath she realized she'd been holding.

The door opened slowly. Ivy Renwick, in a pale pink silk nightgown and peignoir, a sad testimony to the violent end of what was to have been her honeymoon, stood aside and let Lane come in.

"How are you? Did you sleep at all?"

Ivy shook her head and took the handkerchief she'd been holding clenched in her hand and pressed it to her eyes. She sat down on the bed. "Thank you for offering to stay with me last night. You're very kind. I did try to sleep, but in the middle of the night everything is a jumble. You can't think straight."

There was a gentle tap on the door. "Oh, that's the very nice woman who brought a tray for the Holdens," Lane said. "I asked her to stop by. Will you let me ask her to bring you coffee and a little something to eat?"

"Coffee, I guess."

Lane stepped out and said quietly, "Can you bring coffee for the two of us, and maybe some toast and a scrambled egg for Mrs. Renwick? Please put it on our bill. We're in number 26."

Consuela smiled. "Oh, I know that, ma'am. Everybody was talking about the brave lady in number 26!"

Back inside, Lane found Ivy sitting at the dressing table, smoking.

"You know, during the war I lost my brother and a cousin in the Pacific theatre. We were devastated, but I had work, and I just threw myself into it. But now I don't know where to turn. I feel like there's no point to anything. I just feel a confusion in my head, like I can't seem to get a hold of it." She rubbed a temple with her free hand. "Why was he shot?"

It almost seemed a rhetorical question. Lane, sitting on the bed, was silent for a moment. "You have your baby," she suggested gently.

Ivy Renwick turned and looked at her with such sorrow that Lane reached for her hand. "I hadn't even told him yet," she said, tears beginning to pool in her eyes.

"Ivy, yesterday when you came back you said, 'I knew he was crazy.' What did you mean by that? Did you mean Jack, or someone else?"

Ivy gave no answer, and turned away from Lane, holding the heels of her hands to her eyes. "Did I say that? God, I don't even know what I was saying. Just seeing him lying there …" She dissolved into a paroxysm of sobs.

Lane went into the bathroom and found a clean washcloth, which she soaked with hot water and folded into a compress. Ivy took it with a slight nod and held it against her eyes. After a moment, she looked at herself in the dressing table mirror. "God, I look a mess."

CHAPTER SIX

IN THE COLD BASEMENT MORGUE of the police station, Mrs. Watts stood rigidly in front of the remains of her husband. She was dressed in a dark wool coat, her black-gloved hands clenched tightly at her waist. Ames stood back respectfully by the door. He had been anxious about this moment as Darling had usually handled this sort of thing, but the hysterics he feared he might have to handle did not materialize.

"He tried to leave us," she said, staring at her husband's face, which had a lurid greenish hue in the light of the morgue. "He was much older than me, you know. He always thought I would leave him. What happens now?"

To Ames, the woman's calm seemed almost cold, but for the fact that she had burst into tears when he and Terrell had gone to her cottage to break the news. They had dropped the child at her grandmother's, and the first thing Mrs. Watts had asked when they were alone was if he had committed suicide.

"We don't know how he died. We'll have to wait for confirmation, but according to the ambulance medic, he might have had something like a heart attack. There will be a post-mortem. He was robbed, and the car keys are missing, so we suspect someone else was either with him or found him like that and took advantage of the situation. We will need to get information from you regarding his health when you feel up to it. It may take some time to understand how he … what happened." Ames thought about the word painted on the Van Eyck garage. Tina had thought it was Watts. He couldn't bring himself to ask Mrs. Watts about it. It seemed almost unimportant in the face of his death.

With some hesitation, Ames asked, "You said your husband tried to leave you. When was that?"

She turned toward the door, her hands still clutched in front of her, her handbag hanging off her wrist, but she did not look at him. "In September, but I persuaded him that he had a daughter to think about. Thank you for telling me everything you know, Sergeant Ames. Would you be kind enough to drive me back to my mother's? I must think of how I am to tell my daughter that her father is dead."

———

"LET ME ASK you something," Ivy Renwick said. The coffee and breakfast had arrived, and Consuela had organized them at a table by the window, where a small pot of geraniums set an incongruously cheerful tone. Ivy had attempted only a nibble of toast. "Who was that woman he was talking to?"

"Her name is Meg Holden. She and her husband are in the villa right beside us."

"I see." Ivy lit up another cigarette and then stubbed it out almost immediately, pushing the clay ashtray away. "I read recently these might not be good for me. I suppose I have to think of the baby."

"Ivy ..."

"I know. What did I mean? But it's ridiculous, impossible. It's just that his brother, well, Jack didn't know the extent of it. I know that sounds crazy to say, but Ned confided in me ... not that I wanted it, at all." She shuddered theatrically and drew her peignoir close around her.

"Can you bear to talk about it?" asked Lane. If Ivy had information about her husband's brother, she was going to have to tell the police. Lane would have to bring her to the idea.

"I was very sympathetic when Ned got home. He'd been wounded, though I never got the full extent of what happened. Jack wasn't home yet. Ned used to come around sometimes to where I worked. Of course, they wouldn't let him in because he behaved so erratically, and that made him angry. I had to ask him to come in the evening instead. It all started going sideways pretty quickly. He ... he told me he was in love with me and got, well, maudlin, and then quite aggressive. I never had the heart to tell Jack about that part of it. Ned was falling apart on all fronts, drinking and so on, and Jane, that's his wife, had left him. And then their father left the company in Jack's charge."

"Do you think it's possible, Ned ..." Lane didn't finish the sentence.

"Killed him?" Ivy's face crumpled again. She put down her coffee and reached for the napkin Consuela had brought with the eggs. "No, that's ridiculous. I don't see how. Anyway," she hesitated, "he's in Wisconsin."

Lane noted Ivy's denial of the possibility that her brother-in-law was responsible when he could, for example, have had him killed by someone else. She said, "You're going to have to tell that detective what you've told me."

"I know. I will. But what if it's nothing to do with him? It will only make everything worse."

"But if it's not him, you'll be happy to know that," Lane said, "and the police can get on with the job of finding who really killed your husband."

"WHAT HAVE YOU been up to?" Darling asked from his vantage point on the bed, where he had been reading, fully dressed, with his stocking feet crossed.

"Just making sure poor Ivy is all right. I feel sorry for her. She's pregnant, poor thing, and she's desperately unhappy because she hadn't told Jack yet."

"She told you that?" Darling marvelled at the way Lane seemed to manage to get people to confide in her.

"Well, she told me the other night at dinner."

"I bet she did," Darling said, with a touch of irony. "And, how is she coping?"

"Not well, and she's afraid her brother-in-law may have something to do with it, though she denies it. But she did talk about him a bit more. He does sound unbalanced. Angry about his brother taking over the business, professing to be hopelessly in love with her. But before you say anything, I told her she had to tell the detective in charge," Lane said. "Have you had breakfast?"

"No. I was waiting for you. And we'll have to be quick about it. We've had a call from Galloway. He's offered to have Priscilla drive us out to a famous mission church and she's coming in just under an hour."

"Oh," she said. "Do you think it's all right for us to go off? Will the police want to ask us anything else?"

"They need nothing more from you, and the sooner I get you away from here, the less likely you are to learn anything that will require us to be part of the police inquiry. This is in danger of fast becoming a busman's honeymoon, to quote your favourite author." Darling hopped off the bed, tucked in his shirt, and opened the door for Lane with exaggerated gallantry.

At their usual table under the ramada, Lane was delighted to see Consuela come around with the menus. "Darling, this is Miss Ruiz. You remember our cab driver? This is his sister. My husband, Inspector Darling."

Consuela bobbed slightly. "You can call me Chela. Everyone does."

Darling smiled at her. "Very nice to meet you, Chela. I thought your brother said you were on the cleaning staff?"

"Yes, but one of the girls is off sick so they asked me to step in. I think she was upset about ..." Her voice trailed off, and she looked in the direction of the previous day's drama.

"It was a terrible thing," Lane said. "But thank you again for this morning."

When Chela went off to collect their breakfasts, Darling said, "Galloway isn't the only person I heard from. Ames put a call through as well. I thought it was too much to hope he was just going to see how we were getting on, though that would have been extremely impertinent. He's got a peculiar death on his hands. He and the new man, Terrell, are investigating."

"This holiday is becoming more busman-y by the minute. What's it about?"

"Oh, no you don't, you're not getting your hooks into this one. He sends his best, by the way."

SERGEANT MARTINEZ GAZED at the notes he'd taken from the people at the inn, but his mind was elsewhere. Before the shooting, he'd been sitting in the interview room across from James A. Griffin and his lawyer, a man who ate well and was feeling the heat. Griffin was out of prison on a sizeable bail, which he had no trouble producing. Both he and his counsel had been leaning back looking bored and, to Martinez's surprise, confident.

"We've been following up on your finances, and we have solid evidence that you've been taking dirty money from your illicit gambling and funnelling it through your restaurant and other businesses." Martinez mentally crossed his fingers they still had that evidence somewhere. "What I'm interested in is money you've paid out to the Desert Sunrise Nursing Home. Regular payments, every month," he had said to Griffin.

"Really, Martinez, you're grabbing at straws here. My client—"

But Griffin waved his lawyer off. "My mother is in the nursing home, what do you think?"

"She's not, though. I checked. She died four years ago."

"They were good to her. I give them a little something. A donation. I'm grateful, big deal. What are you trying to get at, Martinez?"

"What I'm trying to get at, Mr. Griffin, is that the nursing home tells me they've had no money from you since your mother died. So where is it going?"

Griffin had shrugged. "I give them the money. My money, from the restaurant, which, by the way, is a popular place. It's not my fault they lose it. You should check with them. Maybe someone on that end is pocketing it. Maybe they don't want to pay taxes. How the hell should I know? You haven't got anything on me, or you wouldn't be fishing around my dead mother's rest home."

The lawyer, sweat pooling around his collar, picked up his hat and hauled himself to his feet. "Fishing is right. If you have nothing else, I got places to be."

Martinez sighed. He was fishing. If he couldn't find the evidence he already had, he'd have to get to the bottom of the money going to the nursing home, a difficult prospect if there were no records and the nursing home was denying it had received any money. He was already in trouble with Galloway, who had a temper, over the missing evidence, evidence he knew for certain had been in the file in his desk drawer, which he locked every night when he went home, and then moved to the station files. His failure to adequately track where the missing "donations" were going meant that Galloway was right. The whole case was unravelling, and it would end up being his fault. This murder at the Santa Cruz Inn was going to take up time that he could ill afford, as he knew he would have to investigate the financial activities at the Desert Sunrise Nursing Home and hope to scrape up enough evidence.

He rose to indicate their conversation was over. He did not look at Griffin, but he watched the lawyer who stood outside the door fanning his face with his hat. Griffin got up languidly. He would be smirking. What Martinez did not understand was why.

"I FEEL AWFUL leaving those two women behind like this," Lane said. They stood on the front steps of the inn, waiting for Priscilla Galloway.

"I know you do. It's one of the reasons I love you. If I ever get into a mess, I feel confident you will hate to leave me behind as well." Darling was standing with his hands in his pockets, revelling in being able to wear a short-sleeved sport shirt in November. She had, in fact, risked everything to extract him from a very sticky mess in England the previous June.

A pale-blue Buick with a soft-top pulled up, and Priscilla smiled up at them; she was wearing large sunglasses, and her dark hair was wrapped in an orange scarf. "All ready? I thought of putting the top down, but it's a longish drive, and we'll be battered to death. Hop in." She waved at them with a white-gloved hand.

Darling opened the front passenger door and pulled the seat forward to climb into the back. "It's kind of you to do this, Mrs. Galloway."

Lane settled luxuriously into the plush passenger seat. The car smelled new and gleamed in the morning sun.

Priscilla put the car in gear. "Nonsense, it's a pleasure. Paul doesn't often let me drive the car, so it's doubly nice." She gave a trill of laughter that made Lane turn toward her. It was the kind of unnecessary laughter that nervous people emit, but in Priscilla it struck her as having a brittle quality, as if she wished to fill some void with happy sounds.

"Tell us about this church," Lane said.

Priscilla glanced at her, lips turned in a brief smile. "Well, I mean, really, it's just a church in a desert, but it is old, as old as things get in America. Seventeen something. I quite like it, and it's a day out. There's a very nice Mexican restaurant on the way back we can stop at. Very authentic. I can't help noticing that neither of you has a camera. I'll be sure to snap a picture of you two in front of the place so you'll have a honeymoon picture for your album."

"It's true. I don't know why neither of us has one. Darling?" Lane looked into the back seat, where Darling was occupying himself looking at the part of town they were passing.

"Ames always takes the pictures. I don't think I ever imagined myself in the role of tourist."

Priscilla laughed again. "Wedded to his job, just like Paul. No wonder they're friends. You should be careful, Lane." She sounded as though she was going to add to that observation, but she stopped and lifted her chin and lowered it again, her lips closing tightly for a moment. "I wouldn't say it's the prettiest town, but it's quite pleasant to live here. I like the climate, though it is dreadfully hot in the summer, and I do miss how green England is. We are just getting started on building a pool. You can't live here without one! We've been using the country club till now. That and plenty of ice for drinks."

Lane turned to look at the passing street. Clusters of small houses and dusty streets seemed the dominant theme. In this neighbourhood, at least, no one had pools. The assistant chief's job must pay well, Lane thought, or Priscilla had brought some money into the union.

"Paul told me what happened yesterday. Poor you!" Priscilla said. She slowed and stopped for a traffic light.

"Well, not poor me, really. Poor Mr. Rcnwick who got shot out of the blue, and poor Mrs. Renwick who is widowed now, and poor woman who was standing talking to him when it happened."

"It's absolutely ghastly. I'm glad to take you away from all that. I suppose, Inspector, you wish you were back therc, nosing about for clues."

"I do not. I am sure Paul and his sergeant and the no-doubt excellent officers in the Tucson police will get to the bottom of it. I am, as I have reminded my wife several times, on my honeymoon. Indeed, I am sure it is she who is wishing she were nosing about for clues," said Darling from the back seat.

In a short time, they left the few intermittent houses on the edge of town behind and turned southwest into open desert.

After twenty minutes along the dusty, nearly empty road, the unequal towers of the Mission San Xavier del Bac church materialized before them, white and gleaming against the deep blue of the sky. Lane and Darling were transfixed.

"It's a bit run-down, honestly," Priscilla said. "We're on the local Indian Reservation, and any work done on it was done by them. That hill over there is sacred. Something to do with a stream of water." She pointed to a small hillock with a cross at the top.

But for Lane, the peeling whitewash on the adobe and exposed bricks just added to its interest. "It's fantastic. One hears about Spanish Colonial architecture, but it's more beautiful in life than what I could have imagined! If we're to have a honeymoon photo, I think it ought to be in front of these wonderful doors."

Mesquite trees cast dappled shadows across the dusty roadway and up along the walls of what Priscilla told them was an enclosed garden.

"There are some ledges in the garden. After we've seen the inside of the church, we could sit a few minutes and just get a feel for it. I find it very peaceful."

After standing in the cool, dark interior of the church with his hands clasped behind his back, looking up at the ancient and peeling frescoes, Darling whispered, "I've had enough incense. I'm going to take a run up that hill to look at the surrounding view. I think Priscilla might like to just sit with you for a few moments. I'll be a third wheel."

"Where's he off to?" Priscilla asked.

"He's just off to investigate that sacred hill. I'm for a shady ledge and a peaceful surround, myself."

Two men were talking quietly as they worked in a small adjacent garden, but otherwise the silence was all encompassing. Priscilla and Lane sat together companionably. Lane looked through the branches of the mesquite, past the dark green of its tiny leaves at the intensity of the blue above them.

"Does it ever rain here?" she asked.

"Torrentially. But it doesn't come and stay for months like at home."

"Do you miss it?" Lane asked. "London, I mean."

"All that filthy air and smell of damp wool? Not a bit of it. But ..." Here Priscilla stopped and fell silent. She took out a cigarette, offered one to Lane who shook her head, and lit it, blowing smoke away from Lane. Finally, she spoke with an artificial little laugh. "Well, you trade one lot of disagreeableness for another, don't you?"

Lane waited to see if her companion would explain. Priscilla looked down at her hands, holding them out and then turning them as if she were inspecting her gloves, the smoke from her cigarette curling upward.

"Paul does well. Well, I mean ... I do have everything I could want. Everything I never had. I grew up in the East End, you know. Most of my neighbourhood got bombed to smithereens. I've gone from being utterly poor to quite comfortable, thank you very much. From rain and bad air and outdoor loos to every modern convenience in a warm and sunny place. I'm lucky." She stubbed the cigarette out on the ledge and dropped it on the ground. She didn't sound lucky, Lane thought.

"But?" Lane asked.

Priscilla looked at her and then away, peering upward through the sunglasses that framed her face, giving her an air of Hollywood glamour. Lane marvelled again at her beauty and delicate bone structure. "Well, I mean, life isn't a smooth sail, is it? Paul likes things a certain way, and I work hard to keep things just so for him, as any wife would." She smiled brightly at Lane. "Sometimes I wish I could just jump in a car and drive away. Eat what I want, wear what I want, say what I want. Feel ... well, mustn't grumble. It's the bargain I signed on for."

"Is ..." Lane hesitated. It wasn't her business really, but she had felt a weight of darkness behind Priscilla's sudden admission of a dream of escape, however lightly expressed. "Is Paul, well, I mean, is he kind to you?"

Priscilla turned to her. She smiled broadly, her eyes hidden behind her dark glasses. "Now, whatever can you be thinking?" She stood up abruptly. "I wonder how your Frederick is getting along. I'm famished. I really think you'll like the place I've picked."

CHAPTER SEVEN

THE WATTS COTTAGE WAS UP a winding and rutted road above the Willow Point store. Constable Terrell and Sergeant Ames were on their way to visit Mrs. Watts there, as she had wanted to return to a normal routine as quickly as possible for her daughter.

"You know, I drove out to a garage near Balfour, run by a guy called Van Eyck, the day before yesterday, and someone had painted the word *Bitch* on the garage door," Ames began as they sat on the ferry across to the north shore. "The paint was already dry, so it had happened sometime in the middle of the night. The strange thing is that Tina Van Eyck, the daughter—who is a mechanic there, by the way—believed it was Barney Watts who'd done it. They'd had an unpleasant interaction when he'd brought his car in, and she thought he'd done it for revenge." Ames said all this, carefully avoiding the embarrassment of his own dubious motives for going out there in the first place.

"Coincidence, surely. But I guess you didn't want to ask Mrs. Watts about it when her husband had just died?"

"Yes. It seemed so trivial somehow, after he'd been found dead. Anyway, I don't think Miss Van Eyck could really be so sure. It might have had nothing to do with him."

"HE WAS AWAY a lot, so we were used to making do on our own," Mrs. Watts said. They were sitting at the kitchen table with mugs of coffee. They could hear Sadie, her ten-year-old daughter, moving about in the room above them. She had been kept back from school for the day.

"Away doing what?" Ames asked quietly. Terrell had taken Ames's usual place as note-taker, and Ames was finding it awkward sitting with his hands empty. It did mean, however, that he spent more time observing the woman than he otherwise might. Her husband had clearly been much older—but there was something weary about Amy Watts that aged her beyond her years. Perhaps some of it was grief.

"Well, there was the war. And then when he got back, he got a job at the CPR, mostly at the station in Nelson. He was a section foreman in the yard. And then he'd go for training sessions to the coast. Anyway. We got quite used to making do on our own."

Ames looked around. Her repetition of the phrase "making do" suggested a stark, narrow existence. The kitchen was primly tidy and a little over-warm. Dishes were stacked neatly in the open shelves, and cups hung above the sink. A full wood box was tucked between the wall and the stove. A cat lay on a worn grey blanket folded near the other side of the stove. There were no dishes piled for washing, or surfaces cluttered with pencils or books. An empty laundry rack above the stove was pulled tight to the ceiling. Did she always keep it like this, or had grief made her try to find ways to keep busy?

"What about his health?"

"I don't know. I never knew him to be really ill. A little winded sometimes after chopping wood. Recently he would come home and fall asleep right after dinner, but I assumed that was mostly because he'd been at the bar."

"Who is his doctor?"

"We never had a doctor. Been lucky, I guess."

"So he wasn't taking any sort of medicine?" Ames asked.

"No." Mrs. Watts drew the word out. "But now that you say it, I noticed lately that he wouldn't eat like he used to. Kept saying he had no appetite or was too tired to eat."

"How recently?" Ames asked. Terrell sat with his pencil poised over his notebook.

"The last month or so maybe? I honestly couldn't say. Are you suggesting he was keeping some sort of health problem from me?" She didn't wait for an answer. "It would be like him, actually. He always had to be the strong man. Nothing could ever touch him, he said, since he survived the war. I asked him about why he wasn't eating at first, and he just told me to leave him alone. I stopped asking because he'd get mad."

"Can we talk about yesterday? Was it a normal day for him?"

"Yes. We got up, I made breakfast for both of them, and then he drove off with Sadie. He wasn't feeling well so I

91

made him an extra hot cup of tea. He said he was getting a cold, now that I think of it, and I told him not to go to work, but he was adamant that he felt well enough to work. He drops—" she caught herself, "dropped Sadie off at the school down the hill every day. She usually walks back on her own with Betty Ann who lives farther up the road." She clutched at her mug of coffee, kneading it with nervous fingers. "I don't understand why he was over by the Harrop ferry."

"So he never said anything to you about going over there—business with the railway, anything?"

"No. As far as I knew it was just a day of work."

"Now, your husband . . ." Ames hesitated. He had sat in while Darling asked questions, but now confronted with having to ask personal questions, he felt as though he was watching himself, waiting to say the wrong thing and give offence. Luckily Mrs. Watts leapt into the silence.

"I was sixteen when I met him in '36. He'd have been twenty-nine. We met at a church bazaar, which is a little ironic, considering neither one of us was a churchgoer. I was helping Mum with the jumble sale—I have no idea why he was there. The beer tent, I suppose. I went for a break. It was a hot day, and I went to sit on the grass under a tree. Same tree he was smoking under. I was bowled over, you might say, having a grown man pay attention to me that way. I knew he had a reputation, but I didn't care. Eventually, well, we 'had' to get married. I'm not sure that was what he wanted. I think he'd been used to getting his way, if you know what I mean. He did tell me he had a steady girlfriend before we met, and I sometimes used to wonder who she was. But once Sadie was born, he settled down. She was his pride and joy. It surprised me when he started getting jealous. First he kept on about who I saw when he was away in Europe, and then he got sort of distant, like he was preparing for me to leave. I don't know how many times I told him I never would. For better for worse, I told him."

Ames nodded. "You said he had a reputation. Can you explain what you mean by that?"

Mrs. Watts jerked her head abruptly to look away from them, and then quickly turned back. "He got around a fair bit. He'd been out with more than a few of the girls from school. It didn't bother me, really. I think it made him more attractive."

Terrell cleared his throat, and Ames glanced over at him. He'd told Terrell to feel free to hop in if he thought of something. "Ma'am, some men came back from the war a little altered. Did he show any signs of that? Anything from nightmares to even keeping a kit bag packed and stowed somewhere?"

Frowning, Mrs. Watts glanced toward a box bench by the door. "It's funny you should say that. He didn't have nightmares or anything like some I've heard about. But he was proud of surviving. He'd say he was invincible now. But he did have a bag." She got up and went to the bench and lifted the seat. "Oh. It's gone. He wasn't scheduled to go anywhere, but his bag is gone. It wasn't anything to do with the war, I don't think. He just had it for when he had to travel for work."

"Did he usually take a kit bag, for overalls or work

clothes?" This reminded Ames that they had not yet gone into the trunk. The car had been towed and was now parked in the alley behind the station.

"No. He kept those in a locker at work. I don't know why I didn't notice he was carrying it. In fact, I don't think he was. I always packed a lunch box for the two of them. His is one of those big ones, with a thermos. He had that with him, and Sadie had hers, and her book bag."

Terrell wrote and Ames thought.

"Can you give me the names of his friends or colleagues that he associated with regularly? They might have known his plans. It's possible he was in the car with somebody, though he certainly was driving," Ames said.

Mrs. Watts was silent for a long moment. "I wouldn't even know who they are. He went for a few beers after work sometimes, maybe played cards, but he never let me into his affairs." She sniffed and Ames saw that she was about to cry. "I wondered for a moment if it was this girl he used to hang around with before the war." She bit off the end of the sentence as if she was going to spit it out.

"Which girl was that?" asked Ames.

She tossed her hair and endeavoured to look disdainful. "I don't remember her name, if you want to know the truth. Lived up the lake somewhere. Her dad ran a garage."

"That reminds me," Ames said, glancing briefly at Terrell. "Did your husband take your car for repairs a couple of days ago?"

Frowning, Mrs. Watts said, "I don't know. He could have, I suppose."

"Right," said Ames, wishing he had his notebook in

hand so he could pretend to glance at it. "Do you remember if he went out later that night?"

"Certainly not. Why on earth would he?"

"No particular reason, Mrs. Watts," Ames said. "Just trying to see if there was anything out of the ordinary that might help us understand what happened."

———

"THAT WAS LOVELY," Lane said, leaning back in her chair. "I've never had Mexican food before. It's a delightful place, a bit like pictures I've seen of little Mexican villages."

"I'm glad your initiation began here. It just started up recently, but they do things right. Come. I'll drive you through the centre. You can see where I go to do my shopping." Seeing Darling's face, she added, "I recognize that look. I've seen it on Paul. Eyes glazing over at the thought of shopping. Don't worry, we won't stop. It's right on your way back to the hotel."

They drove along Stone Avenue and Darling said, "It's a little bit like Nelson. I expect it's much bigger, but it has that small-town feel to it."

They stopped at a traffic light, and Lane, who had chosen the back seat this time to allow Darling a better view, noticed a couple arguing outside a restaurant. "Good heavens! It's Meg Holden and ... I don't know who."

As the light changed, Lane and Darling both turned to look out the side window and then the back one. Meg started to walk away and the man, a burly specimen in a brown suit that was a little too small, pulled her arm hard and swung her around to face him. Just when Lane wondered if they ought to intervene, Meg pulled her arm back and rubbed it and then, paradoxically, began to laugh, reaching out to stroke the man's cheek.

"Someone you know?" asked Priscilla, glancing at Lane through the mirror.

"Yes, a bit. She's a guest at the inn. In fact, she was the one standing right next to the poor man who was shot."

Darling turned to look at Lane with a slight inquiring tilt of the chin.

"It's all right, darling," she said, smiling innocently. "I am making nothing of it."

When they were back at the inn, shoes and stockings off, lying on the bed with a fan blowing waves of cool air at them, Darling said, "I actually wonder if we should be making something of it. You told me she was visiting a paramour in the hallway of the hotel, and now she's seen having an argument with yet another man in the street, who, by the way, looks like a movie gangster. It beggars belief that she has three men in her thrall, as interesting as that hair colour is."

Lane pulled herself up to lean on her elbow and looked at him. "Tell me what you're thinking."

"I'm thinking that I, we, should tell Martinez, and here's why: Is it a coincidence she was standing next to Renwick when he was shot? What connection might there be between, say, the man on the street and Renwick?"

"Well, certainly not one Ivy Renwick would recognize." She glanced at her watch. "I suppose the brother is probably here by now if he flew down. What are you going to do?"

"I might call the police station to talk to Martinez."

Lane felt dismay. She sat up. "Oh, darling, let me talk to Meg first. No. No, I can see at once that that is nonsense. I'm just trying to protect her, and I can't even think why. She seems, I don't know what. Not vulnerable, exactly … but a little like a woman whose life is not quite in control."

"With three men on the go? I dare say it's not! Thank you for pulling back from the brink."

DARLING HELD UP a card they had found slipped under their door when they returned. "Now, what shall we do about this?" It was an invitation from the inn for a special cocktail party followed by dinner, with apologies for the disruption of "recent events."

"A free cocktail and dinner? I don't know how you can ask. I'm going to wear my wedding cocktail dress. Maybe white gloves like Priscilla. She looked so glam, don't you think, with the gloves and scarf and glasses?"

"If you say so. She's not a patch on you and, I must say, doesn't look all that happy. There's a bit of the caged bird about her."

"Inspector Darling, that is very inspectory of you. I think you are exactly right. I did try to probe around about whether she was happy, but I must have made a real mess of it because she more or less drew herself up to her full height and gave me the brush off. I'm off to the front desk to pick up some postcards. I leave you in peace to call Martinez."

Walking along the winding path through the garden,

Lane marvelled at how it seemed impossible the horrible events of the day before had ever happened. The sudden tearing of the veil of quiet, moneyed sophistication had revealed the human potential for violence, but it was already beginning to seem distant, with everything hurriedly being returned to its usual quiet routine. Lane reluctantly glanced to where the body had been and saw the blood had been scrubbed away by the anxious hotel staff; an air of normalcy was vigorously restored for all of the guests who had nothing to do with the death in their midst.

She arrived at the door, nodded at a couple sitting under the ramada drinking soft drinks, and went into the hall past the library and the restaurant and up the few steps to the main floor. Out of an unexamined curiosity, she turned down the hallway where she'd first seen Meg Holden embracing the man with the moustache and walked the length of it. There were a couple of offices and a door to the outside at the end of it. She pushed open the door and looked out. It was here that some of the underpinnings of the hotel were kept out of sight: a laundry and a cleaning supply closet, both with their doors open, were on one side of the little patio, and a small gate out to the street on the other. What you might call the servants' entrance, she thought. She was about to turn back when she spotted Chela rinsing a mop in a deep cement sink in the supply room.

"Hello, Chela," she said, stepping into the room. "I see you're back to your regular duties, then."

Chela turned off the tap and said shyly, "Yes, ma'am. Can I get you something?" She looked as though she might have been crying.

"No, no! I was just exploring. I'm sorry to interrupt your work."

Looking suddenly stricken, Chela turned away and made a stab at continuing her mop washing.

"Are you all right?" Lane asked, coming closer and laying a hand on the girl's back.

"It's nothing, ma'am. I just had to clean up ... well, you know." She crossed herself. "It is so terrible. I kept thinking of the blood pouring out of him." She wiped her hands.

"Oh, I am sorry it was you who had to do it! It's so hard to think of someone dying like that. Especially for poor Mrs. Holden. She was right there."

Chela turned away, wiping her hands on her apron, but Lane did not miss the way she clamped her lips shut.

"What is it, Chela?"

"I shouldn't say, ma'am. It's not my place."

Lane turned her gently by the arm. "Look, if you know something, it certainly is your place. I expect that at the moment the police have no idea what happened. Anything might help them."

Looking genuinely frightened, Chela shook her head. "Oh no, it's not about the man who was shot. It's just that Mrs. Holden. I don't think she's a good woman. I've seen her ..." Chela stopped.

"Do you mean with someone who isn't her husband? I saw that too, quite by accident, as I'm sure you did."

"It's just that he's come a few times. He comes in this door so no one sees him and they meet here. Yesterday, and on a couple of other days, she left by this door and was picked up in a car. I didn't see who was driving, but it must have been him. This isn't the way the guests are supposed to go in and out of the hotel. I think she was crazy to marry a man as old as Mr. Holden, but she did, and she took sacred vows. I don't think she should be sneaking around like that."

LANE PULLED ON her cocktail dress and turned to have Darling zip it up. "Oh. I just thought of poor Ivy. She's having to stay on while the police continue the investigation. And given what I've learned about her brother-in-law, she's got her hands full there. Perhaps I should stay back and offer support instead of putting on the bib and tucker for a bang-up night of eating and drinking. In fact, I'm surprised the management are even doing this."

Darling took the opportunity to move her hair and kiss the back of her neck and then zipped up her dress. "Has she asked for your help?"

"Well, no."

"I suspect that if anyone wants your help, they will ask for it. This is a difficult time, and we don't really know much about her, or her relations. I suspect we ought not to interfere." Darling held up two ties, a maroon number with subtle dark stripes and a silver-blue one with a geometric orange design.

"You should get one of these bolo ties we're seeing everywhere. There are some very nice ones in the shop here," she said, looking at what was on offer. "That orange and blue is quite racy. I didn't know you had anything like that."

"There is a lot you don't know about me. For example,

I will be in my grave before I consider a bolo tie. The blue and orange then."

Lane watched him in the mirror, deftly flipping the tie into its full Windsor.

"Could you go look at something else? You're distracting me in ways that will cause us to miss the cocktails," Darling said, looking at her reflection in the mirror.

"Really, darling." She gently kissed his neck in return and then, stepping firmly away, pulled on her gloves. "You never told me what Martinez said when you telephoned him this afternoon."

"He asked me to describe the man, where we saw them, and at what time. Then he thanked me courteously and asked if I would be available should they wish to speak to me further. He also mentioned he'd talked to Renwick's brother—beyond which he told me nothing, before you ask."

CHAPTER EIGHT

September 1947, Kenosha, Wisconsin

"**WELL, THIS IS AN HONOUR.** Ivy let you out of the kennel, did she? What'll you have? Mine's whisky, if you don't mind." Edward Renwick was leaning heavily on the bar, his tie undone and his hair pushed off his forehead in a way that made it stand up in a messy hedge.

"He can have one more, but that's it," the bartender said to Jack Renwick. "If you're the brother he's been talking about, you should get him home."

That was more easily suggested than done. Edward had become truculent, and he glowered when Jack had tried a gentle pull on his sleeve.

"Why don't you leave me the hell alone? Go back to your wife and your golden boy life." He emphasized *wife* with a measure of disdain that made Jack frown.

"Come on, Ned," he tried quietly. "No need to make a spectacle. The barkeeper is going to toss us both in a minute. You can come home, and Ivy can make you some dinner. You don't look like you've had a decent meal in days."

"So considerate," Edward sneered, but he got up slowly, pulling his arm sharply away from his brother's grasp.

Jack threw a bill on the bar and walked out behind his brother. When they were on the street he pointed to where he had parked the car and once again touched him gently, this time on the back to guide his brother in the right direction.

"I told you not to touch me!" Edward seemed to explode and, with an oath, turned and threw a punch that found Jack's cheekbone and caused him to stagger and then fall in an ungainly heap onto the sidewalk.

Jack opened and closed his eyes, trying to get back some focus, and began to push himself off the ground. Edward had started to walk away, and Jack thought he should call him back, but the blow had disoriented him. Finally he was on his feet and looking for his hat, which had tumbled into the street. He put his hand to his cheek and whimpered.

"Ned, for God's sake," he managed, retrieving his hat.

Edward, who had disappeared around the corner, suddenly appeared again, striding toward his brother and then stopping. "You can go back to that so-called wife and your happy little life living on what's mine and leave me alone. What I do is none of your business. I don't need sympathy from you," he said, "or rescue." He spat and turned back down the street and disappeared.

———

DARLING AND LANE entered the library, where a gleaming candlelit bar and waiters crisply attired in white had replaced the usual tea paraphernalia. Smoke rose from cigarettes and spread across the ceiling, and the dim room hummed with quiet conversation punctuated by intermittent peals of laughter. It was a room full of people who might have heard of the tragic events of the last couple of days but had determined to put it out their minds—and were succeeding.

"What'll it be?" Darling asked.

"Something exotic." Lane looked around. "Something like that." She pointed at a woman holding a cocktail glass full of amber liquid with a lemon twist balanced on the rim.

Darling pushed off through the crowd, and Lane, near the fireplace, surveyed the room. Certainly some of the guests she had not seen at any of their previous meals or by the pool. She guessed they had arrived after the shooting and must simply have felt lucky to find themselves fêted on their first night at the expense of the hotel. She could see Darling leaning on the bar, waiting for the drinks, and she smiled at the thought of him as she had first met him: formal, serious, correct, with the tiniest whiff of a dark sense of humour. And now he loved her and let himself be loved by her. She was happy in a way she had never imagined possible. She chided herself for the incongruity of her happiness in the face of recent horrific events and then fell fully to earth.

Standing in the doorway, with a double whisky, neat, was a man who looked so like the recently deceased Renwick that she emitted a little gasp. She was watching the ash accumulating on the cigarette he held loosely in his mouth when Darling made his way back holding his own whisky and the amber drink. "It's called a sidecar," he said, presenting it to her. "Chin-chin."

"Darling, look over there. I realize it's because this room is cast in atmospheric cocktail darkness, but that man looks exactly like Jack Renwick from here. It gave me quite a turn, I can tell you. It must be the brother."

"Shouldn't he be comforting the grieving widow, not here guzzling whisky?" Darling commented, sipping his own.

"This is actually very good. What's it got in it?"

"Sorry, I wasn't paying attention. He looks a bit like someone who's had several already. Didn't you say she said he was a bit of a handful?"

"Yes, quite given to drink, apparently, and professed himself violently in love with her. Ought we to go and, I don't know ... talk to him? I mean, we are probably the only ones here who even know he's just lost his brother. How on earth did he get here so fast?"

"He must have flown. An expensive proposition, but I suppose since his brother was murdered, he wanted to hurry out. I assume the police have already talked to him, and they've obviously found no reason to hold him. I suppose there's no harm," Darling said.

"How do you do?" Lane said, offering her hand when they had made their way through the crowd. "Sorry to barge up like this, but I believe you might be Mr. Renwick? I'm so sorry for what you must be going through."

"Not as sorry as I am," the man said. He'd been leaning against the wall and now pulled himself upright. He stubbed out his cigarette and offered a hand. "Who are you again? And how do you know who I am?"

"Sorry, yes, I should have said. I'm Lane Winslow, and this is my husband Frederick Darling. I was one of the first people on the scene when your brother died. We had been dining with him and Mrs. Renwick only the night before. It was a terrible thing. We're so very sorry. How is Mrs. Renwick doing?"

He released Lane's hand and shook Darling's. "Ned Renwick." He tilted his head to look at the ceiling, sighed, and turned to Lane. "I have no idea in the world how she's doing. She won't see me." He took a drink. "It's only what I deserve, I suppose. Police won't release his body. They questioned me this afternoon, and they don't appear to want to release the idea that I might be the one who shot him. I'm a good shot, or I was, but with the best will in the world I could not have shot him from Wisconsin. I don't really know why she even asked me to come. Especially when she won't talk to me now that I'm here. Insult to injury to be questioned by the police on top of that!"

"Look, I think they'll be calling us to dinner soon. Why not sit with us?" Lane suggested, ignoring a not so subtle elbow from Darling.

"Well, I got no one else, and a pretty woman is always a good companion, begging your pardon, Mr. Darling."

"Inspector," corrected Darling.

The man laughed, whatever he'd already had to drink making him slightly sloppy. "Inspector. That some sort of police title? So you're the fuzz. I suppose you've been sent here to keep an eye on me."

"I am not the American fuzz. I am the Canadian fuzz. I assure you I have no jurisdiction. We are here on holiday," Darling said.

"Well, all right then. Dinner it is."

When they had settled at a table near the door, Renwick looked around, holding his glass as if he would order another whisky, but then put it down. "I can't afford to stay here, but if there's a free dinner and drinks going … " He shrugged. "She can afford it okay," he added bitterly. "She's got the whole pile, now. But you don't want to hear about my troubles. Tell me about yourselves."

Lane, who rather did want to hear about his troubles, smiled. "We're just here for our honeymoon. It's my first time in the United States."

"Jack and Ivy were here for the same thing, though they've been married now for three years. So, what's Canada like?"

"More trees than here," said Darling austerely, resenting that this bitter and vaguely unhinged third party was ruining his dinner.

Renwick laughed. Wine was poured and plates of salad produced. He took up his glass. "To honeymoons, then. And trees. God knows this place could sure use some."

"What do you do in Wisconsin?" Lane asked, then felt guilty immediately as she remembered he'd been, as he would see it, done out of his company.

"I used to work for my father, just like Jack, and Saint Ivy, for that matter, but when I got back stateside from serving our almighty flag, I found myself out on my ass. Dad willed the whole thing over to darling Jack, so now I work at an insurance company that was willing to hire a down-and-out vet."

"Where will you stay while you wait for the police to release the body?" Darling asked, wanting to steer Renwick away from any further maudlin disclosures.

"There's a rooming house in the town. I found it yesterday. I don't know why I bothered to come. She doesn't seem to need me to do anything, so she can be in charge of getting his body home." He waved his fork at the salad. "This is okay, whatever it is. I prefer a good steak, myself. Preferably wild. I hunt back home. In fact, I could be hunting now instead of sitting here like a chump. No offence, ma'am."

"None taken. You've had a dreadful time of it. It sounds like you might not stay on then?" Lane asked.

"I don't know. I'm sure the Equity House Insurance Company will indulge me for a few more days, but I can't look a gift job in the mouth. It depends on Ivy. She and I could have ..." but he didn't finish his thought. "I'm not sorry. I came down to see if she'd see things my way now he's out of the way." He looked at them sharply. "There. You're shocked. I'm just telling the truth."

Lane wasn't shocked. This fit with what Ivy had told her about Ned, but she was surprised to hear him say it out loud. There's the demon drink for you, she thought, wondering what anyone could possibly say after that sort of revelation. She daren't look at Darling, but amazingly, it was he who came to the rescue.

"What sort of hunting do you get up in Wisconsin?"

By the time the dishes of ice cream arrived, Darling was

heartily tired of Ned Renwick's company, but he'd been provided with some food for thought, much to his annoyance. He might have to get involved after all.

———

AMES GOT UP and stretched. A day later and they still hadn't heard from the coroner on cause of death. Ames had asked Gilly to report anything unusual when he'd finished his work at the city morgue. Gilly had, on first look, been inclined to agree with the medic about the heart attack. They'd also contacted the *Nelson Daily News* to report the accident, without any of the details, and put out a request to the public for information.

Ames, who had asked Terrell to come to his office, thought he recognized something of himself in the rookie constable. Ames was finding it strange to have a subordinate, but he thought of how Darling, though inclined to sarcasm, had treated his ideas with respect. They'd been discussing the case, and Terrell had had some good insights. It felt a bit like completing the circle, to be giving Terrell the same respect. Now Terrell was silent, waiting for Ames to sum up.

"So," Ames said, "this is what we've got: Watts appears to have taken a bag of some sort to go away but doesn't tell his wife. Instead of going to work, he drives in the opposite direction and is found dead of apparently natural causes near the Harrop ferry, only his keys are gone, the doors are locked, and someone has swiped the cash out of his wallet and disappeared into thin air. And where's the bag? Locked in the trunk of the car, of course. Well, the car's around back. We can jimmy open the trunk." Ames shook his head. "What I don't have any more is a suspect for the mess on the garage door. But I suppose Miss Van Eyck seemed pretty adamant she didn't want our involvement in the matter, so that's that. I'm starving. I can't think any more. The trunk can wait for half an hour. Why don't we go next door and have a bite? It's our usual place. Great grilled cheese and ham. Maybe someone will call in with something while we're gone."

"Sure. I can do up these notes later."

"WELL, WELL," SAID April. "Look what the cat dragged in. And who have we got here, Sergeant Ames?"

Ames wasn't sure he entirely liked the way she emphasized *sergeant*, but replied cheerfully enough, "This is Constable Terrell. He's new."

"Yes, I guessed as much. Nice to meet you, Constable," said April, beaming. "Start you off with coffees? It's freezing out there! We'll be getting snow any time now."

The two policemen sat at the counter, Terrell rubbing his hands to get some warmth into them.

"Where are you from?" April asked, filling the two thick white mugs she'd slid into place in front of them.

"Nova Scotia."

"You don't say! I guess you two are pretty busy right about now. I read in the paper today that Barney Watts has been found dead. Not before time, if you want my opinion." This she said in a conspiratorial whisper, leaning toward them. "What'll it be, gentlemen?"

"I'll have my usual ham and cheese, grilled," said Ames.

"Quelle surprise," April said. "And you, Constable?"

"I'll have the same, I guess."

"We do have other stuff, you know. Or you could just skip it all and go right to the pie. Apple blackberry today." She smiled winningly.

Terrell smiled back. "Maybe another time."

When she had gone to put the order slip up, Ames turned to Terrell and said in a low voice, "Now what do you think she meant by that? She must know something. She's not usually bloodthirsty like that."

Terrell glanced at April's back. "I'm glad to hear it. And I wondered the same thing."

When the sandwiches came, Ames said, "Have you got a second, April?"

April looked around the café. There were only two booths occupied; it was pushing one-thirty and the lunch crowd had mostly dispersed. "I knew I shouldn't have said anything. You want to know what I meant by that remark about Watts, I suppose."

"You're psychic. That's exactly what we want. Did you know him?"

"No, not exactly. By reputation, more. I have a sister who's six years older than me, and he had a reputation back in the thirties of going after girls way too young for him. I think one of Sandra's friends got into some kind of trouble. Then there was a girl called Tina for a while too, back in ... oh I don't know, way before the war, anyway. He works down at the yards, and I think he has a wife, and maybe even a kid, but that doesn't seem to stop him from tomcatting around. I've heard he's got a girl in town somewhere."

"You don't know who she is?" Terrell asked.

"No, but I hear stuff. Maybe now that this is in the paper, I can chat with some of the regulars, see if they know anything."

"And do you remember your sister's friend's name?"

"Nah, but I can ask Sandra. She's up in Prince George with her husband. I owe her a call. I can do that for you. Maybe I should go into the police force myself after all this," she said, smiling.

"Just say the word," Ames said. He was trying to sound nonchalant, but inside a kind of unfamiliar anxiety had seized him. "We could use a lady police ... person. I saw a few in Vancouver when I was there. I think they mostly have desk jobs."

"Oh, I wouldn't be happy with that. I'd want to be where the action is! When is your boss getting home, anyway? He's the one that inspired my thoughts about becoming a policewoman."

Trying to still a slight wince of disappointment that it wasn't he who had inspired her, Ames said, "Another week and half, two. They went to Arizona. April, that Tina you mentioned. Do you remember her last name?"

April shook her head. "Her dad ran a garage up the lake somewhere, I think." She looked out at the drizzle that had begun to hit the windows. "Bet it's nice in Arizona. You boys better eat up, or it'll be cold."

CHAPTER NINE

A MES SAT IN HIS OFFICE, too stunned to do more than stare at his typewriter. He felt as though he kept hearing April say, "Her dad ran a garage." He remembered seeing Terrell glance up at him briefly, expressionless, when she'd said it. It was exactly what Mrs. Watts had said. A girl whose father ran a garage. He was in a complete state of confusion and, he realized, anger. How could she have lied to him? How could she have pretended she hadn't known Watts when she most certainly had, and possibly intimately?

"Tina," Terrell had said, on the way back to the station. "That's a coincidence if I've ever heard one. Can we assume it's the same Tina? Did Miss Van Eyck say anything to you about her knowing this guy before? Not that it matters. Mrs. Watts says he didn't go out that night."

"She did not," Ames had answered glumly. "But what if it does matter? If Tina thinks he's the one responsible for the painting then—"

"I can't see how it has any bearing on the man's death though, which we still think is natural, in spite of the robbery and the locked car."

AMES WAS GOING to have to go back to take a picture of the paint on the door and explain that they weren't going to be charging Watts, who apparently had an alibi and was now dead—and by the way, was there anything she'd like to add? Feeling terrible about asking the Van Eycks to leave that vile word on the garage door for a photo that the death of Watts had pushed out of his thoughts, he pulled his hat off the stand and buttoned himself into his coat, calling Terrell.

"Let's get that trunk open."

Taking the crowbar that Ames had placed in the police car, he and Terrell stood looking at the trunk. "It's a shame to make a mess of the car," Terrell commented. "It's the only car Mrs. Watts's got."

"Needs must," Ames said, expertly popping the trunk open. There, indeed, was a small military-looking canvas carry bag with a brass clasp and leather handles. Using his handkerchief, Ames pulled it out, leaving Terrell to shut the trunk and stow the crowbar.

"Hello," said Terrell. He'd been about to shut the trunk but stopped. "Look at this." He was pointing at the space where the bag had sat.

Ames leaned in and looked, and then put his finger on the thick rubbery smudge on the floor of the trunk. "Paint," he said. "Black. I'm guessing we don't have to look any further for the garage-door vandal, after all. His wife said he didn't go out that night. It looks like Watts was leading a double life."

Back in his office, Ames used the handkerchief to snap open the clasp. Both of them leaned in, surprised. The topmost layer in the bag consisted of some quite colourful lady's clothes.

HE WASN'T GOING to take Terrell with him. When he got down the stairs, he saw the constable at his desk in the back corner typing his notes. He had piled the clothes in front of him on the desk and was listing them. "Underwear, sir, and two complete changes of clothing for her. Same for him. All new, but no tags. Size 16 R, whatever that is. They look like the woman wearing them would be quite slim. Though his wife is slender, I'm guessing they don't belong to her. This bright-red dress doesn't seem like her sort of style at all. It means, though, that there could have been someone in the car with him. It's not enough clothing to run off for any length of time, but it's enough for a lost weekend."

"And that someone either took advantage of his heart attack to steal his money or fled and someone else did. Listen, I'm going out to ask Miss Van Eyck a couple of questions and let them know they can paint the garage because I still think it's likely Watts was the culprit. I'll stop by Mrs. Watts's and ask about the clothes, just in case. Could you get down to the train station and learn anything you can about his work, his mates, whether he shared his plans with anyone? You know, that sort of thing."

"Yes, sir. I've been doing these notes. Even before the lady's clothing, something has struck me as—"

"Odd?" Ames supplied.

Terrell smiled, "Yes, sir. Mrs. Watts said he'd go to the coast for some sort of training, but I find that kind of, yes, odd, because he was essentially a labourer, even if he was supervising a group. They clean up the yard, move track, shovel coal. I can't imagine these jobs would require them to go anywhere for special training."

"Yes, I see what you mean, but she said he was away a lot after he got back from Europe. Worth looking into because it's strange that this time he didn't tell his wife he was going anywhere. A lost weekend with someone, or going away for good?"

"By the way, sir, Mrs. Watts would like the car back as soon as we are able. It's been hard for her to get around without it as she lives so far out of town."

THE RAIN HAD moved on, and the sky had cleared, bringing with it colder temperatures. Ames bumped down the road to the garage and stopped the car, sitting for a moment looking despondently at the garage doors, which were both shut. The offending word had been covered with an old sheet, but even with the possible sin of her having lied to him about knowing Watts, he could not imagine anyone applying the word to her, or any woman, now that he thought about it. With a sigh, he was about to open the door when a truly disquieting thought hit him like a clap of thunder.

What if Terrell was wrong? What if this did have something to do with Watts's death? If Tina had lied to him about knowing Watts, could she have something to do with his robbery? What if she was the one he was running off with? He sat, staring at the doors, trying to take this idea in. He checked his apprehension and reminded himself he was a police sergeant. He'd have to take this on board and be very cautious.

He heard banging coming from the inside of the garage as he approached. The small door at the side was ajar. The overhead lights barely seemed to penetrate the obscurity of the inside. When his eyes adjusted, Ames saw Tina hammering at the rim of a tyre and Mr. Van Eyck leaning into the engine of a 1927 half-ton Chevy truck. Van Eyck pulled up at the sound of Ames's "Hello."

"Pretty sound, these things. I've kept this one on the road for twenty years." Van Eyck looked for a rag and, not finding it, wiped his hands on his coveralls. "You're here to take the picture," he continued. "Tina! The sergeant is here!"

Tina stopped and stood up straight. "Sergeant," she said by way of greeting.

"Could I have a moment of your time, Miss Van Eyck, outside?"

Something in Ames's voice made her frown. "I suppose so. Why? I thought you were here to take the picture."

"Just step outside, please." He was surprised by how officious he sounded, even to himself.

Outside, Tina watched with her arms crossed, alert now as Ames paused, apparently unable to articulate his first question. She shifted from one foot to the other. "Well, what is it? I have work to do."

"Yes. Me too. First of all, Barney Watts. He likely did this, but he won't be doing any more. We found him dead in his car near the Harrop ferry."

This revelation caused Tina to gasp and lean against the front of the maroon police vehicle. She had blanched and was shaking her head. "Dead? How can he be dead?"

Her pallor startled him and concern outweighed Ames's determination to be the hard and clinical policeman. "Can I get you some water, Miss Van Eyck?" He looked toward the garage, wondering if he should get her father.

Tina saw where he was looking. "No! For God's sake, I don't want him here. I'm fine. I'm just shocked, that's all. How did he die?"

Ames watched her face. Was she pretending, or was she genuinely shocked? He took a breath. "Miss Van Eyck, I have reason to believe you may have known Barney Watts better than you let on last time I was here. Why didn't you say?"

Tina turned away, looking toward the water through the now-skeletal trees. "All right. Yes. God, I can't believe it. I absolutely hated him, but this ..."

"Miss Van Eyck, where were you yesterday afternoon?" Ames regretted it as soon as he'd said it. It sounded far-fetched, but what if she was the one planning to run off with the dead man? In the next instant he knew how unlikely it was and wondered if he was just getting back at her for lying to him about knowing Watts.

She turned and looked at him furiously. "Oh, for Pete's sake, stop being such an ass, Sergeant!"

———

June 1935

TINA SIGHED HAPPILY as she walked down the road to the garage from where the school bus had dropped her off. Last day of school, ever! There had been little rain, and the sun made the grass in the unused fields on either side of the road golden. The line of aspen behind the garage below her was a picture of white bark and green flittering leaves; it was impossible to tell if it was the lake that sparkled or the trees.

She turned at the sound of a car bumping down the road behind her. A customer. She stepped onto the grassy bank on the side to let it go by, but it stopped. A man with black wavy hair leaned out of the window and smiled at her. He wasn't young, but he was very good looking, she thought. His lips were curled into a confident smile that made her feel flushed. His dark blue eyes seemed to bore into her.

"Need a lift?"

His playful tone gave her an unfamiliar confusion, and she felt embarrassed that it must be visible on her face. "It's okay. I'm just going home to the garage."

"Well, that's where I'm going, so hop in."

"But it's just down there," she said. She tried to look away, but his eyes held hers. They were like the blue of the sky above the lake.

"Come on! I'm not going to hurt you," he coaxed. "Come around and hop in." He leaned away from her to push the passenger side door open.

She looked nervously down the hill to where the garage lay basking in the June sun, imagining her father inside working, her mother in the house or out feeding the chickens, and then she went around and got in. The man moved his hat from the seat and tossed it into the back.

But he didn't drive. He put his arm up on the back of the seat so that his hand was near her head. "What's your name, then?"

"Tina," she said, barely above a whisper. She felt the presence of his hand acutely but would not have been able to name what she was feeling. She pushed her hand into her pocket to hold the little embroidered purse her grandmother had given her. It had her name on it. It always made her feel secure.

"Mine's Barney Watts. You can call me Barney. Your dad run that garage?"

"Yes, Mr. Watts." She had never called a grown-up by a first name in her life. His invitation felt like a door opening up into some place she had no business going.

"Barney, I told you," he said, laughing. "You're a pretty thing, I'll say that. School all done now?"

"Yes. I'm graduating this year. Today was the last day." She didn't dare look at him, so she stared at the book bag she had on her lap.

"Well, you're all grown up then. What are you, now, seventeen, eighteen?" His hand had moved, and he fingered a blond curl.

"Sixteen," she said, feeling breathless. He was nothing like the boys at school.

"Sixteen! That's pretty young to be graduating."

"I skipped fifth grade," she said. She wanted to pull her head back, away from his hand, to get out, to have the world be as it was only a few minutes before.

"Pretty and smart! Bet you have a boyfriend. Hey, there's your dad." Mr. Van Eyck had come out of the garage and was standing looking up the road toward them. He pulled his right hand back to the steering wheel and looked at his watch. "I promised him I'd bring the car in by four and it's ten after."

As he put the car into gear and trundled down the road to the garage, Tina exhaled relief slowly so he wouldn't think she'd been nervous.

"What are you going to do now you've done with school?" Barney asked.

"I'm going to help my dad in the garage." She was feeling normal again, happy as they approached the open bay doors where her father stood, just as he always did. She liked working on cars.

"You don't say!" Barney stopped the car and waved at Mr. Van Eyck who had moved to the shade of the bay, hands on hips, watching them, his eyebrows drawn together. Barney went to open his door and then leaned back toward her. "You should let me take you out some time. Pretty girl like you. I could show you a good time like you deserve. Celebrate your graduation. What do you say?" He dropped his voice. "You wait for me at the top of the road next Saturday at eight, eh?" Without waiting for an answer, he got out of the car and waved at her father and called out, "Thanks for doing this. I'm on the road tomorrow, and I'm just not sure about the clutch."

———

121

MARTINEZ SAID, "MARTINEZ" into the receiver, wishing the phone would just stop ringing for five minutes. It never rained, but it poured. Not only was the Griffin business weighing on him, with its attendant anger from Galloway, he had the murder at the Santa Cruz Inn to think about, and he was fielding any number of minor calls about missing animals and a robbery from a tobacco shop in South Tucson, which he had to deal because none of their officers was available and he spoke Spanish.

"Good morning, Sergeant Martinez, this is Inspector Darling. I'm sorry to bother you again. I tried Assistant Chief Galloway and he's not in just now."

Martinez shook his head. He liked the inspector. He'd found himself wishing out loud to his wife the night before that Galloway was more like the inspector. "No trouble at all, sir. How can I help?"

"It's just that my wife and I had dinner with Jack Renwick's brother last night, as he was on his own, and he expressed a great deal of bitterness about his brother, said he was glad he was dead. It seems he was in love with his brother's wife and this would free her up, as he sees it. Unfortunately for him, she doesn't see it that way and has refused to talk to him. He's short of money and is moving out today to a rooming house near the station. He says he has leave from the insurance company he works for, Equity House Insurance Company. I know you interviewed him yesterday, and I certainly don't want to interfere, but I am uneasy about him. He drinks excessively, and he's angry. I'm a bit worried about Mrs. Renwick's safety." He stopped short of recommending any particular course of action, though he wondered how long she was expected to stay on.

"I see," Martinez said. He had written down the name of the insurance company and circled it with a question mark. Renwick had not mentioned it. In fact, he'd said he worked for his brother's company still, in some minor capacity.

When he hung up, he pulled his notes toward him. It seemed to him there were only two possible avenues of inquiry. It was possible Meg Holden had something to do with it. She was standing right next to him; though she certainly hadn't shot him, she might know who had. Darling had called to tell him that she'd been spotted on Stone Avenue talking to a man who was neither her husband nor her lover. Or Jack Renwick's own brother was involved somehow, maybe had him killed. He was after all a man who, by all accounts, hated Jack, was a serious alcoholic, and was in love with his sister-in-law. The latter he considered more likely. In his experience people were most often murdered by someone they knew and very often as the outcome of a contested legacy. The trouble was that, as attractive as he looked for the shooting from every other point of view, he'd not been contacted in Wisconsin until his brother was dead. Furthermore, he had produced his bus ticket from Phoenix for the day after the shooting. He had arrived there by plane from Wisconsin, an expense he said his sister-in-law was going to make up. All he could produce from that leg of the trip was a baggage claim ticket, as he'd lost his airline ticket, but gave the flight number and arrival time in Phoenix, which had checked out.

He drew up a to-do list. Under "Holden" he wrote, "Interview again. Ask Darling's wife for a full description of the man Mrs. Holden was talking to at the hotel." Was it the same man Mrs. Darling had seen her with on the street? He hadn't shared his suspicions with Galloway yet. "Explore any possible connection between Jack Renwick and Meg." Had she become his lover as well? Mr. Holden was rich. He could have had his rival picked off by someone. He smiled wryly at the thought of all these murderers-for-hire he was conjuring up to make these theories work.

Under "Renwick" he wrote, "Call insurance company in Wisconsin to verify Ned Renwick's whereabouts. Re-interview Ivy about Ned Renwick's behaviour toward her." He professed to be in love with her. Had he taken the obsession as far as getting rid of her husband, thus killing two birds at once? Was Mrs. Renwick hiding something else? She had arrived at the scene with bags, saying she'd been shopping, but was that all? Had she been outside the hedge on the street shooting her husband? They'd gone over every speck of ground outside the hotel and had not found either an abandoned weapon or even a bullet casing.

In a state of irritation, he pulled open the drawer of his desk and looked accusingly at the blank space among his files where the Griffin notes and financial evidence ought to be and wrote, "Find who took the damn evidence." Because if he didn't, he'd go to court with only a rickety story about Jimmy Griffin pushing some of his gambling money through the nursing home, which had squeaky clean financial accounts.

The thing that puzzled him the most, really, was that

not only had his typed-up notes gone missing but the notebook in which he'd written his original notes was gone as well. He remembered putting it in the drawer next to the manila folder. The notebook had been full, and though it was not his usual practice, he'd tossed it in where he kept his typewritten notes before he took them for filing. He closed his eyes and saw himself putting the folder into the drawer, and then the notebook, and he saw himself locking the drawer at night when he went home. But he couldn't make the exact connection between the day he'd slipped the notes in and that particular night. He locked that drawer every night. Had he walked to Galloway's office with the folder to talk with him about them? Had he gone to the water cooler still holding the file and left it sitting on something? It shook him to think he couldn't remember clearly. Of course, he knew why he couldn't really remember details about water coolers and other people's desks: because taking the files for central filing was a routine activity, and it's what he would have done.

He got up and went across to where Officer Alba sat. He would send him on the robbery in South Tucson; then he was going to do one more thorough search of the station for his folder.

LANE WAS IN the lobby gazing down at some silver and turquoise bracelets in a glass case. She ought to bring something back for Angela, who'd been so wonderful about organizing her wedding and had been right to pooh-pooh Lane's assertion that she just wanted a simple and discreet wedding. She became aware the woman behind the counter had stopped hovering and had moved away from her to the end of the counter.

"Yes? What do you want?"

The disapproval in her voice made Lane look up to see Chela Ruiz standing uncertainly in the doorway. Lane smiled and said as brightly as possible. "Oh, hello, Chela. How nice to see you."

Chela nodded and looked nervously at the manager. "I have to talk to this lady."

Frowning, the woman looked at Lane. "Madam?"

Lane smiled again. "Yes, of course. I think she's found something I've lost. What a dear! Could you put those earrings aside for me? I think they are just the thing for my friend. I'm in number 26."

"Certainly, madam."

Chela led Lane down the long, carpeted hallway, and out the rear door where the cleaning supplies were kept. "I saw her again, miss. The car came again for her today, only this time I had a look to see who was driving. It wasn't the same man."

Lane glanced toward the gate and then to the street outside. "You mean Mrs. Holden? What do you mean not the same man?"

Chela whispered, "Not the young man she, you know ... This one was older. Not as old as her husband, maybe more like her. She seemed to know him well. He touched her leg when she got into the car."

Was this the man she'd seen Meg talking to in town? "Chela, you have to talk to the police. Could you describe him?"

"Yes, sort of. He was a little heavier; he had a brown suit. He had a big nose, like someone who drinks a lot. But I can't talk to them, miss! That's why I'm telling you. You could talk to them. You could tell them if you think it's important."

Lane shook her head. "I don't know if it's important or not, but she was there when that poor man was shot. I know the police are going to want to know anything that may be out of the ordinary. I've met the sergeant in charge. He's called Martinez. He's very nice and not at all frightening. But he won't be satisfied from hearing anything second-hand from me. If you want, I'll go with you."

Chela surprised Lane by collapsing onto an overturned bucket and beginning to cry. "No, you don't understand. Raúl, he—"

"Your brother? Would he be angry for some reason?"

"It's just that he can't be noticed by the police. He doesn't have a birth certificate. My parents were poor when he was born, and he didn't get one. They're always checking. If they ask him and he can't produce one, they'll deport him."

"Oh." Lane was stymied. "But was he born here?"

"Yes, even my parents and grandparents were. But when people get in trouble and they don't have papers they send them across the border. Some of them have never even been there. They don't even have relatives over there."

"But no one is in trouble here, Chela," Lane said reasonably. "And your brother doesn't have to come into it. He didn't see anything. You did. Do you have a birth certificate?"

Chela nodded, but she looked unconvinced.

"Look. I'll call Sergeant Martinez and we can go

together. He'll be much more interested in solving the murder than talking about Raúl."

It hadn't been easy, but Chela had been persuaded to talk to the police, and Lane hurried back to the room to talk to Darling and call Martinez. Darling, however, was nowhere to be found. She went out and across the grounds to the pool, but he was not among the sunbathers. Muttering "blast!" under her breath, she went back to the room and shuffled through a couple of papers till she found the number Darling had written.

"It happens I was just about to come out there," Martinez said, when she'd explained.

"Oh. Chela works on the cleaning staff here. I'm a bit worried about how the management would view it. We couldn't come there, could we?"

Martinez sighed. "Look, can you give me a rundown of what she said? I need to go there because I have to interview ..." He was about to tell her and then he stopped. "I have to interview someone else there. If what she says is relevant, I'll meet her after she leaves for the day. What time is that, do you know?"

"I think she starts very early, so I suspect probably around four, but I can check for you." Lane went on to tell Martinez about the mystery man Meg Holden seemed to have met more than once. "The thing is, that Mrs. Holden seems to have a young man that she meets as well. Both Chela and I have seen them together, as it happens."

Martinez shook his head at the folly of humans, remembering his own father who had an affair with a woman for nearly the full length of his marriage and even had children with her. It interested him that women could carry on like that as well. "Thank you. Just tell the maid that I will arrange to meet her after work."

"She'll be very relieved, thank you."

Darling, looking as animated as a thoroughly self-contained man could, arrived just as Lane was hanging up the telephone. "They have a tennis pro here," he said.

CHAPTER TEN

———

"**FOR GOD'S SAKE, NED.** I told you. This doesn't change anything." Ivy Renwick folded her gloved hands tightly together and looked with distaste around his room. "How can you stay here? I could have paid for you to stay at the inn. No one would have been any the wiser."

"I would have been. I don't want to be a kept man. All I wanted was what was mine. Anyway, that Canadian couple recognized the family resemblance right away. He's a policeman. Can you beat that? Anyway, I'd hardly be incognito."

Ned sounded petulant, and Ivy felt a rush of impatience and, she realized with surprise, anxiety. She saw again that image of Jack lying dead under the bedspread, and the memory triggered a lurch of sickness. She moved toward the door.

"Look, I think we'd better lay off. I have to get Jack's body home as soon as this nightmare is over, and I have to get to the office to sort things out. This has been a mistake."

"That's my baby in there," Ned said. "Or are you forgetting that?"

"It would be hard to. You remind me every five minutes."

"Look," Ned went back to being conciliatory. "You're right. We should lay off. When this is over, we can get married. You know the board is going to want me to take over the company. They won't want a woman. It's logical, especially if we're married. You'd still be part of the decision making."

Ivy stood by the door looking at him. Could he have picked a more sordid rooming house? He couldn't manage his way out of a paper bag, she thought, let alone the company. She would cope with the board. It amazed her that he didn't know how much they disliked him. He'd been several times to the chairman railing against his brother being in charge. At least one of those times he'd been drunk. No. She felt quite sure of the board. "Of course, darling. We'll talk about it when this is over. In the meantime, don't contact me." She had no intention of talking about anything with him. She looked right, then left when she stepped onto the street, and then realized how shifty she must look, like a criminal trying to avoid detection. She held up her hand for a cab and wondered why she had never seen him before as he really was.

———

MR. VAN EYCK, leaving the garage to go deal with the percolator he'd left on the stove, looked toward the car where Ames and Tina were sitting in the front seat. He smiled. Maybe something would come of it. He liked the young sergeant. But Tina had been pretty prickly on the subject of men since before the war. He wondered if he should invite them in to join him for a cup of coffee but then thought he would just let nature take its course.

He would have been disappointed by the course it was taking. The mood in the car was tense.

"FINE," SHE SAID. "You're right. I didn't tell you the truth! I had a good reason, okay?"

"Perhaps you'd better tell me what really happened between you and Mr. Watts when he came the other day," Ames said as clinically as he could manage.

"I told him to go to hell. There. Are you satisfied?" Tina had an elbow up on the passenger side window frame and was resting her head on her hand, looking angrily out the window.

Ames had nothing to say to this. He wasn't satisfied, but it seemed obvious she hadn't been planning to run off with Watts. She must have been at the garage while he was meeting his end. Obvious or not, he knew he had to ask. "Were you planning to go away with him?"

"Are you out of your mind? I would drown myself in the lake before I spent one minute with him."

"But why didn't you tell me the truth yesterday?"

"You want to know the truth? The truth is that I bet there are a thousand people who would be happy to learn that man is dead. He was a repulsive, manipulating bastard."

"What people?"

"Anyone who has a daughter, believe me. Brothers, mothers, fathers."

"Your father too?"

Tina wheeled on him. "Why would you say that, Daniel? Dad knows nothing about it. I never told him."

Ames sat quietly, his lips pressed together. The use of his first name had stung. She sounded hurt. He was making a hash of this and was now sorry he'd left Terrell behind. He had to keep this professional, but it was getting difficult.

"Never told him what, Miss Van Eyck?"

She held his gaze a moment as if sizing him up. "Look. All you need to know is that we did, yes, have an argument, and I sent him packing. As for yesterday, my dad and I were here most of the time." This was mostly true, she thought. Her dad had gone off in the afternoon, but she'd been there. "Several people came and went during the day. If you want, I can give you their names, since you don't seem to believe me. Otherwise you can just leave us the hell alone!"

Tina got out of the car and slammed the door, causing Ames to wince. He saw her father come to the window at the sound. It was too far away to make out his expression.

SITTING OUTSIDE THE Watts cottage, which was looking tranquil and almost cozy with smoke curling out of its chimney and a light in the front window glowing against the rapidly spreading darkness of the inclement winter afternoon, Ames sighed. More complicated questions and another angry woman to deal with.

Once admitted, Ames stood awkwardly on the mat just inside the door.

"I just have to ask a couple of other questions." Mrs. Watts looked tired, but not particularly sad, which he found surprising. For one thing she smiled at him, an expression that lit up her face and gave a hint at what an attractive woman she must have been before life caught up with her.

"Well, you'd better come in and sit down. I gather you found the bag. Don't worry. I'm prepared for anything. I know this is going to sound horrible, but I find myself almost relieved when all is said and done. He wasn't an easy man, and I suspect I stopped loving him even before Sadie was born. He didn't love me, but I think he loved her, if he was capable at all of love."

Unable to say anything to this, Ames, now sitting uncomfortably at the table, looked down and then cleared his throat. "We did find the bag, yes. We found not only a couple of changes of clothes for him but also a couple of frocks, some lady's underwear." He cleared his throat again. "Blue dress, with flowers and a red one?"

Mrs. Watts's face darkened. "You don't say. Well. I'm not surprised somehow. Not my dresses, Sergeant, I can tell you that." She sat down. "I suppose that explains all his absences." She made a move as if to shut the door on him. "I want the car back. I called the station this morning. I can't do a thing without it."

"Do you have an extra set of keys? We still haven't found any."

"No. I don't think I do. I hadn't thought about that," Mrs. Watts said.

"That shouldn't be a problem. We've almost finished with it. The trunk lock is broken, but I'll get it fixed and then have someone drop it back as soon as possible. I can maybe get a locksmith to make another set of keys while

I'm at it." When she did not respond to his offer, he cleared his throat. "We did find traces of black paint in the trunk, and we now suspect that your husband might have used it to deface the door of a local garage."

Mrs. Watts turned her head away sharply, as if she couldn't trust what she might say. She finally turned to look at him. "That as well. Where? No. Don't tell me. Some sordid mess he got himself into behind my back." Her anger was palpable. "Anything else, Sergeant?"

AMES ARRIVED BACK at the station in a very unsatisfactory state. He reflected on the almost red-hot anger with which Mrs. Watts had responded to the finding of the dresses, and the possibility that her husband had been responsible for defacing a local business. It seemed in direct contradiction to the calm acceptance she appeared to show earlier when she had said she didn't love her husband and suspected he didn't love her. And there was the business of Tina, which he'd also made a mess of.

He thought again about how Darling would have been able to negotiate the problem of an angry witness like Tina, how he dropped his voice, dug in, used a completely neutral courtesy so the witness felt safe and went off the burn. She'd lied about her angry interaction with Watts, who had—or so the working theory suggested—subsequently driven to the garage in the middle of the night and painted it to get back at her. Something his wife hadn't realized he'd done. It hardly seemed to matter now, though it would conclusively clear up the matter of the damage to the garage door. He threw his hat onto the rack and took off his overcoat.

Terrell appeared at the door with his notebook open. "Sir?"

"You have something? More odd things, perhaps?"

Terrell smiled. "Yes indeed, sir."

"Pull up a pew," he said. "I came up empty. Miss Van Eyck wasn't trying to run away with him; she was at the garage all day, she says, and now she's in a snit. And the clothes don't belong to Mrs. Watts, according to her. In fact, she's adapted quite quickly to being a widow. I did tell her about the splodge of paint in the trunk of the car and explained our suspicion about her husband and the paint on the garage door. She was extremely angry, but I don't know if it was at me or her faithless husband." He frowned; a thought about this had bubbled up then and had gone again just as quickly. He sighed. "What have you got?"

Terrell opened his book. "Okay, I talked to the people at the station, including his boss. He does, did, work there as a yardman, which is why that woman coming off the ferry recognized the licence from seeing his car at the station. However, he no longer works as a foreman. He'd been demoted a couple of months back after a conflict arose with the men. When I asked what the conflict was about, he told me he had no idea, but it was clear Watts was no leader, as discipline had become lax and work wasn't getting done.

"So I went and talked to several of the men. They said the whole thing started between him and one of the men. Something about a girl. Someone called Finch. Hang on." He flipped a page. "Yes, here we go. Craig Finch wasn't there today, but I hope to catch him tomorrow. I got his address, though, sir, if we want to go talk to him at home. I got a feeling people knew something, but they weren't that forthcoming." Terrell didn't tell Ames that he'd been told by one of the men to get the police department to send a "real" police officer next time. The courtesy of the foreman made up for it.

Ames frowned. "And what about these trips Watts's wife said he took?"

"Not for work. In fact, according to them he rarely missed a day of work."

"So then, he's spending nights somewhere nearby when he was supposedly away on work trips? And now he is running off with someone for, judging by the contents of the bag, a lost weekend, only he dies of a heart attack and the woman, whoever she is, takes advantage of the situation and robs him and, for good measure, locks him in the car. And goes where? It's just the strangeness of the whole thing."

"My questions exactly, sir."

———

SERGEANT MARTINEZ, FRUSTRATED again by finding no trace of his folder, put his cap on and prepared to go to the inn. He picked up his new notebook, sitting in the wooden tray where he always kept them, and made his way between the desks to the door.

"Sergeant," someone called, and he turned to see young Cooper approaching him with a piece of paper. "I've tracked down the rooming house, sir. I got lucky. I called six and the sixth one was it. He's been there for five days."

"Thanks, Officer Cooper." Martinez frowned and called after him. "Did you say *five* days?"

"Yeah, that's what the landlady, Mrs. Parvis, said. She didn't seem to approve of him much."

"Why, what did she say?"

"She said she ought to show him the door, the way he carries on, but wouldn't say any more. Said, 'He pays his bills,' so I suppose money wins out over whatever it is he does there."

Martinez got into the patrol car and looked at the address. It was about a mile away on Park. Though he was sure that what Cooper had learned must be a mistake, he thought he'd better stop there on the way. Edward Renwick said he had only just arrived from Wisconsin the day before. He'd flown, he said, to Phoenix and taken a bus to Tucson, and even produced some proof of the trip. What did this mean?

"Sergeant Martinez, ma'am," he said when he got to the rooming house, and flashed his badge. "You talked with one of our officers earlier about one of your guests? Edward Renwick?"

"Yes, I did. What's the interest of the police, anyway?" Mrs. Parvis was wearing a handkerchief tied in a turban around her hair, and her plump figure was wrapped in a long apron that ended at the top of her rolled-down stockings and a pair of ancient, stained mules. "Not that I'm surprised," she added.

"Can you tell me how long he's been here?"

The woman turned toward a small table that held a

heavy register. "There, see. He came on the eighth. What are we now? The twelfth? So, five days."

Martinez stepped across the threshold and peered at the book.

"He was gone part of yesterday—no, sorry, the day before, and last night. No need to ask where. He came back today."

"Why no need to ask where?" Martinez asked.

"He was with that hussy, of course! She was sneaking out of here again this morning, thinking I didn't see her."

"I see." Martinez looked down the dingy hall. "Is he here now?"

"No. No doubt drinking somewhere. That seems to be his other occupation. I don't know where he's getting his money, but he can't have much, or he wouldn't be staying here. That woman looks pretty expensive. Maybe she's keeping him."

"Can you describe her?" He looked back at the landlady whose expression was a perfect combination of disapproval and gratification.

"Tall blonde. Expensive perfume. Came the second day he was here."

"How often has she come?" Martinez asked. Could it be Ivy Renwick?

"Nearly every day since he's been here. Today, the day before, in fact, I think they went out together, then I guess he was with her somewhere, and then before that as well, after he first got here. I lost track, honestly. Three, four times at least. First couple of times she was here more than two hours."

She was there on the day of the murder. Martinez ripped a page out of his notebook and wrote his name and the station number on it. "Call when he comes in. Leave a message if I'm not there. I'll put an officer nearby to keep an eye out, as well. In the meantime, can you let me into his room?"

The landlady surveyed him critically for a moment and then shrugged. "On your head be it if he comes home and catches you messing around in his room."

IT HAD BEEN a disappointing venture. The tiny, dingy room yielded little more than a few clothes shoved willy-nilly in two drawers of a tall dresser, a battered suitcase thrown into the closet, and a bag of toiletries sitting open on the dresser. He thanked Mrs. Parvis, who seemed disappointed not to learn something wonderfully shocking about her guest.

Feeling a wave of excitement, Martinez broke the speed limit on his way out of town to the inn. Notwithstanding the lack of anything incriminating in the room, Ivy Renwick had been visiting her brother-in-law at a rooming house when he was supposed to be in Wisconsin on the day her husband was shot dead in front of their honeymoon hotel room. His being able to produce all that 'evidence' of his travel made him look even more suspicious. Why had he produced it unless he had something to cover up? As to a weapon, he could have gotten rid of it anywhere. After all, there was a whole desert, right across the road from the hotel, at his disposal.

"WHY DON'T YOU go? I think I'd better stay here and

support Chela in case Martinez wants to question her. He says he's coming here to interview someone. He didn't say whom, but I'm guessing Meg Holden or Ivy Renwick. That poor woman. She's barely been out of her room since it happened. I should pop over and see her."

"Tennis famously is a game one doesn't play on one's own," Darling said. "And if you mean 'poor' Ivy Renwick, I saw her getting furtively out of a cab not an hour ago from my vantage point at the tennis court."

"It won't be just you, will it? It will be you and the pro. I'd only be in the way."

"That winning smile is not going to mollify me. I'll go make an arrangement with him, and then later, or tomorrow, we'll both go have a lesson."

"Perfect," said Lane, but she was already looking toward Ivy Renwick's room from where they were sitting in the shade outside number 26. Where had she been? "Where do you think she was?" Lane asked Darling. "And why do you say she looked furtive?"

"I'm a police officer. I am trained in furtive. As to her whereabouts, none of our business, I should have thought."

LANE KNOCKED SOFTLY at Ivy Renwick's door. There was a brief shuffling inside and then the door opened just wide enough for Ivy to peer outside.

"Oh, it's you," she said, opening the door a bit more, but not enough to suggest she'd welcome anyone in.

"I just wanted to make sure you're all right. I've felt quite badly about you having to wait here while things get decided after losing your husband," Lane said.

Ivy sighed. "You might as well come in," she said, walking away from the door to the table where they'd drunk coffee two mornings before. She took up a glass of water and drank and then stood with her arms crossed.

"How are you holding up?" Lane asked.

Ivy looked at Lane as if she was thinking of saying something significant and then turned away to look out the window.

"I wish I was home," she said. "I'd like to bury my husband and attend to the factory. I can't count on my brother-in-law to run things. He's useless." She picked up her cigarettes, lit one, and inhaled deeply.

"Oh," Lane said, surprised. "Has he gone back to Wisconsin? We had dinner with him last night. He told us he was moving into a rooming house till this was over."

Ivy looked at her sharply. "Why, what did he say?"

"Just that, and that you wouldn't see him. Given what you told me, I did rather understand why you wouldn't see him."

Ivy shook her head and produced a mirthless smile. "It's all a lot more complicated than that." She stubbed out the barely smoked cigarette. "Thank you for stopping by. I really would like to rest now."

Lane opened her mouth to respond when a sharp rapping on the door made them both jump.

"Mrs. Renwick? It's Sergeant Martinez. I need a moment of your time, please," Martinez called through the closed door.

Ivy Renwick went white and reached for the back of a chair for support. Lane pointed at the door and Ivy nodded.

"Hello, Sergeant Martinez."

Martinez looked surprised to see Lane and asked, "Is Mrs. Renwick here?"

Before Lane could answer, Ivy said wearily, "Yes. Come in, Sergeant."

"I'll leave you to it, then," Lane said, starting through the door. "Let me know if you need anything, Mrs. Renwick."

"Oh, can you stay? Can she stay?" She turned to Martinez. "I'd prefer it."

Surprised, Lane came back into the room and waited for the sergeant's response.

"She can stay," Martinez said, "but I've come to tell you we now know you have not been entirely honest with us, and I'll have to take you down to the station to answer a few questions."

Ivy sat down heavily and looked at her hands.

"If you could get whatever you need, Mrs. Renwick," Martinez said patiently.

Ivy stood up and went to the desk and pulled out the hotel stationery and scribbled something on it. "Mrs. Darling, this is the law office for the business back home. Could you call them, ask them to recommend a legal firm down here, and ask them to send someone immediately to the police station?" She turned to Martinez. "I won't answer questions until a lawyer is there."

Nodding, as if this were par for the course, Martinez said, "That's fine ma'am. We've picked up Mr. Edward Renwick and will be speaking with him for some time, I expect."

Lane followed them out and stood on the sidewalk, waiting for the sergeant to help Ivy into the back of the car.

"Sergeant Martinez," she said when he had closed the

door, "what shall I tell the cleaning woman, Chela Ruiz? Will you be interviewing her?"

"Oh, right. No, I don't think I'll need to at this point. You'd best call Mrs. Renwick that lawyer. She's going to need one."

CHAPTER ELEVEN

——————

WEDNESDAY MORNING, AMES AND TERRELL sat in Ames's office. Ames was tapping the desk with his pencil, and Terrell was waiting, his book open.

"Clearly Barney was not a very nice man," Ames said. He was troubled by what Tina had told him, which was, in retrospect, not much. But she knew Watts and hated him, and then there was what April had said about Watts and young girls. He'd known Tina. Known her how, exactly? What had Watts done that made Tina hate him?

"Yes, sir," said Terrell. "A history of a penchant for young girls, which for the most part is not in itself against the law, but it becomes less and less savoury as he gets older. His wife is a good ten to fifteen years younger than he is, and, in fact, was sixteen when they met, and now we hear he may have been engaged in something with the girlfriend of one of his workmates. And, of course, who belongs to those pretty clothes in the bag?"

"None of this is going to feed the baby. He was robbed, let's say by his passenger, but died what appears to be a natural death. We should concentrate on that," Ames said. "Maybe we were asking the wrong question at the ferry. We need to ask the guy on the ferry if there was a female foot passenger going over to Harrop that day. But it could have been any hitchhiker, really. We're just thinking it was a woman now because of the clothes. Whoever it was must have walked some distance or caught a ride."

"Could we put a notice in the paper and on the radio for anyone seeing a man or woman walking on the road on Monday to contact us?"

"Yes. Then let's go see Finch. If he was arguing with him about a woman, it's possible the woman with Watts was Finch's wife. Then I'll go back out and talk to the ferryman. I might give the scene another look as well. I'm puzzled about the keys."

When Terrell had gone off to the offices of the *Nelson Daily News*, Ames sat for a few minutes more looking at his notes and then decided he needed a cup of coffee to stimulate his thinking.

"Oh, I'm glad you've come in," April said as Ames walked into the diner. She held up a coffee pot and he nodded. "I called my sister to ask"—and here she dropped into a near whisper, looking at the elderly couple sitting at one end of the counter—"about you-know-who. She said he had a real reputation, thought he was the bee's knees. He even was rumoured to have practically forced girls to . . . you know. And she's pretty sure he put at least one girl in the family way. Most of the girls in town learned to stay away from him. According to Sis, he even propositioned her, and she told him where to go."

"You don't say. Thank you for calling her." He could see from the way April hovered that she'd have liked to hear more from him, but it was an ongoing investigation. He was relieved when she was summoned to another table. Besides, he was always slightly embarrassed about the amount of sugar he put in his coffee. He stirred in his customary three spoons and gave himself over to thinking about this new indication of the victim's unsavoury personality.

BACK AT HIS desk, Ames scribbled some notes and thought about Tina. Was she one of the girls Watts had "forced," or even put in the family way? He thought of Tina with a secret child somewhere and dismissed the idea, though the thought of it produced an unpleasant sensation between anger and grievance. Aware that his anxiety about Tina could distort his thinking about Barney Watts's death, he pulled his notepaper toward him and tried to sort what was on it. He had become convinced that a system of note taking he'd learned from an officer in Vancouver might yield results.

He folded the paper in half lengthwise and on the top of the left-hand side he wrote: B. WATTS, DEATH. Underneath he detailed the finding of the car, the tyre marks indicating a sharp and precipitous turn, its final position, the position of the body, the fact of the car being locked, the keys gone, and the wallet empty and cast away. He'd put something about the cause of death when Gilly came through with his report. Finally, he noted the holdall with Barney's clothes and those of a woman, most likely his passenger.

On the right-hand side he wrote WHAT WE KNOW ABOUT B. WATTS. Here he laid out, in point form, his home life, his work— including his demotion, which he had kept from his wife. He sketched out nights away, the argument at work with Finch, and his reputation for pursuing young girls before the war: Tina, his wife, possibly a woman connected to Finch.

Across the bottom third of the page he drew a line and under it wrote NOT KNOWN and listed the location of keys, the reason for the position of the car at the ferry turnoff, the passenger, the reason for the argument with Finch, and who had emptied his wallet.

Staring at the lists, he wondered how the right and left columns were related. It was possible that it really was just Watts's unlucky day, Ames thought. He was happily on his way to a tryst with someone, picked someone up, had a heart attack, and was robbed and left for dead. He put his pencil down. Two possibilities presented themselves: Watts was going somewhere with a woman and began to experience the heart attack. The woman, instead of trying to help him, took advantage of the situation—stole his wallet and locked him in the car so he wouldn't give chase. Not exactly murder, but was there a statute somewhere about not offering aid? Or Watts was alone in the car and on the way to meet someone and had the heart attack; a passing hitchhiker, or motorist for that matter, stopped, saw Watts was dead, helped himself to the wallet and keys, and drove off.

He added to the NOT KNOWN section: "How much

money did he have on him, and where the hell was he going?" He threw his pencil on the table, watched it bounce and roll off the desk, and, cursing, went to retrieve it.

"Chasing mice, Ames?" Sergeant O'Brien had appeared in his doorway and was watching with interest as Ames scrabbled under his desk where his pencil had rolled.

Ames pulled himself out cautiously to avoid hitting his head, stood up dusting his knees, and said with defiant dignity, "Yes, Sergeant O'Brien?" It was unusual for the desk sergeant to haul his considerable frame up the stairs.

"Do you have a moment, Sarge?"

"Have a seat," Ames said, waving his hand graciously at a chair that looked a bit small for his colleague.

O'Brien sank gratefully onto the chair and then pulled it forward. "It's about the young darkie."

Ames could detect no animus. "You mean Constable Terrell," he said firmly.

"Yes. It's just that the other lads, well, I mean, he keeps himself to himself, if you see what I mean."

"Not entirely. Are you saying they don't like him?"

"No. Not exactly. But he doesn't help by being a loner. He doesn't, you know, shoot the breeze and the like, like the rest of them."

Ames looked at O'Brien, feeling a little at sea. "Perhaps he's just hesitant. He is new. Has anyone asked him for a beer? He's a vet. So is Pritchard, isn't he? They could go to the Legion."

O'Brien looked noncommittal. "People say things, you know, out and about."

"For God's sake, O'Brien, what people? What things?"

"You know. They ask about people on the force. Sometimes on the phone I get, 'don't send the darkie.' Like that."

"So you're telling me that the men don't ask him to join them after work because people might disapprove? I'm not surprised he's standoffish. What do you think he hears from people when he does go out?"

"I hadn't thought of that."

"No. I suppose not. How are people going to get used to the idea if we can't even stand by our own? And while we're at it, what do you think the inspector would think about it?"

O'Brien, who had never addressed Ames with any real deference before, heaved himself off the chair and said mildly, "You do have a point, Sarge."

Ames watched O'Brien clomping out the door and shook his head, exhaling a long breath. If there was ever a time he could use the steadying thoughts of Inspector Darling, this was it.

"Sergeant."

Ames heard Terrell's greeting to O'Brien just outside in the hall and winced. Terrell must have overheard part of the conversation.

"Sir?" Terrell said with a quick knock at the door. "Paper will print our request to the public for information.

"Excellent. Next stop, the rail yard. Let's see if we can track down Craig Finch." He stood up, drumming his fingers lightly on his desk, and cleared his throat. "I'm sorry about what you might have just heard, Constable."

Terrell shook his head. "Don't trouble yourself, sir. I've

heard worse. And for what it's worth I thought you handled it well."

"NO, HE HASN'T been at work," the foreman said when they asked after Finch. "Influenza, he says. Between Watts dying and Finch on the sick list, I'm pretty short-handed. Mind you, I don't need anyone spreading germs around here, but he couldn't get back fast enough for me." The foreman lit a cigarette, apparently deciding to extend the break provided by Ames and Terrell turning up.

"Was he at work on Tuesday?" Ames asked. He wasn't sure how relevant this question was as it seemed to him highly unlikely Finch was going anywhere with a man whom he appeared to hate.

The foreman shook his head. "Don't think so. No, because I was short that day as well."

"One of your men said there'd been an argument between Watts and Finch. Did you hear it?" Ames asked.

"Heard about it. Something to do with a woman. Now, I found that surprising. Finch is a married man with kids in high school. Watts is married too, for that matter. All I heard is one of the men heard Finch say, "You stay away from her, or else.""

"Is it possible Finch could have been talking about his wife, or maybe even his daughter?"

The foreman shook his head, an expression of dismay on his face. "I sure wouldn't like to think so. That girl of Finch's is only about sixteen."

"Can we have a look in Watts's locker?"

"No point. His missus came and emptied it out. Took

a couple of bundles of stuff. No reason not to give it to her."

TERRELL KNOCKED ON the door of the small, shabby bungalow on the steep rise that looked down on the Nelson side of the ferry landing. He and Ames could hear someone talking somewhere inside, but no one came. He knocked again, and finally, after a further wait, a woman opened the inner door and looked at them through the screen door. A strong odour of cigarette smoke preceded her. She looked exhausted and unkempt, as if she had not left the house for several days.

"Mrs. Finch? I'm Sergeant Ames, and this is Constable Terrell from the Nelson police. May we have a word?"

The woman's hand jerked to her chest, and her eyes filled with tears. Her voice was desperate. "Oh my God! I was just going to call you! Craig's out looking for her. Something's happened to her, hasn't it?"

———

LANE WAS STANDING outside number 27 deep in thought, having watched Martinez walk across the garden with Ivy Renwick toward the main entrance. He managed somehow to convey the feeling she was going willingly by merely indicating with his hand where she should go. But Lane knew it was as close to an arrest as she had ever seen. What had he found out? It must have been compelling. Was the Holden line of questioning being discarded? She opened the notepaper Ivy had given her and went inside number 26 to place the call to the law firm in Wisconsin. Finally, after what seemed an interminable wait, the desk phone rang. "We have Delany and Pratt on the line, madam." The operator sounded distant and tinny, like she might be on another continent.

It took some time to explain the situation because she didn't know how much they knew about the Renwicks' trip to Tucson, but she made clear that Jack Renwick had been shot and Mrs. Renwick needed the services of a lawyer in Tucson as quickly as possible. She heard the thump of the receiver being put down, muffled voices calling out and, eventually, another voice.

"One of our partners was able to contact a banking lawyer in Phoenix who gave us the name of a firm in Tucson: Davis and Tackman. We will call ahead now. Wait fifteen minutes and then ask for Mr. Rodney Davis."

She waited impatiently for the fifteen minutes to go by and then rang through again to the main desk and asked to be put through to the number she'd been given. While she waited, she imagined the stiff-collared lawyers at Delany and Pratt scurrying madly about, trying to think about what the wrongful death of the president of Renwick's company was going to mean. When she did finally reach Davis, he had not yet received the call, so she was obliged to explain the predicament Ivy Renwick was in and to say that she urgently required a lawyer at the police station.

"Has she been arrested?"

"I don't really know. What I heard was that they were taking her to the station for questioning. She said she would not speak to them without a lawyer."

That call over, Lane sat back and breathed a sigh of

relief. She would go and see how Darling was getting along with the tennis pro. She was making for the door when the telephone rang again.

"I have Canada on the line for you." Lane waited, her brows knitting, trying to move her mind away from the Renwick situation to whatever this was about.

"Hello, Lane Winslow speaking," she said.

"Miss Winslow, it's Sergeant Ames."

"Of course, it is! I'd know that voice anywhere. How nice to hear from you. How are you?"

"I'm well, thank you, at least ... is the inspector there?"

"He's off playing tennis at the moment. I can get him to call you. Is there anything I can help with? Anything to do with your strange case?" she asked, smiling.

"I bet you would have figured it out long before now. No. It's an awkward personnel problem. In fact, I seem to be swimming in awkward problems right now. I've got a situation with Tina Van Eyck." He stopped. Should he tell her about that? She may have some woman's intuition.

"Oh?"

"My case up here has gotten complicated, and I found out Miss Van Eyck was lying to me. I mean, it isn't a murder or anything, just a robbery, and she probably wasn't even involved, but, you know."

"It must have been awkward for you to have to interview her. How did she lie to you?"

"It started with someone painting an ugly word on their garage door in the night. I won't say it, but it was likely directed at her. When I asked her about it, she claimed it was someone she'd had a fight with because he'd made a pass at her when he'd brought his car in. What I found out later was that she actually knew the guy back in the thirties and she hates him because, well, I don't know why. But the point is, she could have told me in the first place. Instead, I had to find out somewhere else. And here's the problem: it turns out the guy probably was going somewhere with a woman when he died. I'm pretty sure it wasn't Miss Van Eyck, but still."

"Why are you sure it wasn't her?"

Ames was silent. "She seems to have—God, I can't believe I'm saying this about her—an alibi. I just want to believe she wasn't planning to run off with him."

"So it sounds like you're worried on three counts: one, she lied to you when you thought you were friends; two, you're worried that if she lied to you she has something to hide; and three, she might have had plans to go somewhere with this man."

Ames took a deep breath, feeling some relief at the clarity Lane was bringing to his dilemma. "That's right. I'm just finding the whole thing difficult because she is hiding something, I'm sure of it, and it could be relevant to the case."

"I certainly see that. It sounds like you're upset because she doesn't seem to trust you."

"Exactly. She suddenly seems to have taken completely against the police, on top of that. There's a crime, and she's not really cooperating. I think she should tell me why she hated the dead man, but what if it had nothing to do with anything?"

"She would be angry at you for forcing her to tell you

something personal that perhaps involved hurt or shame from the past. What do you think the inspector would do?"

Ames answered without hesitation. "He would talk to her gently and impartially. I don't know how to do that, especially when I'm angry."

"And you're angry because you like her, and you wish she trusted you. It is a dilemma. It's hard to be impartial." She paused, but Ames didn't seem to have anything more to add. "I'll get the inspector to call you as soon as possible. Is there a good time?"

"I'll be in and out. We've just learned of a missing teenager, and it might be related to this case. We're calling the local RCMP detachments to be on the lookout, and we have to interview her friends. In retrospect it wasn't that important. Just some office stuff."

———

WHEN AMES HUNG up, he felt slightly better. He looked at his notes, took up his pen, and added another question: "Why is Tina VE really angry at the victim?" All signs were pointing to him being a predatory bastard. Had Tina been one of his victims? He added this to the list of unknowns and then put "Terrell to interview?" in parentheses, and looked at the clock. And, in a surprising and ugly turn, they now saw it was possible that sixteen-year-old Ada Finch had run away because she had been the object of Watts's attentions. No wonder Finch was furious. Ada Finch had two close friends, and he and Terrell would be off to see them at around four, after they got home from school.

LANE FOUND DARLING at the tennis courts making a very good account of himself. She sat on a bench at the edge of the court and admired his serves and returns. It was a revelation to her that he played tennis, as it had been in the summer when she had learned that he was a good dancer. It opened up an avenue of wondering what else she didn't know about him. On the one hand it delighted her to think that there was much yet to learn, and on the other hand it made her wonder how she had married him on such a meagre acquaintance. He stood now, swaying, nimble in the knees, tennis racket at the ready in two hands, waiting for the pro to serve. He was wearing a white short-sleeved shirt and linen trousers, and his arms were beginning to tan. She had a giddy moment of feeling herself married to a complete stranger, so unlike the serious-minded police inspector did he seem at this moment.

"Fault!" he called, in a professional-sounding voice.

She realized that it was she who should submit herself to the teachings of the pro, as she had only played a bit of tennis at Oxford and could not rise to nearly the skill level of her new husband. She lowered her head and looked at the red of the clay.

Of course, it wasn't true, was it? There had been a red clay tennis court at home when she was a child. Her father had insisted both his daughters play and had demanded, as he did on all matters involving their education, they play well. Her sister had taken to it like a duck to water. Lane had merely enjoyed it. She could still hear her father tossing his racket on the table and wiping his face with his handkerchief, saying to no one in particular, "She's absolutely bloody useless. Not a competitive bone in her body."

She looked up to see Darling and the pro shaking hands over the net. "Thank you. That was good fun. I haven't played since I was at university. Not much opportunity now."

"Well, you haven't lost your instincts. Is this your missus?"

"Yes, indeed. Lane, this is Benny. Benny, my wife, Lane. She's very clever, so I expect she's secretly good at tennis and just hasn't told me."

Benny's tanned face lit up with a dazzling smile. "Ma'am," he said, nodding. "Later today? I have a lesson with another guest now, but after lunch I have a free slot."

"Yes, why not?" said Lane. "I haven't played since I was at Oxford in thirty-eight. Not very well, I'm afraid."

"That's what I'm here for," Benny assured her.

"YOU'RE VERY GOOD," Lane said as they strolled along the brick paths back to their room. "I'm honestly waiting with bated breath to see what other skill you pull out of a hat. In fact, I don't think we know each other well enough at all. I'm not sure we didn't marry in haste."

Darling put his arm through hers. "We have leisure. Shall we go engage in a spot of repenting?"

"Not until you call Sergeant Ames. I was on the line to him just before I came to watch you. He said it wasn't urgent, and I know it's expensive, but I expect he'd like to hear from you."

Darling opened the door and stood aside to let her in.

"Well, perhaps he'll pay for it, then. I don't recall inviting Ames on our honeymoon. Why can't he stay where he's put?"

"I'll be outside with my feet up reading about Lord Peter and the nine tailors. And then I have big, very ill Renwick news."

CHAPTER TWELVE

TINA VAN EYCK STOOD LOOKING at the top of her father's head as he leaned into the engine of a '39 Plymouth coupe. She was completely out of sorts. She felt guilty about her treatment of Daniel Ames, and in the next moment this was replaced by a wave of fury at his questioning her like a common criminal. But of course, he has to, she thought. It's his job. She fervently wished she didn't like him so much. He seemed almost too young, though he couldn't be more than a year or two younger than she was. Maybe it was that he was genuine, open. And so damned optimistic. He was more or less what he appeared to be, and you couldn't say that about most men. But he also was a policeman.

She was so muddled that it took her a moment to realize that her father, for the second time, was saying, "Plug wrench, when you feel able."

"Sorry, Dad. A million miles away."

"You certainly were. Is it this business with Watts being

dead?" He pulled himself upright and leaned on the car, looking across the engine at her. "I can't get over the idea that he comes and ruins our paint job and then ends up dead." He stood up straight and said tentatively, "I thought I heard you arguing with him that day."

"Yup. I did. He made a pass at me. The police will want to make something of that, as well." She turned angrily away and reached for the plug wrench, handing it to her father, who took it without taking his eyes off her.

He frowned. "I wish he'd never come. Why would he come, suddenly like that? It's not like there aren't other service stations," her father said bitterly.

"Dad, I don't need you to fight my battles. I've dealt with worse than him."

Mr. Van Eyck shook his head and looked into the engine. "What about that sergeant—aren't you a little sweet on him? You could do worse."

"Look, Dad. I'm not sweet on him, or anyone, so can we just drop it? I had enough agro from men in the old country. And I'm not in the market." Tina had gone to England to join the Auxiliary Territorial Service and had worked as a mechanic for the duration of the war. She'd come back fed up with men. Now she found herself attracted to Sergeant Ames and felt the more foolish for letting her feelings off the reins.

Shrugging, her father leaned back into the engine. "Suit yourself."

Later, Tina took the opportunity provided by a break in the rain to walk down to the lakeshore. In spite of the damp, cold gloominess of November weather, she loved to sit looking out at the lake, winter or summer. It reminded her that her puny human problems were not the only thing in the world. She sat on the top of the tilted, weathered picnic table on the edge of the tiny cove of sand at the bottom of the property and gave herself up to gazing at the expanse of dark water. Today the lake was brooding but utterly quiet except for the gentle singsong lap of the water along the sand. The mountains rose dark and misty on the other side of the lake, suiting her dark mood.

Should she have told Ames? She couldn't bear to remind herself of it. And it wasn't relevant. She turned a yellowed leaf that had lodged on the table in her fingers. The problem was, she hadn't liked lying to Ames. It was in such contrast to the forthright girl she'd always thought herself. But if she'd told him the truth about knowing Watts, she'd have had to explain. And if she explained, it would seem like she had a motive to harm him. No. That wasn't it, and she knew it. It was shame. Pure and simple. A shame she couldn't even confront in herself.

———

LANE SAT UNDER the ramada, white wine in hand. "So what did Amesy want?"

"Not till you tell me the Renwick news."

"Only that Ivy Renwick was as good as arrested by Martinez."

Darling tilted his head, puzzled. "What do you mean, 'as good as'? And how do you know, anyway?"

"As you know, I'd popped over to see if she was all right."

"Of course you had," Darling said, turning his wine glass.

"And," Lane continued firmly, "I'd not been there five minutes when Martinez came by. I tried to make myself scarce, but Ivy insisted I stay. He told her he'd discovered she had not been telling the truth and she was required at the police station for questioning. He also said they were in the process of questioning Ned. She asked me to call her lawyers in Wisconsin and get them to find counsel down here to meet her at the police station. She seemed, I don't know, nervy and hard in a way I hadn't quite seen before."

"It takes a lot of nerve and hardness to kill your husband," Darling suggested.

"You're jumping to conclusions though, aren't you? Thank you," Lane said to the waiter who had deposited a Cobb salad at each of their places. "I'd like to learn to make these fluffy white buns."

"I wouldn't say jumping. You're telling me she's hard, and I saw her coming back this morning from somewhere in a cab, and I absolutely swear she did look furtive. Besides, I liked him—Jack, I mean. He was a straightforward sort of man. He certainly didn't deserve to end up like that."

"And why are they questioning her brother-in-law?" she asked. "Is there a suggestion they are in this together?"

"I think I've learned something about you," Darling said, contemplating her. How lovely she was! "It's not that you are mad to see justice done. It's that you're a nosy Parker, looking for tantalizing gossip everywhere you go."

"Tantalizing gossip, my dear, holds the key to every case. Well, it's out of our hands. Now, Ames."

"Yes. Apparently O'Brien made a rare venture up the stairs to Ames's office to say the lads are troubled by Terrell. He wasn't quite sure whether O'Brien was trying to say they are unhappy to have to work with a coloured police officer, or they aren't sure how to handle the public's misgivings, or if they think he is standoffish."

"How interesting. I'm sure he never expected to have to handle that sort of problem. What did he do?"

"The right thing, as it turns out. He told O'Brien to remind the men that they are part of a unit and need to stand by their own. He also suggested someone take him for a beer. I suggested he get the ball rolling on that one."

"I knew Ames was made of the right stuff."

"Yes. Your regard for each other is legendary. I suspect he's worried some of the men might genuinely be prejudiced and it could interfere with the police work."

Lane nodded. "There's really nothing he can do about that, though, is there? One hopes that Terrell is good at his job and the men will come to rely on him and lose those sorts of prejudices. As it happens, Ames had a little problem to share with me as well."

Darling waited, and when nothing was forthcoming, said, "Yes?"

"I'm just not sure I can say anything."

"Oh, blimey. Not his love life, is it? I'd stay as far away from that as possible. I know I do."

"Yes, I suppose it is that, though not entirely. His strange case is involved as well." Lane went on to tell Darling about Tina lying and Ames feeling betrayed by it. "He came up with the idea that perhaps he was too cross at her to interview her properly. I suspect he might ask Terrell to do it."

"Perhaps I could hire you as the department psychologist," he said. "Now, the murder underfoot here looks like it's well in hand, so no one will need you, and we have a week left on this supposedly relaxing honeymoon. We must make plans. There is a pool to lie by, an as yet unscheduled horse expedition, and your tennis lesson. One or two other things we could do." He leaned over and kissed her softly. "I don't want us to get back and feel regret."

"I'm already inoculated against regret by just being in this lovely place with a lovely person and being able to lie around in a bathing suit in November." Lane looked at her watch. "Right. I'm off to my lesson. Why don't you arrange for something with horses for tomorrow? See if we can get a picnic lunch to take along."

CHELA WAS SITTING outside on a chair in the tiny alcove attached to the cleaning cupboard, having a cigarette, looking over the fence onto the street and farther north at the Catalina Mountains in the distance. The fragrant shade of an oleander provided soothing respite from the noon sun. She loved this moment of quiet. Of course, Raúl would be annoyed to know she was smoking, a thought that filled her with a good-natured rebellion.

She turned at the sound of the door opening and stood up automatically as Mrs. Holden came through. She was wearing a light-blue summer coat and a matching blue hat. Meg stopped when she saw Chela and then smiled broadly.

"Oh, I didn't know anyone was here. This must be your lunchtime. I am so sorry. I know, I know, I shouldn't be using the back door, but my husband, Mr. Holden, is in the lounge, and I'm sneaking off to pick up his birthday present. There'll be a cab here soon."

With that she flipped the latch on the gate and stepped out to wait on the street. Chela watched Mrs. Holden's back. The woman snapped open her handbag and took out a handkerchief, then put it back, and looked nervously both up and down the street. Why, Chela wondered, would the woman offer such an unnecessary and lengthy explanation of her movements to a hotel maid? Curious now, she sat back down on her chair and waited. Either the young man would come or the older one. She bet anything that Mr. Holden was not sitting in the lounge. Her patience was rewarded. The same car that had been driven by the older man pulled up and the passenger door was impatiently pushed open. The man was leaning across the seat saying something to the woman, who still lingered on the sidewalk. This time Chela saw his face and frowned. She'd seen it before, and not just the last time he'd driven up. Somewhere else.

———

THE PARENTS OF Ada Finch's friend Rafaela, who lived two streets above the Finches, would not allow her to be questioned without their being present, and so Ames and Terrell now sat on kitchen chairs with them, feeling the awkwardness of the questions they would have to ask.

"Did Ada say anything to you at any time about a man she might be seeing or any plans she might have?"

Rafaela, a tall girl with dark hair held back with a ribbon, glanced at her parents and looked down.

"Please answer the sergeant," her father said. He stubbed a cigarette he'd lit only moments before into a glass ashtray and looked expressionlessly at his daughter.

If I were Rafaela, Ames thought, I'd be scared to death right now.

"She ... she was seeing a man. She used to go away with him sometimes at night, and she'd tell her parents she was staying here at my house."

Rafaela's father looked thunderous and leaned across at her. "She bloody what?"

Her mother looked down and then put her hand on her husband's arm. "Language, darling."

"Don't 'language' me! Our daughter has been letting that good-for-nothing Finch girl use us as an excuse for her filthy behaviour." He reached over and grabbed his daughter's wrist, causing her to cry out. "I told you to stop seeing her. She's trash. Who is this 'man' anyway? What grade is he in?"

"Sir," Ames said, using his calmest voice. He watched Rafaela's father let go of her wrist and turn away in disgust, fishing for another cigarette in his shirt pocket. "Rafaela, was this a schoolmate that she was seeing?"

The girl shook her head, looking miserable and massaging her wrist. "It wasn't anyone at school. It was a grown man. She said it was someone from her father's work. She was proud of that. She said she'd slipped one over on her dad." She looked nervously toward her father and leaned almost imperceptibly toward her mother.

"Do you know if she was planning to go anywhere with him this last weekend?" Ames asked.

Glancing again at her father, she said, "She told me they were going to run away, that he was getting a divorce and they would get married. He told her not to worry about anything. He'd pick her up in the car and they'd go away."

"Do you know where he picked her up?" Terrell asked.

She looked up at him and then looked down again. "That's the problem. He never did pick her up. She waited and waited, only he didn't come."

"I WOULDN'T LIKE to be that girl right now," Terrell said as they drove back toward the station. They had stopped to see the second friend. She had expressed concern that Ada hadn't been at school but did not seem to be in her confidence. Still, Rafaela had given them plenty of food for thought.

"So, Ada is under the impression that Watts is going to whisk her off to a happily ever after somewhere. Only he never picks her up. She calls Rafaela, in tears, and then goes home, telling her parents she's had a falling out with Rafaela and is staying home after all. The next day she reads the paper and learns, let's assume, that Watts has been found dead, and she disappears." Terrell eased into the parking spot in front of the station.

"And that raises two additional problems. She wasn't the one with Watts when he died, so why does she run away, and to where?"

CHAPTER THIRTEEN

MARTINEZ RUBBED HIS HAND ACROSS his chin, took a deep breath, and looked at Mrs. Renwick. The lawyer sitting next to her, glowering professionally, had already made him angry by balking at the door of the interview room and saying, "Can't we get an American to interview my client?"

He used the pause to glance at the clock and note the time of the interview. "Mrs. Renwick, you are the wife of the deceased, John Philip Renwick?"

"Yes. He was called Jack."

"And you were down here on a honeymoon?"

"Yes."

"When did you arrive in Tucson?"

Mrs. Renwick glanced at Davis, the lawyer. "Six days ago, on the seventh. But you know that. It's on the hotel registry."

"And Mr. Edward Renwick? When did he arrive?"

"How should I know? Haven't your little detectives squirrelled that out? You're wasting my time. My husband was shot in cold blood. Shouldn't you be trying to find his killer?"

The lawyer put his hand on her arm briefly to calm her but said nothing.

"You're right, Mrs. Renwick. Time is being wasted. Let me get to the point. According to the landlady of the rooming house where Mr. Edward Renwick has been staying since November eighth, a woman answering your description has visited him there no fewer than three times. According to her, and she appears to be very observant, the woman stayed longer than two hours on at least two of the occasions and, further, was with him on November eleventh, the day your husband was shot."

Davis looked at his client with pursed his lips and turned to Martinez. "Detective, I wonder if I might have a moment with my client?"

Martinez glanced at the clock on the wall and made a note of the time, closed his notebook, and stood up. "You can stay right here. I'll give you twenty minutes." He resisted saying, "Because you're going to need it."

Leaving an officer outside the door of the interview room, Martinez went back to his desk and sat down to wait, wondering what they would cook up that could possibly alter the inevitable conclusion the facts in hand appeared to lead to. He guessed it would tend in the direction of her being a victim, either of her cruel husband or her Svengali-like brother-in-law. More the other way around, he surmised. She looked as tough as nails.

"Martinez!" It was Galloway, standing at the door of his office.

"Sir?" Martinez got up and went to Galloway.

His boss jerked his chin in the direction of the interview room. "Good job. Quick work. You should have this one in the bag by end of day." He turned to go back into his office and looked back at Martinez. "And don't lose your notes."

Turning back to his desk, Martinez struggled to grasp how he felt. He was on the right track, he was sure of it, and Galloway, like any boss, wanted cases solved and put away. There was a moment of gratification in receiving Galloway's praise, a rare commodity, followed by irritation at his casual jibe.

Back in the interview room, Davis said, "My client wishes to make a statement."

Martinez nodded and made a note of the time. "Go on."

"Officer, I did visit my brother-in-law three times. So accurate. I will be cautious with landladies from now on. Ned, Edward Renwick, came here to appeal to me to intercede with my husband about the company. Their father's will cut Ned out completely. Ned understood that he would never be the head of the company, but he wanted a role. I saw him because I felt sorry for him. He had a bad war. It was my view that he needed to have a role because it would steady him, help him move past his troubles. I tried to intercede, I talked to my husband, begged him to reconsider, but he was adamant. I tried to organize a meeting, but my husband would have nothing to do with it. He was very angry that Ned had presumed to follow us and do an end run through me when we were on our honeymoon. That's it. That's all I have to say." Ivy Renwick folded her hands over her gloves, which lay on her purse, and looked away.

Martinez made his notes. "Can you tell me exactly where you were at twelve thirty on Tuesday?"

"I had gone shopping at Steinfeld's, that big department store downtown, and I stopped in to see Ned to tell him it was out of the question and Jack wouldn't see him. At twelve thirty, I was probably telling him he should go home, find something else to do. I did offer to give him a little financial help on the QT. Neither one of us was out shooting my husband, before you ask."

"Do you have anyone who can corroborate? For example, what time did you arrive at the rooming house?"

"Can't you ask that irrepressibly nosy landlady you have on tap?" Ivy pushed her hair behind her ear.

"We did. She said you left the rooming house a little before noon, and that you arrived about an hour before that, at eleven. Where did you go?"

"Well, isn't she just the most precious thing!" Ivy said furiously. "Look, I was upset. Jack was being unreasonable to start with, and Ned flew off the handle and said he thought the whole thing was my fault, that I had driven a wedge between the two of them and his life was ruined because of me. I needed air. I went back to walk around and calm down. I walked around for an hour, and then when I felt calmer, I took a cab back to the hotel. That's when I saw ..." Here Ivy put her hand to her mouth and turned away with a little sob.

"THIS IS ABSOLUTELY wonderful!" Lane turned to look at Darling, who was riding behind her. They had joined a small group that had been organized out of a working ranch at the base of the Catalina foothills. The desert trail took them along the north side of the dry bed of the Rillito River, and then steadily upward into the foothills on a narrow bridle path. A slight breeze swept up the smell of sage and something Lane could not identify, a medicinal, almost acrid smell. Darling, she thought, had been right. It was good to get away and do something besides lounge at the inn.

"We'll stop here for lunch," the guide said. There was a semicircle of stones set out facing south with a sweeping view of the city far below and a hitching post for the horses.

"I'm going to have a sore bottom," Lane remarked. "I haven't been on a horse since I was about seventeen, and not on one of these western saddles." She looped the reins around the post and kicked her legs a bit to get out the stiffness. They sat side by side munching ham sandwiches and looking down the sweep of the valley that contained Tucson.

"You were seventeen once?" Darling asked.

"I was. Not very prepossessing, I'm afraid. And shy to boot. You would have preferred my sister. Pretty, lively, full of conversation."

"Not as intelligent as you, though, I bet."

"Much more clever. She had friends and could keep them. I was always a bit of a loner." Lane's younger sister had been their father's chosen child because she was outgoing and confident. He had never, Lane thought, been able to cope with Lane's moodiness, so like his own. The irony of her having worked in intelligence during the war came home to her again. She had been a spy, just like him. She, in truth, had no idea what her sister had done in the war. She'd gone to South Africa just before hostilities broke out. Lane had come to believe she would never see her sister again.

She shook off these thoughts and finished her sandwich. She reached into the paper lunch bag. "A chocolate biscuit! How perfect! The valley and city look so lovely from up here, but poor Ivy is languishing in a jail cell somewhere down there by now, I expect."

"If Martinez has been convinced that she indeed had the opportunity and means to shoot her husband, then I expect she is. Now, look over there. A lizard. You don't see those in King's Cove."

CHELA WAS NOT at all easy in her mind. Most days she enjoyed cleaning the rooms, especially the suites. Sometimes the guests left a tip for her, and she liked seeing the clothing and the toiletries of the wealthy guests. Often she unstoppered bottles of perfume to inhale the scent, though she never took the liberty of dabbing any on. Chanel No. 5 had always been her favourite. But today she could not shake the memory of the man she'd seen in the car with Mrs. Holden. She pushed her cleaning supplies to the next room. That poor lady whose husband had died. She really didn't want to work in that room. So close to death. Still, Pepita had been cleaning it since the man was killed and she was all right. She just wished it hadn't been on her list for the day. She told herself sternly that she could not catch death and knocked firmly on the door.

"Cleaning service!"

There was no answer. Chela took out her key and was surprised to find the door unlocked. "Hello? Cleaning service," she called into the room, but there was no answer from the bedroom or the bathroom. The lady must have rushed out and forgotten to lock it, she thought.

It appeared Mrs. Renwick had left in a hurry. A silk robe was lying on the floor, where it had evidently slipped off the bed; clothes were strewn on the unmade bed. Chela looked into the closet and saw, as if drawn by some dark force, the suitcase that must contain the clothes of the dead man. No men's clothes were hanging up. Reluctantly she realized she would have to hang up all of Mrs. Renwick's dresses and sweaters in that closet before she could make up the bed.

Almost holding her breath, as if to avoid the stench of death, she hung the dresses. Her anxiety robbed her of her usual pleasure of admiring the beautifully structured clothes of the wealthy. She picked up two pairs of shoes and went to put them side by side on the floor of the closet, on the opposite side from the dreaded suitcase. She pushed a pair of black and white pumps into the dark space and tried to fit the red sandals in next to them. Something was on the floor behind the shoes blocking their spot. Irritated, she reached in and with a cry pulled her hand away as if it had touched red-hot metal. She was as sure as she had been of anything in her life that she had touched a gun.

THERE WAS A knock on the interview room door. Martinez, who had been watching Mrs. Renwick write out her statement, stood up and opened the door.

"Phone call. You're gonna want to take it, trust me. I'll stay here. You can get it at my desk." The young officer practically winked at him, a circumstance so unusual that Martinez frowned and made his way to the desk.

He looked up sharply and glanced toward the interview room as he listened to the person on the other end of the line. "Please don't touch it or allow anyone else to touch it. An officer will be along as soon as possible. Well, I can't help that, ma'am, please just do as I say," he said.

Martinez returned to the interview room. The young officer got up and grinned at him. "Pretty good, eh?"

Martinez nodded as slightly as he could and waited until his colleague had left. Mrs. Renwick had finished her statement and now sat with her gloves on, her hands folded in front of her.

"Officer, I'm finished, and I should like to return to my hotel. I presume someone can drive me?"

"I'm afraid that won't be possible, Mrs. Renwick. I'm going to have to ask you to remain here. We will be conducting a search of your room."

Ivy Renwick's face went crimson. "This is outrageous. It's bad enough I've been dragged here for this nonsense, you have absolutely no right to search my property. Does he?" She looked at the lawyer furiously.

Davis, who could see plainly that she did not remember his name, chewed his bottom lip. He found the entitled rich difficult to deal with. They always seemed shocked that anything could be pinned on them and outraged that anyone should try. He looked at Martinez. "You will need a warrant, even though the hotel room is not her home, strictly speaking, if it is your intention to go through her things."

Ivy Renwick turned triumphantly back to Martinez.

"I am aware of that. Getting a warrant will, of course, take a bit of time, but I don't think we should have any trouble getting one."

The lawyer turned to Mrs. Renwick. "It will speed matters up if you give your permission." He left unsaid the question, "Is there any reason you don't want your room searched?"

Reluctantly, Ivy Renwick nodded. "Fine. Make it snappy. I'd like to go back and pack and get the hell out of here. You've kept me here long enough. I have a company to run."

AN HOUR LATER, Martinez returned to the interview room, where he had sent a lunch and a cup of coffee in the interim. The coffee was gone, but the lunch was untouched.

"Mrs. Ivy Renwick, I am arresting you for the murder of your husband John Philip Renwick. We will be placing you in custody . . ."

Ivy did not hear the rest. She only heard the loud thrumming of panic inside her head.

CHAPTER FOURTEEN

"WE WILL HAVE TO GO back to Miss Van Eyck," Ames said. "There are unanswered questions there about her interaction with Watts." He made no move from where he sat, his back to Terrell, looking out at the lowering sky. "And where is Gilly with the post-mortem?" He turned and looked accusingly at the door, which remained steadfastly innocent of Gilly coming with information.

"I could go out and do it," Terrell offered. "I've done up the notes from today. You could get busy with the RCMP on the disappearance of Ada Finch. Miss Van Eyck doesn't know me; she might find it easier to tell me the whole story."

CONSTABLE TERRELL SAT next to Tina on the picnic table by the lake. Tina had suggested they sit there because she did not want her father, hard at work in the garage, to overhear. They would have been warmer in the living room, but Tina felt the need to be outside, blown clean, perhaps, by the light gusts that had picked up. The sky promised another evening of rain or even snow if the temperature dropped enough.

"We usually need to find out as much as we can about a person who has been robbed and died like this. Any insight into his life might provide a clue," Terrell said as soothingly as he could.

"Sergeant Ames too chicken to come?" asked Tina.

"There are several interviews in town that need to be completed," Terrell answered.

"I bet. Well, what do you want?"

"I'm just wondering if you could tell me a bit about your earlier relationship with Mr. Watts. I am not at liberty to say, of course, but your information may add to what we already have."

"I didn't have anything to do with him dying, so I don't see how it matters."

"I know," said Terrell, nodding, not indicating what he knew. He waited.

"Look, it's true. I wasn't completely truthful about why he came. He came here to ask, none too nicely, if I'd ever talked to anyone about what happened back then. He was angry and tried to intimidate me, stomping around like an ss man."

"What did he mean by that? Who might you have told about what?"

Tina looked down. "You'll have to know the whole thing, I suppose." She paused and broke a scrap of wood off the table and threw it onto the ground. "I met him when I was sixteen. I was a bit bowled over, I suppose. I'm embarrassed about it now. He was older, good looking, had a car. What kind of a moron does that make me?"

"It makes you a normal sixteen-year-old girl who had no defence against a man like that."

"He asked me out, and I knew it wasn't a good idea. I knew it. I was scared even when I was sneaking out of the house to meet him on the top of the road. But ... I don't know. Why do we do stupid things when we are young?"

"Because we are young. You can't judge yourself against what you'd do now," said Terrell. "Did something happen on that night? Or some other time?"

"I never saw him again after that," Tina said, skirting the question. "Not till he turned up the other day. It knocked ten year's growth off me seeing him. Still acting like he owned the place. Then he had the nerve to say he'd missed me and how pretty I still was, that we should go out sometime. It was all I could do not to slug him with the spanner I was holding. I guess I shouldn't say that. Won't help my case, I expect."

"So something did happen that night you went out?" Terrell prompted.

"He ... he said he was going to show me a good time. I thought that meant we'd go to a bar or out dancing somewhere or something, but he was driving away from town. You can imagine the rest, I suppose. I don't have to spell it out."

"I'm sorry, this is a difficult question, but did he assault you?"

Tina turned away convulsively, got up from the table, and stood looking at the lake. Small whitecaps were just beginning to appear. Like trouble brewing, she thought. It shocked her to hear the word, because she had never said it to herself. She had spent the war fending off advances from drunken servicemen. "Tough Tina" she'd been called. She'd been proud of that reputation. But it hadn't stopped her from falling for a charming Welsh infantryman who turned out to be married.

She turned and looked at Constable Terrell, who was sitting watching her with his head tilted. He looks kind, she thought, but he's a man. He'd be judging her.

"Look, Constable, I'm not proud of myself. I tried to stop it, but he was so strong … I never should have gone off with him. Here's the thing that's really embarrassing: I already knew he had a reputation. I thought I would be different, that he really liked me. I can't have this come out. If my dad ever found out what really happened, he'd have me out on my behind."

"You don't know that. He seems like a very understanding man."

He was right. Her father being an understanding man only made it worse. It would be better to be thrown out. It would only be what she deserved. He would be understanding and angry on her behalf—and wonder why she'd never told him. It would be unbearable. Especially after her idiocy during the war with the married infantryman, she didn't deserve anyone's sympathy, especially not his.

She looked at him and shook her head. "Is there anything else, Constable? You know everything now. I presume neither you nor Sergeant Ames will be bothering us again?"

Almost as an afterthought she looked at the ground and added, "I suppose he'll have to know."

"I'm afraid so, yes. Just one last thing: Did you go to the police at the time?"

Tina stood silently for so long that Constable Terrell had to prompt her. "Miss Van Eyck?"

She turned away to look north at the long stretch of dark, unsettled water. "That's what I don't understand. I did go one afternoon on my own because one of my friends told me it didn't matter that I had put myself in that position, that what Watts did was still wrong. She drove me there. I talked to a guy at the station. He took some notes and said he'd look into it and I should come back the next day. When I went back, he was angry. He asked me why I was lying, trying to get a respectable man in trouble. He called me . . ." Tina turned to look at Terrell and then looked away again. "He called me a little tart who got what I asked for."

Constable Terrell clamped his mouth into a grim line and made a note in his book. He kept his voice as dispassionate as he could. "Do you recall the name of the officer you spoke with?"

"I barely remembered my own name after that. He told me I could get in trouble with the law and that my parents would be dragged through court."

Tina got up and pulled her thick shirt around her body and glanced at Terrell. "That was the end of who I used to be. That day. Not the day it happened. I was terrified by what he said. I decided that I would be tough, that no man would ever tell me what to do except maybe my own father. And I can tell you, when the chance came to leave and work in the old country during the war, I could not have been happier. I thought it was over and I'd got past it, till that bastard walked in the other day throwing his weight around. I don't understand why he came around thinking I'd said something to someone after all this time. I'm glad he's dead. You find that shocking." Tina glanced up at Terrell's face, but could read nothing on it. "This had better be the end of it." She was embarrassed by how peevish that sounded. A man had died, after all.

Terrell shook his head, frowning at the words he'd written. He could see now that it might not be. "I'm sorry, just one thing more. Do you, by any chance, remember the date of your visit to the police station?"

"So you can dredge it up for all to see?" Tina said furiously. "No, thank heavens, I don't. All I can say is that it was June of the year I graduated, 1935."

Terrell made a final note in his book, closed it quietly, and pushed it into his raincoat pocket. "I'm very much obliged to you, Miss Van Eyck. I can't promise you won't get any more visits. It depends on the how the investigation goes. But I will say this: I'm sorry it went so badly when you reported it. That wasn't right. It should never have happened." It shouldn't happen, he thought, but it did. All the time.

Just as they reached the car, he stopped. "Miss Van Eyck, I'm sorry to ask this, and you'll be within your rights not to tell me. Was there any outcome from that meeting when you were sixteen? Pregnancy, that sort of thing?"

Tina reddened. "No, thank God."

AMES HAD LURCHED out of his chair and now stood looking out the window. Rain was coming down again. He could see the little rivulets running along the street below. He imagined them gathering force, turning into a river. Terrell had been reading from his notes about his conversation with Tina Van Eyck.

Ames swore under his breath. "Who the hell would have told a young girl she got what she asked for?"

"It was back in June of '35. How much turnover has there been here since then?"

"God knows. I don't know if Darling was even here then. He might know. I bet he never even started a file, whoever it was. And Tina's right. Why, suddenly, after a decade, did he reappear to ask her if she'd told anyone? Well, Tina's story supports what we've learned about Watts so far," he said finally. "But it still doesn't follow that one of the apparently many young girls he probably violated suddenly up and robbed him as he lay dying. It seems Ada Finch wasn't with him, so we're back to the hitchhiker theory. When did you say those ads in the paper and the radio about hitchhikers would run?"

"They will be in tomorrow's paper, and I think the radio will start this evening."

Ames was about to make another comment when there was a knock on the door. They turned and saw Gilly with a paper in his hand.

"Sorry this took so long. It took some time to complete the tests. I thought you two might be interested in this. Your robbery victim didn't die of a heart attack exactly, though he did have a weak heart as it turns out, and his heart stopped. He died of suffocation, brought on by ingesting a combination of chloroform and very likely strychnine." Gilly, usually staid and understated, said this with something bordering on a triumphant flourish.

"Poison?" Terrell and Ames asked at once.

"Yes indeed. And organ failure. His heart for sure, his kidneys perhaps. As to his heart, the failure came on very suddenly. His inability to breathe is interesting in that context as well. It looks as though his whole system gave up."

"Are you saying ... what are you saying, exactly?" asked Ames.

"I tested his blood for some sort of poison but it's difficult with the tests we have now. It was a sweet bleachy smell that put me on to what possibly happened. Chloroform and strychnine together could produce these symptoms. Chloroform by itself can be dangerous. It's notoriously unreliable, even in competent medical hands. More people than you'd want to think about die on the operating table. A civilian flinging it around could do untold damage. So let's have the murderer use chloroform to subdue him, thus living up to every cliché in the book, by the way, and strychnine soaked in a rag so he would be breathing it in. It could have been followed up with some administered by mouth, though I couldn't swear to it. If it was just the strychnine, he could have inhaled a large enough dose that he would have been dead inside of a couple of hours. But I'm going to say that it was much quicker than that because of his heart stopping. Forensic science is moving along at a good clip. In a couple of years maybe someone will come up with a way to definitively screen the blood, but there's nothing now. However, following on my inhalation theory, I looked for residue of strychnine on his moustache and so on."

"And?" If Watts was poisoned, it would drastically alter the whole complexion of the case.

"A bit on the right side of his mouth in his moustache."

Terrell frowned thoughtfully. "So, someone subdues him with chloroform, then makes him breathe in strychnine?"

"That's about the size of it. Strychnine by itself is not a swift death, and is pretty unpleasant. My guess is if we add a solid dose of chloroform to that hanky, the assailant could have subdued him and then he'd be passively breathing in the strychnine. Pretty elaborate because the chloroform alone probably did it for him with his heart stopping. The killer wouldn't have known that, of course, so he or she, let's be generous here, would want insurance, and wouldn't want his victim thrashing around. I'd say the attack came from behind, by someone who is right-handed. The problem is, a man driving a car, attacked from behind, will have put up a fight no matter how strong the assailant is. I think it's significant that it would have been done by someone behind him. He could have been caught by surprise, gasped, which involves a good strong breath, and speeded up the action of the sedative and the poison."

Ames furrowed his brow. "That might account for that strange smell in the car. I can see the strychnine because it's basically rat poison. Lots of people have it around the house. But how would someone get hold of chloroform? Isn't it for medical use?"

"Things do go missing from hospitals all the time. But, failing that," Gilly added with a slightly ghoulish air, "just mix some household chlorine bleach with rubbing alcohol. It's volatile and dangerous, but it can be done."

———

LANE WAS LYING on the bed, reading and waiting for her turn to have a bath to soothe the stiffness from their day on horseback, when the phone rang. Puzzled—and worried because Lord Peter was even now climbing into the bell tower, a manoeuvre she already knew would do him no good—she put her book down, pulled her robe around her, and went to answer it.

"Lane Winslow speaking."

There was a hesitation at the other end of the line and then a worried voice. "I was hoping to reach a Mrs. Darling. Is she at this number?"

"Oh, yes, of course. I am Mrs. Darling. I don't usually use my married name. Who is calling?"

"My name is Martha Yelland. I'm the head nurse at the St. Mary's Hospital. I'm calling on behalf of one of our patients." Martha lowered her voice. "Mrs. Paul Galloway was brought in very late last night. She's in quite a bad state. She didn't want me to call unless things became really bad, but while she's not on death's door, I feel like someone should know."

"My God! But what about her husband?"

"He brought her in," she said, her voice sounding very compressed.

"Yes, so he must be there with her," Lane tried to understand what was underlying the nurse's strange communication.

"Ma'am, I'm calling because I think she needs a friend right now, and you're the only contact I have. She's in very bad shape, but she managed to tell me you're the only person she can trust. She asked me to call you. I'd best be getting along. It's a busy ward."

Lane hung up the receiver. Why was she the only person Priscilla could trust? She began to throw her clothes on, calling out to the bathroom door, "Darling, something has happened to Priscilla. She's in hospital. I'm going to just pop down and make sure she's all right. You won't mind?"

"Of course I'll mind. Was that Galloway? Why do you need to be hauled out in the middle of the night?" The splashy sound of an irritated man quitting his bath came through the door.

Lane opened the bathroom door just enough to put her head through. "It's not the middle of the night. No, it was a nursing sister from the hospital. Don't get out, darling. It's just the nurse was behaving rather peculiarly. I think she was trying to say something without saying something, if you know what I mean."

"I haven't the first notion what you mean," Darling said, subsiding. "I should come with you."

"No," Lane said hesitantly. "I think this might be something I have to do. I get the feeling Priscilla might barely want me, but certainly not you. It all seems a little cloak and dagger, and Galloway isn't with her. I think—but no, I won't say until I've seen her. The front desk will get me a cab. Don't worry about a thing."

Darling, who felt fully unconvinced about not worrying, grunted and then issued directions for her to hurry home.

LANE WAS DROPPED off in front of an imposing set of buildings far west of the town.

"Not the round one, ma'am. That's for the tuberculosis patients. Do you want me to wait for you? Visiting hours are over; they'll probably kick you out."

"Oh, yes. Please. Do you mind?" Lane said gratefully.

A nurse at reception looked primly at the clock on the wall. "You've left it quite late. There won't be time for a long visit."

"I know. I'm terribly sorry. The person attending my friend called me and asked me to come right away. Sister Yelland I think her name is."

The receptionist smiled suddenly. "I nursed in England during the war. We say *nurse* here, not *sister*. If she called you, it must be important. Up the stairs on the left to the second floor to our critical ward. We'll look the other way if you need a bit more time."

Lane pushed through a set of swinging doors, feeling the claustrophobia the smell of hospitals evoked in her.

"Nurse Yelland?"

A tall, angular woman, made taller and more severe-looking by her starched cap and tightly pinned hair, looked up when Lane introduced herself. "You've come. Thank you. She might still be awake. She's been going in and out of sleep. Morphine does that." Yelland got up and indicated that Lane should follow.

"But what happened to her?" Lane asked. "Was it a car accident?"

Yelland turned to face her and said stiffly, "It wasn't a car, and it wasn't an accident."

"But what, then?"

"I cannot say. Mrs. Galloway refused to say. When Mr. Galloway came in, he said she'd had a bad fall. Slipped on a rug at the top of the stairs. That is what we have on our records." She turned to continue down the hall and then stopped. "She needs rest and quiet. Please don't be too long. I just want her to know she has a friend."

Lane was ushered into a room where the dominant colours were pale beige and green. It was disheartening in its starkness. She stifled a gasp of dismay. Priscilla lay on her back with her eyes closed and her arms outside the covers. Her face was swollen and bruised, her left eye inflamed and puffed shut. Her arms were black and blue, and there was a bandage on her right arm.

Lane pulled up a chair as quietly as she could and gently took her right hand. "Priscilla? It's Lane Winslow."

Priscilla opened her one undamaged eye and turned her head slightly, with a groan. "They've doped me up. Why are you here? I told them not to call you unless it was an emergency."

"Dearest Priscilla, if this is not an emergency, I don't know what is. What happened?"

Closing her eyes, Priscilla was silent for a moment. "I've lost the baby, I know it. I can feel it gone. They haven't told me, but I know."

Lane felt herself blanche. "I'm so sorry. I didn't know

you were pregnant." Lane paused. "Nurse Yelland said you fell down the stairs."

Priscilla attempted a smile. "Yes. My own mother used to 'fall down stairs.' Isn't it ironic? It's hereditary, it seems."

"Paul did this."

"Apparently he didn't like me being pregnant. He didn't marry me so I could ruin myself with brats."

Lane sat holding Priscilla's hand, her mind in turmoil. There must be laws against this sort of thing, she thought desperately. After all, she had contact with a law firm now; maybe Priscilla could get lawyer.

"You just have to think about getting better, now," she said. "Do you have someone you can stay with?"

Priscilla attempted a sarcastic laugh and groaned instead. "Paul is the assistant chief of police. Where would I be safe?" She attempted to adjust her body and then gave it up, grimacing at the pain. "The drugs seem to just make me dozy without actually dealing with the sore bits."

"Shall I get the nurse?" Lane asked.

"Don't bother." She closed her eyes, and Lane wondered if she'd drifted off to sleep, but then her eye opened again. "He's always terribly sorry." Priscilla's voice began to drag with the effect of the drugs.

Lane pressed Priscilla's hand, wanting to stroke her bruised forehead. "Get some rest now. I'll come tomorrow."

Priscilla managed to turn her head slightly to look at her. "I dream sometimes of stealing that beastly car and driving to Phoenix and catching a plane. But ... assistant chief of police ..."

"Ma'am," Nurse Yelland put her head in the door.

"Yes, of course," Lane said. Outside she said to the nurse, "I'll come back tomorrow. Is there anything I should bring?"

"Some hope? She'll be here for a week, easy. No doubt we'll patch her up and send her home."

Lane started toward the stairs and then stopped. "Has she been here before?"

Yelland shook her head. "Nope. But I bet she should have. There are some older bruises on her." She approached Lane with contained fury. "He kicked her until she lost that baby. If you can do anything to get her out of there ... and before you ask, I know who her husband is. A so-called rising star in the force. An anti-corruption crusader. Doesn't that beat all? I'm sorry. I shouldn't be sharing this, but it makes me absolutely livid to see this sort of thing."

DARLING AND LANE sat in bed holding hands. "Why doesn't she leave?" Lane asked. "I don't understand it."

"Perhaps he controls the money. I think the fact you are the only person she could call suggests he controls who she sees. She must have no friends she can trust. And I expect she's afraid. I wonder if that law firm you contacted would be useful here?"

"That's exactly what I thought," Lane said.

He turned to her. "I'm sorry, Lane. He's an absolute bastard. How did I never see that? I'm going to have to re-think everything I know about him."

"I suppose men don't talk about that sort of thing with each other. And he wasn't married when you knew him."

"No. He wasn't. Now I think of it, he was a bit of a 'lad,' I suppose. Somewhat loose talk about the ladies, that sort of thing. I suspect I wasn't comfortable with it, but it's what a lot of men did ... do. I don't think I ever imagined he would be capable of something like this."

"I have to do something," Lane said.

Darling turned to look at her. God almighty, he thought, what now? But he turned out the light and pulled her close.

She lay awake long into the moonless night. Finally dozing, she woke with a start just past three, wondered at her wakefulness, and then remembered Priscilla. She lay staring into the dark, her innards in turmoil. Finally she rose, put on her cardigan and then her robe, and quietly opened the door to step outside.

Shivering at the cold, she closed the door quietly behind her and went into the empty garden. She marvelled at the darkness and the riot of stars above her. The canopy of the sky seemed close enough to touch. They whirled above her in a way that made her think of van Gogh. She went to the pool area and lay on a deck chair so she could look upward, already feeling the cold would not allow her to stay out long in little more than a silk nightdress.

It gives perspective, she thought. We are nothing in the face of this vastness, with our little problems and tiny short lives. But Priscilla's problems were not little, and she had none of the advantage of perspective Lane had—only the claustrophobia of pain and closed doors. The idea came to her as she was getting up to hurry back to the room, driven by the cold. She would talk to Chela first thing in the morning.

THE NIGHT SHIFT officers were beginning to stretch tiredly and stack things on their desks when Martinez came in.

"Morning," he said to Bevan, a young officer who had more than once wondered to Martinez why he had graduated at the top of his class to spend his nights flipping a pencil at his desk, waiting for the phone to ring.

"Sergeant. Pretty quiet last night," Bevan said, "and no visits from the assistant chief, unlike a couple of nights ago."

"Good. You got to relax and catch up, then," Martinez said, moving to his desk and then stopping. "What do you mean about the assistant chief?"

"He was here the night before last. Came in late in a pretty bad temper. Closed himself up in his office. I heard him on the phone. I mean, I heard him raise his voice, but I didn't hear what he was saying."

"What time was this?"

"One, one-thirty? Stayed for about an hour and left again. I'm used to it now. He was here maybe two weeks ago storming around as well. Doesn't talk to me. I'm nobody."

Martinez watched Bevan go back to his desk. He's here practically on his own on the night shift. He shook his head as if to clear it. But the thought persisted. Had another cop taken his notes? Had Bevan? He'd gone over every possible thing he could have done with his notes, and he knew he would not have been careless. The inevitable conclusion meant someone else must have made them disappear. Had Griffin gotten to someone at the station? He'd open up a can of mental worms with this kind of thinking. He'd be suspecting everyone now.

And why was the boss hanging around the station so late? Was it the Griffin case? He had said in no uncertain terms that he wanted a conviction. It was the one thing Martinez had seen Galloway really angry about. But who would he be on the phone with at that time of night? Maybe something at home. He'd seen Galloway with his wife at the Christmas parties. A beautiful woman. Galloway had joked more than once that she was a handful, whatever that was supposed to mean. He couldn't imagine making remarks about his own wife at the police station. Martinez understood that the best policy for someone with his background was to be as correct as possible at all times.

Martinez put Galloway out of his mind and used the momentary solitude in the main office to make one last search for his notes. He would have to begin recreating them and get something very solid on where Griffin was putting his money. He'd better let Galloway know what he suspected, though he knew it wouldn't go over well. With a sinking heart he realized he would also have to interview the Renwick woman about the gun and try again to find out why Edward Renwick had been hanging around town four days before he claimed to have come. He had been promised a ballistics report that morning on the bullets they'd recovered from the victim. That should speed things up.

CHAPTER FIFTEEN

IT WAS DESPERATE, LANE KNEW. And it could cause an irreparable break between herself and Darling. She had walked to the edge of the hotel property before he awoke and stood shivering in the morning cold, watching the golden edge of light on the Catalina Mountains. She had slept little and had felt the confinement of being in a hotel, however luxurious—and even, for a moment, the confinement of being with someone else. On her own, sleepless nights had been a fairly frequent occurrence, especially since the war had ended, and had ranged from long spells of vague anxiety to panic and attacks of violent shivering. She had struggled to try to understand the source of these attacks. Lord knew her intelligence work provided enough fodder for any amount of shell shock. She'd seen men incapacitated by it when she was a child. She never could have imagined she'd be coping with something similar.

She sometimes felt she understood the root of her trauma. It must have originated with the murder of three people in a safe house by Bretagne nationalists in the spring of 1943. Lane's assignment had been to liaise with members of the French underground at a safe house and deliver a coded message. The whole thing had been catastrophic. She'd arrived just after the people inside the farmhouse had been shot, and she had seen the shooters race away on a motorcycle. She'd been unable to protect a fourth person who'd been hiding when his mates were assassinated. But she always stopped short of reliving the whole thing, overwhelmed by the powerlessness and regret of never being able to go back and change what had happened. On her own, at home, she could turn on the light, read, warm up milk, go sit in front of the fire. At least there she could creep out to the sitting room or kitchen and not disturb Darling, though that had not been necessary in the brief weeks they'd been married. His presence did provide a comfort she had not fully expected, but she did not fool herself that her attacks of panic would be gone forever because she was certain that her own sense of guilt would never be gone.

Her relief at seeing the grey light of morning under the edge of the curtain had been profound, and she'd gotten up, dressed quickly, and taken herself outside. She wanted more than anything, she thought, to tell as few lies as possible. Indeed, she had never lied to Darling. It terrified her to think of doing it now. It opened a great black chasm in her mind from which she feared there might be no escape. But what was the alternative? If she told Darling what she was planning, it would create a further rift between himself and Galloway. He would be forced, perhaps, to lie to someone else because of what she had done. She could not possibly put him into that position.

The sun breasted the row of mountains, sending light spilling across the desert, suddenly shaping the peaks with gold and shadow. Praying that he would understand, that he would in the end agree there was no other solution, she turned away from the direct light of the sun. Whatever the outcome, she could not turn her back on Priscilla. The fallout with Darling would have to come later.

———

THERE WAS HOPEFUL news on two fronts the next morning at the Nelson police station. The first was word that Ada Finch had been located. Ada's cousin in Lardeau had hidden her in a barn overnight and then got too frightened to keep up the secret and confessed to her mother, Ada's aunt. She would be back in Nelson by the afternoon. They could interview her and her father, now that it had become a murder investigation, as soon as he had got her home.

"The girl showed some enterprise. She apparently sneaked onto the steamboat and got a lift to Lardeau by water. Her father is driving over to pick her up. He's pretty mad," Terrell said, after taking the call.

In addition, Terrell's advertisements had prompted three calls to the police station. One was from a farmer down the south arm of the lake; he'd picked up a boy who had missed the school bus and brought him into town. Another call was from a man travelling between Kaslo and Nelson who'd seen a man on the road—he couldn't quite remember where—but hadn't stopped to pick him up. A description of the man was requested and given. A third call was from another driver who had seen the same man and had picked him up, about five miles out of town, and deposited him at the local Rexall drug store.

Armed with the description, and restive over the personal turmoil the case was causing him, Ames took up his coat and announced that he was going to track down the second hitchhiker.

"I'll come with you, sir," said Terrell.

The sky had become heavy, and there was a smell of snow in the air as they crossed Baker Street toward the drugstore. The bell on the door rang as they went into the narrow, crowded space. A plump middle-aged woman turned to stare, mainly at Terrell, and then inched away toward the newspaper stand. The pharmacist was on a stepladder fetching something from a high shelf; he came down, putting a small box on the counter.

"Gentlemen. I'll just finish up here and be right with you."

Hoping that no one else would come in, Ames and Terrell waited while the transaction was finished.

"Now then, what can I do for you, Sergeant? Don't usually see you fellows in my pharmacy."

"We're looking for a man who was dropped off here three days ago. He'd caught a ride into town." Ames gave the description and the pharmacist nodded.

"I saw the ad in the newspaper looking for information. That was Wilf Gunderson. I happen to know because he told me he'd missed Stewy's bus and had to walk quite a ways before anyone stopped. He's not in any trouble, is he?"

"Is he a regular customer?"

"Yes, he gets his heart pills here. He's not that old, but he's had a dicky heart since he was a boy."

Terrell looked up from his notes. "Can you tell us where he lives, sir?"

"He lives in a little homestead just this side of Balfour, before you get to that gas station. Lives there on his own since his wife died. Nicest guy you'd care to meet."

"Thanks very much." Ames and Terrell both tipped their hats and went out to stand on the street.

"I'm not too hopeful he's our man," Ames said, "but we'd better head out there. The nicest people you care to meet don't usually go around murdering and robbing people. But he was on the road at the crucial time, so he might have seen something useful. I know we should really be stopping first to tell Mrs. Watts that this has become a murder investigation. I dread it, if I'm honest. And who knows? We might get something from Gunderson that will allow us to tell her we have someone in our sights. We'll stop there on the way back. If we're lucky, we can get back before it snows."

They'd crossed to the north side and had been driving for twenty minutes when they felt a dip in the temperature, Terrell turned up the heat. "Do we have enough information to even find the place?" he asked.

"We'll ask at the store. Mr. Bales is bound to know."

"Are you worried about Miss Van Eyck, sir?"

Ames felt completely transparent. "All those women, Terrell. If the hitchhiker angle doesn't pay off ... now that it's become a murder, I find it hard to imagine that Watts's penchant for young girls wasn't part of this. It seems there are some who have plenty to be angry about. There might be more out there who suffered the . . . treatment Miss Van Eyck did." He could not bring himself to say so violent a word.

"The question is, why now? If he's been happily married for a decade, why would he be suddenly worried that Miss Van Eyck talked, and why would he end up murdered?"

Ames thought about Tina, suddenly confronted after more than a decade by the man who had raped her, and then he shook off the thought. "We know Finch was not at work that afternoon. And we don't really know if Watts has been happily married for a decade. We've only got his wife's word for that. She might be trying to preserve his reputation. Or her own. She knew about the other girls at the beginning, but when she got pregnant, she told us he stayed with her. But who knows? He certainly disappeared from time to time," he said.

"According to Gilly, someone must have been with him in the car, hiding in the back seat. Or did someone follow him and get into the back seat to, I don't know, talk about something? Maybe someone who was blackmailing him about the rape?"

"And that's the other thing. Where was he going? You're suggesting he might have been going to meet a blackmailer, pay him—or her for that matter—off? According to his wife, he drops their little girl off at the school down the hill and he goes to work. Where was he going that day, and why didn't he pick up Ada? It suggests he was murdered before he could get to her. He was certainly driving in the wrong direction to pick her up." Terrell looked up at the sky with a frown. "I really hope this holds off."

GUNDERSON PROVED TO be a genial man in late middle age. He was outside chopping firewood when they pulled up in front of the cabin after a bumpy ride up the hill. He approached the car with a wave and a surprised smile and invited them into his cabin. They sat at a small wooden table.

"I sure don't get much traffic up here," he said again. He seemed very pleased. "Especially the police!" He chuckled.

Ames explained their mission. "We're following up on leads with regards to a recent death near the Harrop ferry. Were you hitchhiking into town on Tuesday morning some time?"

The man laughed. He looked a bit like a young Santa Claus, Ames thought. Bushy hair, bushy beard, twinkling eyes.

"Walking to town, more like. You know Stewy drives that little bus a couple of times a week, and I missed the darn thing. I finally got a ride a ways out of town, six miles or so. I don't remember seeing nothing at the Harrop turnoff. Someone in a hurry to catch the ferry. That's about it. I picked up my pills at the drugstore and then got a lift at the Nelson ferry from someone driving to Argenta. It's too bad that damned steamboat that goes up and down the lake stops all the way up at King's Cove. I coulda taken that, but it would have meant a long walk back."

"What time would you say you passed the ferry turnoff?" Terrell asked.

Gunderson shook his head. "I don't wear a watch. Just got this thing here," he pointed at a rosewood clock that sat in solitary splendour on the mantel of the stone fireplace. "Got it from my grandfather back in Norway. It's how I know when to get down to the bottom of the road to catch the bus. I'd been walking a good while by then. I left here at seven or so."

"Can you remember anything about the car that was in a hurry to catch the ferry?" Terrell looked up from his notes.

"Dark blue maybe? No! I lie. Dark green. Not one of your fancy new cars. A bit older than that thing you fellows pulled up in." He nodded toward the window.

"How many people in the car?" asked Terrell.

"One person. The driver." He paused and frowned. "Well, I thought it was one, but remembering it now, I have this impression of two."

"So it's possible there were two?" Ames followed up.

"Gosh. I wish I could be sure. I was tired from walking. I was probably seeing things that weren't there. Sorry."

WITH AMES WINCING about the undercarriage, Terrell picked his way slowly back down the rutted and little-used road.

"He seems a fairly buoyant kind of person for a widower," Ames remarked, exhaling as they finally reached the turnoff to the main road. "Though I wonder at him chopping wood with a bad heart."

"He did have a sort of shrine to his wife, did you notice it? Near his bed on a little table. Photo and a little flowerpot with some leaves and dried grasses. What I've seen is that some people just have a more positive disposition. Take what life sends them. My gran is like that. When you look at her life, she seems to have lost so much: her husband when she was in her forties, a child to an accident when he was eight, and all the people that die as you get older. All kinds of health problems and she's pretty much house-bound, but she's always got a smile or a cheerful word. She says everything is in the hands of God, and it's a dis-appointment to Him to be downhearted."

"I'm a bit downhearted about where we're going with this murder," Ames admitted. He was going to add, "Sorry, God," but worried that if Terrell was of a religious persua-sion, he might take offence.

"It's true, we haven't had much on the hitchhiking front, except Gunderson does seem to have seen the car and said it appeared to be in a hurry. I'm interested more than ever in who would like to see Watts dead," Ames said.

"Didn't Miss Van Eyck tell you she thought there were plenty who would be pleased by the news? I mean, that list seemed to include anyone associated with a young girl he might have interfered with."

"Yes, I'm pretty certain Craig Finch would be delighted."

Terrell glanced at Ames. "And of course … "

Ames nodded. "The wife, though she seemed genuinely distraught. But by her own admission she hasn't been very happy for a while. The last time I talked to her, she pre-tended to accept that there wasn't much love between them, but that he loved his little girl and that was enough. But she got furious about the suggestion he was running off with someone. I don't think she's as accepting as she pretends to be. I want to ask her about this possible blackmailing angle. Let's see how she takes the news that this is a murder investigation."

———

GALLOWAY STOOD AT his door and bellowed, "Martinez!"

Martinez looked up and rose slowly. He'd seen Galloway barrel in and could see he was in a blacker mood than usual. "Sir," he said.

"Any progress on that murder at the Santa Cruz Inn?"

"We have the wife and the brother-in-law in custody, but the one weapon we've recovered from the hotel closet was not the weapon we're looking for. It was registered to the dead man and hadn't been used. Brand new. Though I think it is relevant, we could be asking ourselves why he brought a gun on his honeymoon."

"Have you tried asking his wife?"

"That's for today, sir. The weapon we are looking for is, based on the bullets recovered, possibly an automatic."

"Get it sewn up." Galloway turned back into his office.

"Sir," said Martinez to his back. He watched the door close and contemplated presenting an angry Galloway with the news he suspected Griffin had a plant in the station. There was nothing for it. He couldn't keep it to himself. They'd all need to be on guard from now on.

"What?" Galloway shouted at Martinez's knock.

Martinez pushed open the door and stood almost at attention in the doorway. "Sir, I think there's something I should talk to you about."

"Well, get in here and talk. I don't have all day. And shut the bloody door."

Wondering why Galloway was so perpetually in a temper, Martinez began. "It's about my notes, sir. I've looked everywhere, and I am convinced I have not mislaid them. The fact is that without those notes, Griffin will get away with all the things we know he's doing. I'm wondering, sir, if there is someone here, on the inside, who has taken them, someone in the pocket of Griffin himself." There. He'd said it.

Galloway leaned forward, his hands clasped in front of him the desk. "That's a serious accusation, Martinez. And pretty convenient for you. Do you have someone in mind?"

"No, sir. But if there is someone on the take, it would mean serious consequences for the department. We already know Griffin has moved money through his restaurant and out through other businesses. If we don't get a conviction, it means a criminal is effectively in charge of this town."

Galloway stood up with a swiftness that unnerved Martinez. He put his hands in his pockets and turned away, looking out the window. He swung around, marched to the door, and looked through his window at the floor of the station. "You're telling me you think someone out there is a quisling."

"It's the only explanation, sir."

"And I suppose you have someone in mind?"

Martinez hesitated. If he said someone's name, he would be breaking the biggest rule of policing: don't betray your fellow cops. But he was a sergeant now. And if there was someone on the take, he couldn't keep his suspicions from his boss. He owed that much to Galloway. "I wonder about someone on the night shift, sir. There would be opportunity to go through desks and files."

Galloway looked out his window onto the shop floor. "Bevan? Cooper? Is that what you're thinking?"

"I know nothing against either of them, sir. But I am certain now it is the only explanation for the disappearance of my notes."

"You mean, besides your incompetence? Well, we'd better keep an eye on them, hadn't we?"

"I TOLD YOU already. I had no idea my husband had bought a gun. He had taken over his father's company. Perhaps he thought he needed protection." Ivy Renwick was exhausted because she had not slept well, and her pale skin showed the deep shadows under her eyes. "How long are you intending to keep me here?"

"You will be arraigned this morning, ma'am. As will Edward Renwick."

She turned to her lawyer. "They have nothing on me. I didn't even know about that gun. I want you to get me out of here. I have enough for whatever bail they demand."

Davis, who had little enthusiasm for the project of defending any Renwick, asked, "And Edward Renwick?"

Ivy flinched and looked irritated. "I have nothing to do with him. He can rot here for all I care."

Martinez made a mental note of this exchange. A new idea had presented itself. He was quite certain that Ivy Renwick and her brother-in-law had been lovers, but her absolute dismissal of him since they had been arrested made him wonder if she, in fact, was innocent, and suspected Edward of having shot her husband. Perhaps a dead husband was not useful to her. It certainly could be to the brother-in-law if the board of their company was inclined to push for a man to be in charge of the company rather than the dead man's wife. His brief acquaintance with the two of them suggested Ivy was far more competent than her hard-drinking brother-in-law, but in his experience, men generally didn't want to put women in charge of things.

GALLOWAY SAT DOWN and leaned back in his chair. The overhead fan turned lazily above him, moving the warm air in an unsatisfactory manner. Muttering an oath, he reached for his cigarettes and lit up. He watched the smoke whirling slowly, giving shape to the movement of air. His dissatisfaction at the moment was not centred on Martinez and the Griffin problem. It was with his wife. He hadn't been wrong, he knew that much. He'd been very clear with her about babies. He couldn't bear the thought of a squalling baby. He'd given her everything she could want, and why not? He loved her. So why had she done it? She knew he didn't want her figure ruined. He'd have to go back to the hospital and make it all okay. Say he was sorry and, of course, forgive her. The nurse had told him she'd lost the baby. She'd be upset about that. He'd have to make that right. He would take her on a nice vacation. She'd like that. She could buy a new wardrobe for it.

He stubbed out his cigarette and looked at his watch. He'd go to the hospital later in the evening. Or tomorrow. Give her a little more time. He didn't look forward to it. He hated hospitals. In the meantime, he had much bigger problems. With this murder at the Santa Cruz Inn and Martinez stumbling about, he'd begun to suspect the whole business of Griffin might be harder to deal with than he thought.

———

Chicago, 1928

MEGAN O'SHAY STOOD in front of the long mirror in the rooming house where she lived with her parents and her three brothers. She was wearing a long silk slip, and her hair had been wrapped in a protective net. Her mother was holding the white satin wedding dress, ready to slide it over Meg's head.

"Arms up," she commanded. "It will be good to get out of this lousy place. You're lucky, you know that? I hope you appreciate it."

"Sure, Ma. I do. Ow! There's still a pin in it. I appreciate you set me up to marry Art so you could get out of this dump."

"Don't talk to your mother like that. You're sixteen. You do what you're told. He's handsome, he's going to be rich. He's better than that trash you've been seeing."

Meg conceded silently. Art was better than Ricky, the

boy from school who had actually cried when she'd told him she was breaking up with him and quitting school to get married. Art was confident, well dressed, smart. He loved her. Her mother had told her she would learn in time to forget Ricky and love Art. Maybe. She had worked her whole life to create a hard shell around her heart. She had actually imagined the shell, like a beautiful oyster shell with iridescent colours. She imagined opening it quickly and putting Ricky inside, hidden forever, because the one thing she knew about Ricky was he really loved her. She drew herself as tall as she could and looked in the mirror.

"Get this thing off," her mother said, pointing at the hair net. "Let's see what you look like with everything."

Meg reached up and pulled off the hair net. Her hair was marcelled perfectly, the golden waves framing her pretty round face. Art is the lucky one, she thought. Her mother pulled the veil off the bed and placed it over her daughter's head.

"You look like Mary Pickford. A real star." She suddenly took her daughter's wrist and pulled her close. "Don't you mess this up! This is our one big chance!"

Meg pulled away, feeling the edge of her shell cutting into the inside of her chest. "Don't you worry, Ma, I won't. You think you arranged this? I got him. He loves me. He's marrying me, and he's taking me far away from here. Do you understand what I'm saying?"

CHAPTER SIXTEEN

————

IT WAS STILL DARK AND very cold at five in the morning when Lane and Raúl pulled up in front of Saint Mary's. Lane had left a hastily scribbled note for Darling on the desk. She hoped it would be enough to let him know she was safe without actually telling him she was spiriting someone away from the city in a clandestine early morning operation.

They found Nurse Yelland just inside the front doors with a wheelchair-bound Priscilla. She was encased in blankets, her face hidden by her dark glasses and a head scarf. With infinite care, she was settled onto the back seat and laid on her side.

"She's still on pain medication," Yelland explained. "But she practised getting up and walking yesterday, and she should be able to manage at the airport. Amazingly she had a visit from her maid yesterday. She felt bad that the missus was in hospital without her toiletries, or even her handbag, and so she brought them along. She wasn't particularly friendly, but she sat for a few minutes with Mrs. Galloway and told me on the way out that at least she'd be able to buy herself a candy bar now. I had a feeling this was not the first time the maid had to deal with this sort of thing. Mrs. Galloway's husband came last evening, but we told him she was sleeping and couldn't see anyone. He looked relieved and said he'd be back today."

Lane had bought a handbag at the hotel gift shop and put a wallet with some money in it, but Priscilla having her own things was much better. She transferred her money to Priscilla's wallet.

"Thank you, Nurse Yelland," Lane said earnestly. "With any luck she will be long gone by the time he comes."

"Think nothing of it. He's only visited her once. Busy man. I'd like to think it was remorse, but I doubt it. There aren't many people who'd do what you're doing. I wish all the women I deal with had a guardian angel like you. You've raised my very jaundiced view of humanity no end."

At that time of morning, the road to Phoenix was quiet. They passed a few large trucks but not much in the way of other cars. At six the stars began to fade, and the sky changed from inky black to streaks of intense orange and yellow. Lane watched with her heart full as this transformation took place. They had passed the bulk of the Catalina Mountains, and now the desert stretched east, with golden light beginning to wash over it.

She turned and looked into the back.

"I think she's asleep," she whispered to Raúl, who had maintained a complete silence, perhaps in honour of the serious business of the morning.

"I'm not asleep," Priscilla contradicted in a muffled voice. "I'm just trying to stay warm. I see I have a little suitcase. What did anyone find to put in it?"

"My sister found some clothes she thought you could use, and this lady did too," Raúl said, looking up at the rear-view mirror.

"Well, that's jolly nice." Priscilla sounded weary. "I'll have to find a way to thank her."

"No, ma'am. There is no need. She is happy to help. You just relax. We'll be at Sky Harbor in about an hour and a half."

LANE WALKED ACROSS the tarmac with Priscilla, providing an arm for support. "Are you sure you are going to be all right?" she asked.

"Yes, quite all right. Don't fuss. My friend in New York has agreed to meet me. Paul knows nothing about her." They had arrived at the stairs into the plane, and she took the railing in her free hand. "Thank you, Mrs. Darling," she said with formality. She was about to go up the stairs when she turned and reached into her purse and pulled something out. "This has your honeymoon picture, do you remember? I was going to keep the rest to hold over Paul if he ever found me. But perhaps someone here can use them." She dropped a roll of film into Lane's hand and started up the steps slowly and then looked back once more. "Thank you. I have a son, you know. I never told you. Perhaps now I will be able to see him."

"I've put my address in Canada in your handbag. Please write and let me know how you're getting on," Lane said,

213

but Priscilla Galloway was already facing away from her, climbing the stairs painfully to whatever future she could make for herself. Lane stayed and watched the plane take off and make a great arc, flying south and then around and away toward the northeast. She thought about Priscilla, delicate and frail, sitting in the plane with her dark glasses on, perhaps thinking of the son she'd left behind somewhere. She is the most solitary figure in the world, Lane thought. She looked at the roll of film in her hand and slipped it into her handbag. What had she meant about holding something over Galloway?

"RAÚL, I DON'T know how to thank you. It was such an enormous thing to ask of you."

Raúl shrugged genially. "It is nothing, ma'am. I hate to see a woman in that position. Anyway, my sister Chela thinks the world of you. She said most of the guests treat her as if she doesn't exist, or they talk loudly to her because they think she won't understand them. The management likes to keep the help strictly out of sight, if you know what I mean. You made a big impression on her."

"We have something in common, as it turns out. We both saw one of the guests meeting a man in secret, so we had something to talk about right away."

"Listen, when you work at a swanky place like that, you see lots of stuff. She knows her job. Clean up and see nothing." Raúl smiled. "She lives near, so I hear about most things. But she's a good girl; she knows not to get involved. You know, she said that same guest was meeting two different men. The last time, yesterday or the day before, she got a good look at an older man who picked her up. She was pretty surprised because she thought she recognized him."

Lane turned her eyes from the passing desert. "Did she? Had she seen him before?"

"Yeah, in the newspaper. She went and checked. A few weeks ago, a local businessman got arrested for something and his mug shot was in the paper. Funny name. Started with a G."

"How extraordinary!" Was this important? Whatever Meg Holden was up to was very likely just a sideshow, and while deplorable or scintillating, depending on your point of view, not relevant to the death of Jack Renwick. She would be interested in what Darling would have to say about it, though—once he got over what she'd just done.

"It just goes to show you that rich people play by different rules," Raúl commented.

Lane got out of the car in front of the Santa Cruz Inn, thanked Raúl again, and was again rebuffed when she tried to press some money on him. She turned to look at the front of the inn. It was quiet and elegant, basking in the late morning sun. In her anxiety she had half expected to find the place in an uproar, that somehow, impossibly, Galloway would have found out his wife was missing and would be striding about demanding answers, but of course, he could have no idea just yet of how his wife had disappeared, even if he was the assistant chief of police. Or perhaps he didn't even know yet. She looked at her watch. Much to her amazement, it was just before noon. Lane was famished. She went in search of her husband. She found him by the pool reading *The Grapes of Wrath*.

"Good book?"

Darling looked up, unsuccessfully trying to hide his relief. "Where the bloody hell have you been?"

Lane, surprised by his vehemence, stopped and looked anxiously at him. "I can't say. Do you mind awfully?"

Darling swung his legs around to the ground and frowned. "As a matter of fact, I do. I woke up and you were nowhere to be found, and no one at the front desk could tell me where you'd gone."

"Aren't you being a little overwrought? I left you a note."

"Please don't tell me how overwrought I can be! And you call this a note?" He pulled out the note he'd shoved between the pages of his book. *Sorry, darling, I've just gone out to help Priscilla. Not sure when I'll be back. Don't worry.* That 'don't worry' must be the crowning understatement! It's after noon. I woke up at six in the bloody morning and you were already gone. I was about to call the police."

Lane stood, dismayed by his anger. It was their first real row as a married couple, and it was, she could see, really her fault. Perhaps she'd been wrong not to include him in the plans, but she'd been concerned about putting him in an awkward position with Galloway. Now she saw the outcome was much worse: she and Darling were in an awkward position with each other. She sat down next to him on the deck chair.

"I wish you wouldn't just go off like that," he said. "I understand you've been on your own and you're used to doing whatever you want, and I even understand that it's probably not fair, as a modern man, for me to expect you to tell me what you're doing all the time. I just honestly don't know if I can live like that. The thing is, now that I have more than just myself to think of, I get worried. There, I've said it. And you can't deny you have form."

"Darling, I'm so sorry to worry you. It's not fair. I know. I wasn't doing anything the least bit dangerous, and I promise I'll tell you everything."

Darling harrumphed and took her hand tentatively. "Well, now I'm sorry, too. All I had this morning was a cup of coffee, because I kept thinking you'd turn up and want to eat breakfast."

"My poor darling. Get dressed, and we'll eat at once," Lane said. She linked her fingers through his and felt a jolt of wanting him as they started back to the room. How complicated it was to love someone. "You're right. I have been so used to just going around doing things on my own without ever having to think of anyone else. I didn't think about you being worried. I promise I won't do things that alarm you like this anymore."

Darling closed the door and pulled her into his arms and kissed her. Even as he succumbed, he smiled inwardly. He doubted she could ever really keep such a promise.

FEELING THE RELIEF of their first fight being behind them, they sat at their favourite table. It had a sense of privacy she particularly wanted at this moment.

Lane leaned toward him. "Look, I saw Raúl this morning, as it happens, and he told me something that might be important."

"Who the devil is Raúl?"

"Don't be silly. You remember, the cab driver, Chela's brother."

"So you went somewhere in a cab."

"Sort of. Yes. Look. I'll just say I asked Raúl to help me get poor Priscilla out of danger. It was perfectly safe. We drove her to the airport in Phoenix."

"You what?"

"It was really nothing. A quick drive there, onto a plane, and off to friends."

"Oh my God," Darling said, shaking his head.

"And here's what's important," Lane pressed on, "he told me Chela realized she recognized the man Meg Holden keeps meeting. Well, one of them. The older one. His mug shot was in the newspaper when he was arrested a couple of weeks ago. He couldn't remember the name she told him, but it started with a G."

Darling looked up sharply. "Griffin, I wonder? When I was at the police station that first day, I met Sergeant Martinez, and Galloway was giving him a bit of a dressing down over losing some notes on the case. He told me later it would be big for his career if he brought Griffin down. He implied that Jimmy Griffin was a local mobster. I must say, having seen Martinez at work here on the Renwick case, I can't fully subscribe to Galloway's comments on his incompetence. But of course, I've learned quite enough about Galloway now to dislike his views on practically everything."

Lane drank her iced tea. "By the way, when I saw Priscilla, she handed me a roll of film. She said our honeymoon photo was on it, but she also said there was something she was going to use against Paul."

Darling frowned. "Against *Galloway*? What does that mean?"

"I don't know. But I feel like Priscilla entrusted me with it, wanted to make sure we got it developed."

Darling was silent. "My hope of a carefree remainder to our honeymoon is fading fast. What do you propose to do?"

"I propose to take it to the front desk."

"And if there are compromising pictures of Galloway?"

"Priscilla won't have been taking pictures of him in the altogether or with other women. I'm going to go out on a limb ..."

"Your favourite perch," he commented.

"Haha. I bet these are pictures taken in social situations. But I do take your point. I could contact Raúl. He'll be discreet and get them done by someone he knows. Now then, about Meg: I wonder if Griffin is the man we saw her with on the street. The one who was pulling her about. You do agree with me that the plot thickens."

"What plot would that be?" asked Darling cautiously.

"The Meg Holden plot. If she's out there meeting a gangster, and she's standing next to poor Renwick when he's felled, it seems to me two and two do add up."

"The trouble is, they add up to five," Darling pointed out. "Or some odder number, if we count your behaviour today. You need a connection between the gangster and Renwick. And you have two people in the slammer who are the most likely to be involved: his nearest and dearest."

Lane sank back. "Of course. You're right, as usual. But it is still singular, if you ask me."

"Well, no one *is* asking you. But it's certainly worth mentioning to Martinez or, under normal circumstances, I would say Galloway."

Lunch concluded, and with Darling in a palpably better frame of mind, Lane thought it might be time to get serious about finding a present to take back to Angela. She ought to look again at the earrings she had on hold at the hotel gift shop and then find other shops in town to see what else was on offer. She had left Darling with the business of phoning Martinez. She tried not to think about Paul Galloway and what would happen when he found out his wife was gone, which he most assuredly would, sooner or later. As she was leaving the gift shop, she found Chela waiting for her, looking worried.

"Hello, is anything the matter?" Lane asked, following Chela down the hall to the cleaning area.

"I saw him again. The young one, I mean. He came to the back gate, but he didn't come in, he just waited. Then Mrs. Holden turned up, and they were talking so I could hear everything." Chela glanced at the door, as if fearful that someone would come out.

"Was something said that worried you?"

"They were kind of fighting, at least I thought so at first, but then he was trying to comfort her and tell her everything would be all right. But she kept saying she was frightened, that she didn't trust him. She said he would stop at nothing if he found out. Then the man said she should run away with him."

"Do you think she meant her husband?" Lane asked.

"I don't know, but she did sound really frightened. Honestly, Mr. Holden wouldn't scare a puppy. I mean, I know he's rich, and who knows how he got that rich, but he seems really nice to her. She spends whatever she wants, and she comes and goes however she wants." Chela managed to infuse a large measure of disapproval into the last sentence.

Lane stood thoughtfully looking at the row of oleander outside the wall. Really, this was gossip, but Chela seemed genuinely worried about it. Why?

"Chela, can you tell me what it is that worries you?"

"I don't know. I just think it is sort of out of control, do you know what I mean? I feel like something bad could happen again. I don't think I can really tell anyone. I'd be fired right away. After all, it's none of my business, but after that other shooting, I'm scared. And besides, they come in and out of this service gate all the time, and they've seen me working here."

It hit Lane how vulnerable Chela was. She had to protect her job and even her undocumented brother. How different their circumstances were! "I understand. Will you let me think about it? I honestly don't know how concerned we should be. I'll talk to my husband, but I promise not to talk to anyone else without letting you know. Can you do something for me? Can you get hold of your brother right away?" Lane wanted to give him the roll of film to develop.

CHAPTER SEVENTEEN

July 10, 1944

PRISCILLA BARR SQUATTED DOWN ON the station platform to button her son's coat, noting how much nicer it was than the one she'd sent him off in the last time. An anxious woman pulling her child along to find the right carriage jostled her, but she scarcely noticed that or the noise of the crowd or the explosive little exhalations of the waiting train. She only had eyes for him.

"Am I going back to the same place, Mummy? To Dave and Paula and Trixie?" Robbie was seven now and was happy to be going back to the village. Being back with his mother had meant being alone in the flat while she went to work because the schools were closed, and he had spent his days fighting back fear and loneliness until she got home every night.

"Yes, darling. You were happy there, weren't you?" She had to lean in to talk to him because the platform at the station was crowded with children and servicemen. Many of the children were crying and begging not to go, but some were silent, trying to be brave for their parents. A few lucky ones were going with their own mothers back to the places in the country where they had been billeted. The threat of a new wave of bombing had engendered a kind of panic that was palpable in the crowd. The stationmaster was shouting out the boarding call and the clamour intensified as parents said all the last-minute things to their children. She reached up tentatively and smoothed down his brown hair.

"Yes, Mummy. Trixie misses me. She has no one to play with."

"I'll see you soon, darling, I promise." She tried to imagine that this was true so that she would not cry or think about her life without him. "Paula and Dave love you very much. They were so happy to learn that you are coming back to them."

Her son smiled. "I love them too. Look. We have to get on. It's important. I will miss the train." He tugged at his little suitcase with one hand and leaned back to pull his mother to her feet. "Come on. You walk me to the stairs."

There was a crowd at the door, but she somehow got Robbie into the train. She watched his back among all the others crowding into the vestibule, and then he seemed to disappear. She couldn't tell one back from the other. She waited, watching the windows for a wave, but the train pulled out, and he was not among the children at the windows waving at their parents.

Priscilla watched till the smoke had cleared. So like him to use the big word "important." He had learned that grown-up way of speaking in Hampshire. She turned, putting her hand on her chest to hold her cardigan against a sudden wind. She pressed hard as if to push her whole hand in to fill the void where her heart had been.

"LAST ORDERS!"

Sergeant Paul Galloway looked up at the publican ringing the bell and, on impulse, took the barmaid's hand. "Just two things. Another pint, and what's your name?" He had leaned at the corner of the bar all night, just to keep her in his sights. He hadn't even planned on this pub, but a couple of the boys from his unit had said the barmaid was pretty, and he'd been bowled over by just how pretty she was. Blue eyes and black hair, petite and curvy. A body like a goddess. But more than that, in spite of her smiles and good-natured chatter, there was something forlorn about her that seized him with an overwhelming urge to protect her.

The barmaid slipped her hand away deftly and pulled his pint. "Drink up," she said. "Your ten minutes is running out."

When the publican began to push them out, he held back. "Yeah, yeah, I'm going. Keep your hair on. Look, miss. I'll be outside. I'll wait all night if I have to," he called.

When she came out, pulling on her jacket and calling goodnight to the publican, the street was empty except for Sergeant Galloway.

"I still don't know your name," he said, tipping his cap and walking along beside her.

"I'm not in the habit of giving it or anything else to pushy men in Yank uniforms."

"Aha! I'm not a pushy Yank, at least I wasn't. I started out as a pushy Londoner. Does that make it better?"

"Not much. Why are you in an American uniform?"

"If I answer that question you have to answer mine. I moved stateside and became an American. What's your name?"

"Look, I don't have to tell you my name. I'd like to go home now and enjoy some peace and quiet. I don't want to be badgered." She'd stopped and looked at him for a moment, appealing, she hoped, to his better nature.

He took her arm gently. "I have two days, miss, and you are the prettiest girl I've ever seen. Ever. I won't sleep tonight or any night if I don't know who you are, if I can't get you to come out with me just once, so you can see I mean it."

"How do you know I'm not married or have a bloke?"

"No ring, and you're not a *bloke* sort of girl. You need a man who can look after you and give you beautiful things. If you were anyone's girlfriend, he'd be here right now wanting to give me a hiding."

Priscilla Barr felt something in her yield to her own longing for security, for protection, for beautiful things. The sheer struggle of her entire life came on her like a wave of exhaustion and she took in a great draught of the muggy night air.

"How do I know you're not married?"

"I'm not married, my luv, but I sure as hell hope to be."

Galloway didn't sleep much that night anyway. Priscilla Barr. Priscilla Barr had agreed to go with him to a club after work the next night, and he was going to go to Selfridges and buy her the most expensive perfume in the house.

———

MEG HOLDEN GOT out of the taxi in front of the Fox Theatre. Looking right and left, she got into the line-up for the afternoon showing of *The Vigilante's Return*. She sat at the back of the house, put her purse down on the seat beside her, and pulled off her gloves. She was feeling relief. Rex had given her the money she had asked for, and it had been safely delivered. He was probably napping right now back at the villa in the inn. She'd sneaked off to see Art, who had seemed distracted and had shooed her away with a peck on the cheek. "You're doing a good job, sweetie," he'd called after her as she was going out the back door. But he'd stood and watched her leave. She tried not to think that meant anything.

"Is this seat taken?" a tall man asked as the lights were going down and the curtain was opening.

"Shh!" Meg said, taking her purse off the seat.

The man reached for her hand and squeezed it. "I don't want to 'shh.' I missed you, honey. I didn't like arguing like we did," he whispered, brushing her cheek with his lips.

She turned her face toward him, the light of the film flickering on her cheek, and they kissed. Her hunger for him made her breathless.

"Baby, it makes no sense you staying with that old guy. Why don't you come with me? I got a lead on a job in Flagstaff. Come on, what's stopping you?"

Someone two rows ahead turned and glared at them. "Shut up, will ya?"

Meg put her head on the man's shoulder and stroked his leg. She couldn't live without him, she knew, but she could not leave. It would just have to be like it always was. She kissed him again.

"I can't," she whispered directly into his ear. "I told you. I never could. I just want things like this. You're happy, aren't you?"

The man jerked away and grabbed her hand, pulling her out of the seat and through the nearby exit.

Meg blinked, shocked at his sudden move, and tried to adjust her eyes to the blinding light of the lobby. Stumbling, she felt her heel catching on the thick carpeting of the short set of stairs that led down to the washrooms.

"What are you doing?" she finally managed. "Let go of me!" She yanked her hand back and rubbed it.

The quiet carpeted hallway was empty. "Now look here, you can't have it every which way! I want to be with you, honest and upfront. I'm tired of sneaking around. Leave that guy and marry me. That's how it has to be. Otherwise we're through."

Meg, dismay flooding through her, put her hands on his chest, the handbag on her wrist clunking against him. "You know I love you, baby. You know I don't think of nobody but you."

"Then you'll come with me."

Meg fell back. "I can't. I just can't. I can't tell you why. You just have to trust me." What would he think if he knew about Art? She suppressed a shudder.

"Trust you? About that. I thought I saw someone following me a week ago. It happened a couple of times. Something to do with you?"

Meg frowned, a new fear gripping her. She could feel it grow from a small nut of panic. It was beginning to spread, and she controlled it by making a fist and taking a deep breath. "It's got nothing to do with me. Rexy wouldn't do nothing like that. He doesn't even know about us! You must have been mistaken."

"How do you know he doesn't know about us? You're all hot for me. I'm surprised he wouldn't see that."

Meg recoiled from the coarseness of his words and his expression. Contempt showed in his blazing eyes and the slight curl of his lip, emphasized by the lift of his moustache.

"Why would you say something like that?" She could feel the tears burning.

The man leaned back and slipped his hands into his pockets. His grey double-breasted suit was expensive and hung on his lean frame attractively. He liked it, and he liked the way he looked in it. He liked that she had paid for it.

"You either come with me now or we're through."

"You'd cut off your own nose to spite your face!" she flung back at him. "You think I have money on my own? There'd be no more nice things if I left Rex."

"There hasn't been anything nice for a while, baby, and I don't need your money. I told you, I love you. I told you that. Now make up your mind." He had gone from debonair to sulky.

Someone came down the stairs and headed for the ladies' powder room and they fell silent, looking at the floor.

"Nothing to say? Okay. See you around." The man pulled himself off the wall he'd been leaning on, put his hat on, and walked up the stairs and through the curtain into the lobby.

Meg stood, congealed with pain and fear in the quiet hallway. She couldn't follow him or call him back. It was more than her life was worth.

GRIFFIN PICKED UP the phone in his office and asked his secretary to put him through.

"Yes?" The voice that answered was curt.

"I thought you were going to take care of things. That sergeant is still grinding away at me. He's found where the other money is going."

"Look, I told you, the case is going nowhere. I've got problems of my own right now, all right? You have to trust me."

"Honestly, I don't care. I did trust you, and I did a favour for you on the basis of it. I'd just as soon not be involved. I don't need another dead body on my hands."

"What do you mean another?"

Griffin sighed. "I had to take care of a little family business, okay? It didn't work out, but at least that cop, Martinez, is going in a good direction on that. Did I tell you I got a photographer? He takes pictures of the restaurant for my advertising flyers. He does some other stuff too. Very smart. I have a couple of nice photos of you and me, you know that? Anyway, I gotta go. I'm leaving this in your capable hands. But I don't have a lot of time. I got a business to run." He slammed down the receiver. It was useful to have a cop in your pocket, but it could be a big pain in ass.

Griffin flung the papers he was holding on the large oak desk that dominated his office at the restaurant. The man in front of him was looking down, trying to hide his fear.

"You're an idiot, you know that? A simple job, that's all I asked of you! Now what are we gonna do? The police are looking for answers. I can't afford to keep them and you on the payroll if you're going to be a jackass. I've got a good mind to toss you at them. One less stupid employee for me. Did you even listen to Hidalgo?"

The man said nothing. It was obvious to him that if Mr. Griffin did feed him to the police, it would just blow back on him, but it would make him even madder to hear that.

There was a long silence. Finally Griffin, perhaps reaching the same conclusion, blew out his breath in disgust. "Get out of here. Keep your nose clean, or I'm sending you to the operation in Albuquerque to get you outta my sight."

When the man had gone, Griffin sat down heavily and closed his eyes. He'd been in tight situations before. Tighter even. His big problem was that he couldn't trust anyone. People used to do exactly what he told them. His wife, his men. Now it seemed like everybody did whatever they wanted. He had a momentary idea that he was getting too old for the whole thing. That he should cash out and move to Florida. His wife would like that. She always used to talk about Florida. He'd forgive her and they'd live the good life in Miami or Tampa. Maybe after the court case. That, at least, was going as planned.

CHAPTER EIGHTEEN

GALLOWAY DROVE INTO THE PARKING lot of St. Mary's and turned off the engine. Staring glumly at the building, he pulled out his cigarettes and lit one. He inhaled a big lungful of smoke and then leaned his arm on the open window. Oddly, though he was assailed by some of the biggest problems he could remember having to confront—his wife was lying inside in a bit of a mess and he was beginning to have anxious doubts about the Griffin business—it was Darling who came to mind.

He'd liked Darling back in Nelson when he arrived from Vancouver in '36. He was studious and paid attention, especially to what he'd said to him. He'd shown young Darling the ropes. Now look at him. An inspector, and no doubt thanks to everything he'd taught him. But instead of being grateful, he seemed—he couldn't find the word. Condescending, almost, as if Darling couldn't quite approve of him. It wasn't anything he said. It was the opposite. It was his silences, his noncommittal nodding, as if butter wouldn't melt. And then he turns up with that beautiful wife. Cultured, smart, from the upper crust. The real deal, not like poor Priscilla with that put-on accent trying to cover her Cockney roots. Darling didn't deserve a woman like that. He wasn't man enough for her, he thought in a sudden flight of fancy.

He flicked his cigarette onto the ground and rolled up the window. Maybe he could get Priscilla out today, get her home. She was making more of a fuss than was absolutely necessary, and he didn't want to have to keep coming to the hospital. He hated hospitals. He'd talk to the doctor about it. Persuade him that she'd be better off at home where everything was familiar and she had a maid to look after her.

The elevator opened on the hushed beige and green floor, the nurse's station directly opposite with two white-capped women busy with papers behind the counter. He wouldn't bother them. He knew what room Priscilla was in. He strode down to the end of the hall and pushed open the door. He was staring at an empty room, cleaned and starched. He frowned and stepped back to look at the number.

"Where's my wife?" he asked quietly, back at the counter. The nurses looked up. "My wife, in 403, where is she?" He spoke louder.

"Keep your voice down, sir. Who is your wife?" one of them said. The other remained silent and looked at him scathingly.

"Mrs. Galloway, Priscilla Galloway. She was in 403. Just tell me where she's been moved to."

"I'm sorry, sir, I can't say."

"You can't say? Do you have any idea who I am? What do you mean you can't say?"

"I presume," said the nurse primly, keeping her voice down, "that you are Mr. Galloway. And I can't say where she is because she checked out yesterday morning."

"She couldn't have. That's ridiculous. I never allowed that. I want to see her doctor."

The second nurse now spoke. "I am Nurse Yelland. I was here when you brought her in. You will have to keep your voice down, or I'll ask you to leave. Your wife checked out yesterday morning, which she had every right to do. I'm afraid we have no idea where she is if she is not at your home. I can certainly fetch the attending physician. He will be able to explain all the medical treatments that were required while she was here." Nurse Yelland's voice rose slightly, as if challenging him.

Galloway could feel the blood rising in his face. "How dare you take that tone with me. Do you know who I am? When I'm finished with you, you won't know what hit you!"

"As you wish, sir. Will I call the attending?" Nurse Yelland answered icily.

Back out in the parking lot, he smoked and paced, trying to stop the panic and rage he was feeling, trying to understand what could have happened. The attending doctor knew nothing of her leaving and, considering the extent of her injuries, would not have recommended it. Yes, they did keep a record of the time people checked out, but she did not say she was leaving. No, she had not consulted him.

Priscilla would never leave him. This was at the centre of all his thoughts. She would never leave him. She loved him. She had said so many times. They'd had bad times before, but she'd never wavered. Anyway, she had no money of her own. He desperately tried to remember who her friends were. Someone at the country club? He thought about the people they met there, golfed with, drank with. He couldn't, not in a million years, go ask one of those arrogant, new-money bastards where his wife was.

———

MRS. WATTS OPENED the door at Terrell's knock. She looked from Terrell to Ames, as if she could scarcely remember who they were. Finally she said, "Yes?"

"Good morning. I'm sorry to disturb you again. There have been new developments in the matter of your husband's death, and we just need to check on a couple of things," Ames said, trying for a tone between unhurried and grave.

She lifted her eyebrows and then backed away from the door to let them in. "Do you want coffee?"

Ames was surprised at what seemed to him to be a lack of curiosity. "No, ma'am, we won't be long. We have had a post-mortem, and I'm sorry to say the results suggest this has become a murder investigation."

At this, Mrs. Watts sat heavily, putting one hand over her mouth and looking down. "Oh my God! I don't understand. I thought he'd had some sort of attack."

"No. He was attacked. Someone held a poisoned cloth of some kind over his mouth."

"But who would want to kill him?" Mrs. Watts looked up, her face white.

"That we don't know, at the moment. But can you tell us if there was anything unusual lately? Had he been more worried recently? A phone call, a letter maybe?"

Had she suddenly blanched? It was difficult to tell in the shadows of the room, Ames thought. "I don't think so. What sort of letter? What are you saying?"

Ames sat down opposite her. "We've learned your husband was possibly planning to run off with a local girl, the underaged daughter of a workmate. He was supposed to be picking her up on the day he was killed, but of course, he never came for her."

Mrs. Watts put her hands over her eyes for a moment and then stood up, her face contorted. "The daughter of a workmate? My husband was not a good man, but he could not have been that stupid. It's nonsense!" She walked towards the sink and leaned forward on it, looking down, then she straightened and turned abruptly. "I've had enough of this. I want his body, and I want to give him a proper funeral. His daughter deserves that."

Ames stood up and shook his head regretfully. "I'm sorry, ma'am, unfortunately we can't release his body until we have a fuller understanding of how he died. I know these are terrible things to hear. Can we call someone? Can we pick up your mother for you? Perhaps she can stay for a bit, or we could take you and your daughter to her?"

"I'm perfectly capable of looking after myself. You're telling me my husband was murdered. Then find his killer. That's what you can do, Sergeant Ames."

"I SHOULD PHONE Inspector Darling and ask whether he remembers Tina coming in to report what happened to her," Ames said, pulling on his beer. They were in the hotel bar, and it was crowded and noisy, as always. Smoke filled the top third of the room, its volume sustained by the cigarettes of a hundred miners, rail workers, and millworkers. But not by the two policemen.

"You don't smoke, sir?" Terrell asked.

"My mom would kill me if I took it up again. She has some crazy idea my dad died of it because he coughed so much before he died."

"Certainly you could phone the inspector. Even if he remembered, though, I'm not sure it would help," Terrell said. "We already know Miss Van Eyck went to the station and got insulted for her troubles. It doesn't answer the question of who was in the car with Watts making him sniff rat poison, or why he went around to the garage to see if Miss Van Eyck had revealed the rape to anyone."

"True enough. I think I just want to find out which policeman it was so I can beat the bastard senseless."

Terrell smiled. "I know what you mean. Bad police work is infuriating. It reflects on all of us. Let me tell you, I know that only too well."

"How so?" Ames asked. "I can't see you ever doing shoddy work. You seem meticulous to a fault."

"Thank you, sir. In my case, if I were dishonest or bungled things, it would reflect on my whole race."

"Oh," Ames said. "I never thought of that. I remember Tina saying once that she had to be twice as good as a man to get half the credit. It must be something like that."

"Just like that," Terrell answered. "Can I get you another?"

"Sure, thanks. It makes you think. There's that business of walking a mile in someone else's shoes. I mean, I don't think most people walk that mile. Or maybe I mean I don't, not as much as I should. I just see the world from my perspective and assume everyone else sees it the same way."

"I think we're all capable of doing that," Terrell said. "But being born coloured, I don't have much of a choice. I sometimes feel like my whole world is dependent on other people's points of view."

Ames nodded. He thanked the waiter for the beer and looked around the room. All men. The women, he knew, had a lounge next door, with a separate entrance, where they could go with their escorts.

"This case is all about the women, isn't it?" he said. "Either he was killed by an angry woman from his past, or by an angry father, brother, or even husband of one of those women. It's still hard for me to imagine women committing murder even after the cases I've seen, but that's because I really do see them as the 'fairer sex.' But what if I tried to see the world from the point of view of a Tina or an Ada Finch? Or even a Mrs. Watts, hearing her husband was planning to run off with a teenager. Maybe when they get angry, they want to beat people up as well."

"I bet they do," laughed Terrell. "I've seen women kill with a look! But the real question is why *now*?" he said, serious again. "What happened just now, why did he suddenly come around asking Tina if she'd said something? As you said, he's been relatively happily married for ten years except for perhaps a few affairs, but something changed that unleashed everything that led to his death. Something or someone spooked him about the past."

"And why be running after Ada? It's unsavoury. He's nearly forty years old. Maybe he thought this was his last chance," Ames mused. "And which happened first, Ada or the warning about the past?"

"And he never gets to her. That's the part I find puzzling. He sets out, his clothes packed and hers too, only he ends up dead by the Harrop ferry."

"Wait," Ames said, "Wait. The clothes. We've been assuming those are Ada's clothes, when we found out they weren't his wife's. Why wouldn't Ada bring her own clothes?"

Terrell nodded. "I see your point, but what if he says, 'I'll buy you lovely new frocks, you don't have to worry about a thing'?"

"Yes. They are brand new. So first we have to see if they are Ada's ... something new she bought for her big escape and handed off to him so she could just go to school as usual with her books and nothing else so as not to raise suspicion. Then if they aren't, we'll have to look into where he got them." Ames looked at his watch. "We can interview her this afternoon. Her parents will never let us interview her without them, so I imagine her dad will leave work to be there. And, do we believe that Mrs. Watts knew nothing, didn't see any change in him? I thought she was a bit all over the map with her response when we told her it was murder."

———

AS MUCH AS he was disinclined to talk to Galloway, Darling knew he would have to share that Chela might have seen Meg Holden with a man who might have been James Griffin. Consequently, an hour after breakfast, he was at the police station with Martinez, sitting in Galloway's office.

Martinez was taking notes, but Galloway, Darling thought, seemed distracted, resistant even.

"So this maid, Chela, is certain about it being Griffin?" Martinez asked.

"I don't see how we can take the word of a Mexican maid, no offence, Martinez. Did you talk to her yourself?" Galloway said.

"No, my wife did." Darling avoided glancing at Martinez to see if he'd taken any offence at Galloway's remark and instead looked steadily at his old mentor

Galloway threw his hand up in a dismissive gesture. "Well, there you are then! A couple of women chattering. Nothing in it."

With infinite effort, Darling suppressed his fury at Galloway's dismissal of women in general and Lane in particular. With the studied calmness he used with recalcitrant witnesses, he asked, "Can you show me a picture of Griffin or describe him? I'm wondering if the man we saw her with in town the other day might be the same man."

"Suit yourself. Martinez, go get the mug shot." This order was delivered in so peremptory a manner that Darling glanced at Martinez, but the sergeant's face was expressionless as he got up to do his boss's bidding.

"Listen, Darling, I'm pretty sure you've got the wrong end of the stick. We've got our man on this one. Martinez has worked hard, God bless him, and he needs a win. Let's not upset the apple cart."

Darling was attempting to formulate a response to this when Galloway spoke again. "When we're finished here, can you stay back? Something's come up with—" but at that moment Martinez was back with a small photo of the classic mug shot: profile and full face.

Darling took the photo and looked at the grainy representation of James A. "Jimmy" Griffin. Could this be the man he and Lane had seen on the street? He'd asked if she wanted to come with him this morning, but for some reason she had resisted. She had claimed the call of poolside and Lord Peter.

"What sort of shape is he?"

"He's five seven, 195 pounds, quite portly."

That would certainly match the shape of the man he'd seen. "Does he have an ill-fitting brown suit, by any chance?"

Martinez smiled. "I'm not sure about a brown one, sir, but every suit I've seen him in seems a little too small."

"I wonder if you can let me have this? I'll show it to my wife and Miss Ruiz. She thought he was the same man she'd seen in the newspaper some weeks ago, but this would confirm it." He addressed this to Martinez, ignoring the sound of Galloway shifting impatiently in his seat.

Martinez got up. "Sure thing. Can you give me a ring?"

"You're just muddying the waters, Darling," Galloway said irritably when Martinez had gone. "Shut the door."

Obligingly, Darling got up and closed the door and then sat down again, trying to look benignly interested.

"Listen, something's happened. Maybe you can help." He paused, as if he might change his mind. "My wife's disappeared. That's a bit strong, perhaps. But she's checked herself out of hospital and gone off and hasn't told me where."

Darling, who wasn't supposed to know anything about Priscilla, feigned surprise as best he might. "Oh. I see. I'm sorry to hear she was in hospital."

"I'm hoping you do see. She had a fall down the stairs. That's why she was in hospital. But you'd seen her before that, when she drove you out to the mission. Did she seem all right? Did she say anything at all to you?"

Darling was becoming aware of a maelstrom of emotions, not all of which were easily identifiable or pleasant. He tried to tackle the foremost: Galloway seemed to think that his wife might have confided in them. All right? Had Priscilla been all right? Looking back, he realized he hadn't thought so for a second. She had seemed both reclusive and fragile somehow with those dark glasses and the scarf and gloves and at the same time overly bright. But she'd been a bit like that the first time he'd met her, when they'd gone to the Galloways for dinner, so he'd assumed that was normal. Had she confided anything? Certainly not to him. And it was at this moment the other anxiety began to take shape. Had she confided in Lane? And in a gawd-help-us moment, he could see the real enormity of Lane spiriting Priscilla away to Phoenix. What if Galloway were to find out?

"She certainly didn't say anything to me, to us. We had a lovely drive to the mission, explored it a bit, and came back for a nice lunch."

Galloway leaned back in his chair and sighed. "I see. Well, I expect she's gone to her friend, Dahlia. She was pretty beat up, and you know what the ladies are like, eh, Darling? A little vain." He laughed unconvincingly. "She just wants to be back to normal before I see her again."

Darling, whose lady was the furthest thing from vain, noted Galloway's use of the phrase "pretty beat up" and then stood up.

"I'm sure that will be the explanation," he said. "I'd best be off. Only a few more days of the holiday, and then it's back to winter! I expect my wife would like to see me." I know I'd jolly well like to see her, he thought. Had she even thought about the danger before she acted?

CHAPTER NINETEEN

O N SATURDAY AFTERNOON, AMES, TERRELL, and the stony-faced Craig Finch sat at the kitchen table of the small house. Ada was there too. They were looking at what seemed, in this severe context, the highly inappropriate and garish pile of ladies' frocks and underwear.

"Well?" asked her father coldly.

Ada shook her head dumbly, glancing miserably at the pile of clothes and then looking down at the table.

"Miss Finch, did Barney Watts say he would buy any clothes for you?" Ames asked.

Ada looked desperately at her father and then down again.

"Answer the bloody question!" her father thundered.

Looking frantically toward the door, Ada managed, "He said ..."

"Don't look for your mother to come and save you. She's with your gran at the hospital. Now, what did that bastard say?"

Ames wished Finch wouldn't browbeat his daughter, but he did not interfere, thinking perhaps he'd have no better luck himself with some gentler tactic. "Miss Finch?"

"He'd take care of everything, but—"

Finch jumped up, took up what clothes he could gather in his fist, and shook them in his daughter's face. "So he was proposing to dress you up like a tart in this garbage? I don't suppose you have any bloody idea what would have happened next, do you?"

Ames half stood. "Mr. Finch." His voice was soothing, causing Finch to drop the clothes and sit down angrily. "Miss Finch, but *what*?"

"I already gave him some of my clothes. He told me to so I wouldn't have to take anything but my schoolbooks so it wouldn't look, uh, suspicious." She stopped and looked miserably at her father.

"There will be plenty of suspicion to go around from now on," her father said. "Have you finished, officers? Ada has her homework, which she'll have lots of time to do because she won't be leaving this house after school for the rest of her natural life!"

"Mr. Finch, can we have a word with you on your own?"

"Now what? Get up to your room," Finch said to his daughter. He waited till she was out of the room and part- way up the steps and then turned back to the police-men. "What?"

"We understand you had a violent disagreement with Watts at your workplace. Is that true?" Ames asked.

"What of it?" Finch said truculently. "People get into arguments all the time."

"Yes, but you were overheard to say something along the lines of 'stay away from her'. It suggests that you knew he had designs on your daughter. So it shouldn't have been such a big surprise that he might have been going to run away with her. Can you tell us where you were Tuesday afternoon?"

"I was home, sick."

"Can anyone verify that?" Ames tried to keep his voice mild.

"My bloody wife can verify it. What the hell are you driving at? I didn't do anything to him. Believe me, though, if he'd managed to get her away, I wouldn't answer for my actions! I'm not surprised he's dead!"

"WHEW!" TERRELL SAID, navigating down the narrow street after this stormy interview. "That poor kid. I used to think it would be fun to have a daughter, but I'm not so sure now. There's just too much awful stuff that can happen to them. I'm inclined to believe him, by the way. Of course, his wife will just confirm he was sick at home."

"And would a man with a short fuse like that go to all this trouble with poisoned handkerchiefs? He'd much more likely shoot him in a fit of rage. Still, he's on our list. The question of the clothes is puzzling me. What do we have? According to her, the clothes weren't for her, but maybe they were. Maybe her father was right: Finch intended to dress Ada up, try to make her look older so as not to arouse suspicion if they were planning to run away somewhere."

"If Ada gave Watts her own clothes, where are they now?"

"Keep driving. Let's stop at the train station and see if he kept another locker or something. I can't imagine that he'd risk bringing a bunch of teenager's clothes to his place of work, but they weren't in the car or at his house. At least, Mrs. Watts didn't mention them," Ames said.

The foreman at the station shook his head. "Just the empty one you saw."

Back at the police station, Terrell handed Sergeant O'Brien, the deskman, the keys to the car and said to Ames, "Look, sir, why don't I pop out to the dress shops with this stuff and see if I can find out who bought it. I think it's pretty obvious, but at least we could dot that i, as it were."

Ames nodded, but he didn't tell Terrell what he was going to spend the next hour doing because, he realized later in the file room, he was slightly embarrassed about it.

———

"HELLO, DARLING," LANE said, when her husband's shadow loomed across her deck chair. There were two children splashing about in the pool while their mother sat on the edge with her feet in the water, calling out to them not to go to the deep end.

Darling took off his hat, pulled a nearby deck chair closer, and sat down. "I've heard a most extraordinary story," he said.

"Do tell," she said, smiling. The shade from her sun hat fell becomingly across her face, but he firmly ignored that.

"I went down to the Tucson police station, as you know, to tell Martinez and Galloway about Chela seeing Meg's older male friend's mug shot in the paper. Martinez took it seriously and Galloway pooh-poohed it. Then Galloway asked me to stay back for a word. Can you guess what that word was?"

"Haven't the foggiest," she said.

"He told me his wife had checked out of the hospital on her own and disappeared. He wondered, don't you know, if she'd seemed all right to us on our little trip to the mission. I confess, I was stymied. For one thing I had to pretend I didn't know she'd been in the hospital, and for another I wasn't sure what confidences she could have shared that would be in any way connected to her later hospitalization and disappearance. Did she confide in you, perhaps while you two were sitting in the shade of the mission garden?"

"That's interesting, because you know, there was a moment when I thought she might confide in me. In fact, I tried to encourage it, but she gave an artificial little laugh and brushed me off. I wasn't very convinced. And when it comes down to it, I don't think I was that surprised to learn he'd put her in the hospital."

"I can't tell you how little I enjoyed pretending I knew nothing about her disappearance from that hospital."

———

TERRELL TRUDGED THROUGH a barrage of sleety rain to the three main dress shops in town and was relieved to have some luck at the third.

"Yes, those are from our shop. The dresses, I mean, not the underwear. It happens I do remember because I myself really liked that blue dress. I asked the lady who bought it if she was going on vacation and she said she was. She said they were driving down to California."

"Do you remember her name or anything about her? Or the day they were purchased?"

"Oh." The saleswoman stopped and frowned. "I'd have to go through my sales slips to find the exact date, but I would say within the last month? I didn't get her name, but I do remember her. A pretty blonde with very curly hair. In her early thirties or late twenties perhaps, but quite young looking for all that. Yea high." She held her hand up at Terrell's chin level. "These are size 16 R. They were meant for quite a slender woman, which she was."

"Eye colour?"

"Honestly, I couldn't tell you. Dark green, brown. Not notably blue or anything."

"Thank you. If you could give your sales slips a quick look and give me a call at the station, that would be helpful, thank you. Ask for Constable Terrell."

"By the way, Constable, I can save you some trouble on that other purchase. It came from Grace's down the end of the street, near the gas station, and it was bought the same day because the lady had a bag from there."

Terrell smiled and tipped his hat as he left the shop, looking with a sigh at the two cold, wet blocks he'd have to traverse to get to the store.

"WHAT ARE YOU looking for, Sergeant? I thought there were rats in here," Sergeant O'Brien said, looking into the file room.

Ames was seated in front of a three-drawer filing cabinet. The records room was windowless and dusty. Sneezing explosively, Ames said, "I'm looking for what I'm pretty sure isn't here: a file containing information about a young woman, a girl really, who might have come here to report an assault in probably late June of '35."

"Why shouldn't it be there? We've always kept pretty good records."

"Because it's likely the girl was sent away with some harsh words from the officer she talked to. You know, blaming her for it, refusing to take it seriously."

O'Brien, not one for standing, settled his bulk with a "humph" into a chair in front of the small table, which was the only other furniture in the room. "I can't see that, can you? How young was she?"

"Sixteen."

"Well, there you are then. A sixteen-year-old would have come in with a parent, and no parent would put up with the daughter being dismissed like that."

Ames pulled another file folder out, opened it, scanned the pages, and tossed it back in, then turned to O'Brien. "That's the thing, she didn't come in with a parent. She didn't want her parents to know. Were you here in '35?"

"I was. The inspector wasn't here yet. He came in '36. Was it an old guy, do you know? Higgs retired that year. If it was him, I can see it. He was a tad old-fashioned, and didn't much like keeping records, especially toward the end. And Sergeant Galloway was here then, but he left in '37. Moved down south somewhere stateside because he didn't like the cold. He was okay. A little full of himself but well liked. He used to play poker with a group of guys every week. Said that's how he kept his ear to the ground. Took Darling under his wing." He chuckled and pushed himself upright. "He did pretty well at cards, as I recall. Got a round at the bar out of him more than once. Anyway, I'll give it a think, see if something comes to mind. Gotta get back to the desk. I suggest you come up for air soon. The dust in here will kill you. And I couldn't swear to there being no rats here, either."

O'BRIEN HAD JUST reached his desk when Terrell pushed the door open and removed his sodden hat, shaking it onto the doormat.

"Don't you look like a drowned muskrat," O'Brien commented, watching him peel off his rubber overshoes and gingerly hang his soaking raincoat on the coat rack.

"I feel like one. Is Sergeant Ames in?"

"He's gone upstairs after spending a couple of happy hours in the file room getting dust up his nose. Police work, eh?"

Terrell smiled wanly and went up in search of Ames. He already knew that Ames wasn't going to like hearing what he'd learned from the dress-shop expedition.

———

"OH, MY GOD," Darling said, pushing his hand through his hair. "Can I not leave you alone for a minute?" He was again prey to very mixed feelings. On the one hand, he felt unabashed admiration for his wife's unwavering sense of justice, and on the other, anxiety about what it would all mean.

"Darling, if you had seen her, you would not have hesitated. And after all, she asked for my help. And Chela helped me get hold of her brother. He used his own car so that the taxi couldn't be traced, and he had a day off coming anyway. He was magnificent and wouldn't take a cent."

"Of course, you were right. Of course, you were. I just wish you'd told me ahead of time. I can just see my whole married life unfolding before me, with you bashing off to rescue the halt and the lame, leaving me in the dark."

"I so nearly did tell you, but at the time I worried that you would be in the position of knowing and having to lie to Galloway. I don't think you are all that comfortable with lying."

"What worries me is that you are," Darling said, taking her hand and looking at it despondently. He thought about her wartime career in intelligence. Surely a good deal of lying would have been required.

But Lane took both his hands and looked at him earnestly. "I am not. I have never lied to you about anything. And I never will. I thought you knew that." She dropped his hands and looked away toward the children who had come out of the pool and were being rubbed down, shivering and laughing. She was immediately sorry she'd said it. It was too big, and it wasn't fair because while she hadn't lied, she'd kept him out. "I'm sorry. That was unfair. I did keep you out of it. I can see that it's almost a form of lying."

"That makes two of us. I'm sorry as well. I don't imagine for a minute that you'd be comfortable lying, but I will admit, I don't like being ... maybe *not trusted* is a better way to look at it. I can even confess that in looking back on my conversation with Galloway, I am glad I didn't know ahead of time. It would have made for an awful awkwardness. I think what I'm saying is that I do want to know before you go haring off on rescue missions, should this become a fixture of our marriage, and I want you to trust me to handle the outcomes."

"I do love you," she said, leaning in to kiss him gently. "Shall we go riding this afternoon? I'd love to see the city from up high again. It's convincing me that we might even get a couple of horses when we get home. What do you think?"

"Well, yes to the ride this afternoon, certainly. I just have to show Miss Ruiz this photo. And you too for that matter. Does this look like the man we saw Meg Holden talking to on the street? I didn't get a good enough look at his face. I think I was concentrating more on his grabbing her arm like that."

Lane took the photo he'd pulled out of the manila envelope. "We were almost half a block away by the time I tumbled to the realization it was Meg Holden. Certainly the shape of the head looks right, but I don't think I could swear to it in court. But Chela saw him very close up, so she'll know for sure. Who is he?"

"He's a bit of a local gangster, and if Mrs. Holden is very chummy with him, I suspect that means something."

GALLOWAY SAT ON the patio of his home, nursing his fourth scotch and waiting for Fernanda to cook his dinner. She'd looked disapprovingly at him when he'd ordered her to just bring the bottle and set it down on the table beside him, but then, she looked disapprovingly at him all the time. He should dismiss her. He looked at his watch. It was nearly eight and starting to get cold. She'd serve dinner and then go home. He could feel a wave of anxiety about being alone and pushed it aside. The Griffin situation had seemed in the bag. What was the meaning of Darling's so-called information? It would, he was absolutely sure, come to nothing.

Galloway turned to the problem of his wife. He'd made up the name "Dahlia" when he was talking to Darling, but there must be a Dahlia of sorts somewhere who knew where she was—or was even hiding her. He started again to run through the people they knew at the club when Fernanda called.

"*Señor jefe*. It is on the table."

Galloway got up, surprised at how light-headed he felt. He said nothing to the maid but shook his hand at her in a shooing motion when she asked if there was anything else. He listened until he heard the back door close, and only when he was sure she had left, did he turn to his dinner.

Priscilla would be back. He even felt half convinced that he'd been right when he told Darling that she was just waiting till she looked more like her old self. She couldn't survive a second on her own, he knew that. She had no money for starters, and there wasn't a single woman at the club who would risk her husband's career by sheltering the wife of the assistant chief of police.

He was the assistant chief of police, dammit. He'd use good old police procedures to track her down. If it did turn out to be one of the women at the club, well, he'd see what ought to be done about that.

CHAPTER TWENTY

TERRELL HAD BEEN RIGHT. AMES was not the least bit happy about the information he'd brought from the dress shops. Both sales ladies had remembered the woman who'd made the purchases in particular because of the curly blond hair. The second shopkeeper had made a point of how yellow it was.

"Tina Van Eyck," Ames said miserably after a very long moment.

Terrell, however, had been quite convinced of her candour after his interview by the lake. "We don't know that, though, do we? There must be scores of pretty blondes in their late twenties in town."

"Probably none who had a relationship with him when they were teenagers. He was never planning to take Ada Finch anywhere. He was going off with Tina. She's lied to us right from the start."

Terrell was silent and then spoke. "I'm not sure you can call being raped a relationship. Anyway, why would he tell

Ada Finch he was going to take her away somewhere if he'd been planning to run off with Miss Van Eyck?"

Ames winced. "I suppose. But we've only got Tina's word for what he did to her when she was sixteen. There's no trace of her supposed report to the police. There's nothing for it; we're going to have to go out there. Maybe even bring her back for questioning. We're going to have to learn a good deal more about that whole business." No fear or favour, he thought, feeling completely unsettled.

"If we're going out anyway," Terrell said, "let's stop at the cottage and find out from Mrs. Watts if Ada's clothes were among the things she took from his locker." He was not at all convinced by the Tina Van Eyck theory and hoped that circumstances would support him.

THE WEATHER MADE Sunday morning as moody as the previous day. Heavy black clouds seemed to cap the valley, locking out the light. The lake was a menacing dark green, the wind causing the ferry to rock on the crossing. Ames looked balefully out at the trees on the other side of the road that were bending in the gale, throwing off the last of their dying leaves.

There was little but the most necessary traffic on the road, which instead of the usual dust now cast up a fine rain of mud from the tyres of the vehicles ahead of them. The road up the hill to the Watts cottage was a series of wet craters, and Ames winced with every jostle and bump.

Rain was coming down in earnest when the two men stood on the small porch knocking on the door. They'd been relieved to see smoke coming out of the chimney as they pulled to a stop on the overgrown grass in front of the cottage.

"You again." Mrs. Watts stood with the door only half open, as if she would resist asking them in, but then she stood back. "You'd better have news. Or my car."

The policemen stood on the doormat, hats in hand. "We won't stay, Mrs. Watts. We just wondered if you could tell us what you found in your husband's locker when you cleared it out."

She hesitated. "Nothing unexpected. His boiler suit, a towel, some toiletries, a couple of extra shirts. Why?"

Ames could feel, rather than see, the infinitesimal glance Terrell gave him. "We know he was planning to run off with that girl. We were wondering if there might have been anything in the locker that might have something to do with this."

Mrs. Watts frowned and stepped back. She looked behind her and then back at them. "He must have been planning it for months. I thought it might be—" She stopped, then said, "If he was with someone, you have your murderer then, don't you?" She glared at them.

Had she been about to say who she thought it might be? Ames wondered. "I'm not at liberty to say, ma'am. Now did you find girl's clothing among the items from the locker?"

Her lips moved marginally into an expression of disgust. "No, I did not. If you must know, I can't bear to have his things around. I've been burning everything."

"And you had no notion prior to our telling you that he might have been planning to go off with anyone?" Ames asked.

"No. Why should I? Do you think I would have let it happen if I'd known?"

"I wonder if you've made sure to check the pockets in the garments?" Terrell asked suddenly.

"To see if there was any money in them? Ha! He'd have it squirrelled away for that hussy, wouldn't he? As it happens, we've been going short lately."

"I meant more—did you find any notes, names, destination, receipts, that sort of thing?"

"Not a thing," she said. "What about the car?"

"The trouble is, we haven't located the keys yet. I'm not sure if a locksmith can make one, but that might take some time. We could have it towed back here, but unless you have spare keys, it won't do you much good," Ames said.

She sighed. "Good day, then."

TINA LOOKED AT the two men, her jaw working, her lips clamped, her right hand holding a spanner in a manner Ames was far from easy about.

"If I'm to understand you, you think I went into town to two different shops and bought myself some fancy clothes to run off with a man I hated even more than I hate you right now?" She turned when she heard her father come into the bay with a cup of coffee. "It's all right, Dad. I'll take care of this."

Mr. Van Eyck paused, looking anxiously at the three people talking in the dim light next to the black Chrysler he'd been working on, and then turned away. Tina glared at the police.

"I'm sorry, Miss Van Eyck, we have to ask. The fact is, someone fitting your description was seen buying the clothes that we found in the trunk of Watts's car. A car in which he was subsequently found murdered." Ames could feel the bitter overtones of his delivery and wished he could be dispassionate, but his failure to find any record of a sixteen-year-old Tina reporting an assault to the police now loomed large. She could have made that up as well.

"So I murdered him now, too, did I? Which is it? Did I murder him or plan to run off with him?"

Terrell cleared his throat. "We are only trying to eliminate people from our inquiry, Miss Van Eyck. Do you have a recent photo we could use? That should take care of it for now. We can show it to the dress-shop people."

"Unbelievable!" she said, storming off.

The two men stood with their hands behind their backs, both wondering if she was coming back, and then she exploded back into the bay holding a small, folded identity card.

"It's my Auxiliary Territorial Service identification. I'd like it back, if you please." She pointedly handed it to Terrell, who flipped it open. The picture inside was of a younger Tina, her head slightly tilted, wearing a khaki cap, her hair cut shoulder length, the curls ballooning out from under the cap behind her ears. It was a good likeness.

"One more thing, Miss Van Eyck. Have you given any thought to who you might have talked to at the police station? Have you remembered anything since we spoke?" Terrell asked.

Here Tina looked down. "I thought I was so close the other day. I remember he was a big man. I feel like it's a Scottish name, but I've tried all 'Mac' anythings and nothing is sticking."

"Could you keep at it and give us a call if anything comes to you?" he said.

They were about to return to the car when Ames stopped. "Miss Van Eyck, do you keep rat poison on the premises?"

"I don't know. You'd have to ask my dad. Dad! Have you got a minute? The sergeant here wants to know if we keep rat poison here." She did not disguise the sarcasm in her tone.

"I ALMOST BELIEVE she made him up," Ames said glumly when they were bumping up the road from the garage. "The policeman she supposedly told about the rape." Even as he said it, he couldn't believe her capable of that kind of lie. She was short tempered, standoffish, yes, but in his heart, he believed she was a straight shooter.

"She provided us with her identity card with no difficulty." Terrell hesitated. "Can I ask, sir, why you seem so, well, off kilter with this one? It seems sort of personal somehow. No offence meant."

Ames sighed. "None taken. If you must know, I dated her. Well, once. I took her to Darling's wedding. If this gets out to anyone at the station, I'll be coming for you!" He groaned inwardly at having said even this much to Terrell, new as he was and a subordinate.

"You can certainly count on me to keep your personal confidences, sir."

"I had been hoping to go out with her again, if you must know, not that she seemed inclined. And now there's this. I just don't think we can afford to trust her."

"I must say, I find her credible, sir. Her anger at him seems very genuine, so I can't imagine she would have been planning to run off with him, especially as he'd apparently promised Ada Finch he wanted to run off with her."

"Angry enough to kill him, though?" Ames asked. "Her father said they don't keep poison, but he may not know if she bought any. We should have searched the premises."

"See, I think you might be overcompensating because you want to be impartial. If this were someone else, who'd just freely given us an identity paper to show the shopkeepers, what would your response be?"

"All right, all right. You've made your point. I would assume they must be innocent. I'm not even sure I believe she did anything, either. But we do have to keep an open mind. We can't leave any stone unturned."

An open mind includes not assuming someone is guilty, Terrell thought, but he didn't say it. Sleet was turning to wet snow, and he was forced to drive slowly as the windshield wipers struggled to keep a triangular patch of window clear.

"And Darling is lying around like a grandee in the sun, not a care in the world," Ames muttered.

———

REX HOLDEN WAS a patient man. As he saw it, he was old, he'd accumulated what he wanted in life, and he was entitled to live off his successes and enjoy what he could. He'd enjoyed his wife Meg very much. She was giddy and pretty and never, ever difficult. And she showed him affection that he'd never expected to know again after his wife of forty years had died at the end of the war. He'd warded off the dire warnings of his country club friends, ignored the raised eyebrow of the justice of the peace, and had really quite enjoyed showering gifts and money on his young wife.

But the recent increasing spate of absences had raised some misgivings in him. He had been sitting by the pool with the newspaper and had watched his neighbours in number 26 talking. Now *that* was a beautiful woman, and she had been a champion when that man had been shot, he thought. So kind to Meg, so practical. He could see, could almost feel, the depth of the bond between her and her husband. At the restaurant they talked intently, laughing or serious, but always talking. Not like so many couples who sat silently looking away from each other, having long ago exhausted any conversation.

He had to confess, he missed that close companionship. He'd had that with his first wife, Velma. And he had to admit he was beginning to mind Meg skittering about all the time, God only knew where.

As if his thoughts took form, Meg appeared at the gate to the pool, dressed in a purple suit that hugged her generous figure attractively. She lifted her hand and twiddled her fingers in his direction.

"Hello, sweetie! How's the water?"

He couldn't see her eyes behind her dark glasses, but

he felt himself relax at the sight of her. Maybe they could have a little talk now.

"It's grand. Want to come in?"

"I just have to get some money for the cab. He's waiting outside. Do you have your wallet with you?"

Holden reached over to the side table where his room key, wallet, and an empty glass that had held lemonade were placed and extracted a couple of dollars.

Meg hurried over and took the money. "I'll be right back, sweetie, and come and lie on that deck chair. Don't let anyone else take it!"

Holden watched her going back to the door of the hotel, her perfect legs in the perfect silk stockings he kept her supplied with. But he did wonder. Where had she been this time?

LANE WAS BACK in the laundry area with Chela. If the haughty front-desk people only knew the number of times she'd been here, she thought. They were sitting side by side on wooden chairs, in the shade of the oleander. The picture of Griffin was lying on Chela's lap. Darling had come with Lane, and when Chela had indeed identified the man, he'd retreated to the room to telephone Martinez.

"So he really is a criminal."

"I don't really know for sure. Certainly this is a police picture, but I don't know if he's been convicted of anything in a court." Lane said. "The one good thing is that it might be enough you have identified him; hopefully Martinez won't ever need to talk to you."

Chela was about to answer when she looked up, startled.

An equally startled young man had swung the back gate open and had come up the three short steps, clearly not expecting to see anyone. He stopped abruptly and looked at them, and then looked up toward the door into the building.

Chela stood up, exerting some authority in her own realm. "Can I help you, sir?"

"No." He hesitated, clearly nonplussed. "I mean ... no." He looked anxiously again at the doorway, as if expecting someone to come through.

"The front door to the hotel is over that way," Chela said. She had moved to the gate and was holding it open.

Without a word, the man turned and went back onto the street.

"That's him," Chela whispered, back in her chair by Lane. "The younger one."

"He clearly was expecting to meet her," Lane agreed.

Chela shook her head. "She's got her nice old husband, and she's got him, and now she's got this guy." She held up the photo.

As if on cue, Meg Holden came through the door and, like the young man, stopped dead at seeing Lane and Chela. "Oh," she said. "I ..." She looked toward the gate. "I came to see if you found my ... my bracelet. I think it fell off the dresser, and I can't find it."

"I didn't clean your room, ma'am, but I can ask the girl who did," Chela said.

Meg Holden, who had been glancing nervously toward the street, seemed only to be half attending, but at the last moment she looked at Chela and then blanched, putting her hand to her chest. She opened and closed her mouth as if to speak, but no sound came out. Her eyes were riveted on the photo Chela was still holding.

THAT EVENING ON the rooftop patio, Lane and Darling stood together with matching gin and tonics, looking at the setting sun.

"Would a person get tired of having to see that every evening?" he wondered.

"We should ask a local. I don't think I would. I don't get tired of looking at the lake in its many moods. In fact, I almost miss it, cold and dark as the winter is up there. You know that moment on a cold morning when the air is fresh on your face and you are looking at the skeleton of a tree against the grey, brooding sky?"

"I confess I have not parsed the winter views so finely. In town, I have been used to looking at murky smoke rising from my neighbour's chimney across the alley. It is not as uplifting as what you are describing."

"Look, there's Mr. Holden all on his own. I wonder if Meg has had the vapours and taken to her bed. I've never seen anyone so shocked as when she saw that mug shot of Mr. Griffin. I don't think we need any more proof they're connected somehow." Lane began to move toward Holden.

Darling wanted to utter a warning, but it was too late. There she was, smiling and wishing their neighbour a good evening.

"You remember Mr. Holden, darling? His wife is feeling quite unwell, so I've asked him to join us for dinner."

"Splendid," said Darling, raising his glass with feigned enthusiasm.

Inside the dining room, dinner ordered, Lane rested her chin on her hands and smiled at Rex Holden. "I'm sorry Mrs. Holden can't be here. But I'm sure they can take something to her room."

"I guess she's still upset over watching that poor fellow get shot," Holden said. "I thought she was getting over it some. She loves to shop, so I've been encouraging her to go. It seems to cheer her up."

Lane paused. She could think of no suitable response to Meg being cheered up by shopping. "You know I never asked where you are from," she said.

"Just up the road in Phoenix. Meg's got an aunt down here who's not doing so well, so I thought we could make a little vacation out of visiting her. She's been seeing her quite a lot. She's not well off, so fortunately I'm able to help out. Meg's moved her into a better house and made sure she gets regular medical care."

"That's wonderful," Lane said, smiling warmly. She studiously ignored Darling's penetrating gaze. "Lovely dinner," she continued. "I've never had chicken fricassee before."

"I know people wonder," Mr. Holden said. "I'm sure you must. She is younger than me, I'll give you that. I was happily married for forty years, and I don't mind saying I was lonely when Velma died. Meg came along just when I thought I'd be alone for the rest of my life. She's a little rough around the edges. I can see my pals at the club looking at her. They can't decide whether to look down on her or be jealous!"

"Well, I think it's rather wonderful, don't you, darling?"

"**DO YOU THINK** you'll marry again if I die?" Lane asked, sitting in front of the mirror in her new silk dressing gown. She'd been urged to buy it by her friend Angela in King's Cove, who had said no woman should be without a trousseau on her honeymoon. It was fine in this climate, but Lane wondered how useful it would be in the dead of a snowy Kootenay winter. Her warm, thick flannel dressing gown was more the thing.

Darling, who was already in bed with a book on his chest—one he wasn't reading because he found the sight of his wife brushing her hair quite transfixing—shrugged thoughtfully. "Only if I can find a woman with hair that colour. And as much as I look forward to that, I'd urge you to reconsider putting yourself in any position likely to lead to your death. You have a weakness for it that I don't approve of."

The banging on their door made them both jump. Darling looked at the clock: ten after ten. Lane pulled her dressing gown across her and tied the belt as she hurried to answer the door.

Rex Holden was standing on the mat, looking distraught and breathing heavily in a way that didn't sound at all healthy. "She's gone," he managed. "Packed up everything and gone."

CHAPTER TWENTY-ONE

June 1936

JANE VAN EYCK CONTEMPLATED HER two hours of sleep. She was slumped at the kitchen table, feeling as if all the curling pins she'd put in her hair the night before were boring into her skull. She lifted the mug of black coffee she'd had cooling in front of her and drank. It was bitter. She pulled the curtains to watch the gentle coming of dawn along the lake, pink and fresh, the sun hidden by the mountains but already casting a warm glow into the sky. Nature goes on, she thought, in spite of our little human troubles. Deriving no comfort from it, she turned away from the view and looked down the hall toward where her family slept. There was no getting around it: she was dying.

She wondered now if she'd been right not to tell him. It might have been less lonely. But then he would have had a whole year of anxiety and misery, said a practical voice in her head. It was better this way. In fact, if only she could manage to go away and die on her own, everyone could be spared. As it was, she didn't really know how it would come. She had known all along. She knew the doctor would want to tell her husband and not her, but she demanded to know and swore him to secrecy. She couldn't bear the thought of her husband having to cope with her death.

The doctor had told her she would become weak and that would be the time to go into the hospital. They could make her comfortable there, ease her passing. The doctor had disapproved in the strongest terms of her decision not to tell her husband. He'd said he had half a mind to break his promise and do it himself.

At least put your affairs in order, he'd said. Jane looked around the small kitchen and through into the sitting room, where light was beginning to colour the walls. She had so few affairs to put in order. The biggest affairs were her husband and Tina, and they were in order. Tina seemed, though Jane could not for a minute understand it, to enjoy working on cars alongside her father. That would be especially good when she had gone. They had a bond. They could support each other.

The one affair to put in order, she thought, was telling him what had happened to Tina. She wouldn't ask permission to break her promise. Someone on this earth needed to know in case, one day, Tina wasn't as okay as she so defiantly claimed to be.

———

AMES WAS SPENDING dawn at the beach, a quiet place with only the whispering lap of water to accompany his confusion. He sometimes came here to think after a sleepless night, and he usually had sleepless nights over some rocky problem with a girl. He picked up a handful of sand that wasn't covered with a patch of freezing snow from the late-night fall and tossed it into the still water along the edge, watching the wavelets moving out in a circle. Elephant Mountain, across the narrow band of water, was just beginning to light up. Topmost in his mind was that nothing could ever again be on the same footing with Tina Van Eyck. He thought of the day it had all started when he'd gone out to the garage on a flimsy pretext in the hopes of getting her to go out with him again. She'd rebuffed him completely, but then had laughed, made a joke, as if it still might be possible.

Now nothing was possible. The dress-shop keeper had looked at the photo and said, "Nope, not her. This woman had a thinner face." His own anxieties had been relieved by this proof that she had been telling the truth, but he had delivered a deathblow to any regard she might have for him. Had he done the right thing? Yes, he thought, he had. But had he done it the right way? He didn't think so. He'd failed absolutely to maintain the polite distance Darling seemed to manage so effortlessly.

Darling had arrested Miss Winslow on the suspicion of murder when they'd first met but had been so professional that a year and a half later they were actually married. Would he ever be like Darling? He'd been angry and afraid. Why? He'd felt betrayed, as if Tina had lied to him about who she was, and his resentment came out in every word he'd said to her and every look he'd given her. There would be no coming back from that. He stood in front of the lake now, pulling his overcoat tightly around himself, his heart wrestling with the conflicting feelings of uplift at the beauty of the morning and confusion about why it mattered so much to him that Tina would never speak to him again.

———

"POOR MAN," LANE said. "He's really in shock." They were the only people on the outside patio. The other guests were breakfasting inside because of the lingering chill in the morning air.

"Why would he keep that amount of money on him? Eight hundred dollars will get her quite far," Darling said.

Lane pulled her cardigan around her. "Brrr. I feel like we are putting on a brave Canadian face. It's not that warm out here."

"Buck up! The sun will start doing its job in no time. Look, I think you ought to tell Holden what you know."

"It's going to sound as if we've been spying on her the whole time, but of course, you're right. It's not fair to leave him ignorant of his wife's activities."

"And you haven't been spying?"

THEY FOUND HOLDEN'S suite door open, and Lane knocked gently on it.

"Mr. Holden?"

Holden came to the door with a folded shirt in his hand. "Just packing up. Might as well head back to Phoenix." He motioned them in. Two large leather suitcases were open on the bed. He tossed the shirt into one of them and then put his hands in his pockets and looked listlessly around the room. Even in his grief, he looked dapper, with a pressed white Egyptian cotton shirt and a dark blue silk scarf carefully tied at the neck.

"I just have to admit I've been had. My friends warned me, but I wouldn't hear a word said against her. My fault. What I don't understand is why she took off. She knew I was fond of her, and I would have supported her and left her nicely set up for that matter. I'm an old man. I don't pretend she really loved me, but I'm sure she appreciated the security I gave her. She's had a dreadful life. Grew up in awful poverty in Chicago. I can't help worrying about where she will go. Of course, if she runs out of money and comes back, I will probably take her back. I'll try to understand her a little better. We can make up, I'm sure of it."

Darling looked at Lane, and Lane cleared her throat.

"It is possible she did have somewhere to go," Lane began gently.

GALLOWAY WOKE FEELING groggy. His eyes were swollen and blurry, and he had a headache. He'd drunk too much and he knew it. In the light of the morning, he was unable to recapture the clarity he'd had the night before and now felt only a kind of messy confusion. He tried to stave off the growing sense of alarm this feeling was engendering.

Standing at the kitchen sink, he poured a glass of water

and winced at the acrid taste it had in his mouth. Morning sunlight was beginning to saturate the patio wall, and for a moment, he was comforted by what he had. He'd made it after all: assistant chief of police and, without a doubt, next in line for chief. He'd done that. He'd managed this house, his job, his wife. He'd done everything he had to. It had been laughably easy.

He turned away from the view of the patio with its orange trees and Talavera tiles and reached for the coffee pot. Immediately his mood darkened again, and for one moment he was almost able to name what he was feeling—he recoiled from it as he would from a burning building.

He started with the easy part of his list. He had Griffin. That wouldn't change, provided Martinez didn't mess the whole thing up. There was a promotion he shouldn't have encouraged, he thought bitterly. He'd go in today and nail down the loose ends. His confidence began to assert itself with the smell of the coffee percolating on the stove. He had always managed to get what he wanted, what he needed. That ability would never leave him. After that, he'd tackle the hospital. Someone there knew something—he was sure of it.

———

The day before

"HEY!"

Startled, Hidalgo scrambled up clumsily and knocked over the chair, trying to shake the shock and sleep out of his head. What was she doing there?

"I've seen you, you know. What do you think you're

doing?"

In desperation he pointed toward the field. "*Yo soy—*"

"Uh huh. Don't try that Spanish stuff on me. You work for him, don't you?"

"Who?" he tried.

"My husband. You think I don't see you following me around? How long have you been spying on me?"

Hidalgo looked anxiously across the road to see if anyone had come out to listen. Mr. Griffin would kill him as it was for blowing his cover. She was pretty when she got mad. Her blue eyes were flashing, and her blond hair fluttered around her face like a halo. She was wearing a red sundress that certainly did justice to her figure.

"I've been here since you and him," he nodded his head toward the hotel, "came down here."

To his amazement she blanched and stepped back, nearly unbalancing on a rock. She looked up and down the road. "The whole time?"

"Yes, ma'am."

"And you report to him, everything you've seen?"

"The truth is, I don't see much, so not much to tell." He wasn't going to tell her he'd seen and reported the young man.

"You're lying. I can see you are."

"He's just looking after you, miss. Making sure you're all right."

"And you're lying again. Well, I bet he'd be interested in the fact that I've seen you. Sticking out like a sore thumb isn't a good quality in a mob spy. But we ain't going to play it like that." She began to pace, covering up a growing panic. "You stay here. I'm coming out with an envelope with one hundred dollars in it. And then I'm going to tell you what you're going to say him."

MEG WAS REALLY frightened. After talking to her husband's man, she had sought refuge in a little lounge off the silent, carpeted hallway. She had to get away. She knew that now. He couldn't be trusted. He'd kill her next. Taking a couple of deep breaths, she closed her eyes and tried to still the pounding of her heart. She couldn't do this sort of thing anymore. Her eyes flew open. She looked at her watch and put her hands firmly on the arms of the chair she was in. She knew where his money was. He was going out to meet, God, she couldn't remember who, but that gave her time. She'd leave here, hide out for a day in case they checked the bus and train stations, and then she'd be off, away from him for good. With a new resolution, she pushed herself out of the chair and walked quickly back to the villa. Chicago. She could start there.

GRIFFIN FROWNED AT the memory of his shock and subsequent rage. It hadn't been his finest hour. That's when you make mistakes.

He thought about her now. It wasn't like he hadn't enjoyed a fling or two. There was a lot of temptation when you ran a popular restaurant with entertainment. He and Meg, they'd been partners right from the get-go. She'd been good at the job. What was a little transgression in the bigger scheme of things? The idea of Florida rose again. Just the two of them in an apartment looking out at the ocean, enjoying a retirement they'd more than earned. Or he could start a little restaurant there, legit. She could be at the front till she started to lose her figure.

Almost laughing, he straightened up. The answer was right in front of him the whole time. He'd put his money into Florida real estate. Get a start on that retirement plan. He put his Cuban out carefully, saving the remains for later, and pulled open a drawer, looking for his notepad. He found it under a pile of papers on the desk. Just as he managed to locate a pencil, he heard someone in the hall, followed by a tentative knock.

"Yes, what is it?"

Hidalgo pushed the door open and hesitated. "She's left, sir. She got in a cab outside the hotel with two suitcases. I did follow it, like you asked."

Griffin frowned. "And you followed the cab to where?"

"I lost them."

"You lost them? Are you a complete imbecile? No one could lose a cab in Tucson!"

"I must have been speeding. I got pulled over. By the time the cop had written the ticket it was gone."

———

GALLOWAY LEANED AGAINST the car with his arms crossed, his dark glasses protecting his eyes from the glare of the sun. The hospital loomed before him. He hadn't been on the beat for years. This was a job for a rookie. A guy like Bevan. Taking in a deep breath, he made for the back entrance.

The older maintenance man working there looked at his badge expressionlessly. "What can I do for you?"

"I want to know who was on the early shift last Sunday"

"Can I ask why?"

Feigning an affability he did not feel, he said, "We're pursuing a missing persons case. Last known to be at this hospital."

The man, who had been the shift supervisor that very day, nodded. "I think you want Smitty. He mentioned seeing someone leaving before it was even light. None of our business what they do up there, but it might be something. He's not on shift till Thursday, though, if you want to talk to him."

"I'll take his address, thanks," Galloway said. He was feeling the same sense of growing satisfaction he always had when he knew he'd get what he needed. He was like a damn Mountie, he thought. He always got his man.

———

O'BRIEN PICKED UP the phone to call upstairs. When Ames answered, O'Brien started to say, "Ames," but corrected himself—the kid had earned his stripes after all. "Sergeant, I think I may have something here. I went back to the file room with one of the boys because I thought it could use a sweep and a dusting. For good measure I had him make sure all the files were in order, not that anyone goes in there much, especially for the pre-war files. Anyway, he found a '35 file in the '33 section. An assault report. The officer had written the name of the alleged assailant, then crossed it out. It apparently didn't pan out. Someone wrote 'no foundation' and signed it off."

"I'll be right down," Ames said.

"I hoped you'd say that," O'Brien murmured as he hung up the phone and settled his bulk more comfortably on his chair. He adjusted his glasses to see if he could remember whose signature that was. He could hear Ames clattering down the stairs. Oh, to be a young eager beaver, he thought, with no envy whatsoever.

"Let's see," Ames said, holding out his hand. There it was. "Tina Van Eyck, aged sixteen, reported assault by local man B. Watts. No parent, no corroboration, no foundation." "Who is this?" he asked, pointing at the scribble that constituted the signature.

"I was just trying to figure that out. I recognize the signature, but I just can't remember who it belonged to."

Ames peered at it closely. "It certainly isn't *Mac* anything. Miss Van Eyck thought the name was Scottish. This is just a scribble. And whoever it was didn't bother printing his name where he was supposed to."

"I'll mull it over. It might come to me. I hope not in the middle of the night. I like my sleep."

Ames smiled briefly. O'Brien liked all the comforts. "I wonder why it was misfiled like that?"

"Well, that anyone could do," O'Brien pointed out. "It wasn't the only one. Nothing so bad as two years, but there were a couple that needed re-filing. That room has terrible lighting."

"Thanks. This is something, anyway." Ames started back up the stairs when he heard O'Brien exclaim.

"No, hold up."

When he turned around O'Brien was looking at the signature again.

"That's Paul. It's gotta be."

"Paul?" asked Ames, coming back down.

"Sergeant Galloway. I told you about him. Took Darling under his wing when he came here."

"What was he like?" Ames asked. He'd certainly ignored a genuine assault report.

"He was okay. He had a thing about not wasting police time. Worked hard. Unmarried, so he had nothing to go home to. He probably annoyed more than one member of the public because, when he got his teeth on the bit, he'd really go at it till he got his man. Good rate of conviction."

"Why did he leave? When did he leave?"

"He left in '37. As to why, your guess is as good as mine. Said it was too cold and too small. Knowing him, I'm guessing he didn't find the women glamorous enough. Ambitious fellow, all the way around."

"He doesn't sound like the sort of person Inspector Darling would take to," Ames said doubtfully.

"That's true enough. I don't think Darling picked up too many of his habits. But he was younger and wanted to do a good job, and Sergeant Galloway seemed to really like him. But he was like a pit bull when he thought he had someone."

"A zealous cop like that could make mistakes," Ames said. He was thinking of his own recent myopia.

"No, he was pretty solid. Wait. I mistake me. There was an arson conviction that got turned over after he left. I think there was another fire, and Darling in his usual plodding way found the right guy. But the evidence looked good enough. No one would blame Galloway for that mistake."

Ames sat thoughtfully at his desk, blaming Galloway for his mistake with Tina. He wondered if he should try to reach Darling and ask him about the guy—but he knew that if he did, he'd get an earful about interfering with Lane and Darling's honeymoon yet again. On the other hand, Tina had been ill-treated and he, at least, could right justice, even if only a little, after stumbling about making such a mess of it.

CHAPTER TWENTY-TWO

"YOU'RE ALL I NEED," DARLING said with asperity into the phone. "Now what do you want?"

"I'm sorry, sir. I couldn't think of another way," Ames said.

"Waiting till I got back? Solving it yourself? Putting O'Brien or Terrell on to it? Your lack of imagination is astounding. We are back in less than a week. What couldn't wait?"

Ames plunged in, bringing Darling up to date with the developments, especially as they involved Tina Van Eyck, which, in spite of himself, Darling found interesting. "So, I went on a search for the file and I couldn't find it, but O'Brien found it misfiled. It turns out she had reported the assault to someone called Galloway who dismissed her out of hand. I think you knew him, before he left. I just wondered if he ever mentioned the case, or if there's anything you could tell me about him. Why did he leave here?"

Darling's mouth worked. He'd been thinking quite a lot about Galloway himself. He too, given what he knew now, wondered if there was anything more to Galloway's abrupt departure in '37.

"Sir?"

"Yes, Ames, I'm here. Off the top, I can tell you he never spoke of the case. I am heartily sorry he would have dismissed a report of a violent assault. Was she ..." but he wasn't able to finish his question.

"Yes, sir," Ames said shortly.

"And this is related to your current investigation?"

"Yes. The man involved has been murdered."

"I see. Do you think Miss Van Eyck is implicated?"

Ames felt the air go out of him. This was really the crux of what he thought of as his own misdeeds. "I honestly don't think so, but I've been very determined to not let the fact that I know her blind me. It was a decade ago, but he's been up to no good recently, apparently planning to run off with a local high-school girl. I just feel awfully bad because I had to question Tina, and I wasn't at my best. I should have let Terrell do it. He's good and he has no stake in this, if you see what I mean. Now I just feel I owe it to her to get to the bottom of it."

"Ah. I gather she's not talking to you, then. It's a rotten thing to have happened to her, and having you blundering around being officious must have compounded the offence."

"It didn't help," Ames admitted. "We did have one lead about a woman fitting her description, but it turned out to be someone else. It doesn't put her right out of the picture, I suppose, but it's becoming less likely."

"I wish I could help. I can tell you this," Darling said, "if she'd seen any other policeman in our force, she'd have been treated differently. At least, I hope so. She just had bad luck." Darling hesitated, looking through the bedroom curtain at the hotel guests strolling in the garden. The sun had finally warmed the place up, and the guests were in summer clothes again. Should he tell Ames he had Paul Galloway right to hand? He was vaguely aware of some embarrassment at his having chosen Tucson for their honeymoon partly on the basis of Galloway having been an old comrade. A comrade with clay feet.

"Look, Ames, keep your eye on the prize here. You're trying to find out who killed Watts. I can tell you for absolutely certain it wasn't Galloway, however repellent he is. As it happens, he is the assistant chief of police here in Tucson and has been here the whole time. So, who have you got lined up?"

"He's there, sir? How is it that—"

"Never mind. He just is."

"I see." He didn't. "Well, there's the father of the teen-aged girl and—"

"No, Ames, a rhetorical question. I don't actually want to know. I'm on my honeymoon. You and Terrell can run along and sort it."

"Yes, sir." Before he could stop himself, Ames added, "Did you used to gamble sir?"

"Certainly not."

"O'Brien told me that Sergeant Galloway seemed to be an okay guy who stood people drinks after work and gambled a bit. I was wondering, if you played cards with him anytime, you might know who else he played with. I'm wondering if he played cards with the dead guy. When he was still alive, obviously."

Darling almost smiled at his end of the line. This was how he did it, he thought. Ames bumbled around and then asked an interesting question.

"Sorry, I can't help you. I really never took to it. But it's not the dimmest question you ever asked, I'll say that."

Darling hung up the phone and tapped his fingers on it thoughtfully. Galloway was an absolute ass—that was plain and had been all along. So, why had he left Nelson so suddenly in '37? Just the weather?

Darling went back to the pool to join Lane, his mind full of grim thoughts about how much more disreputable Galloway could prove to be. He found her looking contentedly into middle distance, her book closed on the table next to her.

"Finished it, have you?" he asked, settling onto the deck chair.

"I have. I shall have to go find another, though I won't find another Dorothy L. Sayers, which is sad, because it's what I'm in the mood for now. Actually, I'd better find something short and snappy. Our Arizona idyll is almost over. Who was on the telephone? I admit I keep expecting your chum Galloway to call up and shout angry questions about where his wife is."

"It was Ames, but funnily enough, Galloway did come into it."

Lane sat up and looked at him. "He never! How?"

Darling related what he had learned from Ames. "I bet poor Amesy could use the Winslow shoulder to cry on just

284

now. Tina's is very cold at the moment, and he feels, not without reason, that he's made a mess of everything."

"Poor Tina! An experience like that at sixteen and having to soldier through it for the rest of her life only to have it all exposed in this horrible way. No wonder she's angry; she has felt no control over any of it, either then or now."

"Is that what is making her angry, do you think? Having no control, not just Ames's inept approach to the whole thing? I never considered that," Darling said thoughtfully.

"It would make me angry. In fact, I'd say not having control of their own lives in general is what makes women angry. Into every woman's life a bungling official must fall, but not being able to be in charge of how she gets to deal with it must be absolutely infuriating. And in Tina's case, she was barely out of childhood, and has spent all those years finding a way to live with this horrible experience, and then it all comes spilling out for everyone to see."

Darling was silent, digesting this. It was a new, discomfiting thought to him. How much control men had of their own lives, and those of others, and how little many women had by contrast. Lane had worked hard to regain control of her life, from her family, from British Intelligence, from her manipulative wartime lover, Angus Dunn. He felt a flush of gratitude at her agreeing to give up any measure of her independence to marry him, for suddenly it seemed the greatest gift he'd ever received.

"A man like Galloway," Lane said, interrupting Darling's thoughts, "abuses his wife, dismisses the suffering of a young girl. That is the stuff of a bad man. I wonder, don't you know, if there's more. What's on those photos Priscilla took? I almost can't imagine how a man who behaves that way toward women could be honest. If he already believes he has a right to behave that way to his wife, he must believe he has the right to other things as well—the petty cash, for example, or anything in *his* police station or even *his town*."

"Can I interject into this brilliant analysis, that I love you?"

She smiled. "You always say that."

"I always mean it, now more than ever. I've been wondering something similar," Darling said. "I've been wondering why he really left Nelson. Looking back, his departure now seems somewhat precipitous—though I may be imagining that because of what I'm learning. Ames may have stumbled, in his puppy dog way, into a useful thought: he wondered if Galloway's gambling was an issue and if the thoroughly repellent man who is now the corpse in the case Ames is working gambled with him."

"That might account for why Galloway sent Tina off with a flea in her ear."

"Exactly. I still can't get over how spectacularly wrong I was about him. How could I, even as young and callow as I was, be fooled by a slick, arrogant man like that?"

"Darling, I wouldn't spend a single calorie worrying about that. You are with a woman who wasted years on a man just like that. I think it's a good indication that being dazzled and fooled can happen to anybody. In fact," she said, brightening, "anybody who is young and optimistic and wants to believe only the good in the world. The trick, I think, is not to be embittered by the experience, but to be able—though older, sadder, wiser—to still love someone and be optimistic in their company."

"Is that you saying you love me?"

"It could well be," she said, getting up and kissing him gently on the top of the head. "I'm going to take this book back and look for a quick Agatha Christie. Then I think we should consider going somewhere in town for a bit of a sight-see and some lunch at one of these Mexican places. We've not much time left here."

———

TERRELL AND AMES were at a window booth at the café.

"I can see why you always get the grilled ham and cheese sandwich. It's hard to beat," Terrell said, making rapid inroads on his. He was looking forward to April coming to tell them what sort of pie they had on today.

"Funny Galloway being in the very place the boss has gone for his honeymoon. But the inspector is right. If Galloway didn't actually kill Watts, he's not really relevant, except I can't shake the question of why he dismissed Miss Van Eyck like that."

"You're thinking he gambled with Watts and was covering for his buddy," Terrell said.

"Yes, exactly. But even then, it seems like a very long line between that and his being found dead a week ago. That's more than ten years later."

"You're right there," Terrell said, popping the last of his sandwich into his mouth. "He's been lying low being a respectable husband and father, but maybe he hasn't really changed, and sooner or later he was going to want to relive his youth or something by suddenly going after his work buddy's daughter, Ada."

Ames nodded. "Exactly. So in that situation, Craig Finch would possibly want to kill him, and so might his own wife for that matter."

"But don't forget, he decides to revisit the Van Eyck garage, wanting to know if Tina ever talked. I wish we knew why."

"I need more coffee today. I have not been sleeping well," Ames said, lifting his cup toward April, who was wiping the counter. "Thanks, April."

April nodded, filling Terrell's cup as well. "Care to know about our pies today, Constable Terrell?"

"That I would," Terrell said.

"Apple and pumpkin."

"Pumpkin sounds good. My gran used to make it. Let's see how this holds up."

"Really," Ames said when April had retreated to fetch the pie. "You two are as obvious as the side of a barn." And on consideration, he wondered if it wasn't such a bad idea. He and April had had a brief relationship, which he had ended by dating Violet Harding, another disaster. He admired April, after all, but she wasn't really for him. Maybe Terrell, an honest, kind man who so far appeared to be a darned good policeman, would be a better match.

"I'll pop down to the rail yard and see if anyone remembers a regular card game. That at least might explain why Galloway ignored"—he almost said Tina—"Miss Van Eyck. She might appreciate knowing it wasn't her, if you see what

288

I mean. And who knows, maybe some of Watts's absences were for card games. Perhaps he cheated enough to have someone want to kill him."

———

GRIFFIN WAS BROODING in his office. The restaurant had done good business the night before, the card games in the back room were as full as ever, but even as he was smiling and shaking hands and patting backs, he had felt the dark shadow of worry. The court case was in two days, his wife had left, and he had felt an unwelcome touch of insolence in the man he'd put in charge of keeping an eye on her. He was not used to feeling like he hadn't quite got a hold on things.

He pulled open the bottom drawer of his desk and took out the bottle, splashing some of its golden liquid into the glass in front of him. Surprisingly, as he analyzed things with the help of the bourbon, it was Hidalgo's behaviour that most puzzled him. Had he detected a hint of satisfaction in his spy, as if he was happy she had given him the slip? At least the court case was going to be fine. It was a nuisance to have to go sit in court, but there was no evidence, and it might even be great publicity for his business. His wife would be back. She'd always come back. She'd run out of cash. That gigolo she'd taken up with was no doubt broke, so he was no real threat. He refused to think about that slip-up. Best focus on her. Her stupidity was in leaving Holden. What the hell had she been thinking?

He gulped what was in his glass and winced. He'd come to the edge of the cliff where his control of events was shaky. His rage over her had propelled him to make his first really big mistake. He still teased at his anxiety over how near he'd come to catastrophe. Though he'd been saved by what he could only call a miracle, it was the fact that he hadn't engineered the miracle that was causing much of the disquiet. He'd nearly banned one of his best men over it, and now, for reasons he couldn't understand, a man he'd trusted completely, who'd never put a foot wrong—hell, he'd put him in charge of his wife, for God's sake—had a tone he couldn't quite put his finger on.

With a wave of anxiety, he wondered now if he should have permanently gotten rid of the guy, as reliable as he'd been over the years. He shook his head and pulled open the drawer again. The one thing he learned from his dad was that you can't litter the place with bodies. In the long run, one of them will always come back to haunt you. He held up his glass to his dear old dad, who'd had to die so that he might live smart.

CHAPTER TWENTY-THREE

DARLING AND LANE CLIMBED INTO the cab at the front of the inn, and Darling gave the cabby the instructions. They were just pulling into the narrow street when Lane saw a bank of clouds beginning to pile up in the west.

"Do you think it will rain today?" she asked the cabby. "It does seem cooler. I wonder if I should get my cardigan?"

The cabby stopped, backed up a few yards, and parked near the steps to the front door.

"That's a good idea, ma'am. It can get cold if it rains. The hotel might have some umbrellas too."

Lane got out of the car. A movement in the row of cars that was parked farther up the street caught her eye. Was the car blue? She shook her head, surprised, and hurried in to collect a sweater and umbrellas.

Once on the road again, she glanced out the back window. No flash of blue. It had been two years since the war had ended. Would she ever get over her professional vigilance? They were deposited on Church Avenue near the courthouse and given instructions for a pleasant historical walkabout and a suggestion for an authentic Mexican restaurant nearby.

"Now," said Darling when they were standing gazing up at the courthouse. "What's going on?"

"It's all these men coming and going. It's clearly worried Chela, especially when she learned one of them is a criminal." She tried, even as she was talking about it, to put her finger on why it worried her so much. "I mean, out here in the open air, it really is just probably typical misbehaviour you'd get at any hotel. I think I let her make me feel a bit jumpy. I mean, for a moment I even thought we were being followed from the hotel. The whole thing is ridiculous."

Darling weighed this. Lane had been trained in whatever the heck it was intelligence people had to do. He'd not known her to be ridiculous about anything. More disturbing to him was that it triggered an already brewing misgiving of his own, namely that trouble would come from Lane's having helped Priscilla escape. He turned to her.

"I've never known you to be ridiculous. What made you think someone might be following us? Come, let's walk around this confection of a building and see it from all angles." He guided them along the front of the courthouse, but he began to watch the street.

"It's just that when we stopped and went back to the hotel to fetch my cardigan, I saw what I thought was a blue car beginning to pull out and then stop as well. I told myself it was errant nonsense, of course."

"Not errant enough not to keep an eye on the rear window, I couldn't help noticing."

"Yes, but who and why would anyone be following us?"

"I don't know. You were witness to a murder, you kidnapped the assistant chief of police's wife, you've been spying on a guest who might be associated with a mobster ..."

Lane laughed. "I have not been spying on the guests. I just stumbled on that woman and her lover, and the rest was just Paúl's sister worrying. And I can see you are scanning the horizon in search of enemies. Come. Let's finish our tour of these lovely old buildings and find that restaurant before it starts raining. I propose to leave you over coffee and a newspaper after lunch and pop into a few local shops. You will be spared every horror associated with shopping."

As per her promise, Lane left Darling at their small window table with coffee and the local newspaper. Darling turned to the crime-watch section and learned that Ivy and Edward Renwick had been arraigned subsequent to the death of Jack Renwick, Ivy's husband and Edward's brother, at an expensive local hotel. It interested him that Ivy Renwick had been released on a sizeable but unnamed bail on the condition that she remain in Tucson, but Ned Renwick had been remanded in custody. What did this mean? Had Martinez found stronger evidence linking him to the killing? According to the article, Edward had lied about being in Wisconsin when the murder took place, and there was some evidence of an association between the wife of the dead man and her brother-in-law. The reporter had also managed to get hold of the fact there'd been a poorly hidden dispute between the two brothers over the ownership of their father's electric company.

This certainly put any possible involvement of Meg Holden and any of her improbable lovers into further doubt. He noted also that James Griffin would be on trial in two days on corruption charges related to his restaurant. He wondered about going to the public gallery for that. It might be interesting to see how the American system worked. His mind wandered further to what the relationship might be between Meg Holden and Griffin. He ordered more coffee and looked at his watch. Lane had been gone for over forty minutes, and he quailed at having to prolong his stay nursing cups of coffee for much longer.

Twenty minutes later, Darling paid the bill, got up, and went out onto the street. The promised rain had not yet materialized, but the afternoon felt ominously dark. Ought he to go looking for her? She would come back and be annoyed to find him not there. He moved slowly along the street looking into shop windows, trying to still his growing misgivings.

After a further half hour, Darling had moved from growing annoyance to actual anxiety. He looked up and then down the street, locked in indecision. He had no idea where she might have gone, but he was increasingly certain she would not have stayed away as long as this. She was much too courteous to make him wait. People passed him, bound who knew where, with parcels and friends, chatting and smiling, some on their own with worried faces. Two young women were laughing uncontrollably and, in his mind, were untroubled. He felt the envy of the burdened. None of them was Lane.

Would she have gone back to the inn? He could scarcely imagine she would have gone back without coming to fetch him. Well, it was the one solid move he could make. He crossed the street, breaking into a trot because the streetcar was coming faster than he bargained for, and went into a phone booth on the corner. He fumbled with the phone book, found the number for the hotel, and fished in his pocket for change. Worried he might have missed Lane at the restaurant, he looked through the phone box windows at the street. He found a nickel and put it into the machine, waited, and then dialled. His head swivelled when he saw a young woman pass. She wasn't Lane. The wait seemed interminable.

"Santa Cruz Inn. Good afternoon." An efficient, businesslike voice.

"Hello. This is Inspector Frederick Darling. I'm staying in number 26 with my wife."

The voice warmed up. "Of course, Inspector Darling. How can I help?"

"Could you just check to see if my wife is back at the hotel? We seem to have crossed wires about where to meet."

"I haven't seen her come in, sir. I can send one of the girls to check. Would you like to hold?"

"Yes, I'll hold, thank you." He already had a sinking feeling he was wasting his time. She would not be there. He scanned the street anxiously while he waited. He could hear the hotel receptionist speaking to someone and then doing something with paper. A banging sound, like a chair hitting the edge of the counter. A long silence.

He glanced at his watch. The bloodless data of his watch face engendered a spike of anxiety. It was ticking well past an hour and a half. "Hello? Inspector Darling? I'm sorry, but your wife doesn't appear to be here. Is there somewhere I can reach you if she does come in?"

"No." Darling paused. What to say? "If she does come in, just let her know I'm on my way back."

He pushed open the door, the sound of traffic seeming to burst on him after the silence of the booth. He felt disoriented by it and tried to place himself on a north–south axis but couldn't remember which way the streets ran. A certainty lodged itself in his mind: they had been followed. Lane's instinct had been right.

He would ask the way to the police station, but he knew it would be futile. In Nelson he would have told anyone calling to say their wife had been missing for an hour and a half to wait for at least twelve hours before sounding the alarm. There was no reason the Tucson police would be interested in a story about his wife not coming back from a shopping trip. But Martinez might be interested because the one clear possibility was that someone had thought Lane had seen something incriminating about someone on the day of the murder.

He went into every likely shop on the street and it appeared she had spent a good deal of time in a shop that sold clothing and Mexican weaving just around the corner from the restaurant.

"She was very interested in one of the shawls, but said she was going to look a bit more and might be back. That was, oh, an hour ago, easily. I'm afraid I didn't see where she went after that."

Conscious of time passing, Darling checked for likely businesses Lane would have visited, but no one had seen her. It was as if she'd gone up in smoke.

MARTINEZ SAT FROWNING and then shook his head. "It seems very unlikely to me, sir. Though we haven't found the weapon yet, I'm fairly certain we have our man, and woman, for that matter."

Darling sat back, his lips set in a grim line. "It's been more than three hours now, Sergeant Martinez. I can tell you for a certainty my wife would never have disappeared for that length of time without letting me know."

"Listen, I can put out a missing persons on her, of course. I think we should give it a little longer. My advice is that you go on back. For all you know she's come back and is waiting for you."

"Is Assistant Chief Galloway in?" Darling momentarily considered going over Martinez's head, but even as he asked, he knew the sergeant was following established police procedure.

"He isn't, sir. He hasn't been in today." Martinez glanced towards Galloway's office. Where was Galloway?

THE ROOM WAS desolate in its silence. Darling walked into the bathroom and then back again, stopping at the dresser. He picked up Lane's hairbrush, put it down, and looked toward the wardrobe, where he took up a handful of her cocktail dress—the one she'd married him in—and held it to his nose breathing in, his hands clutching tightly at the skirt, hearing it swish as he pulled at it. A kind of despair he had not thought possible flooded him. It was robbing him of any ability to act, he could see that. He closed the wardrobe firmly and went to sit at the desk. Pulling open the drawer he took out stationery and pen. He could occupy himself making notes, thinking through things, like she did. He was about to close the drawer when he saw her black notebook. He'd never asked to see it, and she'd never offered. He went to push it back, but his anguish drove him to open it instead.

Land and sky, here they balance
On a golden edge.
Heaven and earth, I am like that mystic
Of the Middle Ages, who looks with wonder
At the terrifying expanse above him.
My hand half raised to reach out,
Pulled to touch the starry eternity
That threatens to engulf.
And yet, it is not fear I feel
But yearning.

THERE WERE CROSSINGS out and additions. Darling imagined Lane whittling the poem—somewhere away from him in a place she kept only unto herself, words and partial words falling around her while she found her way to clarity. Desolation threatened to engulf him again. He closed the notebook and held it momentarily in his hand. He had read her poetry before and wondered at it, at the singular act of isolation that was required to write it. Even a Lane who went off somewhere he couldn't follow to write was a

Lane he devoutly wished for at this moment, rather than the one who seemed to have been snatched off the face of the earth, as if, he thought fancifully, into the very firmament she described.

He closed the drawer gently, picked up the phone, and was put through to the police department. Martinez wasn't immediately available but would be called to the phone the minute he was free. Darling waited.

"Inspector Darling. I hope you are calling to tell me she is with you."

"I am calling to tell you she is not, and I am not satisfied to wait any longer."

"As it happens, Assistant Chief Galloway came in shortly after you left, and I spoke with him about it. We were preparing to mobilize in the event she was still missing. The boss has specifically said he wishes to take charge. I will let him know you have called, and I believe his first action will be to have you brought here."

"I appreciate that. Tell him I am grateful." He didn't feel grateful. He only felt frightened, and the prospect of having to go anywhere with Galloway did nothing to make him feel better.

———

ELEANOR ARMSTRONG, POSTMISTRESS of King's Cove and a dear friend of her neighbour Lane, was looking out the window a little disconsolately. She felt bad about her mood—after all, who could be truly unhappy with a daily companion like her husband, Kenny? She could see him outside chopping wood for the stove, dressed in his ancient black wool pants and his thick maroon sweater with the rolled collar, his inevitable costume until it got too cold to go out without a jacket. She had knitted the sweater for him a few years after they married, and she thought it rather sweet he still reached for it on a cold autumn morning. Alexandra, their west highland terrier puppy, had gone out to help with the wood and now sat alertly watching and shivering intermittently.

I should knit her a little sweater, Eleanor thought. It cheered her up to think of having a project. The fact was she was missing Lane Winslow and, she amended her thought hastily, her nice husband, Inspector Darling. They were only gone for three weeks, but she had become used to Lane coming around to the post office, exclaiming over Alexandra, eating sandwiches or scones, and drinking tea.

Sighing, she picked up a sheet of newspaper she was about to consign to the wood box to start tomorrow morning's fire when something caught her attention. She brought the paper closer and looked at the date. She glanced out the window and saw that Kenny had taken up an armful of wood and was making his way back to the house, Alexandra running ahead to clear the way. Eleanor opened the door and pushed the screen door to let them through.

"That should keep us a little longer." He dumped the wood into the wood box and wiped his face with his handkerchief.

"Did you see this?" Eleanor asked, holding up the paper. "I don't know how I missed it. Do you remember when we were going into town last Tuesday and we stopped to pick that woman up? We had to squeeze her into the cab with us. Blond thing."

"I do. Why is the paper interested?"

"It's not the paper, it's the police. I wonder if it's to do with that fellow they found dead in the car at the ferry?"

Kenny looked hopefully toward the sink where the kettle had stalled after being filled. "Why don't you put that thing on, and I'll go let them know. I hope it's not too late! I bet Lane and her fellow will be sad to have missed the action! It doesn't seem like a proper case unless she's at the centre of it."

"I'LL LET HIM know, sir," O'Brien said into the phone. "Can he phone you if he wants to follow up?"

Assured that he could, O'Brien put the receiver in the cradle and then looked up the stairs, contemplating a good loud shout. Considering the men on shift were quietly catching up on paperwork, he picked the receiver back up and dialled upstairs to Ames.

"Sarge, we've had a call from up the lake. A Mr. and Mrs. Armstrong did pick up a woman hitchhiking on the day in question. Blonde, curly hair, ever so nice. Knew it couldn't be anything, but thought it was their duty to call. Dropped her about two miles north of Willow Point."

"Armstrong? From King's Cove?" Ames asked.

"That's the place."

"Did they say where they picked her up?"

"Sorry, I missed that bit. You could give them a ring back. Poor things probably have nothing to do all day. It'd be a treat."

Ames smiled momentarily, thinking of the unceasing

industry of everyone up in King's Cove, and thanked O'Brien. His mood fell again immediately. A woman with curly blond hair. He picked up the phone.

"Oh, no, dear me no, certainly not Miss Van Eyck. Nothing like. I remember her from the wedding, of course," said Eleanor in answer to his anxiously asked question.

Relieved, though logic would have told him immediately that it couldn't have been Tina, already exonerated at the dress shop, Ames asked, "Do you remember where you picked her up?"

"Yes, Mr. Armstrong and I were trying to remember. I'd say it was between Balfour and the Harrop ferry turnoff somewhere. She'd gotten a lift, she said, to visit her friend up the lake, and her husband was supposed to pick her up, only he hadn't arrived, so she thought she'd better get back on her own."

AMES LEANED BACK in his chair and rubbed his chin. "Not very helpful," he said to Terrell, who sat opposite. "For one thing, the woman was farther down the road from the ferry. For another . . . I don't know. I haven't got another."

"It is singular that she had curly blond hair. That's twice now that a woman is described as having curly blond hair."

"Okay, let's assume it is the same woman who bought the clothes. That puts her right in the middle of the thing, especially as we are looking for someone who might have left the car and had to get a lift back. Why is she coming from farther away when she gets picked up? It's as if she's continued down the lake and then turned around and comes back. Where does she go?"

"Maybe nowhere," suggested Terrell. "Maybe she wants to throw off the scent."

"Possibly. But here's the other thing. This woman has twice been described as, well, a *woman*, not some young thing like Ada Finch, which is where the victim's tastes clearly lay," Ames said.

"They could be two entirely different curly blondes," Terrell suggested. "I imagine the local beauty shops turn out a lot of curly blondes who aren't that young but are trying to look it."

"So, he's either killed by a curly blonde, or, and we haven't pursued this yet, someone he cheats at cards, or . . . or what about some other woman from his past . . . a blonde who was young once, had been seduced and discarded and never forgot, and has come back to get her revenge?" Ames said, animated again.

The phone on the desk jangled, and Ames picked it up impatiently. "Yes?"

It was O'Brien. "Sarge, I think you better come down here. A fellow has come in to confess to murdering Barney Watts."

CHAPTER TWENTY-FOUR

THE PAIN WAS SHARP AND excruciating. Lane instinctively reached for the back of her head and found she could not. She had a momentary delusion that she was in a pram that rocked as it travelled, except she could not understand why someone would be yodelling. She opened her eyes slowly and was looking at the back of a car seat. She was lying on her side. She tried again to move her hands, if for nothing else but to locate and comfort the pounding pain at the back of her head. It was then she realized she they were bound behind her. Clarity began to reassert itself. The loud yodelling continued, and someone was ineptly yodelling along. Now she could feel the rope binding her ankles.

Closing her eyes, she tried to remember what must have happened before this moment. She'd been having lunch with Darling and said she was going to look into the nearby shops. She struggled to recall the exact trajectory of her movements. She had looked at the shops along the street the restaurant had been on and then turned the corner. She tried to bring to mind the name of the street she had turned onto but then discarded the effort as not essential. She had gone into a small dress shop and looked at a shawl. There was a black and white one with a beautifully woven fringe. She had been told it was a traditional Mexican r-something. Then that was it. She had come out of the shop, intending to look at other shops for shawls and then return for the black and white one. That was all that would come. No, wait. She opened her eyes. She remembered a sudden feeling of being closely followed, perhaps by two figures?

Judging by the pain, she must have been coshed and bundled into this car. She moved her legs onto the floor and struggled into a sitting position. The pain in her head surged. The yodeller was now singing, playing a guitar. Someone was sawing on a fiddle. The driver, who'd been singing along, stopped at Lane's sudden appearance in the rear-view mirror and reached up to adjust it so he could see her better.

"Where are you taking me?" Lane leaned forward with some difficulty to talk to the driver. At least her voice still worked. He was wearing a cowboy hat and sported a bushy moustache. He looked like someone who ought to be easy-going and kindly, except for the coldness in his blue eyes.

"Good morning! Where am I taking you? Well now, that would be telling, wouldn't it?" The driver had an easy delivery as if he plucked people off the street every day of the week and spirited them out of town—for out of town they were going.

Lane felt a momentary dismay. Was it morning? No. Late afternoon. Probably not long after she'd been at the shop. She was in the thrall of a sarcastic kidnapper. Wonderful. She looked with alarm at the passing landscape where the final sparse smattering of houses was disappearing. She could see the Catalina Mountains, where their riding expedition had gone just a few days before. So, they were going north, climbing a ridge that skirted the foothills. To Phoenix? But no. The driver turned east along a winding road.

"You've no right to take me anywhere. Who are you?"

"Would you shut up? Don't make me sorry I didn't throw a gag on you," the man said loudly over the radio. He reached over and turned the radio down. The yodelling song was ending. Lane leaned back and watched the passing scene out the window. She could see the town, maddeningly down the hill, its small compact centre of office buildings rising like beacons in what was otherwise a vast sea of flat desert. Somewhere down there, Darling must be going absolutely mad, she thought. It was pointless to imagine rescue. She had been a block away around the corner from the restaurant when she'd been struck and bundled unceremoniously into the car. It was done in moments. She imagined it must have taken two people to get her into the car and tie her so quickly. Now there was only the driver. "That was Mr. Hank Snow with "Lonesome Blue Yodel," here on KVOA from the Grand Ole Opry. Stay tuned for the NBC news."

Irritated, the driver turned the radio off, leaving only the sound of the car on the gravel road. Lane considered another approach.

"Why have you kidnapped me?"

"That's a little strong, isn't it?" the driver said, looking into the mirror with a touch of a smirk.

More sarcasm. "Not from where I'm sitting." She turned her head away to look at the city way below and then winced at the sharp pain at the back of her head.

The smirk turned into a chuckle. "Pretty and funny. You got it all."

Lane, not wanting to indulge this type of conversation, fell silent again. They had moved far enough east that they appeared to be above the outskirts of the city. Abruptly the driver turned north again, and began a winding climb into the mountains. Lane looked out the rear window, trying to orient herself, but the city had disappeared behind the folds of mountains.

The saguaros gave way to a few deciduous trees and then to evergreens, a sign that they'd driven up into a more temperate zone. The car slowed and performed a hairpin turn onto a smaller, very bumpy road. They were headed west again, dropping slightly as they moved slowly parallel to the road they'd left. It seemed interminable. Lane kept her eye on the south, but the descending hills and the thicker cover of trees was making it difficult to calculate how far away from the city they were.

Finally they came to a stop. The sudden silence after the jarring ride made Lane feel as if something were pressing against her ears. The man leaned back, took out a pack of cigarettes, rapped one out, and stuck it in his mouth. Lane looked around, moving her head gingerly, trying to ascertain why they'd come to a halt. There was a cabin some fifty feet away, surrounded by pine trees that threw shade on a porch that ran the length of the front. Two rocking chairs gave an air of domesticity and comfort. Hardly the prison she thought she might be bound for. Still, she was bound.

"Are you going to untie me?"

The man took a long drag on his cigarette then exhaled, filling the closed car with a choking smoke. With a sigh he opened the door and got out, stretching and then spitting. "Come on then," he said, opening her door. "Legs." He waved his hand, indicating she should push her ankles in his direction so he could untie the rope. She hoped her skirt wasn't riding up. He did not do the same for her arms. Longing to rub her ankles to get the circulation back, Lane struggled out of the car and rubbed one ankle against the other, thankful to be in the open air. The pain in her head engendered a wave of nausea. She breathed in deeply.

If it was meant to be her prison, it was an incongruously beautiful place. The black clouds hanging over the city had not completely blocked out the sun here, and though it was cold, the air had a sparkling freshness that seemed to emanate from the branches of trees that bobbed gently in the almost imperceptible breeze. Gulping air, as if fearful she would soon be deprived of it, Lane saw the view from the property, down a great cascade of overlapping hills, sky rising like a spreading dome, an intense blue in this clean air, dotted intermittently with puffy cumulus clouds. Though she could not see it, Tucson must be directly below them, or a bit west of where they were.

The man tossed his spent cigarette onto the ground and

took her arm, wrangling her up the stairs to the front door. "Come on. Up we go."

The cabin looked new. The door opened onto a generous sitting room with a massive stone fireplace and leather furniture. Navajo blankets were folded over the backs of several chairs. The head of a bighorn sheep adorned one wall, and a shelf with one or two books but plenty of half-full bottles of various expensive whiskies occupied one side of the fireplace. This was someone's vacation cabin, she thought. Someone with plenty of money.

"This is nice," she said, trying to keep sarcasm out of her own voice. No need to enrage this man.

"Glad you think so." He steered her across the room, opened a door and pushed her in. "Nicest room in the house," he said, and then closed the door. She could hear the key turn in the lock with a maddening clarity. The man stood for a moment outside the door, as if waiting for her to protest, and then she heard his footsteps receding, she hoped in the direction of the kitchen. Perhaps he would be humane enough to bring her water. And some aspirin. At home an unused cabin would have the water turned off in the winter. She prayed it wasn't so here.

She turned with a sigh to look about her cell—a large bedroom with its own bathroom. There was a double bed with a handmade quilt and a thick wool blanket folded at the bottom end. That was useful anyway, she thought. She couldn't tell how long she was meant to be staying, but at this altitude it must be considerably colder at night than in town, and that was cold enough. No electricity.

Everything here would be a lot easier to negotiate if her hands were not tied behind her back.

A window over the bed looked out over an ascending rocky treed hill. Even with hands, it would be a challenge to navigate, as the window was covered on the outside with an elaborate ironwork grill, no doubt, she thought bleakly, of some expensive Spanish Colonial design.

She sat with a thump on the bed and groaned at the pain that shot through the back of her head. She tried to feel her way along the rope tied around her hands. Her hands were crossed and face up and she could not feel where the knot was. Probably under her wrist where she could not reach it. The key in the door startled her, as if she'd been caught misbehaving, and she sat perfectly still and waited.

Holding a tray with a glass of water and a plate of sandwiches, the man came in and pushed the door shut with his foot. "Don't say I never did anything for you. I'll put these over here in case you're hungry."

"How do you expect me to eat with no hands?" Lane asked crossly.

"Keep your hair on. I'm gonna take the rope off. Don't try any funny stuff. I have a gun in my belt and I'm not afraid to use it." He pulled her to her feet and turned her so he could attend to the rope.

Her hands freed, Lane began to massage her wrists, wincing as she realized her shoulders also hurt.

"Why am I here? How long am I supposed to stay here?"

"Look, honey, I got no idea. I just do what I'm told." He turned and moved toward the door.

"By whom?" Lane asked.

"You'll be fine here overnight. Plenty of covers on that bed," he said turning to her briefly and then letting himself out and locking the door behind him.

"Hey!" Lane called. "How about some aspirin?" But she got no reply. She put her hand up to feel her head and encountered a sizeable lump on the right side at the base of her skull. She gingerly pressed and held it in the hopes of reducing the swelling and looked longingly at the glass of water on the dresser. If she were to be here overnight, she'd have to husband her resources. She turned on the bathroom tap, and after a cough, a blob of water spit out, quite the wrong colour. She let it run while she inspected the bathroom window. It was high, clamped shut, and grated, just like the bedroom window. More worrisome, it was already getting dark outside. She looked with alarm at her watch and saw it was already ten to five. Soon, the temperature would drop even further, and she would be freezing in total darkness.

The water was running clear and she poured out the water she'd been given and refilled it from the tap. No point in taking risks. She stood by the door listening. She could hear her captor moving about, opening and shutting drawers, slamming cupboards. Then his footsteps approaching. She jumped away from the door and stood by the bed.

The man unlocked the door and threw a small yellow tin of aspirin on the bed beside her. "It's all I could find," he said, as if the search been an irritation that was making him late. He closed and locked the door again.

She wished she had charge of the key, particularly if her

captor was spending the night. But then she heard footsteps going way from her. The front door opening and then closing. Was that another key turning in a lock? She put her ear to the door. The car starting and then slowly disappearing back along the road up the hill.

Kicking the door in irritation, she considered her situation. She was in the American southwest, locked in a log cabin with nothing but a sandwich for company, and soon it would be dark. She wished now she'd chosen a Zane Grey at the inn library. Surely something in one of those books would speak to her situation.

———

"MR. VAN EYCK," Ames said, surprised. "You'd better come upstairs."

Terrell settled him into a chair at the desk and Ames sat down and watched him, clasping his hands on the desk. "Now, what's all this?" he asked, and then thought, God, I'm starting to sound like O'Brien.

Marcus Van Eyck looked nervously at Terrell, who had remained standing.

"I'll get another chair from the next office, sir," Terrell said, "and bring my notebook."

Mr. Van Eyck sat looking down at his hands, his mouth working. He looked up when Terrell came back in with the chair and shifted his own chair slightly to make more room. The noise of the scraping of the chair on the floor was loud in the expectant silence.

Ames was about to speak when Van Eyck spoke up.

"You mustn't be hard on Tina. She doesn't even know." He looked at Ames in a way that suggested he was appealing to him personally on her behalf.

"Doesn't know what, Mr. Van Eyck?" Ames asked. He was genuinely puzzled.

"She doesn't know that I know. I've known for years. Her mother told me just before she died in '37. She didn't think it was right Tina should have that burden all on her own. I should have done something then, but then the war started, and Tina left, and I suppose he must have too. When it was all over and she was back, it was like the whole world had changed, wasn't it? She was like a new person, that's for sure. Confident, sure of herself, a heck of a mechanic. If she had any kind of a bad time in the old country, she'd learned how to handle it. I didn't give it one thought till she had that argument with that Watts the other day."

Ames sat for a moment after this rush of words. He could hear Terrell's pencil on the surface of his notebook. Where to start? "So when you say you knew, do you mean about what happened to Tina when she was just out of school?"

"Being raped by someone? I know you're reluctant to say the word, Constable Ames, I mean, sorry, Sergeant Ames. I was. I couldn't bear to say it or even think it, but when I saw her with him, I knew he must be the one. She was like a wolverine. I was proud of her, Sergeant, and I thought, if she can bear it and defend herself like that, I've got no right to pretend it was anything but what it was. Honestly, it's like they say, 'a little child shall lead them.' I felt powerless before, and then I knew I could never leave

313

her alone with it ever again."

"But you didn't tell her you knew?" Ames clarified.

"Oh, God no. Can you imagine what it would have felt like for her to know her father knew something like that had happened to her? When I woke up the next morning and saw that word smeared across our bay doors, something snapped."

"Can we just take a step back, Mr. Van Eyck? Were you aware she'd come here to the police to report the—the rape?"

Van Eyck nodded and took a big intake of breath. "Yeah. She, the wife, I mean, told me that. By the time my wife told me, that bastard had left the police, but I never forgot his name, Galloway, Sergeant Galloway." He cleared his throat, as if he was unused to such a barrage of talking.

"Let me get you a glass of water." Terrell stood and put his notebook on his chair. Ames and Van Eyck sat quietly. They could hear Terrell walk to the top of the stairs and call down for one of the constables to bring water and then return, trying to sit as unobtrusively as possible, taking up his notebook again.

"So, can you tell me what happened on the day Barney Watts was killed?"

Van Eyck took a deep breath, as if he'd been preparing for this moment. "I checked the address we had for him in our records, and I drove there the next day and waited on the road to see if he would come down. When he did, I followed him. I thought he would head into town to work because he told me he worked in the rail yard, but I think he saw me. He drove away toward the north. He knew I was after him. He tried to get away by turning down the road to the ferry and realized he was trapped. I pushed him off the road and he was dazed. That's how I got in and I killed him. There. I'm prepared to sign a statement."

The door opened cautiously, and a glass of water was produced. Van Eyck took it and drank it down in three gulps and then put the glass down and looked expectantly at Ames.

Ames rubbed the side of his neck and glanced at Terrell, who was looking studiously down at his notebook. "Of course. I can get Constable Terrell to prepare it. Can you just clarify how you killed him? It's best to get the whole thing down."

Van Eyck looked up, pursed his lips, and then nodded. "Yes, of course. He had his window rolled down, and I reached in, and I guess I just got overcome with it all and I strangled him before I knew what I was doing."

"And you did what with the window?"

"The window?" Van Eyck paused, looking puzzled. "Oh, yes. I see what you mean. "I ... I went around the passenger side and rolled it up."

"And did you do anything else? Take anything?"

"I just got out of there. I thought the ferry might come over and someone getting off might see me."

Ames stood up. "Thank you, Mr. Van Eyck. I'll have you sit downstairs while Constable Terrell types up your statement."

Frowning, Van Eyck said, "Aren't you going to lock me up?"

"Mr. Van Eyck, unless you've been parading around town in a blond wig, then probably not."

HAVING DEPOSITED MARCUS Van Eyck, protesting volubly about not being locked up, onto a chair in the waiting area before the front desk, Terrell returned. "Well, well. What was all that about?"

"It could only be that he thinks Tina did it, and he's trying to protect her. It's certainly what Darling would call a cliché. He's got exactly enough details from the newspaper to put together his story, but he clearly does not know how Watts really died," Ames said.

"You're most certainly right. What I wonder is why he thinks Tina did it? Wasn't she in the garage with him at the time it must have happened? She must have done something that aroused his fear. He claims they've never talked about the assault, but he obviously saw her in action giving Watts what-for when he came in. And we have our question answered about whether this is the first time since before the war that he came to the garage. But something must have convinced him that she did it. I guess I'd best go type this up."

It was only after Ames, left alone in his office, had put his feet on his desk, a position that usually expressed nonchalance and a relaxed view of the world, but now gave no pleasure at all, that he thought, "Oh, my God! That's it!"

CHAPTER TWENTY-FIVE

LANE WAS QUIETLY GRATEFUL WHEN she finally began to feel sleep steal over her. The dark was not as absolute as she thought it might be, as somewhere out of her view from the window, the moon was waxing and throwing a cool luminescence across the landscape. It obliterated colour, and the parts of the hilly folds that caught the light highlighted the inky sinister blackness of what lay in shadow. What was absolute was the cold. She had taken her sandwich to bed, praying it was only what appeared to be roast beef and not laced with something lethal—if they'd wanted to kill her they could have done it outright any number of times, she reasoned—and piled the covers around her while she ate, contemplating who "they" could be.

It was ridiculous to try to sleep when it was only eight thirty at night, but she lay, trying to hold all the warmth she could until—perhaps from the tension of trying desperately to imagine which of her provocations, as outlined by Darling, had got her into this mess—she began to feel exhaustion replace the alert trepidation she'd been in the grip of. She settled on the mob boss because of the men who kidnapped her. They seemed like mob henchmen from fiction. But knowing about Meg Holden's movements seemed the least of her sins. Surely this reaction was more in keeping with a man whose wife has been helped to escape. She discounted her involvement with the Renwicks in any way. The law had dealt with both of them. It was with these thoughts becoming more entangled and fantastical in her head that she finally drifted off.

When the noise penetrated, she woke slowly into complete blackness. The moon had disappeared somewhere, and now only darkness prevailed. She lay stock still, waiting to understand what had woken her. She pulled her hand out from under the covers and tried to see the time, but it was impossible. There was more noise. A door closing. Something being dumped on the floor. She sat up now, alert, reluctant to move from the warmth of her covers, but looking desperately around in the darkness to find a defensive weapon. The glass was beside her on the bedside table. A good solid model with a heavy base. If need be, she could use it. She drank down the rest of the water and waited. Again more noise and then from under the door an intermittent light. Someone with a flashlight.

Lane nearly jumped out of her own skin when whoever it was tried to open the bedroom door, rattling it angrily. And then through the pounding of her own fear, she heard an oath, loudly uttered by a woman's voice.

"Who's there?" Lane called loudly.

"What?" The woman on the other side of the door

sounded irritated.

"I'm locked in here! Can you open the door?" Lane called. If the woman, whoever she was, attacked her, she felt more comfortable about being able to fend her off with the water glass.

"Who the hell are you?" The door handle rattled again. "Just wait." Lane could see the light of the flashlight dancing away from where it had shone through the crack at the bottom of the door. More noise. Drawers, cupboards. Finally, the sound of a skeleton key going into a lock, and a flashlight shining full on her face, causing her to throw her arms across her eyes.

"Hey, are you that lady from the hotel? Number 26?"

"Yes," Lane offered. "Could you turn the flashlight so it's not in my eyes?"

"Oh. Sorry. I didn't expect no one to be here."

"Mrs. Holden?" Lane ventured. Once her initial panic died down, she recognized the voice. She threw the covers off, sat on the bed, shivering, and pulled the blanket around her. Her head throbbed with a dull pain. The aspirin had only taken care of the sharper pounding.

"What in the hell are you doing here?" Meg Holden asked. She stood the flashlight on its end so the light shone toward the roof and threw a faint light around the room. "All the damn kerosene lamps are gone for some reason."

"I feel I should ask the same question. Is this cabin yours, Mrs. Holden, or your husband's?" She struggled to imagine why the benign Mr. Holden should want to imprison her on the side of a mountain.

"Lord, no! It belongs to that idiot, the assistant chief

319

of police. My husband and I get to use it for little holidays. As is only right. We practically paid for the thing. Not that I love a vacation in the middle of nowhere."

Lane shook her head, trying to clear it. "So Mr. Holden had me kidnapped? I don't understand. Is he a friend of Galloway's?" What on earth could any of this mean in the context of what she thought she knew?

"Rex? He wouldn't hurt a flea." Meg was smiling, almost sadly, Lane thought. "He's not like any of the others. But we got bigger problems. I had to get away 'cause of that Renwick. Artie thinks I know, and he won't stop at nothin' to stop me talking if he thinks I've tried to run away, which I have." She sat down next to Lane and clenched her hands on her lap. "I bet he's down there thinking, oh, she'll come back. She always does. Not this time, buddy!"

Lane momentarily gave up trying to make any sense at all of this bewildering speech. Who was Artie? "How did you get here? I didn't hear a car." Of course, she'd been asleep, but hope bloomed at the thought of a car. They could drive away from this place.

"I had the cab drop me at the top of the hill, just in case someone was here. It's coming back in the morning for me. It's a horrible hike in these shoes!" She held her foot out away from the bed, and Lane saw she was wearing very pretty red and white Oxford high heels. Most unsuitable for a nighttime hike. No car, then. She looked at her watch. It was quarter after four. She groaned silently, resisting the urge to throw herself back on the bed. She had often been in untoward places at this time of night in France during the war, after all.

"Why come here?" Lane asked. "It seems an out-of-the-way place to run off to."

"Because, dearie, no one is supposed to be here! This place sits empty from October to May. I figured I had time to collect what is mine, have a good sleep, and really get away, all the way back to Chicago. My luggage is stowed at the bus station. Finding you here sure doesn't help! It means someone is coming back for you, or to do something to you, I don't know. Who brought you here?" She looked at Lane, frowning.

"I've no idea. I must confess, I thought it must have something to do with James Griffin, because the man seemed sort of like a henchman, if you see what I mean."

"That's Artie's style, all right," Meg agreed. "He's not going to leave well enough alone, I can see that now." She stood up and bustled toward the door and then turned abruptly and came back. "Did you see something? Is that what happened? You saw his man shooting? No, wait. You didn't see nothing. Did the man who brought you here have a gun? Big tall guy, cowboy boots and moustache?"

Something about what Meg had just said bothered Lane. But she couldn't put her finger on it. The pain in her head wasn't helping.

"Well?" said Meg.

"Sorry. Yes, a cowboy. That sounds like him. Who is he? How worried should I be?"

"We should both be very worried, honey. We gotta skedaddle. He's probably the one who shot that Mr. Renwick."

GALLOWAY DOWNED HIS neat whisky and clunked his glass onto the tiled counter. By the time they'd arrived at the home of Tucson's assistant chief of police after futile hours driving around the city, Darling had known the man wasn't right. Galloway wasn't just drunk; he'd come unhinged somehow. Unmoored. As though that one act of defiance by his wife had dislodged something deep inside him. He had been silent and unresponsive in the car, but Darling guessed that the whiskey would change that soon enough. That he was somehow involved in Lane's disappearance seemed certain. But what to do about it?

Galloway poured himself another whiskey. Then he smiled and looked at Darling. "You wanting me to help find your wife. I can't get over the irony of it all." He offered the bottle to Darling. "As it happens, I want help finding my wife too. Isn't that a coincidence? And I expect when I know where mine is, you'll find the lovely Mrs. Darling as well."

"What are you saying?" Darling asked.

Galloway had not picked up his glass. He now leaned across the counter bringing his face close to Darling's. "I'm saying that I want to know where my bloody wife is. I'm saying that I know damn well your wife had something to do with getting her away from the hospital—the advantages of being a policeman—and I'm saying that if you don't tell me, I will get it from her." He picked up his drink and swirled it around. "This is going to seem a bit crude to you, Darling, gentleman police inspector that you are, but I'm finished with subtleties." He reached into his jacket and pulled a revolver out of the holster he had strapped onto his upper body. "I mean business, you see."

Darling looked at him steadily, stilling the flutter of panic that felt like it could overwhelm him. "Where have you taken her?"

"Oh, marvellous. We could play at this all night. That's my question, though, isn't it?"

"The thing is, Galloway, whatever you've done, it's pointless. She actually has no idea where your wife is. It's possible Priscilla expected a response like this and wanted to make sure no one knew, so you see, neither I nor my wife can be of any help."

"You're lying. But that's all right. Your wife won't be so reluctant when we go see her. Trust me. She'll have had time to think about her answer."

"You've used one of your men to kidnap my wife?" Darling, not of a religious persuasion, prayed the hotel concierge had done what he asked.

"One of my men? Don't be an ass! I didn't get where I am today without some more biddable, let's say, connections." He took up his glass again, draining the contents.

"You might as well have a drink, Darling, and sit down. It's a waiting game now. I've got someone picking us up before dawn." He looked at his watch in an exaggerated manner, like an actor trying to reach the back of the house with this gesture, and then collapsed onto the bar stool.

LANE'S HEAD WAS full of questions, but Meg was focused on the business of the moment: getting out before the cowboy came back.

"I stashed a little money and a change of clothes here a couple of times ago. Things were a little rough between me and Artie, and I thought I might have to make tracks." Meg took the flashlight and went toward the kitchen, leaving Lane in the dark.

How apt, Lane thought. In the dark. Why should things have been "a little rough" between Meg Holden and Artie? Hurriedly she put her shoes on and tied the laces. Also not appropriate for a hike, she realized, but sturdier than what Meg was wearing. She felt her way through the sitting room toward the kitchen and could see the flashlight bobbing around inside a cupboard.

"Here, hold this thing. I need all my hands."

Lane took the flashlight and pointed it toward where Meg was kneeling, pulling a board out of the back of what appeared to be some sort of larder.

"Take this. I put some boots back here somewhere." She handed Lane a cloth bag that smelled primarily of mildew, and even in the dark Lane could feel the layer of dust. "Got 'em!"

Emptying the bag onto the sofa, Meg shone the flashlight on its contents. Lane could see blue jeans and some sort of brown slacks and at least two plaid shirts. "These might be a little big, but better than that dress you got." She held up the pair of the jeans. "Damn!" she exclaimed suddenly. "The flashlight's going. Okay, I've got the cash."

The flashlight was indeed going. Lane could see the light was wavering, fading in and out. This whole thing would be more difficult to accomplish in the dark. Meg flicked it off and continued changing, chucking her dress onto the floor and pulling her cardigan over the plaid shirt.

Lane followed suit, and like Meg, pulled the trousers over her stockings. They'd need every layer in this cold. She tucked her silk slip into the jeans. "Too bad you didn't have the foresight to put away two pairs of boots," she said.

Meg had collapsed onto the sofa and seemed to be doing something in her handbag. Lane sat next to her and waited, praying that Meg knew what she was doing.

"I put a little money away, and with the money I took from Rex, I should be able to get as far away as I need to. Now, I need to think." Meg had snapped the bag shut and sat looking straight ahead.

The sofa was facing the window, and the open curtains only compounded the sense of darkness, though Lane was beginning to become accustomed to it and could see Meg's outline, sitting very still in a way she had not imagined possible for Meg, staring as if she could see something outside.

Fearful that her rescuer had lost her nerve, Lane said, "What is your plan?"

"We're gonna have to hike back to town. I don't know what you're doing, but I'm catching a bus outta here."

Lane wished she could remember how far they had driven to get up here. It had taken well over an hour. They'd be hiking in the dark and not, she realized, on the road. They would have to cut across the countryside, steeply down and westward in the hopes of meeting the main road. Walking back along the arterial road that got them here would be a dangerous waste of time and take them far in the wrong direction. The whole thing would take hours. Hours when they could be exposed once the sun rose and they reconnected with the main road. She tried to see her watch but saw only the outline of it on her wrist. She guessed that it was about four thirty in the morning. She tried to imagine what sort of cover there'd be if whoever it was came back early in the morning and found them gone and guessed which direction they were going. They'd have a bit of time once the kidnappers showed up, discovered she was gone, tried to assess the situation of the clothes on the floor, and decided how to track them. They needed to put as much distance as possible between them and the cabin before then.

"Look, get rid of this stuff. We don't want them to know you've been here," she commanded, picking up the clothes Meg had dropped on the floor. "We have to move quickly if we are going to make any headway before dawn."

Meg took the clothes she was handed and felt her way to the kitchen. Lane hurried to the bedroom and dumped everything out of her handbag and took up her passport, her wallet, all the change she had, and her room key and distributed them into her pockets. She didn't want to be hampered by a handbag. About to turn away, she snatched up her handkerchief. Almost smiling, she remembered her German governess telling her a well-brought-up girl never left the house without a handkerchief. They were good for all kinds of emergencies. She was sure her governess had never anticipated a night flight from armed men in cowboy country. As a quick afterthought, she opened the wardrobe and felt inside. With a cry of triumph, she called out, "I've found a couple of jackets!"

She pulled them off the hangers. One was a man's flight jacket with a thick shearling lining, and the other was some sort of fur jacket.

Meg was at the door. She had switched on the flashlight, which momentarily beamed with its old intensity and then began to flicker again. She reached for the fur. "I think this will fit just fine. I'll need it when I get to back east."

Happy at Meg's choice, Lane put on the flight jacket, and though she fairly swam in it, zipped it up, and counted herself lucky. "Do you have those keys? We should lock this room. They might as well imagine I'm still in there. Maybe they'll stop and make some coffee while they think of what to do with me."

Meg found the keys, locked the room after some messing about with the wrong keys, took them to a cupboard by the fireplace, and then thought better of it. She pushed the keys into the lock of the front door, locked it, and then left the keys, trying to turn the main key past the lock position to jam the lock.

"No," said Lane. "That will alert them something is wrong. Let's lock the door as we leave, like he did."

Meg shrugged and Lane could see her nodding in the dark. "Good point." She started for the door.

"That handbag might get in the way. I shoved everything I have in my pockets," Lane suggested.

Meg stopped and then shook her head. "I love this purse. Rex gave it to me. And it's real expensive."

The cold smacked them cleanly as they stepped outside. The sky was reeling with stars in the space above the forest, a great alien canopy that took Lane's breath away. While it was dark, the night had a kind of luminescence that seemed to shimmer. It was easier to see the outlines of things as they looked out toward where the city lay below. The trees, the road, the boulders.

"Well, here goes nothin'," Meg said.

God, Lane thought, I hope not nothin'.

CHAPTER TWENTY-SIX

I**T WAS THE HAIR. IT** was something to do with the hair.
Ames paced his office. A curly blond woman bought the
clothes; she was the hitchhiker picked up by the
Armstrongs. A blonde in her late twenties or early thirties.
A blonde who was not Tina Van Eyck. But it was Tina
whom Mr. Van Eyck wanted to protect. Why?

With a bound he was out of his office and down the
stairs to the main office where Marcus Van Eyck still sat
glumly, waiting to sign his statement.

"Mr. Van Eyck, do you mind? I have a couple more
questions." He waved his hand toward the interview room.
On their way past Terrell's desk, he mimed writing on a
pad and signalled Terrell to follow them.

Once they were settled, Ames put his hands in front of
him on the table and looked at Van Eyck, who was sitting
back in his chair, as if unconsciously trying to pull as far away
as possible from whatever was coming. "Now then, I think
you'd better tell us why you think Tina killed Barney Watts."

Van Eyck's eyes widened almost imperceptibly. He shook his head. "I don't think that. I don't think that because I did it, I told you. I want my statement, and I want whatever is supposed to happen next to happen. I won't sign anything except what I said."

"Listen, I appreciate a father wanting to protect his daughter. But lying isn't going to get us any closer to who is actually responsible."

There was a silence while Van Eyck, with a puzzled expression looked from one policeman to the other. "I don't understand," he said finally.

"If I'm honest, neither do I. But I know one thing: you didn't do it. You don't even know how he died, though you have the details of the car right. I'm guessing you did see the scene, maybe, and found something that made you think Tina was involved. How's my guess?"

Crossing his arms, Van Eyck looked away from Ames.

"Look, Mr. Van Eyck, this isn't going to get us anywhere. We both know it wasn't you, and if it's any help, we don't think it was Tina. The question is why you think it was. And before you continue down this road, lying about what you've seen obstructs our ability to solve this case, and that is a crime. If you're so anxious to spend time in a cell, we may yet be able to arrange it."

Van Eyck looked back at Ames, a glimmer of something like hope in his eyes. "Then why was this officer out to the garage to talk to her all those times?" He indicated Terrell with a lift of his chin.

Terrell made a small movement, but Ames lifted his hand slightly. "Let's start again, shall we? How about we go over the whole thing again, and this time you tell us the truth."

———

August 1936

BARNEY WATTS LEANED over and kissed Amy. They were parked near the beach. A string of lights along the pier reflected on the nearly still surface of the water. They had parked under the trees, which blocked out the light from the town behind.

"You're sweeter than all them other girls," he said, running his mouth across her forehead and then back to her lips.

Slapping him lightly on the leg, Amy smiled in the darkness and then whispered, "What other girls? I thought I was your girl." She ran her hand along his leg, causing him to take a sharp intake of breath. He put his hand on hers and pressed it into his thigh. "You tell me. You seem to know everything."

She pulled her hand away abruptly and sat back on the seat. "You were seen last summer with that Tina and who knows how many others. You got a reputation."

Barney frowned in the darkness, feeling a flutter of alarm at her tone, but said lightly, "Like you said, last summer. Why you bringing her up? Wouldn't I be with her if I wanted her? She's cold. I'm with you." He tried to pull her back to him, but she resisted.

"I just gotta check. She's stuck up and she's been acting weird. She knows about us, I just know it, the way she looked at me when I saw her in town. She's disgusting, working in a garage like that! I don't even know what you see in her."

He grabbed the top of her arm suddenly and swung her so she faced him. "I don't 'see' anything in her. Did she say anything to you?"

"You're hurting me! No, she didn't. She's too stuck up to talk to anyone. People just know stuff."

"What do you mean? What have you been telling people?" Anger competed with fear in his voice.

"What do you think I am? I haven't been telling anyone anything. But it's all gonna have to come out. You're going to marry me."

He let go of her arm and reached into his shirt pocket for a cigarette and lit it with his lighter, illuminating his face for a moment. He pushed the lighter into his trouser pocket and leaned out the window, blowing smoke into the night air. He didn't offer Amy one.

"You can ignore me all you want. We're getting married. You have to marry me."

There was such a steel tone in this statement that Barney turned to stare at her. She was sitting with her arms crossed looking out the front window, her mouth set.

"What is that supposed to mean?"

"It means I'm expecting, and it's yours. Obviously. Did you knock her up as well?"

"Would you shut up about her?" Barney threw the cigarette out the window and put the car into gear, but it was only relief he felt. They'd been talking at crossed purposes. "I'm dropping you off."

"You're not dropping me anywhere. I'm staying right here till you marry me. If you don't, everyone in this whole town, including your boss, is gonna know what you've been up to, going after all those girls in school." This was a sore point with Amy. It wasn't just Tina; she knew of several other girls, one as young as fourteen. But there was something special about Tina, she was sure of it, and she hated her for it. She had the upper hand now, though, and Tina was going to know it.

TINA LOOKED UP from where she was working, sweeping the inside of a truck being picked up later that day. It had been dry all summer, and a cloud of dust obscured the car coming down the road. She stood up, looking with growing fury and fear at the car. It was the cream-coloured '33 Buick Barney Watts drove. She dropped the hand broom and sped toward the garage. She couldn't see him. Her dad could deal with him. Just outside the bay door, she reached into her pocket and pulled out her handkerchief to put over her mouth. She felt like she might be sick. She rushed to the small toilet in the garage.

"Dad, get that!" she called desperately. She slammed the bathroom door shut and stood breathing heavily, trying to fight back the fear and nausea. Succeeding somehow, she leaned against the door. She heard her father come into the bay.

"Hey, Tina. It's some friend of yours from school. She just wants to have a word."

She? Tina opened the door, pulling out a bobby pin and pinning a lock of hair that had fallen forward. She strolled as nonchalantly as she could toward the car, parked right outside the door. Amy Donald was standing outside the car, one foot on the running board, gazing around at the property. She looked at Tina as she came through the door.

"Amy," Tina said. Why was she driving Barney's car? "You got a new car."

"Very funny. You know perfectly well whose car this is. I just came to tell you I'm getting married. I thought you'd like to know." She pulled a cigarette out of her purse and lit it, throwing the burning match into the grass.

Tina stomped on the match furiously. "You trying to set the whole place on fire? Why should I care you're getting married? You never even finished school. I'm not surprised you're getting married. What else can you do?"

"I won't be going back because I'm having a baby."

Her pride in this seemed nonsensical to Tina. "I gather it's Barney's work. I heard you were going out with him. He's an ass. I wish you a long and happy life."

Amy dropped the nonchalance. "I'm here to tell you to keep away from him. He's mine now. You can't pretend you don't like him."

Tina was knocked back by this speech and stared at Amy in genuine surprise. "I can't pretend I do like him. I can't pretend I do anything but hate him. You're making a huge mistake. You have no idea what he's really like!"

Amy turned and got into the car and revved the engine. She looked at Tina as she put it into gear. "Oh?" was all she said as she peeled into the turn that would take her back up to the road.

THE EVERGREENS WERE slightly smaller and more distantly spaced than the intensely packed forest cover Lane was used to around King's Cove. The ground was relatively clear, and there was a thick soft carpet of dried pine needles that would hide their progress from anyone but a professional tracker. It initially made their descent easier despite the dark. Lane explained to Meg that she wanted them to move both down and westward, while putting as much distance between themselves and the cabin as possible. They were motivated to move quickly because of the cold, and Lane was impressed with what she thought of as Meg's stoutheartedness. Seeing her at the hotel in those little suits and high heels, she would not have thought of her hiking competently in boots down a mountain at night.

The vegetation began to change, at first imperceptibly and then more obviously. The evergreens thinned out, with leafless deciduous trees in small patches, and farther down, as the grey light of the coming dawn spread across from the east, they could see the dim shapes of saguaros standing guard along the descending hills far below them.

Lane pulled to a stop. "Let's just stop a second and get our bearings." They'd been walking for over an hour, and she could hear Meg breathing hard. She had unclasped the fur jacket. "I realize the main road to the cabin turnoff is above us. I can't really remember where it turned east because I was a bit stunned. Your friend hit me over the head and knocked me out."

"See, that's what I don't understand. What the hell does Artie want with you? It makes no sense. Unless he thought you saw the shooting, then, okay. But if he thought that, he wouldn't have dragged you up the mountain and made sure you had a sandwich. He would have driven you up the mountain and popped a bullet in you and left you."

That was the second time Meg Holden had suggested that Artie—whoever he was—was responsible for the shooting. Why? "So, I'm confused. When you say Artie, who—"

"James Arthur Griffin. I never liked the name James. He's my husband. Unfortunately." She dragged out the last word in disgust.

Lane could see Meg clearly in the grey light. "I thought Rex was your husband."

"Oh, honey, it's way too complicated to get into now. The real question is why you're here. Did you see who shot Renwick?"

"No, of course not. I'm as puzzled as you. Wait, didn't you say that was Paul Galloway's cabin?" Would the assistant chief of police be working hand in glove with the biggest crook in town?

"Yeah. We use it sometimes when he's not here. He is never here at the same time, for obvious reasons, but he's been pretty good. Artie's managed to stay out of the slammer thanks to him. It's not cheap, but it's worth it."

"What do you mean, 'not cheap'? Does Griffin pay Galloway to keep him out of trouble?"

Suddenly cautious, Meg shrugged. "Honestly, I don't get his business dealings. I just stay out of the way and try to look pretty. Should we keep going?"

Thus equipped with a multitude of things to think about, Lane followed Meg, wanting to have her set the pace. The way was more visible with the lighter sky, and not a moment too soon, the terrain had changed from soft forest floor to steep and rocky inclines. They followed a narrow descending vale, much slowed down by the precipitous and rugged terrain, often having to scramble over and down boulders. Unfortunately, it was pulling them due south, and Lane wanted to try to push west. The one comforting thing was that they could now see the very eastern edge of the city far below and across the plain. It gave Lane some hope. Perhaps at the end of this narrow cleft they could veer west again. In the meantime, her mind was humming.

So, Galloway was collecting money to protect the criminal, the apparently murderous criminal, James Griffin. Artie. That established a link between Galloway and Griffin, a link she had not even been considering. She'd been wondering about a link between Griffin and Renwick. It didn't surprise her. It was abundantly evident now that Galloway had engineered her kidnapping in retaliation, she was now absolutely certain, for helping Priscilla. The question was, what was he planning to do with her? With a shudder, she guessed: try to find out where his wife was—by fair means or foul.

She was about to ask Meg about what connection there might be between Griffin and Renwick when a chill gripped her heart. Even now, far down there somewhere in the city, Darling had gone to the police, to Martinez, maybe even to Galloway, to ask for his help in finding her.

FOR REASONS HE could not readily pinpoint, Ames was becoming anxious. A sense of impending doom was not something he was used to, being of a primarily sunny disposition, but he was afraid, and he could not pull the threads together in his mind to identify exactly what he feared.

"Look, Mr. Van Eyck, you're going to have to stop this. Something is very wrong here, and we're wasting time with you instead of trying to find the real killer. For the last time, why in God's name did you think it was Tina?" Ames sensed, rather than saw, Terrell look up at his growing impatient tone.

"Okay. Some of what I said before is true. I did want to kill him. I couldn't believe he'd have the temerity to come back to our garage after what he'd done. I could hear Tina yelling at him, and I came in and saw the smirk on his face, which only disappeared after she waved a wrench at him. He backed his car up and turned around, and Tina threw the wrench in the corner and stormed out. She likes to go sit on a picnic table near the lakeshore when she's upset. I decided that was the last straw. I was going to have it out with him. I'd go the next day so she wouldn't suspect anything. If she knew, she'd only tell me to leave it. Good riddance to bad rubbish, she'd say. But I couldn't. When we woke up and saw that terrible word written all over our garage, I just had to try to keep calm, pretend I didn't know who'd done it. I saw her talking to you up by the car.

"I called the train station and was told Watts was on the afternoon shift that day, and later I tried to find Tina to tell her that I was going into town for supplies. This was all after you came around that morning. When I couldn't find her, I went and parked at the bottom of the road that goes up to his place. I honestly don't know what I thought I was going to do. I just waited. I figured I could follow him to work and then confront him. Only when the car came down it turned away from town. I waited and followed at a distance and saw the car turn toward the Harrop ferry. That's when I saw her. She'd been in the back, hiding, I guess. Her head popped up right behind Watts so he wouldn't have seen, and then went down again. I stopped there and then off the side of the main road, trying to think what to do. Why was he going to Harrop? What was she doing with him? Trees were blocking my view, so I couldn't see, but I knew if I saw cars coming onto the road, it would mean the ferry was on this side. After some time, I don't know how long, when I didn't see any traffic coming out onto the road from Harrop, I drove slowly forward, and I saw the car off the side of the road, and he was in it. The rain was pelting down. I parked behind his car and went and knocked on the window. I thought he was asleep, but then I understood. He looked dead." Van Eyck stopped, as though he had not breathed properly during his whole narrative. "I couldn't see her anywhere. I called her, but it was like she had vanished."

Terrell scribbled feverishly. "Something about what you saw made you think it was Tina who killed him," Ames prompted.

Van Eyck nodded. "She was in the back of the car. I saw her. And that wasn't all. Later, when I was looking in the window at him, I caught sight of this little change purse Tina used to have back when she was in school. It was lying just out of sight on the driver's side. Her grandmother gave it to her when she was a child. A little pink thing with her name embroidered on it. As soon as I saw it, I knew. I grabbed it and drove off in a hurry. First I was going to go farther up the lake and throw it in the water and see if I could catch up to Tina. But I didn't see her, and I just drove home and hid the purse and waited for Tina. I just couldn't think straight. I couldn't see how she'd pulled it off, but somehow she had. And that's it. That's all I can tell you."

"Where is the purse now?" Ames asked.

"I have a barrel where I burn garbage around the back. I buried it there, knowing it would go up in the next burning."

Terrell suddenly leaned forward. "You seem very sure it was Tina in the car with Watts."

Van Eyck frowned. "The hair. I mean it was just a flash. I couldn't sort in my head how she would have got in without him knowing. I think at one point I wondered if she'd hidden in the back of the car, or if they'd agreed to meet along the way, and he stopped and picked her up and I just missed it. I wasn't following him really closely because there wasn't much traffic, and I thought he'd see me. And the rain was heavy, so I might not even have seen if he stopped."

"So, no sign of Tina. And the ferry hadn't come over yet, so you knew she couldn't have gone over to the other side of the lake. Did you think she might have hidden in the forest?"

Van Eyck shook his head, his expression puzzled. "I did call and search, but it was like she had vanished. Part of me couldn't believe it would be her, but when I saw the purse, I panicked."

THEY'D SENT VAN Eyck home, giving him strict instructions to recover the purse and bring it back to them forthwith, and now Ames and Terrell sat musing in Ames's office.

"The purse isn't necessarily a bad sign, sir," Terrell said.

"It's hardly a good one." Ames, who'd been leaning back, clumped his chair down heavily and picked up the phone. He heard it ringing on the other side. "I'm sure the blonde in the car wasn't Tina. It's too much of a coincidence that the blonde buying the clothes wouldn't be the blonde who killed him. But still ..." He heard it picked up. "Van Eyck garage."

"Miss Van Eyck. It's Sergeant Ames. I need you to answer a question. Do you own a little change purse with your name embroidered on it?" He looked over the receiver at Terrell, who was looking askance at him, forming an unspoken "What?" with his mouth.

A long silence followed. Finally, in a voice as far as possible from the confident voice of the Tina he knew, she said, "Why?"

"Is it yours?" Ames was insistent.

"Yes. I mean, it was. I lost it before the war. It was something my grandmother gave me. I don't understand. Why do—"

"When before the war? Do you remember exactly?"

Another silence.

"Tina, this is important."

"I lost it the night—the night I went out with Watts. He pushed me out of the car at the top of my road. I had to try to straighten up before I got to the house, and that's when I knew it was gone. It must have fallen out of my pocket when ..."

"You didn't keep it in your purse?"

"No. I always put it in my pocket. What's going on?"

Ames felt his anxiety spiking into fear. "Look, Tina, I don't know what is going on, but your father has been to see us. I won't explain now, but he's on his way home. He's going to come back, and I want you to come back with him. Do you understand?"

"Of course, I understand. I'm not an imbecile. Why was he there, anyway?"

"I can explain later, just come back with him, okay?"

"All right, all right. I hear a car. Customer. Gotta run."

"Tina!" But she'd hung up the phone.

A young officer knocked and put his head around the door. "Sarge, that car at the back you wanted the trunk fixed on and keys made, so it could be driven back across the lake? It's gone."

CHAPTER TWENTY-SEVEN

MARTINEZ SAT AT HIS DESK, the photographs splayed before him like a bad hand of cards. They'd been delivered by a cab driver shortly after the assistant chief had left to pick up Darling. A couple of nice pictures of Inspector Darling and his wife out at the mission. These he had set aside. The rest. He shook his head, unbelieving. Paul Galloway with his arms around a couple of girls at the club, on the game he was sure. Galloway and James Griffin at the bar in the restaurant. Galloway and Griffin in what Martinez assumed was Galloway's house, Galloway and Griffin, Galloway and Griffin A couple of pals. Had Galloway's wife taken these without her husband knowing? She must have. He'd never have allowed such compromising photographs. He shook his head. What must have been going on in that marriage? The ticking of the clock on the wall seemed loud in the silence. It had been hours since Galloway had gone to fetch Darling at the hotel. What could they be doing? Galloway had distinctly said he was bringing Darling back to the station so they could begin to plan the search. It was a quiet night for a change. Only one drunk had been brought in, and it was already ten at night. God bless Tuesdays. He found Bevan leaning back in his chair, putting in some procrastination, while a partially written report stared back from the desk.

"Hey, Bev, have you heard from Galloway? He was picking up that Canadian inspector because his wife went missing. He told you about that?"

Bevan produced a puzzled expression. "News to me. Boss said nothing about a missing woman. Just hightailed it out with his usual cheerful and charming good night. I lie, of course. He took off without a word, as usual."

"He said," Martinez began. "Never mind." He turned and started back to his desk, and then on an impulse, he looked right and left, opened the door to Galloway's office, and slid in. He stood for a moment in the dark taking in the enormity of his invasion. It felt like a monstrous violation, after all that he owed Galloway. But nothing added up anymore. He looked behind him at the closed door. Who was he kidding? Nothing had added up for a while. Not Galloway lying to him about having alerted everyone, or saying he was bringing Darling right back, not all those chummy photos of Galloway and Griffin, and he thought, with a thump in his chest, not his missing evidence and notes.

Crossing himself quickly and offering up a prayer to the Virgin, Martinez darted around Galloway's desk and sat in his chair. There was a small desk lamp and he switched it on, his head beginning to fill with the excuses he'd use if Galloway found him there. But it was unthinkable, what he was thinking. Galloway couldn't have spirited away his paperwork. The one thing he was always going on about was the importance of putting Griffin behind bars finally and for good.

In the end it had been simple: Galloway had exercised caution and opted not to destroy the evidence—after all, he might decide to terminate his partnership with Griffin, but he had exercised no caution in the storing of it. Martinez had found it tossed at the very back of the lowest drawer of his file cabinet. He hadn't even bothered to lock the cabinet, so confident was he that no one would dare breach the sanctity of his office.

Martinez looked at it and then put it back. What should he do? Anxious now about the amount of time he'd spent in the office, he pushed the drawer shut quietly and then turned out the desk lamp and felt his way to the door. Taking a deep breath, he opened it a crack. He could see Bevan's back and no one else on the floor. He breathed a sigh of relief and returned to his desk. It was time to try to understand what it meant and what, if anything, it had to do with the disappearance that afternoon, a lifetime ago, of the beautiful wife of the Canadian inspector

"GOOD. NOW I feel we'll get to the bottom of this." Galloway pulled his car up behind that of a tall man with a cowboy hat and a penchant for loud music. "Turn off that racket!" Galloway commanded.

The tall man leaned into the car slowly and switched off the engine. He bent to brush some dust off the top of his cowboy boots, deliberately not looking at Galloway. "Whatever you say, Chief." He didn't appear to like being ordered around by a policeman.

Darling bounded out of the car and rushed up the stairs. A cold grey light heralded the coming dawn, and it made the log cabin seem as abandoned as any he'd ever seen in the Kootenay valley. What had they done with her?

"Where's my wife?" he demanded. "Lane!" He turned the handle of the locked door.

"Don't get excited, there, partner. She's fine. I put her in a very nice room with a sandwich and a glass of water," the tall man drawled. "I even found her some aspirin. I mighta hit her a little hard. It took her a while to wake up and she did have a bit of a lump." He chuckled and then moved in front of Darling and unlocked the door. Galloway was standing by his car, smoking.

Supressing a desire to punch the man, Darling pushed into the empty living room calling furiously, "Lane? Are you all right?"

The tall man strolled to a closed door and put the key in, turning it with a smile. "It's a shame we have to wake her. Here you go." He held the door open for Darling to precede him, but in the same instant saw his prisoner was not there. A dress, some pens, a lipstick, a compact were scattered across the unmade bed, lying near an open and empty handbag. Lane's dress. Lane's handbag.

Darling lunged for it and then threw it back onto the bed, turning to say something to her jailer, but he was already outside—shouting. "She ain't here!"

Darling ran to the porch. Galloway had launched himself

off the car and was tossing his cigarette into the bush.

"What have you done, you bloody moron?" Galloway shouted, pushing angrily past the tall man to look into the empty house.

"Look, I did exactly what you told me to do. I locked her in that room and gave her something to eat. She couldn't have got out without someone helping her." At this, the tall man turned and began to look through the living room and kitchen, trying to find any disturbance in things as he had left them the night before.

Galloway was back outside, walking along the road, looking for evidence of anyone passing, but then he shook his head. They'd passed no one on the road down to the cabin. With an oath, he ran back and began to look around the yard, searching for evidence his guest had gone somewhere on foot, but the scrub, dried pine needles, and rocky terrain gave nothing away.

Darling was looking as well, trying to imagine what she would do if she really had gotten away. He could very nearly smile at the thought of her doing a Houdini act and fleeing into the night, if he weren't so terrified. He glanced sideways at Galloway who was kicking the tyre of the car. He seemed completely unhinged.

Darling thought about where Lane would go, and he tried not to look toward the south, through the stand of evergreens and down the side of the mountain. She certainly wouldn't go back up the isolated road that had brought them here. Too much danger of meeting her jailer on his return. The quickest way to put distance between herself and the cabin was south, straight down the mountain. He was sober in an instant. What would this mean? He knew Galloway was armed, and he suspected the tall man was as well. And, though they had not said so, he was effectively their prisoner.

Galloway strode back into the bedroom, pulling up the bedclothes and scattering things onto the floor. He pulled open the wardrobe and uttered another curse.

"My flight jacket is gone! And Priscilla's fur jacket. Someone must have come here and let her out." He shouted for the other man. That means they must have planned to hike down, he thought. "You go down the mountain on foot. When you find her, march her to the road. We'll pick you up. She wouldn't have left in the dark, so she hasn't gone far. And try not to kill her! What a bloody waste of time!" He took out his revolver and pointed it at Darling. "You're coming with me. Who the bloody hell is with her?" he said, almost to himself.

THE SUN WAS up now, and the long shadows began to give way to a blanched landscape. The steep descending gully they were in fanned out finally, and they could see more of the city below. Lane stopped to assess where they were and how far from the nearest road.

"I'm tired. Can we rest?" Meg said.

Lane was about to point to a ledge just below them but the shot and then the bullet striking an outcrop not five feet away from them wiped every thought away.

"Down!" she shouted, grabbing at Meg and hauling her to the ground. Her heart pounding, she waited, unconsciously spitting dust out of her mouth. Meg was lying next to her, her eyes wide with fear, her handbag over her head. Lane put her finger to her mouth and lifted her head; she saw they were lying behind a slight rocky rise. Could she risk trying to see where their attacker was?

They were on the eastern side of the narrow, steep-sided gully they'd been descending, which now seemed like folly. She wished they'd picked the other side, as they'd have had more of a chance to escape to the road. Nothing for it. She pushed herself partway up with her arms and looked up at the terrain they had descended. The gunman was much farther away than she had imagined, still a small figure.

But he was a small figure, who by his movements carried a rifle in one hand and field glasses in another. "Damn. He's still far from us but he has field glasses. And a rifle. We're like fish in a barrel."

"Wonderful. I'm lying here with a fur and an expensive purse getting shot at instead of sitting in comfort on a Greyhound bus getting out of here."

"Damn! I can't bloody see him now." Lane swivelled her head to look directly down from where they were. There was an outcrop that rose like a great wall of rock some fifteen feet below and to the east of their position. If they could get behind that, there'd be a reprieve.

Another shot, this time striking much farther west, on the other side of the gully. Lane frowned. What had he seen? She strained her eyes and then, with jolt of panic, saw what he was looking at. Below them, and farther to the west on more open ground, she could see a group of about seven riders following a trail. She looked back up the valley. The shooter was a little closer but still far enough away that he might have mistaken the riding party for his fleeing prisoner—or perhaps he had thought she might be among them.

"See that ridge? We have to get behind it. You go as fast as you can. Keep low. He's distracted by that riding party."

Meg shook her head as if she were going to refuse to move, then she got on her hands and knees and began to crawl toward the ridge. There was another shot. It sang into the echoing space. A bird rose in a frightened flutter from behind them somewhere. Meg had stopped and then resumed crawling toward the ridge, moving more quickly.

The shots had spooked the riding party, which was now whirling away in a cloud of dust. The shooter was watching them, perhaps realizing his mistake. It would take only a moment for him to begin looking for them again. Lane looked down and saw that Meg had nearly gained the ridge and was now on her feet lurching toward cover. Her foot slipped, sending a cascade of pebbles down the hill that seemed to Lane as loud as the gunshots they were trying to avoid. She glanced quickly at the figure with the gun. He was still looking away toward the west, perhaps trying to ascertain if one of the riders might be her. It was now or never. She crawled backwards down the incline toward the ridge, trying to keep him in sight and then lunged the last steps and collapsed next to Meg.

They sat silently, waiting for another shot. None came, but now they could hear the faint crunch of his descent.

"Why is he trying to kill us?" Lane asked in a whisper,

more rhetorically than not.

"Because that's what he does," Meg whispered back with irritation. She was looking at the palms of her hands, which were scrapped and abraded. "Ow!"

From where they were, they could see plainly that the riding party was beating a hasty retreat and disappearing over a hill toward town. Lane had a sinking feeling. It was as if they were being abandoned, for they were now trapped on the side of a hill with a gunman getting closer and no help from anywhere. The next shot was closer. Had he seen them? She had to think of a way out.

MARTINEZ HAD WATCHED the dawn come and tried to imagine what had happened. Why had Galloway not returned with Inspector Darling? Had they gone off on their own to try to find Darling's wife? They hadn't taken one of the police vehicles. He picked up the phone and called the hotel. There was no answer at Darling's room. Should he call Galloway's house? This threw him into a quandary. He didn't want to wake and alarm his wife. He hardly knew how to think about Galloway now. He would have to keep things clear in his head. Galloway had sounded concerned when he told him about Darling's wife being missing. And Galloway had no idea that Martinez had found the missing evidence, so in theory there should be no overt change in their relationship. He could deal with Galloway as he always had.

Telling himself to forget the hidden Griffin evidence for the moment, he looked at his watch, picked up the phone again, and dialled Galloway's number. Maybe there was a maid. After four rings, a woman who sounded as if she'd made a laboured run to the phone answered. "Galloway residence."

"This is Sergeant Martinez. I need to get hold of the assistant chief. Is he there?"

"I will check. One moment."

The woman spoke with a Spanish accent. He heard the phone receiver put down on a hard surface and then receding footsteps, slow receding footsteps. He pounded a pencil on his desk anxiously. After what seemed an interminable delay, the receiver was taken up.

"He's not here. I don't think he slept here last night, either. Have you tried the station? He spends a lot of time there since his wife has been gone."

Martinez blinked. Gone? His wife left him? Galloway had said nothing about this. But he had heard the assistant chief had been burning the midnight oil down at the station the last few nights.

He spoke to the maid in Spanish. "I'm at the station. He left here last night to pick someone up, and he was supposed to come back. When did his wife leave, again?" It wasn't entirely relevant, but Martinez couldn't help asking.

"I shouldn't really say, but it was a couple of days ago. She left the hospital, and God go with her. I knew she would be strong enough one day. I think her friend from Canada maybe helped her. She sure doesn't have any other friends."

"Listen, I'm sorry, I didn't ask your name."

"Fernanda Alvarez."

"It sounds like you might be worried about him, yes?

Listen, Miss Alvarez, do you know if he took his car?"

She reverted to English. "I couldn't care nothing about him. I was going to give him notice today anyway. With his wife gone, there's not so much a point in my being here. She wasn't the nicest person, but with what he was doing to her, I wouldn't be either. His car, that new one he's so proud of? It isn't in the carport, so I guess that's the one he's in."

Martinez hung up the phone and sat in a daze, his hand resting on the receiver. He tried to put what he had learned into some kind of order. Galloway's wife had been in the hospital. Why? Fernanda implied Galloway was "doing" something bad to her. Had he been hurting her? He suddenly knew it was entirely possible. And then she left the hospital, possibly helped by Darling's wife. Helped how? Had she helped her escape from Galloway?

And now, Darling's wife was missing. Had Galloway found out and spirited her away somewhere?

Martinez shook his head. It made no sense. How would he do it? Would he take the risk of somehow making someone disappear? Darling had said they'd been eating, and she'd gone shopping and she hadn't come back. Wait. He also said she thought they'd been followed. Had he hired someone? The photographs and the missing Griffin evidence weighed on him. What was Galloway getting out of the deal? Suddenly the car they'd all admired so much when he first drove it to work came to mind. He'd wondered at the time how much money an assistant chief might make to belong to a country club and drive a car like that. Unless he was taking money for services rendered. Or money and services? Did these include the use of Griffin's henchmen when he needed them?

The trouble was Martinez was powerless to deal with whatever was happening. Even if Galloway had kidnapped the whole Darling clan and then some, he had no idea where they might have gone.

The phone rang, making him jerk his hand off the receiver momentarily as if it were burning. "Yes? Tucson police, Sergeant Martinez."

"Martinez, it's Jim Hazeltine from the sheriff's office. We've had a call from the Mariposa Dude Ranch, and we just can't get to it. Both of us are out on other calls. A group was out early on horseback in the upper foothills, and they had to bring them back in a hurry. Some idiot is out there shooting the place up with a rifle. Hunting way too close to civilization. Would you mind going out to take care of it?"

CHAPTER TWENTY-EIGHT

"**W**HAT'S HE SHOOTING AT? I don't think he sees us," Meg said. She was crunched down in the narrow space they had found, where the ridge was split along a parallel, her knees pulled up.

"I agree. I don't think he does see us. But he might have seen our movement out of the corner of his eye and knows we're around here. I'm beginning to think he's just trying to pin us down. Or flush us out. I wish I could see where he is," Lane said, frustrated by not knowing, fearful that he would figure it out and come up this hill and find them. They'd be sitting ducks wedged into this rock formation.

Very slowly she rose and edged forward to where she could see a portion of the terrain below. There was no movement in the limited section visible to her. Then she nearly jumped when a lizard scampered across the rocks in front of her.

"What are you doing?" Meg whispered frantically.

Lane only held her hand up and moved forward another foot. She was at the edge of the outcrop. She gasped and pulled back. The cowboy was just below them at the bottom of the gully, looking up the opposite incline. Then something made her look again. In the middle distance, the dust of a passing car. The road! They'd come so close. She frowned at the man, who now seemed to be looking toward the road with his field glasses. He let the glasses hang loose at his neck and fired two shots into the air. He turned back to the task of scanning the terrain, slowly turning toward where Lane was observing him.

She held her breath and pulled back. The dust had settled on the road. Those two shots had been a signal: "I'm over here." Maybe even, "I've got them cornered." Whoever was driving the car had stopped. She pulled back to consider a course of action. It was only a matter of time. She sat down next to Meg.

"There's a car out on the road. Those last two shots were a signal; the gunman thinks he's got us. That means it's Galloway or Griffin or someone. That man with the rifle, is he one of your husband's men?"

"Yeah," Meg sighed. "That's Idaho."

"He's really called Idaho? Okay. So that means Griffin had me snatched off the street. Do you know why?"

"How should I know? He might think you saw who shot that Mr. Renwick or figured it out somehow. Though I don't know why he'd bring you up here." She thought for a moment. "You know, Paul is in up to his eyeballs with Artie. Maybe he got Artie to pick you up. What would Paul want you for?"

Lane sat back, her hand on her forehead. So she'd been right. He had found out somehow that she'd helped Priscilla get away. She could feel part of her mind trying to trace how he could have done it. Had the nurse talked? She didn't think so. Nurse Yelland was one of the most implacable people she'd ever met. But someone else must have, a cleaner at the hospital perhaps. It made little difference at this point. She pulled her attention back to the current situation.

"Look, I don't think either one of them wants us dead, though I can't say the same for your chum Idaho out there. You're Mrs. Griffin, after all, and Galloway thinks I have information he needs."

Meg shook her head. "You don't know Artie. If he thinks I know something, something he doesn't want me to know, he'd get rid of me. And Paul Galloway? Probably worse. He's a dirty cop. He has more to cover up. Now I'm sitting up here on the side of a mountain with a sore butt and a man trying to shoot me because Paul wants you! If I'd known that, I would have skedaddled long before this!" She turned away staring glumly at the wall of rock directly in front of her and crossed her arms. "You know, I tried to leave him before. I was gonna go back and find an old sweetheart from when I was a kid. He was called Ricky. Turns out he was killed in the Pacific. He's the only person I ever really loved. But Rex, he's a real sweetie. It's too bad, really." She sighed and adjusted how she was sitting. The ground was rocky and uncomfortable. "Anyway, I don't want Artie to find me. Even if he doesn't want me dead, he's turned into a crazy jealous bastard. I want out."

Lane's thoughts were churning. "Do you mean that?"

Meg wheeled on her, her voice nearly coming out of the whisper they'd been using. "Of course I do! I think he had that poor Mr. Renwick shot. I can't trust him."

"Why would he have Renwick shot? They arrested his brother for it." That's when fog cleared, and she finally put it together. The thing that had bothered her in the cabin. "Wait, if your real husband is Griffin, then Mr. Holden ... Oh, I see."

"Okay, you figured it out. That's what I do. I'm a grifter. Now I'm sick of it. I want some peace and quiet."

"But why do you think he was responsible for Renwick's death?"

Meg shook her head. "Not one hundred percent, but maybe ninety-nine. Artie is pretty jealous. Maybe. I don't know."

"Did he think Renwick was your boyfriend? Just a case of mistaken identity?" Lane was appalled at the idea that a completely innocent bystander might have been shot in some sort of lover's quarrel.

"I wish I'd stayed with Rex. He would have helped me out of this. He really loved me! Not a jealous bone in his body."

Not able to make complete sense of this, Lane was about to speak when she turned toward the gully. They could hear a muttered curse and a sliding sound much nearer to where they were hiding. It would be only moments before he found them.

Time had run out. Lane knew what she had to do. Meg was right. Even if she were a grifter, she didn't deserve to get shot for helping Lane escape. She turned to Meg and put her hand on her arm. "Look. Don't move. Don't say anything. Don't come out till you've heard everyone leave, including the car. And good luck."

With that Lane got up, took up the flight jacket she'd been sitting on, and walked into the open from their hideout with her arms up.

"All right. I'm coming down," she called loudly. "No need to shoot the place up."

He must have felt there was a need, because he waited till Lanc was most of the way down the hill and fired one more shot.

May 1943

LANE TRIED TO pull Claude away from the doorway, but he was clinging to the frame, digging his nails in, his knuckles white. "Claude, we have to go! When they realize they have missed one person they will comc back."

He wheeled on her. "What chancc do we have? You don't even have a revolver. What kind of a spy are you?" Tears splashed on his blue jacket. He took one last look at the three people who'd been tied and executed where they sat, and then let her lead him away.

They ran to the edge of the property. It was still early, barely past dawn, so the road was empty. They could hear a dog barking in the village just around the bend. But Lane could also hear a woman shouting. She sounded familiar. Who was she? *She wanted to shift her head to hear better but couldn't seem to move it.* On the other side of the road, they headed quickly to the small forest that lay at the top of a rise. They were halfway up the hill when Lane heard the motorcycle returning. She pulled Claude down among the stands of dead grasses. It was the two she'd seen leaving when she'd been making her way to the safe house. They turned back into the property, jumped off the machine, and began to search. One of them shouted to the other that he was an *imbécile* for not checking the outdoor privy the first time.

"Now!" said Lane. "They're busy. We have a few moments." They bolted into the wood and continued up the hill. Lane breathed with the regular rhythm she had taught herself so she could move quickly over long distances. *She could still hear the woman, who sounded angry now, and wanted her to stop.* At the top, the trees dwindled, and they could see the open country below them. Her thoughts clouded. She could hear the motorcycle as if it had come straight up the hill behind them. *And then the woman shouting, really close now.* She turned but saw only darkness. That shot—she knew it was the one that killed Claude. He had stood up just at the wrong time. It was her fault. She could not stop the well of anguish that grew in her at this. But it wasn't Claude who was down. She was—she could feel where the bullet struck her in the side. At one and the same time she felt the searing pain and the surge of relief that she had not been responsible for Claude's death.

"Get up!"

———

LANE OPENED HER eyes. She felt herself lying on the ground, a rock pressing into her neck, her arm high above her being pulled.

"Get up. I barely grazed you. And that's just because you've been a pain in the ass."

"Let her go, you bastard!"

Lane heard but didn't see the rock that struck the gunman with a soft thud on the shoulder. She was still dazed, and though it was dawning on her that she was not in France, she had a momentary sense that it was Claude who'd been struck. But who was the woman shouting?

She felt herself being helped up. She tried experimentally to move her feet and found she could. "It's okay. I think I can walk," she said. Her mouth felt unfamiliar, as if someone else was talking. She instinctively put her right hand to her left side, and then pulled it away, whimpering at the pain. She tried to focus. She was with a cowboy and a woman going somewhere. It was coming back. She could hear angry male shouts nearby. The voice sounded familiar, but she couldn't place it.

She'd been running from someone with that woman from the hotel. She suppressed an instinct to look back, as her memory came swooping home. Meg should be there, hiding, Lane thought, her heart sinking. Meg wasn't hiding. She was helping her limp across the desert to the road, and she was saying something shrill and very ill-considered to the man with the gun.

Lane tried to turn her head to see where he was, but it hurt. She thought she could hear him walking behind them. The angry, "Would you shut up?" confirmed it.

"Meg," she tried. "You should have stayed."

"You're right about that! But I just got sick of Idaho beating up on people who can't fight back. Look at you. He shot you for no good goddamn reason!"

Lane could see the car she'd been kidnapped in parked up on the road, Paul Galloway leaning on it watching, a cigarette in his hand, a gun trained on Darling, and she was overwhelmed with dread. It had all been for nothing, just like Meg had said.

———

AMY WATTS STOOD in the woodshed dangling the letter in her hand, looking out the door at the utter dreariness and cold. She'd have to burn it, of course, though she had an impulse to keep it. It had proved her right, which made it kind of a prize. What had Barney sent to get a response like this? And to whom? Sighing, she lifted it up and reread it. He must have been trying to get money out of him. He'd been gambling his paycheques away steadily. She'd known about the gambling. Had fought with him, had cajoled him, had begged him. But this, and those … well, she didn't even know what to call them. Prizes? Tokens? A change purse, a ribbon, a chain bracelet. She walked slowly back to the house, which now had a strangely hollow feeling as if it had been wilfully deserted by Barney. He'd finally left her after all, just as she'd feared all those years.

She thought of him opening the envelope, being disappointed by its thinness, and seeing these words: "Don't you dare communicate with me again. I was prepared to forget how I protected you from that Tina, but now it's come up again, hasn't it?" And then an incomprehensible signature. When Amy had first found it, she had turned it over and over, trying to understand who sent it. Barney must have destroyed the envelope. Now it didn't matter. All that mattered is that it had to be burned, just like the clothes and everything else she'd burned to free herself from Barney Watts. She opened the grate with the lifter and watched the flames dancing inside the stove. She dropped the letter in and closed the grate.

"WHAT DO YOU want?" Tina stood in the doorway, her hands on her hips. This was all she needed.

"Hello, Tina." Amy got out of the car and looked around as if she were a big-city buyer. "I guess you heard, Barney's dead."

"I heard, yes. I wish I could say I was sorry. I know you have a little girl. It must be hard. I am sorry about that."

"Thanks. That means nothing, coming from you. You were planning all along to take him from me." Amy cocked her head sideways and looked at Tina. "I never did understand what he saw in you. Look at you. A grease monkey with a floozy's hair."

Tina frowned, feeling like the ground was sliding underfoot. "I honestly have no idea what you're talking about, Amy. I told you ten years ago that I hated him. I still hate him, even dead as he is."

Amy sneered. "Right. That's why he came here the other day, I suppose. That's why he kept that little memento you gave him. He tried to hide it, but I saw it one day stuffed at the back of a shelf in the woodshed."

Tina knew instantly. The purse. Taking a deep breath, she shook her head. "Look, Amy, I never told you this. I should have, but I was young and frightened. He raped me. I was sixteen, and he drove me up some dark road somewhere and he raped me. He had his hand over my mouth so I couldn't breathe or scream. I was sixteen, do you understand? I didn't even know if he was going to kill me. He drove me back and pushed me out of the car at the top of that drive," Tina said, pointed angrily toward the road, "and left me like a piece of garbage he was throwing away. I wouldn't run away with him for all the tea in China. I'd as soon kill him. I never gave him that purse. I thought I'd lost it, but it must have fallen out of my pocket and he kept it. Anyway, he only came here to find out if I'd ever told anyone about the rape. Why would he think, after all this time, I would have told anyone?"

Amy nodded, her lips clamped together. "What a liar," she said. "What an unbelievable lying bitch you are."

Tina glanced at the bay doors and turned back. "It was you."

"Of course it was me. As soon as I learned he'd come here. Then I took care of him."

Tina backed away, slowly. She felt as if her insides had melted. Where was her father? She wanted to close her eyes, to think. Amy had just said she'd "taken care" of Barney. Had she killed him? If so, she wouldn't admit it unless she was planning to kill her as well.

"Look, Amy. I don't know what you're saying. But if you killed him, you should talk to the police. They'd understand. He was a bad man. Life with him must have been no picnic. You'd get off."

Tears formed in Amy's eyes. She opened her purse and pulled out a handgun. "That's where you're wrong, Tina. It was a picnic. He was sweet and worked hard and loved Sadie. I know he could never do what you say he did. Never. I knew he was up to something when he started staying late, disappearing on the weekend. I got the letter, and right away I knew it was true. Then I found the purse. See, he never forgot you."

Tina backed into the garage, trying to think. What letter was she talking about? "Amy, you can't shoot me. Don't be ridiculous. My dad could be back any minute. The police know something is up. Sergeant Ames—"

"Shoot you? I'm not going to shoot you. Way too messy and noisy. Now get in the car. Here, I'll even let you drive"

"SERGEANT AMES? TINA'S not here. I don't understand it. The bay doors are open, and the trouble lamp she was using for an engine repair is still on inside the car. I've looked all over. She didn't even take her jacket."

"Don't move. Stay by the phone in case she calls. We're coming right out."

Ames hung up the phone, his hand shaking, and then picked it up again, asking O'Brien to put him through to the Watts house. A woman answered.

"Mrs. Watts?" He wanted to be relieved, but he already knew it wasn't her.

"No, this is her mother. I'm looking after Sadie, but Amy should have been home long before now. I was wondering if she had an accident or something. Maybe I should call the police."

"This is the police. Where did she say she was going?"

"Just into town to get groceries, but—"

"Into town," he said, "in what?" Ames felt his chest compress.

"In the car. She said you finally gave it back. And, well, the thing is ... it's just ..."

"What is it?" Ames asked impatiently. This was maddening.

"Well, I went up to her room to get something and all the drawers were pulled out and most of her clothes were gone. I'm worried that she ... I mean, she hasn't been the same since Barney died. What if she ran away or something? I can't look after Sadie on my own."

"Terrell!" Ames bellowed, hurtling down the stairs.

Terrell was up and by the door, pulling his cap on.

"Keys!" Ames shouted. "O'Brien. Alert all the local RCMP detachments. We're looking for a dark green 1940 Chevrolet coupe, one, or possibly two, women."

"Sarge," said O'Brien briskly, picking up the phone.

Ames was almost out the door, when he turned again. "And get a warrant to search the Watts house. Get two of the boys out there, first road going up the hill after Willow Point. House at the top. Ransack the place looking for any kind of poison, bottles of something, rat killer, bleach, alcohol, you name it. Outbuildings. Everything."

O'Brien nodded and then turned back to the phone.

"IT WAS THAT damn curly blond hair," Ames said, running his hand through his own hair. The ferry had been on the Nelson side, so they were now on the short ride across, the ferry engine thrumming underneath them. The icy rain of the last couple of days had turned to a steadily falling icy snow. "Curly hair buying clothes, curly hair hitchhiking, curly hair in the car, and then the purse, which Tina said she lost the night Watts assaulted her. It was Amy Watts in some sort of wig, I'm sure of it. What I don't understand is why she fixated on Tina. After all, he seemed to be up to his usual trick of going after high-school girls."

"TURN UP HERE," Amy commanded, leaning forward, trying to see up the little road she wanted them to take. She waved the gun toward an ascending turnoff.

Tina made the sharp turn up the hill, hardly daring to believe her luck. Amy must not know that King's Cove was hidden among the trees on this hillside.

Amy was leaning forward, looking at the options. As Tina started to turn up toward the church, Amy saw the steeple. "No. Damn! Go this way!"

Tina pulled the wheel sharply to straighten the car and go where she was directed. She felt her heart freeze. This road was barely wide enough for one vehicle—rutted, winding, and icy, it climbed steadily uphill. Worse, she had no idea where it would take them. Perhaps to some isolated place where Tina could carry out whatever plan she had. Tina, whose mind had been whirring, tried to adjust to the new terrain, desperately trying to think of how to get away or use the small wrench she had in the back pocket of her coveralls.

If Amy's idea was to shoot her in the close quarters of the car, she might be able to wrestle the gun away before she got the shot off, though those were very long odds. Amy held the gun on her, not shifting it even for a moment. If she yanked the steering wheel hard at one of the corners, she might unsettle her, but it was dangerous gambit on this narrow bit of slippery road because a steep gully dropped precipitously through underbrush down toward a creek fifteen feet below.

Everything happened at once. Out of the corner of her eye, Tina saw Amy reach into her handbag with a gloved hand and pull out a thickly folded men's handkerchief that filled the car with a choking smell, and at the same instant, as they turned a corner, a tractor loomed up, coming right at them. Tina had no time to do anything except slam on the brakes, but the tractor's driver—an old man with a horrified expression and a cigarette clinging to the corner of his open mouth—could not react in time. He ran head-on into the car, his tractor sliding on the ice, pushing the car back toward the curve in the road.

Shaken, Tina became aware that Amy had screamed and was bent over trying to find something on the floor. The gun! She pulled frantically on the handle of her own door and managed to push it open just as Amy found what she was looking for. Tina launched herself out of the car, falling partway down the gully until a fallen tree covered with a fresh layer of snow stopped her. She lay dazed, her back in excruciating pain, waiting for the gunshot. Instead she heard an angry voice.

"What the blazes do you think you're doing? Bloody women! Put that down and get out! Who told you you could drive up this road?"

Trying to ignore the agony in her back, Tina scrambled as quickly as she could back to the road. Her hands were freezing, and it was hard to get purchase. The old man had Amy backed against the crumpled front of the car and was holding her at bay with a rifle. "She was going to kill me," Tina stuttered.

"Could have killed everyone driving up this road the wrong way," the old man said angrily. "Bloody ruined my tractor." He narrowed his gaze on Amy. " Oh no you don't! You stay right there. You," he said to Tina, "get the rope on the back of the tractor. And pick up that revolver. Don't want it going off."

Tina limped around the tractor, found a coil of grey and fraying rope, and brought it back to where the old man was standing, his glaring gaze never leaving his prisoner.

"Can you use a rifle?" he asked, not looking at Tina.

"Yes."

"Good. You take this and you pull the trigger if she tries to move." He slowly transferred the rifle to Tina, keeping it trained on Amy, and only then looked at Tina. "Hey, don't I know you?" But he didn't wait for an answer. He strode in his rubber boots to where Amy stood with her hands up against the car, her face a mask of angry defeat.

AMES WAS SURPRISED to see Marcus Van Eyck at the top of the drive, waving frantically as the car began to slow down. Not waiting for the car to come to a complete stop, he was in the back, closing the door. "She's all right! She's in King's Cove with the Bertollis." Van Eyck collapsed back on the seat after this effort.

Ames had turned to Terrell. "The King's Cove turnoff is about three miles past the Balfour store. Step on it!" He turned around to see Marcus Van Eyck taking a deep breath and looking out the window. "She called you?"

"She said that Watts woman was going to kill her. Luckily an old man in a tractor slammed into them, and somehow they disarmed her and tied her up. What does this mean?"

"It means Tina has caught the person who murdered Barney Watts," said Ames, his feelings a mixture of relief and admiration, but also regret that he had not been able to effect a daring rescue. This, he thought, must be how Darling feels all the time.

CHAPTER TWENTY-NINE

MEG WAS PRACTICALLY DRAGGING LANE the last feet up over the steep gravelly lip to the road. Idaho impatiently took one side of her to get her the rest of the way.

"How did you get this far, anyway?" he said angrily.

She wanted to tell him she worked for the French Foreign Legion, but she could see Galloway, still training his gun at Darling's head. Best not annoy Idaho with any angry sarcasm.

Idaho lifted his head and frowned. And then Lane and Meg heard it too. A new sound. Sirens from at least two cars, somewhere well past the outskirts of the city and coming north in a hurry. "Come on, get a move on." He took her arm in a painful grip and hurried her forward.

UP ON THE road, Galloway and Darling heard the sirens as well.

"What the devil?" Galloway put his hand to the rim of his hat to block out the sun that pushed blindingly across the landscape from high in the east and looked down the long road. The sirens were definitely coming in their direction. Why? They had been standing watching the progress of Idaho's hunt and Lane's emergence from the ridge, Galloway tauntingly handing Darling the field glasses from time to time so he could see clearly the humiliation of Lane's capture.

When the shot had sounded, Darling had been watching only her face through the field glasses. He hadn't seen the man raise his rifle. She'd been talking to the man with the rifle and then she dropped like a rock out of the sight of the field glasses. Darling frantically tried to find her and then threw the binoculars aside and started toward Lane. Galloway had put out his hand and grabbed him by the elbow, hard.

"No you don't." Darling had wrestled to get out of his grip, furious, and felt his arm pulled behind him, his elbow screaming at being yanked into some unnatural position.

"There now. You can calm down. She's getting up. Let's just wait here for them, shall we? She looks shaken up. I don't think I'll have too much trouble getting her to tell me where she took my wife."

"Let me go, you bastard!" And then he too turned to look down the road at the rising wail of the sirens.

Idaho hurried the last few yards to where the car was parked and pushed Lane toward the two men and then turned his attention to Meg, who was leaning against the car, recovering her breath from the effort of helping Lane get to the road.

"The boss is not happy about you," he said to her, but

he had his eye on the approaching police cars.

"I'm not too happy about him, so that makes two of us," she retorted. And then, feeling his hand take her upper arm, she pulled it away. "And you can keep your hands off me. You're nothing but a bully."

"I'll be dealing with you later, missy!" he hissed.

"You can't help yourself, can you?" Meg folded her arms and turned to look at Lane. Darling had pulled free of Galloway and enfolded her in his arms. That's what I need, Meg thought. Someone who loves me just like that. Not for the first time in the last twenty-four hours, her mind turned to Rex Holden. He had loved her just like that. Just like Ricky had.

Lane winced in Darling's embrace and he let go, holding her out so he could scan her.

"When you went down like that, I ..."

"I'm fine, darling. Don't make a fuss. He just grazed me. But I've ruined a perfectly good pair of shoes."

"I don't believe you. You went down like a ton of bricks."

"Thank you very much, I'm sure." Lane tried to smile, but she had been hit and it was beginning to hurt like the dickens. She could feel dampness growing just where her lower rib was. She tried to still the natural panic this engendered. It was probably, as she had told Darling, only a graze. She'd have a sore rib and maybe a handsome scar.

"In the car, both of you," Galloway said, waving his revolver in their direction. Two vehicles from the Tucson Police Department were almost upon them.

"What the hell is going on?" Idaho asked of no one in particular, looking angrily at the rising cloud of dust. "What have you done?" He directed this question at Galloway.

Lane and Darling used the distraction to scuttle around to the rear of the car. Meg joined them. Idaho and Galloway were both armed. If there was going to be gunfire, it was as well to have a place to duck.

The two police cars pulled to a stop, aligned so they blocked any exit on the road. Galloway turned to Idaho. "I don't know why they're here, so you're going to have to play your part. I'm going to put you under arrest. We can sort things out later."

"Sorry, buddy. I've been playing my part. No one is arresting me!"

"Don't be an ass! If they think you're holding any of us hostage they'll shoot you! Just play along!"

Among the officers who leapt out of the car was Martinez. He surveyed the scene, trying to make sense of it. He could see Inspector Darling and his wife and—for some reason—Mrs. Holden standing behind the car.

"What the devil are you doing here, Martinez?" Galloway said.

"Sheriff's office called in a report from a local dude ranch of someone shooting a powerful rifle up in this valley, sir." He kept his voice professional.

"Well, as you can see, I got here before you, and I got him, so you can pack him up and take him right back to town. We can add kidnapping Mrs. Darling to his charges as well."

Martinez's eyes flickered toward a slight movement behind Galloway. Darling was looking directly at him and shaking his head.

"What I see, sir, is that the man you've supposedly apprehended is still holding a firearm. Why are Mrs. Holden, Inspector Darling, and his wife here?"

Galloway took a step toward Martinez, his face suffused with rage. "Who are you to be asking the questions? I made you. You do what you're told, or I'll have you out flipping tortillas for a living."

"*Tortillas*, sir. The double l is pronounced *y*." Martinez felt something inside him harden into resolution. "Can you just explain again why this man, one of Jimmy Griffin's men, is here and still holding a firearm with you and these others, sir?"

Galloway went to take another step toward Martinez, pulling up his revolver as if he just discovered it in his hand, but he was stopped by Martinez, who pointed his own gun directly at Galloway's chest.

"Put that down please, sir," Martinez said, pointing toward the hood of the car.

Galloway wheeled on Idaho and shouted at the police who were watching this drama unfold. "Arrest this man and take Martinez's firearm. This nonsense has gone on long enough!"

The police began to shuffle, and Martinez put up his hand. "Hold it right there." He turned to Galloway. "It *has* gone on long enough. I found the evidence against Griffin, where you hid it, sir. I've got photographs of you with him in various social situations. It seems you've been collaborating with the biggest mob man this city has ever seen. I don't know why, or for how long, but I think it neutralizes your ability to order people around."

Darling saw a movement from Idaho, his rifle beginning

to swing upward into position toward Martinez. If he got that shot off, Martinez would be dead and there'd be a hail of bullets from the heavily armed throng gathered around the cars. He lunged out from behind the car at Idaho, knocking him off balance, and tumbling them both backwards over the shoulder of the road into the gully.

The big cowboy landed hard with Darling's weight driving all the wind from him in a sick woof. He gasped for breath, rolled to one side, then tried to rise but felt the barrel of his own rifle poke him between the shoulder blades. "Okay, okay," he said, then settled face down in the gully and, without being told, put his hands behind his head.

Galloway turned, uncertain now, first aiming his revolver at Darling and then at Martinez.

"No, sir. Put it down. I briefed all these gentlemen before we left and put out an APB. Everyone in the department knows what you've been up to. I've also had James Griffin re-arrested for good measure."

Meg watched as Idaho was handcuffed and folded into the back of one of the cars and then, with a sigh, approached Martinez.

"You seem to be in charge around here now," she said. "I should probably tell you, he likely was the one who shot that poor Mr. Renwick."

Martinez frowned and turned to look at Idaho scowling in the back of the car. "Is that right? Why do you say that?"

"Oh, it's a long story, hon. You'd better bring me in too. I can probably help you. I'm married to Artie, or as you call him, James Griffin. As to why he shot him, it's because

Artie found out about my boyfriend, and that stupid jackass thought it was Renwick, just because we were standing together having a chat."

DARLING AND LANE sat at dinner, bracing martinis before them.

"This is something they do very well in this country," Lane said, holding up her glass, and then grimacing. Her ribs, now bandaged, were throbbing faintly underneath the painkiller she had taken. She took a sip and then put her glass down.

Somehow, they'd all been got down the hill and sorted out. Martinez had been surprised to learn from Meg that it was Idaho who likely shot Renwick under orders from Griffin. The mobster heard from his spy that Meg was playing outside the lines of their arrangement to fleece Holden.

"You know what absolutely astounds me?" Darling said.

"What's that?"

"Martinez told me that, among the papers he'd found in Galloway's office, there was a letter from someone called Watts threatening to reveal something that went on while he was in Nelson in the thirties just before I arrived there. It was a blackmail letter, effectively, demanding cash." Darling took a sip of his martini. "And wasn't Watts the name of the man that got killed just now that Ames is dealing with?"

He was making normal conversation with his wife, but his insides were in turmoil. He'd paced anxiously at the hospital waiting for the doctor to finish treating Lane.

Even hearing that the bullet had only grazed her scarcely soothed his anxiety. She'd been sent home with a packet of painkillers after she had refused to spend the night to get a proper rest.

"We can phone Ames in the morning. It would be a shocking coincidence, certainly. But maybe not so much. I mean, you and Galloway used to work together in the Nelson police force. If he is crooked here, he was crooked there too."

"God, don't remind me," Darling said glumly, grimacing at the strength of the martini.

"Cheer up! You accomplished something you normally are deprived of, saving the day and rescuing me—well, and all of us really, by subduing that cowboy. A dangerous killer by all accounts."

"Thank you for pointing that out. It was not difficult. I put into it all of the rage I had bottled up at watching him shoot you while you were giving yourself up. I think it is one of the most satisfactory moments of my career."

"Yes, it was funny, his shooting me like that. Ordinary soldiers seemed for the most part to understand the rules during the war. I wonder if the ones who shot people giving themselves up in combat ended up in gangs in civvy street?" She put her glass down and grew silent then.

"What is it?" Darling asked.

"You know, when I got hit, I think I passed out for a minute, maybe from the shock of it. Certainly not from this flesh wound. But I was suddenly back there, you know. In France, in '43. I can't really give you the details of why I was there, but I was supposed to meet some people in a safe house, only I found the dog shot outside and three of the four people I was expecting to see were dead. I probably narrowly missed the killers, but I managed to throw myself on the ground as they rode away on a motorcycle. It turns out there was one man hiding in the outside privy. He was beside himself, furious at me for not being armed. I worried that the motorcycle would come back, and it took everything I had to persuade him to get away. When I was lying there, today I mean, I thought I was back in France and that he had been shot and it was my fault. Only as I was coming to did I realize it was I who had been hit. I felt such a relief, I can't tell you, to be free for that one moment of the guilt over the thought that I'd caused his death."

Darling sat, holding her hand, realizing the importance of this moment. In his heart he did not believe he would ever really learn about the details of her war, and yet these few had been shaken out of her by ... he wasn't really sure what. Perhaps by being shot herself?

"What did happen to him in the end?"

Lane looked down and took a deep breath. "That's the thing, you see. He was shot as we were fleeing. They did come back. He was behind me and he went down. I lay, terrified, waiting for my turn, but they disappeared on the bike again. I realized, of course, they hadn't known about me, so they hadn't bothered to look any further. They must have figured out that they'd missed one and gone back for him. I have believed it was my fault ever since."

"How could it have been? You know that, surely." He wanted to say that it was nonsense, but he'd seen policemen suffering the same sort of trauma after violent incidents, and he knew logic didn't come into it.

She so wanted to tell him. How before she'd left on that particular mission, she'd been offered a revolver and had said absolutely not. If the Germans had found her, it would have been the final proof that she was not the local French girl she was pretending to be. She'd have been done for. She wasn't the only one. Lots of the women didn't want them. The great advantage for the women of special operations was that the enemy never believed women would do the work they did. If they were armed it put them in much greater danger. Claude had told her the British were useless if they did not come with guns, but he had been angry about his friends. She had only come with information, she didn't even know what kind, it was all coded, but he wasn't having it. She had always thought, if only she had been armed, he might have been spared.

"Do I?" she said. "I think I do. But guilt doesn't hang on reason. It is a great dark pool inside that reminds you, in your blackest moments, that you were spared and someone else wasn't. I don't think I quite know yet how to live with it."

Darling pulled both of her hands into his. "I think what I fear most is that one of the ways you live with it is to constantly put yourself in danger, until one day ..."

"Look, darling. Let me clear one thing up: I've always been like this. Do you think I would have signed up for the sort of work I did if I wasn't a little inured to the danger? And though I tell you I'm not sure how one lives with that sort of guilt, I *have* lived with it. I have turned my face firmly to the future, hoping that time would do its healing-all-wounds best. I couldn't have married you if I didn't believe in that. But I do sometimes have very bad nights, and I think the loss of that man is why. I should perhaps have told you what happens to me sometimes, but I don't know when it will strike. I think I worried that what happened today would usher in another episode of nighttime horrors. Perhaps I should have told you before. You might not have wanted me under the circumstances."

"I'm afraid there are no circumstances under which I would not want you," Darling said.

"And if it's any consolation," Lane pushed on, not wanting to accept the glow of warmth his words caused her just yet, "I actually think today I realized a little bit more that his death was not my fault. I don't think it means I'm over it completely, but it really is the first time I've seen more clearly that it is, oh I don't know, not about fault and more about circumstance. For example, I refused to take a weapon. It was the right choice. And even if I had had one, it would have been nearly impossible for him, say, to shoot and actually kill even one of his pursuers, speeding as they were on their motorcycle, and for all I know he wasn't a very good shot. He certainly wasn't army trained. So, you see, I think I'm beginning to understand logic might actually come into it."

Darling sat back and looked at the dining room with its hushed atmosphere and thick white tablecloths. Outside, lanterns illuminated the paths to the rooms and suites, and the fountain was lit, the water playing and catching the light. "Not much of a honeymoon," he said, "what with one thing and another."

"I don't know. I haven't anything to compare it to. It was better than poor Mr. Renwick's. With everything else going on in his life, the crowning tragic insult is that he should have been killed simply because he was mistaken for someone else. What do you think will happen with Ivy and the hapless brother-in-law?"

"Once it's clear neither of them had anything to do with the death, I suppose they'll be off back to Wisconsin. She looks like someone who eats brothers-in-law for breakfast. She'll land on her feet and before long we'll be reading about her in the business section of the newspaper. Do you mind terribly about the extra day?"

"Not at all. Once we've done our statements, I intend to spend the entire rest of the day in a lounge chair reading Zane Grey. Better late than never, I always say. What I'm wondering about is what will happen to Meg."

CHAPTER THIRTY

WHEN THEY ARRIVED AT THE police station the next morning, the place was abuzz with activity. Galloway's office was crowded with policemen—Lane was happy to see one woman among them—all going through his drawers and boxing and labelling things. Martinez led them to his desk and asked them to sit down.

"Thanks for coming down. I know this held up your trip back home. Everything is ready for you," Martinez said, sitting heavily in his chair. His exhaustion was palpable. "How are you doing, Mrs. Darling?"

"Quite all right," Lane said, smiling. "It was a flesh wound. I imagine I'll have sore ribs for a while, and then it will be like it never happened."

Martinez nodded.

"Anyway," she continued, "There's a shawl I want to get before I go. I'll cheer myself up with that. In fact, I was on my way to buy it when I got pulled into that car."

"You're taking it very well, ma'am."

"For what it's worth, Sergeant Martinez, I thought you were very brave. I imagine it took everything you had to stand up to your boss like that."

"Thank you. Just my duty, and I have Inspector Darling to thank, I think, for the photographs. They arrived in an envelope yesterday from the Santa Cruz Inn. They were brought by a cab driver." He pulled out the envelope in which the pictures had come and removed two of them. "I guess you'd like these?"

One photograph showed Lane and Darling standing, arm in arm, squinting very slightly from the sun, in front of the door of the San Xavier del Bac mission church door. In the second one, they were laughing at something. Priscilla Galloway had caught them as they prepared for the more formal picture, a lovely natural shot of them happy in each other's company. Lane held this second picture an extra moment. What must it have been like for Priscilla to look through a lens framing two people in a world so far from her own?

Martinez pulled out a third picture and held it up. "The rest were more or less variations on this theme." The photograph showed a crowded restaurant full of smoke and people laughing and drinking. On one side the corner of a stage was visible, and just beside it were Griffin and Galloway talking cozily together, holding cigarettes and martini glasses. "It's how I realized what must have happened to my notes on the case. Galloway was protecting Griffin, in exchange for, I'm not sure what, but we're bound to find out. You know, I had no idea he was married. Galloway knew though. He sure wasn't going to tell me.

And when the Renwicks turned out to be a perfect fit for the crime, he must have thought he could keep Griffin out of it."

He reached for a file and now placed two pieces of paper in front of Lane and one in front of Darling. "These are your statements from yesterday. Could you just read them and sign there at the bottom? Let me know if anything needs to be changed."

This task accomplished, Martinez wished them the very best of luck, and Lane and Darling made their way into the street. It was sunny, but significantly cooler temperatures in the shade spoke of the coming winter.

"I really would like to buy a shawl I saw. I know where the shop is. Do you mind?"

"I don't, but I'm going with you," Darling said firmly.

THEY HAD PACKED everything they could and were about to head to the pool for a last swim when there was a tentative knock at the door. Lane went to open it and found Rex Holden on the welcome mat.

"Mr. Holden, how lovely to see you. I thought you'd packed up and gone home. Do come in. We're just packing ourselves. We're off tomorrow."

Holden took off his hat and held it in his hands. "I'll surprise you I think, but I wanted to thank you. Meg has come back to me."

Lane looked at him with gratifying surprise. She was certain Meg would have been charged with something. Perhaps she had been freed in exchange for information about Griffin. "Goodness. That's good news? I'm sorry

385

about sounding doubtful, but I'd have thought perhaps you felt well rid of her."

Holden smiled sheepishly. "I know now what was going on. I could have filed charges of some sort against her, but she called me from the police station and asked to meet me. She said she was going to get on the Greyhound bus, and then changed her mind. She confessed to me all about the scheme. It was a bit humbling, really."

"But you've taken her back?"

"Well, that's why I've come. She told me how you two had made an escape down the hill and she said something you did made her change her mind. No, no. I don't need to know what it is. But you know, at heart she's good, and I think she genuinely cares for me. I don't know. I'm not getting any younger, and she makes me happy. I imagine the law will be quite forgiving now she's talked about James Griffin's activities. They only asked that she be prepared to appear at his trial to testify, and then they'll let her go. She'll get a divorce and we'll get married, legally this time."

Lane smiled. "I think you're right about her. And she's terribly brave. She rescued me when she didn't have to, and she was very plucky clattering around in the desert in the middle of the night. And you know, she stood up to Griffin's quite ferocious gunman when she saw him shoot me. And she did say she cares for you. I told her to leave her purse behind when we were running away, but she wouldn't hear of it. You gave it to her, she said."

———

"THAT POOR KIDDIE," Ames said, surveying the collection of things taken from the Watts house. "Look at this stuff. I don't understand how a mother could carry on like this. Did she really think she'd get away with it? That she and Sadie would live happily ever after?"

Terrell picked up the blond wig and then put it back down next to the poison Amy Watts had used to kill her husband. "I don't really understand it either. I wonder if she was just going along, doing one thing at a time, and not thinking about the possible consequences. She finds that little purse of Miss Van Eyck's carefully saved in the shed. She sees a letter from an ex-cop that threatens to expose her husband's 'involvement' with Tina if he ever contacts him again. She doesn't know about the background of the rape. She just thinks he's really going to run away with Miss Van Eyck. She conceives somehow the idea that she can kill him and blame Miss Van Eyck, and as she goes along, each step seems to go without a hitch. If she'd managed to kill Miss Van Eyck as well, she probably would have assumed her troubles would be at an end."

Ames shuddered involuntarily. "It's no wonder he was jammed against the driver-side door like that—he was trying to get away. Miss Van Eyck could so easily have been next, though that handkerchief trick would have been much harder to pull off if she wasn't behind Tina the way she had been behind her husband. I bet she had her gun when she killed her husband as well. Perhaps made herself known, told him she had a gun, and he'd better do what she wanted. Made him drive to the ferry; he tried to shake her by driving towards the water, but she made him turn and then she applied the cloth while the car was still moving. I suppose she was squeamish about shooting and thought she could use the same method with Tina."

"Well, Miss Van Eyck wasn't killed, sir. That's the main thing. You know, I have a theory about the locked car doors."

"Just one of the things that didn't make a lot of sense. What is it?"

"Well, typically, as Mr. Gillingham said, strychnine doesn't kill right away, and even subduing him and suffocating him, she might have been afraid that he might somehow survive if someone found him in time. She might have thought that locking the car doors and taking the keys would slow down any would-be rescuers."

"And identify her as his attacker. Well, she's not talking, even to her lawyer, apparently, so it's as good a theory as any."

"I'll catalogue all this stuff, shall I?"

"Yes, thanks, Constable. And good work."

Terrell smiled, and it crossed Ames's mind as he watched him leave the office that April wouldn't have a chance against that smile.

———

"I STILL CAN'T understand how I was taken in by him," Darling said. They were in the dining car having lunch as the train hurtled across the desert heading west. They had left the inn that morning after saying goodbye to Chela and had been driven to the station by Raúl, who had insisted on it. "It's really shaken up my sense of myself. What other ghastly misjudgements have I made or will I continue to make? I mean, it was right in front of me. The way he talked about women, even the arson arrest. When I think about it now, I can see it was hurried. He probably thought he had the right man, I'll give him the benefit of the doubt, but now I see that for him arresting someone was proof of guilt. He never questioned his own judgement for a second. I feel nothing but embarrassment when I think of those things now. What did I think that was? Manliness? Or at least a kind of manliness, maybe."

"What were the good things about him?" Lane asked. "Maybe they outweighed the bad, made it seem trivial."

Darling nodded, digging his fork into a piece of chocolate cake. "This is quite good. One of us should learn to make it. I bet Mrs. Hughes could teach you. Or me," he added. "That's a kind question, so let me think," Darling continued. "He was generous, high energy, and extremely kind to me, certainly, as the new man. It seemed as though he was loyal to the force and the men. He was quite easy to like, really. I suppose he could have changed over the years, through the war, and I wouldn't have seen it. He certainly was not a well man towards the end. He was someone who seemed to think he had complete control of things, and then clearly began to unravel. I wondered at first how he thought he'd get away with it all. I imagine now that he'd gone down the road of kidnapping you to find out where Priscilla was, and didn't foresee the rest of it but had supreme confidence in his own ability to ride it out. Even on the side of the road he was scheming. He would pretend he'd arrested Idaho, charge him with your kidnapping, and maybe even get rid of Martinez for insubordination. He didn't know about the photographs, and he didn't count on Martinez not backing down. Old Mackenzie was in charge in Nelson when Galloway was there. Had been for twenty years. Poor man had to come back and take the helm again during the war because I was in the Air Force. I wonder what he thought of Galloway."

"I think," Lane said slowly, "I think it is easy to like someone who is energetic and generous. They do not invite suspicion because they appear to be completely open. I do it all the time. Perhaps as one gets older one can see past that more often. Are you worried you have some innate lack of judgement that will hurt your police work?"

"Oh, I don't know. I think I'm feeling guilty because it's clear now he was on the take in Nelson as well, though I guess we'll never know exactly what Watts thought he had on him. According to Ames, Watts regularly ran through his pay, and was heavily in debt, which is why he was trying to get money out of Galloway. But most of all I feel guilty because he managed to carry you off like that. If I'd never brought you here, we could have had a perfectly pleasant honeymoon in Niagara Falls or somewhere. Isn't that what normal people do?"

"On the whole, I think I like that you can suffer such self-doubt. I expect it's what makes you more thoughtful and relieves you of the burden of always thinking you are right about everything. I'm sure it's why I fell in love with you."

"**GOOD JOB, YOU** two." Darling was at his desk with Ames and Terrell lined up before him.

"Thank you, sir," Terrell said. "Sergeant Ames is the one, if I may say so."

"Very creditable, Constable Terrell. Ames has said the same of you. I'm not sure I can take much more of this self-effacing goo, so the two of you can run along and find some more crime to fight." Darling waved his hand dismissively and stacked the considerable pile of papers that comprised the report on the Watts murder.

Ames, earnestly hoping for a respite from crime fighting for a day or two, collapsed on the chair in his office. He'd managed to stave off any reflection about yet another catastrophic failure in his romantic life by occupying himself with tidying up the loose ends on the Watts business and learning from Darling about the fate of Galloway in Tucson. He had felt it was only fair that Tina Van Eyck should know that the policeman who had dismissed her so cruelly had got his own comeuppance. Firmly putting aside the officiousness and insensitivity he was certain he'd shown during the investigation, and the embarrassing "Thank God!" that had flown unbidden from his lips when he'd seen Tina evidently in one piece in front of the fire at the Bertollis' cabin, Ames had made the trek up the lake to the garage.

Mr. Van Eyck had brightened at the sight of him pulling up in front of the now pristine bay doors gleaming in the snowy morning, but Tina had looked decidedly unwelcoming and had thanked him coolly for taking the trouble of coming out. And that was that, he thought. He could not shake his feeling that this failure was harder than the others.

He was about to put his feet on his desk to try to return himself to a state of nonchalance when his phone rang.

"Someone here to see you, Sarge. A Miss Van Eyck. Shall I send her up?"

LANE HAD BEEN invited by Angela to come for coffee, so she stopped by the post office on her way. Eleanor Armstrong handed her an airmail letter.

"From the United States," she said, intrigued.

Lane peered at it. There was no return address. Just a name: Priscilla Barr. It took only a moment. Priscilla. Using her maiden name. "Thank you," she said, using it to wave. She could hear someone coming up the steps. It was Mabel Hughes. "Lovely buns, Mabel. I'll be along soon for my baking lesson."

When she was back on the road, she took a deep breath and opened the letter. It was brief.

My dear Mrs. Darling,

I write only to let you know that I have arrived safely and am where I cannot easily be found by Paul, were he at liberty to look. I had thought I would have to delay going to England to see my son because it would be the first thing Paul would think of. I think I may safely go now. I have not seen my son for three years. I doubt he will even know me. I want to thank you for your kindness to me. I can never repay it. I happened to see a small article in the Tribune on a back page and was gratified

*to learn that the roll of film I gave you proved useful. I
do hope the honeymoon picture I took is as lovely as it
looked in the viewfinder.*

*I remain yours faithfully,
Priscilla Barr*

SHE'D HAD A lovely walk through the snow, her spirits
elevated by Priscilla's letter. She'd been planning to go by
the road but had opted instead to take the path that cut
diagonally through the meadow, which in the summer was
full of wildflowers and was now covered with a pristine
layer of white. Lane had nearly given in to the desire to lie
on the ground to watch the tiny flakes descend and drink
in the absolute quiet of this winter day. But she knew
Angela was waiting, and besides, her bullet-grazed ribs
were still too sensitive for her to flop around in the snow.

They sat now in front of the fire, cups of coffee and a
plate of raisin cookies before them.

"You have no idea what you missed, gallivanting off to
Arizona like that! I had a murderer right here in this very
living room! Robin Harris held her at the end of his rifle
till the police got here. It was too awful!" Angela said
with relish.

Lane laughed. "Robin must have been in heaven. I've
always suspected he wants nothing more than to hold
someone at gunpoint. He must have felt the murderer
justified his worldview."

"Robin was absolutely furious because he was bouncing
away down the hill trying to get home from the upper

orchard when that car came around the corner at speed going the wrong way and smashed into him. The front of his tractor is stove in, and he's going to have to get a new one."

"Poor Robin. Does he have enough money for that sort of thing?"

"He's an absolute miser! I'm sure he has thousands stashed away somewhere. Those two policemen, Sergeant Ames and Constable Terrell, were brilliant. I can't believe you were lounging around a swimming pool in a swanky hotel and missed it all!"

"I can't either," Lane said, smiling. She wondered whether raisin cookies would be hard to make.

"I felt a little sorry for Sergeant Ames. I know he brought that Van Eyck girl to your wedding and he looked quite soft on her, and of course, he was so obviously relieved she was okay after her ordeal, but she seemed to want nothing to do with him!"

"YOU'LL NEVER GUESS what happened at the station today," Darling said, after tossing his hat on a coat hook in the hallway and throwing himself gratefully in front of the fire burning brightly in the Franklin.

"I cannot," said Lane, handing him a scotch.

"Tina Van Eyck came to visit Ames."

"With a view to beating him about the head? Angela said she was very cool toward him when they arrested that woman who killed her husband."

"No. With a view to bringing him some flowers. There. I've astounded you."

"You have, indeed! Well, well, well, Amesy. Cheers!"

ACKNOWLEDGEMENTS

I'VE ALWAYS BEEN A SLAVE to the magic of books. Open a book and fan through the pages, and you are airing what is still one of the miracles of our human inventiveness. I still can't believe I get to write them.

No one creates one of these small miracles alone. Thank you to my faithful first readers, who give me vital feedback about whether anyone is going to like the book: Sasha Bley-Vroman, Nickie Bertolotti, Gerald Miller. And with this book, I am delighted to have had the help of old school chum David Nix. He was critical in helping with important historical and geographical details about the Tucson setting. I am very grateful to a retired (and very modest) Tucson lawman for details about the early Tucson Police and the long-vanished Tucson police station, to my doctor friend Dr. Jeff Fine, who gives invaluable help with making the many means of murder seem medically plausible, to Gregg Parsons for his help with vintage cars, and to Ellen Wheeler for her help in connecting me to critical sources. Any errors about any of these things are mine alone.

A huge thanks to the wonderful team at TouchWood Editions! Publisher Taryn Boyd, who has inspired me to keep writing with her steadfast and delighted belief in Lane Winslow; publicist Tori Elliott, who has an enormous job with scores of authors, but always makes me feel there is no one else in the world but me; and new in-house editor Kate Kennedy, whom I already feel I could never do without.

Special thanks to editors Claire Philipson, Warren Layberry, and Renée Layberry, whose close reading and wonderful editing make me look like a genius. And those covers! Margaret Hanson has created a stunning set of covers that are the talk of every book event I've ever been to. Huge thanks to the designers at TouchWood Editions who have worked their fabulous tricks to make the books such an attractive set to have on a shelf.

Thanks to my family: my husband, Terry, who likes nothing more than to stroll in the woods enjoying nature, but must instead listen to me trying out new ideas; my son, Biski, who is unabashedly in favour of my books; my two utterly impressive grandsons, Tyson and Teo; and my loveliest of daughters-in-law, Tammy—all of whom inspire me to carry on writing.

And I cannot forget the readers to whom I am indebted more than I can say. So very many of you reach out with notes, questions, and all manner of kindnesses, and many of you have taken the brave step of telling me about your own lives, inspired by what you have read in the pages of my books. I am deeply honoured by your support and by your willingness to share your own important stories.

IONA WHISHAW was born in British Columbia. After living her early years in the Kootenays, she spent her formative years living and learning in Mexico, Nicaragua, and the US. She travelled extensively for pleasure and education before settling in the Vancouver area. Throughout her roles as youth worker, social worker, teacher, and award-winning high school principal, her love of writing remained consistent, and compelled her to obtain her master's in creative writing from the University of British Columbia. Iona has published short fiction, poetry, poetry translation, and one children's book, *Henry and the Cow Problem*. *A Killer in King's Cove* was her first adult novel. Her heroine, Lane Winslow, was inspired by Iona's mother who, like her father before her, was a wartime spy. Visit ionawhishaw.com to find out more.